AFRIC

Eileen Enwright Hodgetts

PRELUDE

In the Congo Rain Forest 1963; the Simba rebellion

The woman brought her son to the convent set deep in the forest.

"Take him," she said in French.

The Belgian nun replied in Lingala, the local language. "Where is his father?"

"He is gone," said the woman. "They have all gone."

The small boy gripped his mother's hand as the nun studied him.

"Was his father a white man?" the nun asked.

"Yes," said the mother. "I did not wish it, but he forced me."

The nun showed no surprise. "Do you know where he was from?" she asked.

The woman shook her head. "He was a white man," she repeated, "from the mines; but they are gone now."

"We are also going," said the nun; "we cannot stay here; we will all be killed."

"Take him with you," said the mother. "I cannot keep him; he is not of our tribe; he cannot be accepted. The Simbas will kill him."

"They will kill all of us," said the nun.

The mother shook her head. "They say that the Americans are coming," she said, "they will save you."

"Was his father an American?" the nun asked.

"He was white," the woman said, "and he spoke to me in English."

"Then let us hope that the Americans will take him," said the nun.

The mother tried to release the boy's hand; he tightened his grip.

"You go," said the mother. "I cannot keep you." She pried her hand free of his grasp and turned from him. He watched her walk away into the cool green depths of the forest.

"Come inside," said the nun. There was no kindness in her voice. She led him through the open gates and for the first time in his short life he saw the brick buildings of the Belgian colonists, the chapel of the nuns, and the statue of the white woman, the mother of the god they worshipped.

The nun took him into a small room, empty of furniture. A little of the friendly green forest sunlight sifted into the room through a barred window. He stood in the light and waited patiently. His mother had told him to be obedient to the nuns; if they wanted him to wait; he would wait.

The sound of a vehicle engine filtered in through the window, and then women's voices calling and responding in French, the language of the colonists. Doors banged, the engine roared, and then the sound faded away. The boy continued to wait. He waited until the light faded from the room and the night insects began to swarm. He was hungry, tired, and thirsty; perhaps the nun had forgotten about him. He approached the door with caution; should he go outside? He pushed the door open and looked outside. Moonlight filtered through the canopy of trees revealing the empty courtyard; the open gates and the dirt track that led back into the safety of the forest.

Two shadowy figures made their way towards him out of the depths of the forest, a tall man and a child walking side by side. They entered through the open gate. The moonlight fell on the man's face, an African face but not of the boy's tribe; a face criss-crossed with a pattern of tribal markings, and beside him a skinny boy; also not of his tribe.

The man spoke to him in Lingala, calling him forward to stand in the light, and then grunting in surprise at the lightness of his skin.

"Where are the nuns?" the boy asked.

"Gone," said the man. "By now they will be dead; the Simbas are coming this way."

"I want to go home," said the boy.

"You have no home," said the man.

"My mother___"

"I told you," said the man, "the Simbas are coming; they will kill your mother."

"The Americans___"

"They will not want you," said the man.

He turned to the other boy, the one who had entered the compound with him. "I will keep one of you," he said, "but not both of you." His hands were large and strong and he gripped each of the boys by

3

the back of the neck as he pushed them into the little room where the faint moonlight trickled through the window.

"I will keep one of you," he said again. "I will keep the one that is alive when the sun rises."

He turned away from them, stepped outside, and the boy heard the sound of a wooden bar dropping into place to lock the door.

In the morning the man opened the door and looked inside; he saw blood, so much blood. The small boy; the child of the white father, was alive, the other boy was not. Gunfire rattled in the distance, the Simbas were coming. The witchdoctor and his new apprentice walked away from the convent and the sound of battle and into the deep forest.

CHAPTER ONE

Swot Jensen: Present Day Uganda, East Africa,

The last thing in the world Swot Jensen wanted to be was awake, but even Swot, in all her misery, couldn't sleep through the noise outside her room because it had become even louder than the sound of rain drumming on the tin roof. The room was stiflingly hot because the power had gone out in the middle of the night, and the fan was no longer moving the moist air. She wanted to pull the sheet over her head and sleep through the whole thing; in fact, she wanted to sleep until it was time to leave; until her grandmother was ready to admit defeat and take her home. Unfortunately the drooping mosquito net had plastered itself against her face and once she had swatted it away she was wide awake.

She sat up and looked out of the window into the dreary cement compound. She could see her grandfather, magnificent in a snowy white shirt and striped tie. His blue black African face was shiny with sweat and distorted with fury, but his eyes were invisible behind his sunglasses. Sunglasses! They hadn't seen the sun in three days. Swot's grandmother was an equally arresting figure, standing ankle deep in mud, her pink skin glowing as she confronted the man she claimed as her husband. Her cloud of pale hair was curling itself into long white ringlets under the constant deluge of rain. Her tie dyed skirt was spattered with mud and a once-white, fringed shawl was slung around her shoulders. She looked, Swot thought, as she must have looked some fifty years before in the Summer of Love; just a little older, but, from what Swot could tell, no wiser.

Swot had no interest in joining in the argument that she had seen enacted daily since their arrival, but she was interested in the other source of sound. A large African woman, wrapped in brightly colored cloth, was beating on the crippled kid. That's what Swot called him in her own mind. "the crippled kid"; not exactly politically correct but it was Swot's mind and she felt she had the right to fill it with whatever thoughts she wanted to think. The kid was hopping on one foot because the fat woman had already kicked away his pathetic homemade crutch, and he was screaming in outrage at the woman who was trying to tie something around his neck; something that he kept grabbing from her and throwing into the mud from which she would retrieve it with more shouting, or cursing, and try again. The boy's eyes were wide with terror. He was just a little kid, maybe eleven or twelve years old, and the woman was big and very strong. Well, Swot knew something about being little, and overlooked, and she felt for the poor kid. She marched out of the room, barefooted it across the compound and with one well-placed shove, pushed the fat woman into the mud. The woman landed on her large backside with a satisfyingly loud squelch.

Silence fell. They all turned to look at Swot. "I'm going back to bed," she said to her grandmother.

"Swot," she said, "what's wrong?"

"What's wrong?" Swot shouted back. "What isn't wrong, that's what I'd like to know, and my name isn't Swot, it's Sarah."

She reached down and grabbed the object that the fat woman was holding. It was a little leather bag on a string. "He doesn't want to wear it," she said. "He told you that last night. Now leave him alone."

She could see that the fat woman was gathering her breath to express her outrage, and out of the corner of her eye she could see her grandmother headed for her to hug her or hit her, Swot didn't know which. That's the way it was with Swot's grandmother, not that Swot could ever call her grandmother, or gran, or anything warm and cuddly. She was allowed to call her Brenda, because, as she had explained to Swot as soon Swot was old enough to speak, Brenda was her name.

So, Brenda was coming at Swot, the crippled kid was hopping back to his seat on the verandah, and the fat woman was preparing to blast Swot in a language Swot didn't understand, when someone interrupted the moment by pounding on the huge metal gates that enclosed Swot's grandfather's compound.

Everyone in the compound stood and watched as the guard opened the man door and looked outside. They then continued to wait in expectant silence while he pulled back the bolts and opened the gates wide enough to admit a man on a motorcycle. Dressed in blue jeans and a gray tee shirt, spattered with mud and wearing an enormous crash helmet, the man skidded to a halt, and succeeded in doing what everyone else had avoided doing so far; he splashed mud on Swot's grandfather's tie. Her grandfather remained impassive behind his dark glasses while two of his henchmen stepped forward to grab the motorcycle. They didn't have to worry. The rider had already dropped the motorcycle to the ground and was tugging off his helmet. A shock of white hair appeared and then a sun browned, once white face. He turned to face the shocked little tableau.

"They've killed the Peace Corps worker," he shouted in a voice that was pure Virginia. "They dumped him on my front porch."

"Another one of John Kennedy's ideas gone bad," Swot's grandmother muttered. She approached the white man and looked him full in the face. There was what Swot could only think of as a "pregnant" pause.

"Rory Marsden," she gasped.

"Songbird," he said, in a tone of disbelief.

Songbird? When, Swot wondered, had Brenda been called Songbird?

"What did you do with my cows?" Grandmother Brenda Songbird

asked.

"What cows?" the man asked.

"The wedding cows," Brenda said.

"We ate them," the man said impatiently. "What are you doing here?"

Brenda turned to Swot's grandfather. "He didn't return them; he ate them," she said, "so we're still married."

Swot's grandfather flicked the mud off his tie, took Brenda by the shoulders and more or less lifted her out of the way. He was now face to face with the elderly white man. "Tell me again," he said in his deep rumbling African voice.

"It was years ago," said Rory the white man. "What is she doing here?"

"Never mind about her," said the grandfather, "tell me about the Peace Corps worker".

"Multiple stab wounds;" Rory said angrily, "dumped on my porch. It looked like he'd been in a hell of a fight."

He hesitated and his voice softened. "He was just a kid," he said; "a really nice kid. Why do they have to go so crazy when they come here?"

He splashed through the mud to the verandah where Swot stood. "Welcome to Africa," he said, and then he sat down suddenly on the cement as though his legs had given way.

"Hi," said Swot.

Rory looked at Swot's grandmother, "Is she with you?" he asked.

"She's my granddaughter," said Brenda, "and she's a genius."

Swot winced. Why did Brenda have to keep saying that?

"Are you?" Rory asked, looking at Swot.

"Yes," said Swot, "but I am also a person." She glared at her grandmother. "I am not just defined by the fact that I am intelligent," she said.

"No, of course not," said Brenda, "but she did graduate from college last month, and she is only eighteen. She finished High School at fourteen."

"So she's the daughter of___", said Rory.

"Monica; she's the daughter of my daughter Monica, and Herbert is

Monica's father, so he is Swot's grandfather."

"Family reunion?" Rory asked.

"Some reunion," said Swot. She couldn't think of anything else to say on the subject of her grandmother's reunion with the husband she had not seen in the past fifty years, so she turned her back on Rory Marsden and went back into her room, slamming the door behind her. She sat down on the bed and buried her head in her hands. So she was a genius, so what? Life would have been so much easier if she had been born beautiful instead of smart but the mirror didn't lie; it only confirmed her own opinion of herself, horrible hair, mud colored eyes, skinny legs; a loser in the gene pool.

Her reflections on her own lack of beauty were interrupted by someone knocking on the door; a very timid kind of knocking – nothing that could possibly emanate from Brenda who pounded loudly whenever she wanted Swot to join in the ongoing family squabble. Swot opened the door and admitted the crippled kid who hopped over to the bed and sat down. His earlier terror had passed, now he just looked incredibly sad.

"He was my friend," he said, in careful, soft-spoken English.

Swot dragged her mind away from the contemplation of her own shortcomings and gave some thought to the fact that Rory Marsden had come to report a violent death; the death of a Peace Corps worker.

"Who was he?" she asked

"Zach," the boy said. "He was really nice. He was not a fighter. He would never be in a fight. He'd come into the village every night and play football with the kids, and sometimes he'd just sit and talk with me. He was going to help me get my leg fixed. He said he knew a doctor."

"Oh!" Swot didn't really know what else to say. Her high I.Q. and her rapid progress through high school and college had left her with no friends her own age and no experience at offering sympathy or putting herself in someone else's shoes, but obviously something was required of her.

"I'm sorry," she said.

The boy said nothing and continued to sit on her bed looking dejectedly down at his twisted leg.

The silence grew uncomfortably long. Swot searched for something else to say and realized that she didn't even know the boy's name; so she asked him.

"I'm Matthew," he told her. "I am in S1."

Swot had no idea what that meant or why that was significant, but she pressed on.

"I'm Sarah," she said.

"Your grandmother calls you Swot," said Matthew.

"It's a nickname," she said. "A swot is someone who studies hard, but actually I don't need to study."

"Your grandmother says you're a genius," said Matthew, "I wish I was a genius."

"No, you don't," said Swot, "it's highly overrated. I would give anything to be normal."

"So would I," said Matthew.

Nice going, Swot said to herself, he can't even walk properly and I'm complaining about the fact that I'm brilliantly clever and I don't even have to work hard in school; very tactful.

She was grasping for something to say when the need to speak was cut off by a loud clanking sound outside, which finally settled down to the steady roar of an engine."

"The generator," Matthew said; "now your fan will work."

It did. The blades started to move, and the moist air began to circulate,

"Why have they turned it on now," Swot asked, "why not last night?"

"They will be charging their phones so they can call Kampala," Matthew said, "to report the murder."

So Matthew was calling it murder. He was probably correct; apparently the Peace Corps worker had been stabbed like a pin cushion and his body has been dumped at someone's door so even if he had brought it on himself by getting into a fight, it was still technically murder.

"Who would want to kill him?" she asked.

9

"I don't know," said Matthew. He paused and then he said, "Is your grandmother really the first wife?"

"That's what she says," Swot replied.

"If she is the first wife," Matthew said, "then she will be senior wife, and responsible for our discipline; is she kind?"

"Kind?" said Swot, "I don't know, I've never thought about it; she's not unkind, she's just careless. "

"I think that would be better," said Matthew.

He hopped to the door. Swot followed him out and very nearly tripped over a bundle of extension cords draped across the verandah. She traced them back to an orange generator that was running noisily in the corner of the compound. Like a web of umbilical cords all of the wires sprouted phone chargers and phones, with a person attached to each phone. The whole mess was supplying power to every one of Swot's grandfather's male compatriots and they were all engaged in loud conversation, shouting above the noise of the generator. Rory Marsden was shouting louder than anyone else in his Virginia English. Swot gathered from his side of the conversation that he was talking to the US Embassy and the conversation was not going well.

"Zach", he shouted. "That's all I know. Don't you have records? He's one of yours."

He paused, listening. "Nyalawa'" he shouted. 'Rory Marsden, Nyalawa. Dammit man, you know where I am. "Another pause.

"You can't just leave him here," he said. "I know it's tricky, but someone has to be told. The kid has parents. Just do your best but keep my name out of it. "

A long pause.

"Who?" he said questioningly, and then "I don't know. You're supposed to know these things. You're supposed to tell me. I can't do everything for you."

He cupped a hand over his other ear and strained to hear what was being said by the Embassy official. He shook his head. "I've lost the signal," he said.

Swot looked around the compound, thinking what a strange conversation she had just heard, although, of course, she had only heard one side of it. Nonetheless something seemed a little off. She wondered if anyone else had noticed, but all the other people were staring at their phones, and shaking their heads. One by one they crossed to the verandah and laid down the phones, still attached to their umbilical cords. Someone turned off the generator. All was silent except for the steady drip of water from the roof onto the muddy ground.

CHAPTER TWO
Matthew, the Crippled Kid

Matthew wondered what the American girl was thinking. She had not looked happy since the day she arrived, and now she looked downright miserable. He really wanted to like her because she was the only person in the house who had ever stood up for him; but she had an angry expression on her face all the time and she stared at everyone as though she was daring them to speak to her. He thought she might have been quite pretty if she would only smile, but so far he hadn't seen her smile; not even once.

Matthew knew his father was a man of great importance with the best house in the whole district, and the senior mother had been told to give the best rooms to the American girl and her grandmother; but Matthew could tell that the girl didn't appreciate this kindness. Perhaps she didn't understand how secure she was behind the high brick walls of the compound and with the guards who traveled everywhere with Matthew's father; perhaps she was not angry; perhaps she was just afraid.

After the generator was turned off they all stood in silence waiting for Matthew's father to speak. Mr. Rory, the American, put his phone back into his pocket. Two of the boys who worked for Matthew's father had picked up Mr. Rory's motorcycle and were holding onto it for him. Matthew wished he could have helped them; as a son of the house, and the only boy who was not away at school, he should have been included, but, as usual, he was ignored. No one ever expected him to do anything useful; he was just a nuisance, reduced to staying in the kitchen with the women. "You'll need to send someone to fetch the body," said Mr. Rory.

Matthew thought that he was addressing his important father, but the senior mother, who always wanted to be in charge of everyone, interrupted and answered the white man with no respect. He knew that she liked to show off the fact that she spoke very good English, almost as good as Matthew's, and very much better than most of the other wives.

"You will not bring him here," she said and her whole fat body trembled in indignation. "Not to this house. He's one of yours. You keep him."

"He's lying in my yard," Mr. Rory protested. "Someone needs to get him out of there."

"The police," she said.

Mr. Rory shook his head. "They have no vehicle," he said, and then he turned to the American girl and said softly, "God, sometimes I hate this place,"

The girl actually smiled, as though she was pleased to find someone who agreed with her. Matthew thought she looked much better when she smiled but he was sorry to think that she hated the house where she had been given such hospitality, and he was even more sorry to find that Mr. Rory also hated being with them. Matthew's family had always treated Mr. Rory with respect, and he had no reason to hate them, and he also had no reason to take the Lord's name in vain.

Matthew felt bad about the idea of Zach, the Peace Corps worker, lying out in the rain in Mr. Rory's yard. He had liked Zach, and he couldn't imagine who would want to kill him.

"I've taken photos for evidence, and I called the local chairman," Mr. Rory said. "The chairman came and looked. No one knows anything, or at least no one's talking. We have to move him."

"Yes, we do," said Matthew's father. "We will take care of it Mr. Rory. I'm sorry that we don't have any real police detectives to come out like they do on American television, but that's not our way. If he was one of us, we would expect his family to come for him. We shall have to keep him now until the Embassy comes and takes him. He will have to be taken to the Clinic."

"No," the senior mother said, interrupting her husband yet again.

"The clinic is for maternity. He can't be there. What if a woman needs to deliver?"

Matthew's father looked at her; Matthew knew that look; sometimes he had been on the receiving end of that look. He was secretly pleased to see his senior mother fall silent and stare at the ground.

With a snap of his fingers Matthew's father dispatched four men, and moments later they roared out of the gate in a double cab pickup.

Silence fell again. Matthew knew that no one, not even the Americans, would speak until his father gave permission. For a few moments the big man was silent and then he snapped his fingers again. "We shall meet in the dining room," he announced. He looked at Mr. Rory. "Do you want to be present?"

"Of course," Rory said.

Mr. Rory gestured to the two boys who were holding his motorcycle and they wheeled it into the shelter of the gatehouse and propped it up on its stand. Mr. Rory followed Matthew's father and his guards into the main house; a place Matthew was not normally allowed to enter. He saw that the old white lady, the one who had claimed to be his father's senior wife, was also following them. "You're going to need my help," she said. His father shrugged his shoulders but he allowed her in through the door. When the senior mother also tried to follow, one of the guards turned her back at the door.

As she retreated, holding onto what little dignity she had left, a burst of laughter came from the kitchen, adding anger to indignity. Of course she was already angry about the way the white girl had pushed her into the mud, so now that her husband was nowhere in sight she was ready to pick a fight. Matthew knew she was ready to take her anger out on him but the American girl was already prepared for her. "Touch me or touch that kid again," she said, "and I'll put you back in the mud."

Matthew giggled; he didn't mean to; he was too old to giggle like a girl, but he just couldn't help himself. The American girl kept a perfectly straight face and didn't even look at him. The senior mother veered away and waddled off in the direction of the kitchen, pretending that nothing had happened. Matthew knew that the kitchen girls were going to feel the sharp side of her tongue, but at least he had been spared. He hoped that she wouldn't take her anger out on his mother.

He didn't want to go to the kitchen, and he would never be allowed in the house, so he hobbled over to the verandah and sat with his legs dangling over the edge. The American girl sat down beside him. She smiled, just slightly. He thought she had an interesting face. He didn't really know how white girls were supposed to look; this was the first one he had ever met. He had been told that she was actually part African, but he couldn't tell which part it was. Her hair was kind of brownish, and very curly, but not tight curls like everyone else; and her eyes were not brown but they were not light like Mr. Rory's eyes; they were more like the color of mud; he had certainly never seen eyes like that before. She had nice even white teeth, and her skin was really pale. She didn't look like an African, but she didn't look like any white girl he had ever seen in a picture. He wished that she had looked less miserable; it was hard to think of something to say to her.

"So who are you?" she asked. "Are you my cousin or my uncle?"

"I am your uncle," he said, "because I am the child of your grandfather."

"And that fat women, is she your mother?"

"No," said Matthew, shocked at the very idea, "she is the senior wife of my father, and, therefore, she is the senior mother of all the children, but she is not my real mother, not my birth mother; my mother is Jubilee, and she is very nice, and she helps me when she can."

The white girl sniffed disapprovingly. "Polygamy," she said, "I just don't get it."

"It is not a good thing," said Matthew, "but it is our way."

"Well, it's ridiculous," said the American, "but it's nothing to do with me. So, do I have to call you Uncle Matthew?"

"I don't think so," he said.

"Then I'll just call you Matthew," she said, "and you can call me

Swot."

"Does your name really mean that you are a clever person?" he asked.

"No," she said, "it just means that my grandmother has a cruel sense of humor, so let's not talk about her. Tell me about that fat woman, your senior mother as you called her; what's she got against you?"

Matthew thought of the many things that his senior mother objected to, the first being that he was the child of Jubilee, the prettiest of the wives, and not the child of one of the other wives. He thought that situation would be difficult to explain to this girl from so far away and such a different culture who had already declared that their customs were ridiculous, so he settled on the most obvious problem.

"It's because of my leg, "he said, "I can't work like the other children. She wants me to be cured. She doesn't like that I can't work."

"Well, it's not your fault," Swot said.

"She blames me because I won't wear the charm she bought from the witchdoctor." he said. He had no idea where the American girl stood on the question of witchdoctors and their powers; did they even have witchdoctors in America?

"Oh," said Swot, "is that what's in the little bag?"

"It's evil," Matthew said, "but she paid the witchdoctor for it, and she says I must wear it." He straightened his thin shoulders. "I will not wear it," he said firmly. "I don't believe in such things. I am a Christian. I am born again. Are you?"

"Am I what?"

"Born again?"

"Well," said Swot, "that's a difficult question."

Matthew wondered why the question would be so difficult. In his experience a person was either born again, or they were not born again, or possibly they were Catholic, in which case she would have said so; and she would be wearing a Virgin Mary medal or some such symbol.

"I don't want to offend you," said Swot, "but I prefer to rely on my own judgment and not on some distant creator, or some unreliable old book of myths."

Matthew stared at her; he had never heard anyone say such a thing. Book of myths; did she mean the Bible?

"So what did happen to your leg?" the girl asked, changing the subject abruptly. "Were you born like that?"

Matthew shook his head. "I broke it," he said, "when I was five. I was climbing for jackfruit and I fell out of the tree."

He remembered what it had felt like to climb; and he remembered the pain when he fell; he remembered everything.

"So there's nothing genetically wrong," said Swot, not sounding at all sympathetic to the pain he had endured. "If it was just a break, why is it so bad now?

"My father was away," Matthew said, "and that woman, the senior wife, she said that there was no money for a doctor. My mother begged her to do something, but she refused. Now she says she has given money to the witch doctor to heal me."

Swot looked at Matthew's twisted leg. "How's a witchdoctor going to heal that?" she asked.

"He can't," said Matthew, "but Jesus can."

The girl took a deep breath as though she was hesitant to speak, and then she said "It's not up to Jesus to heal you. I'm sure it would be nice if he did, or even could, but what you really need is an orthopedic surgeon."

Matthew nodded his head enthusiastically. "That's what Zach said. He said he knew someone who would help me. He was going to take me to Kampala to see him." The disappointment robbed Matthew of words. There was no more to say

"Why?" said Swot. "Why would someone kill him? He sounds like a nice kid. You liked him, didn't you?"

"Yes," said Matthew.

"I'm sorry about your leg," Swot said.

"So am I," said Matthew.

"Well," said the American girl, springing to her feet, "I'm not sitting out here in the rain any longer. Come on inside."

"Into your room?" Matthew asked.

"Sure, why not?" said Swot. "You can sit on my bed; it's more comfortable than the cement."

Matthew scrambled to a standing position; his senior mother was nowhere in sight so he followed Swot into her room.

Swot Jensen

The high powered meeting in the dining room droned on, although Swot couldn't imagine what they could be saying to each other because no one in the room had any real information, and no way to obtain any. The cell phones remained untouched with their useless umbilical cords attached to the non-generating generator. The rain showed no signs of abating, and Grandfather Herbert's extended family continued to turn the compound into a quagmire. A couple of mangy looking dogs installed themselves on the remaining patches of dry cement under the overhanging eaves, an oily smoke curled from the kitchen fire, and a goat that had been bleating somewhere beyond the wall suddenly ceased its noise. Swot assumed, from her experience of the past couple of nights, that they would be having goat for dinner.

Matthew sat on Swot's bed swinging his legs in apparent contentment, leading her to conclude that he was simply happy to be out of the rain, with a comfortable place to rest and out of sight of the Senior Fat Cow. They didn't make conversation. Swot had nothing more to say to him. What they were not going to do, so far as Swot was concerned, was to discuss Jesus and whether or not Swot was born again. She was of the opinion that being born once was enough of a burden, and she couldn't trust any kind of Savior who would decree that in a family of beautiful people, she should be born so mud ugly.

Matthew lay back on the bed and drifted off to sleep. Swot left him alone. Sleeping like that he seemed so very young and so very unfortunate. His arms and legs were stick thin, but his belly protruded through his worn shirt. She knew enough to know that the protruding belly was not a sign of overeating, just a sign that he had a gutful of worms; probably not a good idea to let him sleep on her bed, but what the heck; he looked really comfortable, and goodness knows what kind of bed he usually found for himself. She imagined that he might normally sleep curled up like a dog in the kitchen somewhere.

Her bedroom door swung open with a sudden jerk and banged against the wall. Matthew jerked upright, eyes wide, and Swot took a defensive step backwards. Her grandfather entered the room, looked around, jerked his thumb at Matthew, and then plopped himself down on the bed as Matthew was scuttling out the door.

"How are you, Sarah?" he asked.

"I'm fine, thank you," she said, a little breathlessly. His large presence in the small room was distinctly intimidating.

"How are you?" she added.

"I am well," he said.

They stared at each other in silence.

"What was the boy doing here?" he asked eventually.

"Just talking to me. He was sorry about the Peace Corps worker; apparently Zach had promised him that he would find someone to fix his leg."

"Ah yes," said Grandfather Herbert.

Silence again.

Swot decided not to be afraid of him. What could he do to her? Really what could he do?

"Why don't you get someone to fix his leg? "she asked.

"We do not have good doctors here," he replied.

"There are doctors in Kampala."

He nodded. "One day," he said, "it might be arranged."

"Why not now?" she persisted. "Do you know what that boy has to go through?"

"He is more fortunate than some," said her grandfather. "I am not here to talk about him. I want to talk about you."

He stared at her again. "I see no family resemblance," he said eventually. "You look like no one in my family."

"I have a lot of mixed up genes," she said. "I don't look like anyone in my family either; they're all Swedish, blonde hair, blue eyes."

"Your grandmother tells me that you are a genius. Is that true?"

She shrugged her shoulders. "It's not important," she said.

"But it's true?" he persisted.

"Yes," she said. "When it comes to school work, I'm a genius. I've already finished college."

"Remarkable," he said; "truly remarkable. Such intelligence is wasted on a girl, but if you have it, then you must use it."

"I intend to," Swot said, deciding not to take up the argument as to whether intelligence was wasted on girls. This was a man who seemed to think that Matthew shouldn't be concerned that he had only one good leg, and that it was okay for his fat senior wife to beat up on all the children. Swot could see little point in arguing with a man like that. It wasn't as though she had to stay there for long, or be under his control. If that were ever to be the case, then things would be a little different.

Her grandfather continued to stare at her. "You don't look intelligent," he said.

"Well I am," she assured him.

"Yes, that's what your grandmother said."

The conversation seemed to be going around in circles and Swot had no idea how to move it forward.

"Are you enjoying your visit?" he asked.

Swot searched for an honest answer. "I don't like the rain," she said.

"The rain is very much needed," he replied, "but it is too much; there has been severe flooding. Lives have been lost; it us an unfortunate situation." His English was excellent but strangely pedantic, as though he was reading from a period novel. "The death of this young American has caused a severe problem; one that may require your genius to solve."

"I can't do anything," Swot said. "I don't know anything about anything that goes on here."

"You will use your intelligence," he declared.

At that moment a shadow darkened the doorway and Brenda strolled into the room, and plopped herself down on the bed next to Grandfather Herbert. He eyed her mistrustfully and moved himself away until there was a good twelve inches of blanket between them.

"I told him you could solve the problem," Brenda said. "They were all sitting in there not knowing what to do, and I told them that you were smarter than the whole pack of them combined, and you like to solve puzzles, and you read a lot of crime fiction."

"There's a lot more to solving crimes than reading crime stories," Swot said.

Brenda waved her hand dismissively. "Swot," she said, "you're the smartest thing here. These Africans have no idea what to do about it, and Rory is being less than helpful. You know, I used to think he was pretty smart, but living here must have rotted his brain."

Swot looked at her grandfather. "Brenda," she said, "I don't think you can just make sweeping statements like "these Africans don't know what to do," it sounds very condescending."

"Oh, I don't mean it like that," said Brenda.

"She means that we are not accustomed to murder," said Grandfather Herbert.

"Well, I wouldn't say that either," Brenda said. "You have plenty of murders. What about Idi Amin, and Joseph Kony, and ..."

"I personally am not accustomed to having people murdered in my village," said Swot's grandfather. "And certainly I have no experience of white people being murdered here. Really I doubt if it was murder. I imagine that he had been in a fight with another white person, and that person killed him; most certainly another white person."

"Now why on earth would you say that?" Brenda asked.

"Because most of us know what side our bread is buttered," said Herbert, "and we know better than to kill Americans, or even to oppose them in any way; it brings about international repercussions and ruins the tourist trade."

Swot looked out the window at the gloomy skies, and the miasma of red muddy mist, and wondered just how much tourist trade found its way to Nawalyo.

"Well," said Brenda, scooting a little closer to the grandfather's immaculately pressed trouser leg, "it's you or no one Swot."

"Why?"

"Because we're cut off. It's like one of those Agatha Christie mysteries where they're all on an island somewhere and no one can get away, and the murderer is one of them."

"The murderer is not here," said Swot's grandfather.

"He could be," Brenda said.

"What do you mean by cut off?" Swot asked, thinking of the long road back to Kampala, and the airport; and the flight back to the States. How could she be cut off from her escape route?

"The storms," said Brenda, "it's been storming for days."

"I am aware of that," said Swot, "all I've seen since I arrived is rain, mud, and more rain; and thunder and lightning."

"It has destroyed the infrastructure," Swot's grandfather said, for the second time.

"It's bad," said Brenda, "people have died."

"From rain?" said Swot.

"Landslides," said Brenda. "Apparently the rain has caused mudslides; whole villages have been destroyed; people have been struck by lightning."

"Oh," said Swot. Really, what was she supposed to say; was she supposed to do something, if so, what?

"We assume that the cell tower has collapsed," said Grandfather Herbert, "because there is no signal. We have become accustomed to communicating by cell phone."

"But we can go by road to Kampala, can't we?" said Swot, thinking that the damage caused by the storms would be a good reason to leave the district; in fact, a good reason to leave the country.

"You're not listening," said Brenda, who seemed energized and excited by the disaster taking place around them. "We're cut off. Do you remember the road we came in on, through the swamp?"

"It was dark," said Swot.

"Well, there's only one road in from Kampala," Brenda said, "and it goes through a swamp and across a bridge. The bridge is gone."

"Gone?"

"Washed away," said Swot's grandfather, "There is no way for a vehicle to reach the Kampala road; no vehicle can even leave this district. I have sent messengers on foot and they will cross when they are able. The cell phone tower is not functioning, and we have no way to contact Police Headquarters. We are alone with the problem of the boy's murder."

"So what do you want me to do about it?" Swot asked. Her mind was still struggling to accept the fact that they were cut off from the road to Kampala. She had hated the city from her one brief glimpse of it, but over the past couple of days it had occupied all her thoughts. If she could get to Kampala, she could get to the airport. Kampala had electricity, and hotels, and taxis and even white people. Kampala had become a desirable objective; one that was now out of her reach.

"Ask questions," said Brenda enthusiastically. "I could help you. You know, ask who was the last person to see the boy alive, and did he have any enemies, or had he been messing around with the girls, things like that."

""Anyone can do that," Swot said. "You don't need me for that."

"But you're so good at solving puzzles," Brenda said. "You'll be able to put two and two together and make..."

"Five," Swot suggested, "or perhaps three. And if by some miracle I reach a conclusion and find the killer, what do you expect me to do about it? I don't want to be stuck in this god forsaken village with a murderer breathing down my neck."

"You already are," said Grandfather Herbert. "We cannot leave, and thus the murderer cannot leave. Whoever he is, he is still here."

"You said it was probably a white person," Swot argued. "Why don't you just round up all the white people?"

"See," said Brenda triumphantly, "she's already thinking about it. She'll get to the bottom of this."

"I spoke too easily," said the grandfather. "It might not be a white person; it could possibly be someone who has been annoyed by this boy, Zach. He was an annoying boy."

"Who did he annoy?" Swot asked.

"He annoyed the women," said Grandfather Herbert. "He is a boy; he knows nothing, he has never traveled beyond the borders of his own country, and yet he comes here and starts to tell the women how to feed their children; what they must eat, what they must not eat. All he knows is what he has in a little book written by someone in Washington who has never lived a day amongst us. He tells the women that everything they do is wrong, and then he starts to teach the children; telling them that they have rights."

"It's like I told you, "Brenda said," One of JFK's brilliant ideas. It was okay at the time, but do you really think that modern Africans want to be told what to do by rich little white kids who are still wet behind the ears?

"Exactly," said her grandfather. "That's exactly what I mean."

Brenda and Herbert smiled at each other and for a moment it seemed that they had a genuine affection for each other. Swot tried to image what it had been like fifty years before when Grandmother Songbird, decked in beads and tie-dye, her hair bleached golden by the African sun had burst onto the scene in newly independent Uganda. She thought about her grandfather who had no doubt been a stunningly attractive young African man, finally given carte blanche to associate on equal terms with a wild, free spirited, and very rich, white girl. Should Swot really be surprised that the result had been the birth of her mother? But many years had come and gone since then and, although Brenda had the luxury of being an ageing hippie, Swot's grandfather had become something else entirely; a man of dignity and position, with multiple wives, and some apparently sinister sources of income. Swot could not for a moment imagine that his need to be surrounded at all times by men in dark glasses, and pickup trucks full of soldiers was a result of him being "Mr. Nice Guy".

"So you're saying that plenty of people had a reason to resent this kid, Zach." Swot said.

"To resent him, yes," said Grandfather, "but to kill him; no I cannot imagine that any of my people would want to kill him just because he paid no attention to our culture. No, there is a deeper reason. He has done something to make a real enemy."

"Like what?" she asked.

"I don't know," said her grandfather. "I have not been apprised of all his activities. He stayed in the village with the peasants. He never came here. It's possible that Mr. Rory knows something, but I know nothing."

"Suppose he was just drinking and got into a fight," Swot said. "He probably wasn't old enough to drink in the States but when he came here he found out that no one cared so he probably got drunk. Maybe he was a mean drunk, some people are."

"I don't know anything about that," said Grandfather.

"No, and neither do I," Swot said, "so what makes you think I can get to the bottom of it?"

"I told him you could," Brenda said. "Come on Swot, you know what you're like when you want to know something. "

"When I want to know something, I look it up on the internet," Swot said. "I don't see any internet around here."

Brenda smiled happily. "That's the whole point," she said. "I brought you here to experience real life, without phones and I-pads and hours spent on the computer. You have to learn to talk to people, Sarah; just talk to them."

"Not my strong point," Swot replied.

Her grandmother's reply was interrupted by another commotion outside in the muddy compound. They all walked to the door and looked out. It seemed that Matthew had once again run afoul of the senior wife and he was hiding behind his mother while the fat woman berated both of them at the top of her considerable lungs. As soon as they sensed the grandfather's presence, they fell silent. Matthew's mother, Jubilee, sank to her knees in the mud, her head bowed in submission and the other wives appeared at the door of the cookhouse, looking on with interest to see what would happen next. One or two of them glanced in Brenda's direction.

Brenda drew herself up to a dignified height, her blonde head held high, and looked down her long thin nose. The senior wife looked back with a mixture of sullen resentment and genuine fear.

"Enough," said Grandfather Herbert. "I will have no more quarrelling women under my roof. If you cannot solve your problems, I will send you all back to your parents, and I will keep only my first wife, this mazungu woman." He indicated Brenda with a not particularly respectful jerk of his head.

"She's not your wife," said the fat woman.

"I am," said Brenda. "I was his wife long before any of you were even born. He gave many cows for me."

The senior wife glared at her sullenly. "You have no parents, no family;" she said, "how could he give cows?"

"He gave them to my traveling companions," said Brenda, "on behalf of my family."

"And now they are grazing on the green, green hills of Cleveland," Swot added maliciously.

The wives drew in a combined gasp of amazement. "Your cows are in America?" one of them said.

"Yes," said Brenda. "The cows have been accepted by my parents and they are in America. That makes me his true wife."

"America is a long way. How can cows go on a plane?" they asked.

"They went on a ship," said Brenda.

Swot heard a rumbling noise coming from her grandfather and realized that he was suppressing a deep belly laugh as Brenda dug herself in deeper and deeper.

"They went to Mombasa on the train," Brenda declared, her rhythms of speech becoming that of a story teller, with perhaps, Swot thought, a touch of Kipling. "In those far off days when the British ruled here, the train ran from Kampala to the coast, and everyone could travel in comfort, and the great ships came to Mombasa to bring passengers and carry cargo. Those were in the days when all the roads in Uganda were paved, and every house had electricity...."

"Careful," said Grandfather Herbert under his breath, "we no longer speak well of colonialism".

"Well the country certainly looked a lot better than it does now," Brenda said.

"That," said Herbert "is a discussion for another day, but please feel free to go ahead and tell my wives how you are going to run the household and maintain the peace."

"I will," said Brenda. "I'll just need some time to think about it."

"Of course you do," said Grandfather Herbert.

Swot looked at Matthew, still hiding behind his mother and realized that this conversation that she found so hilarious was deadly serious for him. For all he knew, the strange white woman was now going to be given permission to beat him and treat him like dirt, and who knows what else she might expect of him.

"I'll do it," Swot said impulsively. "I'll be your detective. I'll go and ask questions, but only on one condition."

"And what is that?" asked her grandfather.

"I want him with me at all times," she said, pointing to Matthew. "I want him to go everywhere with me and be my translator."

"I'll give you one of my men," said Grandfather Herbert, "that boy will command no respect."

"But he'll tell me the truth," Swot argued, "and I don't want one of your men. Quite frankly they scare the crap out of me, and I'm betting they scare the crap out of everyone else, so I don't want one of them. I want Matthew."

"Very well," said Grandfather Herbert.

"And one more condition," she added.

"Yes?"

"If I, or rather Matthew and I, find the murderer, or find out what happened, you will allow Matthew to go to Kampala and have his leg fixed."

Swot's grandfather looked down at her from his superior height, his eyes invisible behind the dark lenses of his sunglasses. "Very well," he said. "I agree. If you find the murderer, he will have his operation."

"I'll need a vehicle," Swot said, "and a driver, but no one scary."

"All of my people are what you like to call scary," Grandfather Herbert said with a slight smile.

"Well pick the least scary," said Swot, "and tell him to leave off the sunglasses. "

"We should start immediately," said Brenda.

"We?"

"I'm coming with you."

"I thought you had to stay here and be in charge of your husband's harem," Swot said.

"Oh please!" Brenda rolled her eyes at Swot. "I have absolutely no idea what's going on here."

Grandfather Herbert looked at Swot for a long moment, and then he marched out into the courtyard summoning his henchmen with a snap of his fingers.

Rory came out of the dining room and retrieved his motorcycle. He smashed the crash helmet down on his head and roared out of the gate spraying mud in all directions.

"Oh," Swot said. "I planned to ask him some questions."

"We will," said Brenda. "We'll question him at the scene of the crime; that's what happens in all good detective stories."

"And when's the last time you read a detective story?" Swot asked.

"You'd be surprised," said Brenda. "And it will do you good, young lady, to remember that you are not the only one in the family with brains. I'm not short of intelligence. I have poor impulse control, and maybe a few damaged memory cells, you know, from the sixties, but I am not unintelligent."

One of the immaculately suited henchmen climbed into the black SUV and started the engine.

"Let's go," Swot said, beckoning Matthew towards her, but Matthew's mother caught hold of him and dragged him away.

"Hey, Matthew," Swot shouted, "you're coming with me."

He looked back as his mother dragged him towards one of the small mud brick houses. "She says I have to have a clean shirt," he said, "and she says you should wear a skirt. I will be back very soon."

"A skirt?"

The fat woman, Swot had not bothered to ask her name, looked at her contemptuously. "You are not dressed," she said. "It is disrespectful."

Swot looked down at her bare feet and cotton pajama trousers. The fat woman was actually correct; Swot was still wearing the same clothes she had been wearing when she was rudely awakened by Rory's arrival and dramatic declaration that the Peace Corps worker had been murdered.

"You need a skirt," said Brenda.

"I didn't pack one," Swot said. "I have jeans, and shorts."

"Look around you," Brenda said. "Do you see anyone wearing jeans or shorts?"

Swot looked around. Brenda was, of course, correct. The women wore dresses, or at least layers of bright cloth wound around their waists. None of them were revealing either their legs or their arms, although they didn't seem to care so much about showing off their bosoms, even to the extent that one had held a baby clamped to her breast during the entire time that she had watched the events in the compound. Swot surveyed the compound. It seemed that Matthew was the only boy at home; the other children were all girls, in tattered short sleeved dresses. Most of the dresses were not even buttoned at the back, and the waist strings were hanging down, trailing in the mud, but they were definitely dresses.

"In this country girls wear dresses," Brenda said.

"Hey, I saw women in Kampala in jeans and pants," Swot protested.

""Not here," said Brenda, "not up country. I don't think that's changed in all the years I've been gone. If you want the women to talk to you and respect you, you need to wear a skirt and act like a woman."

Swot looked at her in surprise; she was actually receiving words of wisdom from her hippy grandmother. This was something new. Brenda smiled. "Herbert's mother let me know how I was expected to dress," she said. "She was an awful woman and I absolutely hated her, and I think she definitely felt the same way about me, but she was right about the clothes. My goodness, I don't know how we managed to survive as long as we did; six stupid white kids in an old VW bus; we didn't carry a lot of cash, but we had cameras, and radios and all kinds of attractive stuff, and we girls were good looking It was okay when we were all together, we kind of kept an eye on each other, but when the others left I had to learn to live like an African wife, and I had to dress like one. I 'm telling you from bitter experience that if you want people to talk to you and trust you and if you want to get anywhere with this investigation, you'd better respect the culture. So you can begin by putting on a skirt. I'll give you one of mine."

"No one's interested in me," Swot mumbled, "I don't think I'm going to be driving the men wild with lust."

"Oh shut up," said Brenda, "and stop feeling sorry for yourself. I'm not talking about lust; I'm talking about trying to fit in. Dressed the way you are at the moment, you are nothing but a walking insult to the culture, so let's do something about it."

Stunned into silence, Swot followed Brenda into her bedroom where Brenda opened her suitcase and handed her a flimsy peasant skirt and a tee shirt.

"Put them on, and let's get going," she said.

"Brenda," Swot asked, "why did you do it?"

"Do what?"

"Marry Herbert?"

"Oh, that's easy," she said. "We'd been weeks on the road, bumping our way up from Cape Town and I was in love with Africa; the colors, the smells, the people; I was crazy in love with it all and I wanted to own a piece of it. Having sex with an African seemed to be the best way to do it."

"But you married him," Swot said. "Why not just have sex with him? I thought you were all about free love."

"I was," she said, "but he wasn't. He wanted to marry me. He had his reasons, mostly to do with the fact that I was rich and white, and I might be his ticket out of here. You cannot possibly believe how handsome he was, and how badly I wanted to go to bed with him."

"That's enough," Swot said, pulling the tee shirt over her head. "That's too much information."

"You started it," Brenda said as she ushered Swot out of the door. She chuckled to herself. "Africa is very sexy," she said, "just you wait and see."

Swot walked out onto the verandah, feeling the light fabric of the skirt floating around her ankles. She found herself picking up a corner of the skirt to keep it out of the mud, feeling suddenly feminine. She wondered how she looked to the people around her. For her this was an entirely new sensation; for the first time in her life she considered that maybe she was not just plain ugly, maybe she was exotically attractive. She stood up straight and held her shoulders back, thrusting out what little bosom she possessed. She looked at the other women in the compound, with their glowing brown skin, their dark secretive eyes, and their generous curved bodies. Her confidence deserted her. Obviously she was missing

some very important African genes. Her shoulders slumped again.
Well, at least she had brains.

CHAPTER THREE

Swot didn't get her own way; the black SUV was not only driven by
a scary dude in sunglasses, another scary dude in sunglasses was
also riding along in the front seat, and a large scary looking gun of
some sort was cradled in the crook of his arm.
She protested, of course. "Come on," she said, "why do we have to
drive around with guns? Who on earth wants to shoot me."
"No one wants to shoot you," said her grandfather, "but
unfortunately you are riding in my car, and there are people who
would very much like to shoot me."
"Perhaps we could walk," Swot said.
"You are welcome to walk," he replied, "but if you do you will be
followed by children and beggars, you will be driven into the ditch
by passing traffic, and you will be eaten alive by mosquitos. But,
you are welcome to walk."
"We'll ride," said Brenda, scrambling into the back seat of the car.
Matthew climbed after her with great enthusiasm. He was wearing
clean shorts, a very white shirt, and a big grin; probably just
delighted to be going anywhere at all away from his stepmother.
The vehicle bumped and splashed its way out of the compound and
onto the red mud road; if it could be called a road. The driver took
up a position in the center of the slippery track presumably, Swot
thought, to keep them out of the deep ditches on either side. She
wondered what would happen if another vehicle came from the
opposite direction and it was only a few seconds before she found
out. A battered truck loaded down with what looked like green
bananas came at them out of the rain, also riding on the crown of
the road. Their driver stuck to his path and for a few moments they
were involved in a game of demolition derby chicken. Before they
could actually collide with each other the shotgun guard wound
down his window and extended the barrel of his shotgun. The
approaching truck veered off the road and into the ditch, tipping at
an impossible angle. The guard wound up the window and they

blew past the wrecked vehicle.

"Shouldn't we help them;" Swot asked, "we just drove them off the road?"

"They are accustomed," said the guard, resettling his weapon between his knees.

Swot saw that they had been passing fields of some kind of crops. She had no idea what was being grown, but she could see that the land was somewhat cultivated and protected by hedges. After a few minutes they left the crops behind and passed into what Swot could only think of as jungle. The trees closed in around them, brushing against the sides of the SUV. If someone were to come the other way now their previous intimidation technique wasn't going to work; someone would have to stop, and someone would have to back up. Swot was pretty certain who would be doing the stopping and backing up, and it wouldn't be her grandfather's driver..

They rounded a corner, a maneuver that left Swot terrified because the driver barely slowed as they went around the curve. Ahead of them three men stood in the road. They were wearing uniforms of some kind and they carried weapons. Swot noticed that the shotgun guard in the front seat squared his shoulders and muttered something to the driver. The driver increased speed. The men in the road stood their ground for a moment, and then stepped aside, and within seconds they were lost from sight among the trees. The guard muttered something to the driver; the driver replied. The muttering continued for some minutes as the vehicle flew down the tunnel of green jungle, spraying mud in all directions. The guard turned round and looked at Swot and her grandmother and then muttered something else to the driver.

"What are you talking about?" Brenda asked impatiently.

"It's nothing," said the guard.

"Oh it's something," Brenda retorted. "Who were those men?"

"It is nothing to worry about," the guard replied, but he kept his hand on his weapon.

"I'll decide what to worry about and what not to worry about," Brenda told him. "Who were they?"

"Bad characters," the driver said.

"Bad characters?" Brenda said. "What kind of bad characters, and by the way, what is your name?

"I am called Mugabe," the guard replied.

"Well, Mugabe," said Brenda, "don't speak to me as if I was eight years old. I am your boss's wife and don't you forget it."

Mugabe muttered under his breath, and Brenda was wise enough not to ask him for a translation.

"Well?" she said.

"They are from Matapa's Army," said Mugabe.

Swot waited, but no further information was forthcoming. She looked at Matthew.

"Who's Matapa? "Swot asked.

"Bad," said Matthew, "very bad. Everyone is frightened of Matapa."

Mugabe turned around and made a kind of clicking sound that frightened Matthew into silence.

"Hey, "Swot said, "don't be shushing him; he's just trying to tell us what's going on."

The guard took off his sunglasses and looked Swot in the eye.

"Matapa," he said, in his deep African voice," is a terrorist committed to the destabilization of Uganda. He commands a small army and he relies on intimidation to keep his people loyal. He captures children and makes them into soldiers. He takes girls, such as yourself, as sex slaves. "He looked at Brenda and then at Matthew. "Old people and cripples are of no use to him," he said, "so they are killed. He burns villages, and crops, he rapes, he steals, and he moves so swiftly that he cannot be caught."

"He uses magic," the driver added over his shoulder. "Witchcraft and curses."

"Well," Swot squeaked in a small voice, "thank you for telling me."

"Never heard of him," said Brenda.

"He is wanted by the International Criminal Court," Mugabe said, "but they will never catch him."

The driver looked over his shoulder again, "We were not aware that he was in this district," he said. "This is not a good thing."

"And he was just there in the middle of the road?" Swot said. "Are you going to tell someone?"

The guard adjusted his grip on his weapon. "When service is restored, we will phone Kampala," he said, "but by the time they come, he will be gone. Tonight the people will suffer and then he will move on."

"Can't anyone do anything about him?" Swot asked. "Do you just let it happen?"

Mugabe shrugged his shoulders. "He will not touch us," he said.

"Yeah, well, it's not just about us, is it?" Swot said. "What about people who don't have big black cars and guards with guns?"

"They will pray," said Matthew.

"Oh, sure," she said, "praying; that'll do the trick."

"Jesus is their only hope," Matthew said firmly.

"God, I hate this country," Swot muttered and then she settled back in her seat and scanned the trees and jungle on either side for men with guns. She relaxed a little when they finally arrived at a paved road; or at least a road that had been paved once upon a time, although obviously not recently. They sped down the relatively smooth road into a small town and an actual crossroads with an actual traffic light, although it was not actually working. The driver blew through the crossroads without stopping. People took one look at the black SUV and scattered out of his way. Brenda was staring out of the window.

"I remember this place," she said. She turned to Swot, "this is Budeka; we camped here. She shook her head. "There was almost nothing here and now look at it. Everything's changed."

"Fifty years, Swot said.

"Don't rub it in," she replied. "We were so ridiculously young."

A strange expression came over Brenda's face; if Swot hadn't known her better she would have said that she looked tearful; but this was Brenda, and Brenda was never tearful.

January 1963 Uganda East Africa: Hippies in a VW Bus

Most of the good people of Budeka were sleeping when the six spoiled white kids arrived in their sunshine yellow Volkswagen bus.

The only people awake were the two Uganda Police Force officers who guarded the town jail, and the three noisy drunks who had just been admitted to the cells; their excuses for public drunkenness falling upon deaf ears. "Yes, we should celebrate that Uganda is now a free and independent country, and we no longer answer to a British Governor and British police commanders; but that was three months ago. Why are you still drinking?" The drunks might have replied that they were drinking because they had nothing else to do; they had been employed by the colonial power and now the colonial power was gone, and so was their pay check; and no one seemed able to tell them where they should now look for job security.

The mini-bus rolled erratically down the single main street. Rory Marsden was driving because he was slightly less intoxicated than the five other kids in the car; and he wasn't high, not even slightly high, which was more than could be said for the three girls giggling uncontrollably in the back seat.

Rory jabbed his elbow into the skinny ribs of the boy next to him. "Wanna stop here?" he asked.

Ben Goldstein poked his head out of the window. "Is there a hotel?"

"I don't know," said Rory.

Tommy Girard leaned forward from the rear seat. "Isn't it marked on your map?" he asked blinking himself into semi-wakefulness. "I thought everything was on your map?"

"We're off the map," said Rory, "we've been off the map for days in case you haven't noticed."

"We're lost," said Annie; "how about that? Rory got us all lost."

For some reason, possibly connected to the amount of alcohol they had all imbibed, the passengers found the idea hilarious. Lost; that's what they came for; they came to get lost; they came to get away from everything familiar, and this was it, the end of everything familiar..

"We can just stop here," said Ben, "this looks like a nice place."

"It looks like the back of beyond," said Tommy.

"Just stop," Ben insisted.

"Where," said Rory, "where do you want me to stop? I can't see a damned thing."

"Over there," Tommy said. "Looks like a field of some sort. We can just stop here."

"Looks like a park," said Rory, focusing his tired eyes on the dim outline of some sort of statue, and perhaps some ornamental railings. He wasn't sure about the statue, but railings probably were not a good idea.

"Go for it," Ben yelled causing the blonde girl in the back seat to sit up and pay attention.

"Where are we?" asked Brenda, who preferred to be called Songbird. "Is there a bathroom?"

"There's bushes," said Rory.

Brenda waved a dismissive hand. "Okay, bushes. Bushes are okay." The headlights of the VW, dim because they were coated in red African road dust, picked out a gap in the railings. Rory was incapable of assessing whether or not the gap was wide enough. He gunned the engine and ploughed across the road, through a ditch and through the gap, scraping both sides of the mini-bus as he went.

"Okay," said Ben. "Let's camp here."

The grinding of metal on metal awoke Mr. and Mrs. Fred Fowler, lately employed by Her Majesty's Government to oversee the education of the natives; and now, with the arrival of independence, not employed by anyone. They were not heavy sleepers. Mrs. Fowler had become convinced that they would soon be murdered in their beds, the way white people had been murdered in Kenya, and were still being murdered in the Congo. Mr. Fowler sprung from the bed and pulled his WWII service pistol from under the pillow. He approached the window and cautiously parted the curtains. He looked at the VW bus that had come to rest beside the ornamental grave marker of the first Missionary Bishop of Budeka. He saw three girls stumble out from the back seat, and run giggling into the bushes where they appeared to be squatting and.....

He climbed back into bed beside his wife and returned the pistol to its original position. "Disgraceful," he said.

"I hope they didn't wake Margaret," said Mrs. Fowler, "she seems like a nervous little thing."

"She'll settle down," said Mr. Fowler, "once she meets the children." In the guest room, the room that Mrs. Fowler had hoped would be a nursery, the new missionary school teacher stirred in her sleep, dimly aware of noises outside. With a head full of spiky curlers, she was having trouble finding a comfortable place on the pillow, but she wanted to look her best in the morning; for the children.
"Americans," Mr. Fowler said to his wife.
"Oh dear," said Mrs. Fowler.

CHAPTER FOUR

Swot watched as her grandmother's expression turned from an unusual wistfulness to her usual determination. She suspected that Brenda had been lost in old memories of the first time she had seen this place; in the days when she had been Songbird Carter, child of privilege, with all boundaries removed.
"Wait," said Brenda slapping the driver's shoulder.
He turned angrily in his seat. "What?" he asked.
"Soldiers," Brenda said. "Look over there; there's soldiers."
"UPDF," said Mugabe "they are of no concern; they are from our own defence forces.
"Soldiers," Brenda said with exaggerated patience, "from your army. Doesn't that suggest something to you?"
Mugabe turned to look at her; his expression concealed by his sunglasses.
"Tell them about what we saw," Brenda said.
"I think it would serve no purpose," said Mugabe.
"I don't care what you think," Brenda insisted; "just stop and tell them."
Mugabe and the driver had yet another muttered conversation. It was obvious to Swot that the driver did not want to stop and he in fact continued to drive ahead through the crowded street while Mugabe's voice became increasingly insistent. Swot had been wondering who was actually in charge of the vehicle and now it became obvious that, in whatever way her grandfather ranked his Mafioso henchmen, Mugabe was the senior. The driver brought the SUV to a halt and then started to back up staring into the

rearview mirror but never actually turning to see what was happening behind him. Swot looked out of the rear window and saw people scurrying out of the way and cars swerving to avoid their vehicle; but no one touched them and no one dared to complain.

The soldiers, there were just two of them, were standing outside of a busy little storefront whose owner had spread his wares across the sidewalk and onto the curb. One of the men had slung his weapon across his shoulder and was intent on examining a display of electric fans; the other was engrossed in reading a newspaper. They looked up disinterestedly when the SUV came to a halt beside them. Habati, the driver wound down his window and called to them. They approached warily. The driver began to speak and once again Swot didn't understand a word he said. If I have to stay in this country much longer, she said to herself, I will have to learn their ridiculous language; but that wasn't going to happen because she wasn't going to stay; as soon as they could get their bridge fixed, or road mended or whatever the problem was, she would be out of there.

The driver and the soldiers talked at length, with the driver maintaining a very low key drone to his voice, and the soldiers occasionally shrugging their shoulders. One of them finally came forward and peered in through the window.

"Matapa dangerous man," he said. "You be careful."

The driver wound the window up again and inserted the SUV forcefully into the flow of traffic.

"Hey, wait a minute," Brenda said. "What happened, what are they going to do?"

"There is nothing they can do," said Mugabe. "We have done as you asked Madame Brenda; we have told them."

"Well, shouldn't they call in reinforcements or something?" Brenda asked.

Mugabe wearily removed his glasses so that Swot could see the long-suffering expression on his face.

"They are a group of five soldiers," he said. "They were traveling by taxi to their barracks in Entebbe but they have been stopped by the floods. They are cut off, just as we are."

"Well, don't they have radios or something?" Brenda asked. "If they called up reinforcements now____"

"No radios," said Mugabe, "cell phone only, and like us they have no service."

"But should they___? "Brenda started to say.

"There is nothing they can do," Mugabe repeated. "What purpose would it serve for them to walk down the road looking for Matapa? They will not find him, and if he finds them, he will kill them. They will stay here in town and wait for the road to be repaired and then they will report what we have told them."

"That's no way to run an army," Brenda protested.

"Perhaps you Americans would like to give us assistance," said Mugabe.

"It wasn't like this when I was here before," Brenda complained.

"That was under colonialism," said Mugabe, "we prefer to have our freedom."

He replaced his sunglasses and turned to face the front, and silence reigned until they reached Rory Marsden's house.

Rory was sitting on his wide front porch. As they pulled in through the high metal gates that surrounded his compound, the rain suddenly ceased and the blazing sun started to bake the moisture out of the ground in waves of sticky heat. Ominous dark clouds still loomed at them from the surrounding mountains, but for the moment at least Swot could climb out of the car without being drenched.

Swot decided that the only description she could come up with for Rory's house was "cute" which she knew was a strange word to use for a mud brick residence in the heart of darkest Africa, but that's what it was; it was cute and incredibly British looking. It stood at the end of a mud road that showed signs of once having been paved. The overwhelming feature of the neighborhood was a rundown miniature gothic cathedral with a rusted tin roof, a leaning bell tower, stained glass windows, and a large statue of the Virgin Mary, so presumably, Swot thought, a Catholic church. An overgrown graveyard surrounded the little cathedral, and beyond the graveyard were several small bungalows, obviously built for the colonial British and one larger residence with wide verandahs and an arched entryway and a sign that said Speke Guest House. Apart from Rory's house and the Guest House, everything was suffering from rot and neglect, and seemed to be sinking back into the mud from which it was built. However Rory's house had been plastered and painted with whitewash, his lawn was mowed, his roof showed no signs of rust, and there appeared to be glass in all the windows.

"We're on the *boma*," Mugabe announced as they pulled up in front of the house. "I think the Madame will be comfortable here." Something in his tone discouraged Swot from asking him a question so she asked Matthew "What's a *boma*?"

"It's the word we use for the place where white people used to live," he said. "In colonial times they all lived here, and Africans lived elsewhere."

"They tried to make a little England," said Brenda, "and look where it got them. I remember this place. When I was here before all of this was in good condition. I don't know what's happened here." The driver turned to look at Brenda. "The British left," he said, "and we have looked after things the African way. All of this now is ours."

And you're welcome to it, Swot thought. It was very hard for her to include herself in anything African. Although the evidence was right in front of her; her grandfather was most certainly an African, but that didn't make her any more appreciative of the steamy heat, the all-pervading mud, the potholed road, and the pathetic derelict buildings; she felt much more in tune with Rory Marsden's level of maintenance.

"Did you bring a notebook?" Brenda asked her as they approached the front porch.

"No."

"So how are you going to ask questions?"

"I don't even know what questions to ask," Swot complained.

"I have a notebook," said Matthew, "and I think we should ask him where the body was found."

"First we should ask him where he gets his money;" Brenda said, "he's living like a king."

Rory came down off the porch to greet them. He was wearing a clean white tee shirt, denim shorts and flip-flops. He gestured towards the house. "Remember this place?" he asked Brenda.

"Oh I do," said Brenda. "Those miserable people from England were living here. What were they called?"

"Mr. and Mrs. Fowler," said Rory.

"That's right," she said, "the Fowlers. We scandalized them, didn't we?"

"I think we scandalized everyone;" Rory said, "'sometimes I even scandalized myself."

He looked at Swot, and then at Matthew. "Well, this is it," he said. "This is where I found him."

"Right here?" Swot asked, stepping back.

"No, just over there, under the avocado tree."

Matthew produced his notebook and started to write."

"What time did you find him, Mr. Rory?" he asked.

"Sun up," said Rory.

"Dawn," Swot translated.

Matthew nodded. "Were the gates still locked?" he asked.

Rory looked at him in surprise. "Good question, kid," he said. "And yes, the gates were still locked."

They all turned and looked at the high metal gates. They were standing open, but Swot imagined that they would make a formidable barrier once they were closed. The entire property was enclosed with a barbed wire fence.

"So," Swot said, "we can assume that he wasn't brought here in a vehicle."

"No, I suppose not," said Rory.

"Someone killed him and then dragged him through the barbed wire fence and onto your property," Swot said. She stopped to think about that. Someone dragged the body of this poor innocent American do-gooder through the surrounding weeds and then heaved him over the barbed wire fence; that was really sick.

"Perhaps they cut the wire," Matthew said.

Swot had to admit that the kid was thinking far more clearly than she was, and she was supposed to be the resident genius.

"Yeah, they cut it," Rory said. "I can show you where."

"We could look," Swot said, "but I'm not sure how that would help."

"Clues," said Brenda, urging her forward. "You look for clues."

"Like what?" Swot asked wearily.

Brenda grabbed her arm and suddenly she wasn't Brenda the free spirit, she was Brenda, the grandmother whose mission in life was to spur Swot into action and to ensure that she made something of herself. "Come on, Swot, "she said, "don't give up already. I want your grandfather to be proud of you. You can do this, I know you can."

"Well, you know more than I do," Swot said sullenly.

"Perhaps we will find clothing caught on the wire, or perhaps footprints," said Matthew hopefully, and then Swot remembered why she was here. She really didn't care who had killed the American kid, but if she could solve the mystery, then Matthew would get his operation.

"Sorry," Swot said. "I'm just a bit distracted. I guess I'm still thinking about Matapa."

"Matapa?" said Rory.

"We saw some of his men," Brenda said.

"Where?" Rory was suddenly very attentive.

"A couple of miles outside of town," Brenda said.

"How many?" Rory asked.

"Three," Swot replied.

"What did your guard say?" Rory asked.

"Not much," Swot replied. "He didn't want to talk about it."

"No one wants to talk about Matapa," said Rory. "Matapa is a political hot potato."

"Who is he?" Swot asked.

"Well," said Rory, "if this was Somalia, I suppose you would call him a warlord, although I personally think he's just an evil son of a bitch. Let me talk to your driver; what's his name?"

"I don't know the driver's name," Swot admitted, "but the guard is called Mugabe."

Rory walked over to where Mugabe was leaning against the hood of the SUV. The driver door was open and she could see the driver inside, reading a newspaper. She couldn't hear what either Rory or Mugabe was saying but Rory seemed to become increasingly agitated. Finally he turned and walked back to Swot.

"If Matapa is here, then things are not what I thought," he said. He looked at Swot and then gestured across the vegetable patch towards the fence. "That's where they cut the fence," he said. "Go knock yourself out."

"Why should you knock yourself out?" Matthew asked.

"He means we should go and see for ourselves," Swot said.

"Aren't you coming with us?' Brenda asked.

Rory shook his head. "I have to go inside and do something," he said.

"I'll come inside," Brenda offered, "I want to see what you've done with the place."

"Some other time," Rory said. "Go with them." He gestured to Mugabe. "You need to go with them," he said.

Mugabe picked up his deadly looking weapon and came across the lawn towards them. He didn't move fast, and he certainly didn't give the impression of hurrying, but somehow he exuded strength and purpose in the way he planted his polished black shoes on the ground; the way he held his shoulders; the way his head turned slowly from side to side, sweeping the landscape. Swot had always thought that she was not attracted to the strong silent type, and she hated to be a cliché, but somewhere deep in a very private place, well below the waistline, she was finding Mugabe and his strongman act, extremely sexy and she was feeling quite distracted as she set off through the rows of corn. She was surprised to find that she actually enjoyed the way the long skirt she was wearing floated around her legs. She admitted to herself that she felt feminine, in a sort of "you Tarzan me Jane" kind of way, which was not the way she should have been feeling as they approached the place where the body of the kid had been dragged onto the property.

Even though he was hopping on one crutch, Matthew was way ahead of her, and Brenda was somewhere behind commenting loudly on Rory's lack of manners. "What's he got in there anyway?" she asked.

"He's probably got an African wife and a bunch of kids," Swot said. "Perhaps he thinks you'll be jealous or something."

"Jealous," she said. ""Why should I be jealous? We were finished with each other by the time we got to Uganda."

"So you___?"

"Sure," said Brenda. "Everyone slept with everyone. We were free spirits."

"So by the time you got here you'd run out of white guys?" Swot asked.

"That's a crude way of putting it," Brenda replied. "It's just that I found your grandfather to be much more attractive than Rory."

Swot looked sideways at Mugabe prowling through the garden like a panther and she really couldn't think of anything else to say.

Brenda turned and looked back at Rory's house. "That's a really big aerial," she said. "I'm wondering if he has a radio."

"I shouldn't think so," Swot replied. "If he had a radio he could have radioed the Embassy instead of yelling at them down the phone. And anyway there's no electricity."

"I assume he has a generator," Brenda said. "There's something going on with him."

Matthew had arrived at the gap in the fence, and Swot could see where the grass and weeds had been beaten down.

"They came through here," he said. He started to draw a sketch in his little notebook. My God, Swot thought, he was taking this very seriously; but of course he had something at stake. If they did find the killer, she wondered, would her grandfather, his father, follow through on the promise?

"They came across that field," Matthew said, heading for the gap in the fence.

Mugabe growled something at him and Matthew stopped in his tracks.

"I have to see where they came from," he insisted.

Mugabe reached out a large hand and pulled Matthew to the rear, practically toppling him in the process; then Mugabe went through the fence with Matthew hopping along behind him.

Swot and Brenda dutifully followed the tracks for a short distance until they came to the road. After that there was nothing to see; the road was a muddy mess of tire tracks and footprints, and no way to tell where the nameless faceless people who had knifed Zach and dragged him into Rory Marsden's yard had come from. .

"Wait a minute," Swot said. "We need to go back and look at the place where Rory found him"

"Why?" asked Matthew.

"Because," she said, "we don't know if he was killed somewhere else, or if he was alive when they brought him here, and that would mean they killed him in Rory's yard. If they did, then there would be a lot of blood."

Matthew nodded enthusiastically. "We go back," he said, and he started hobbling along the road towards Rory's main gate. "Thank you Sarah," he said. "You have started to think."

"Yeah," Swot said, "sorry kid. I'll try to be more help. I know this is important."

"Very important," he said. "and not just for me. It's important for Zach, and for Zach's family; I expect they want to know who killed him. "

Swot hadn't really thought about Zach's family back in the United States. Where did he come from anyway? She imagined him as a sort of white bread guy from somewhere like Kansas City, or Indianapolis; somewhere where people lived safe, boring lives; yeah, just a kid looking for an adventure before he settled down to be as boring as his parents. Did they even know their son was dead? She'd heard Rory shouting down the telephone to the Embassy, but he didn't give them Zach's last name, and then the phone had shut down. She looked back at the house with not just one but two aerials mounted on the roof, plus a satellite dish. Maybe he did have a short wave radio, or maybe he had a satellite phone; but he obviously didn't want to use either of them.

They went back through the metal gates and Mugabe returned to propping himself up against the hood of the SUV and looking sexily vigilant. Swot gave herself a mental telling off; she was not, repeat not, interested in Mugabe. She was certainly not interested in repeating her grandmother's mistake and producing a child who had no idea who she really was; and really she was not interested in sex. She knew that last thought was not quite true. She was an eighteen year old girl who had read more than her fair share of romantic novels; she was quite interested in sex in theory, but not in practice; in fact no practice at all.

In the few minutes since they had left Rory's compound additional visitors had arrived, but Rory had not reappeared from the house. A battered little Suzuki station wagon was parked next to the Mercedes and an African priest in a black suit and a shining white collar was climbing out. He was followed by an African nun in a blue dress and a white veil. They all stared at each other and Swot wondered who was going to make the introductions. She didn't think her grandmother was on very good terms with the church.

"Who is that?" Swot whispered to Matthew.

"I don't know," said Matthew. "He is Catholic."

"And you're not?" she asked.

"No," he replied firmly, and Swot wondered if she had somehow insulted him.

"He is from here in town," Matthew added, "I don't know his name, but you should call him Father; that's what they like to be called."

"Okay," Swot said, "and what about the woman; the nun?"

"Oh, that's Sister Angela, she is the midwife from Nawalyo."

"Okay," Swot said. She looked at her grandmother. "Say hello Father," she urged.

"Hello Father," Brenda said.

The priest stared at her. She stared back.

"I know you," the priest said.

"I doubt that very much," said Brenda.

"Yes, yes, I remember," the priest said, and he was grinning from ear to ear. "You came, the year of Independence."

"Yes..."

"I was a small boy but I remember. We were all celebrating because the British were going, and then you came, Americans in a bright yellow van. I had never seen an American. Don't you remember; we followed you everywhere?"

"I remember children following us," Brenda said."

"That was me, I was one of the kids following you," the priest said. He extended his hand. "I am now called Father Amos."

"I am still called Brenda," said Brenda.

"Yeah, "Swot said, "but you used to be called Songbird."

"Songbird," Father Amos grinned again. "I remember. Ah, there was something else. Now what was it? There was some kind of trouble."

Rory interrupted the priest's train of thought by coming out onto his porch where he was immediately spotted by Sister Angela. She launched into an angry tirade which Rory deflected with an eloquent shrug of his shoulders and the constant repetition of the phrase "it's nothing to do with me."

Although Sister Angela's English was very heavily accented and her indignation caused her to speak very fast, Swot quickly got the gist of her complaint; the body of the murdered boy had been placed in the clinic in Nawalyo; the clinic where she, Sister Angela, was called upon to deliver babies. What was more important, she wanted to know, new life or a dead boy? Was it just because he was white that he was allowed to occupy the clinic and risk the lives of newborn babies? "I knew him," she said in conclusion. "He would not want this."

"We would like to bury him," said Father Amos. "My church will offer land. We didn't like his mission, or the fact that he had been sent here to tell us how to do what we already knew how to do, but we liked him. He was a good boy with good intentions. I think that many would come to his funeral."

Rory sighed and for first time Swot saw his face soften. From the moment he had stormed into Swot's grandfather's compound she had thought of him as a cold, angry, self-absorbed man but now she saw empathy on his face; empathy and understanding.

"I think he would have liked that," Rory said. "I think that he would want to be buried here; he loved it here and he thought he was doing good."

"He was a good boy," said Father Amos.

"Yes," said Rory. "but he was an American boy, and when American boys get killed in Africa, they can't just be buried and forgotten about. As soon as the bridge is fixed there are going to be Embassy people out here asking questions, and they'll want to see the body." He stopped looking at Sister Angela and looked at Swot. "You need to see the body," he said.

"No, I don't," Swot assured him.

"If you want to find out who killed him, you need to see how he was killed."

"Multiple stab wounds, that's what you said."

"But that on its own tells you nothing," Rory said. "The shape of the wounds would tell you the shape of the weapons and____"

Swot looked up at the satellite dish on his roof. "You've been watching American t.v.," she said. "Is it Bones, or CSI?"

"Mr. Rory," said Sister Angela., "what about the mothers? I have mothers who are ready to deliver. We don't know when the bridge will be mended. It could be months."

"The Embassy people will find a way across," Rory said. "Heck, for all I know they'll send a helicopter. He was a Peace Corps worker; they're not going to just leave him here. The parents are going to be complaining and it's bad publicity for the program."

"They'll send troops won't they?" Swot asked.

"Soldiers?" queried Sister Angela. "Why should they send soldiers for just one boy?"

"No, not for the boy," Swot said. "for Matapa."

"Matapa," said Sister Angela. "Matapa is here?"

"We saw him Swot said, "well, probably not him, but some of his men."

Sister Angela's face had taken on a gray tone. "What shall we do?" she asked.

Father Amos was shaking his head. "What does he want?"

"To kill, to rape, to take our children," said Sister Angela.

"We saw some soldiers in town," Swot said.

Sister Angela barely glanced at her. "Soldiers do nothing," she said.

"Surely if you warn people they could be ready," Swot said. "I mean, how many people does he have with him?"

"How many does he need?" asked Sister Angela. "Our people are defenseless."

"We'll do our best to warn people, but what can they do? They run to the bush but he finds them," said Father Amos. He pulled a cell phone from his pocket and looked at it forlornly. "Still no service," he said.

Father Amos headed towards his little vehicle with Sister Angela following close behind. Obviously the news that Matapa was in the area took precedence over the fact that the dead boy was in the clinic. Before Father Amos could start his engine another person came through the gates of Rory's compound; a white woman on a bicycle; Swot didn't know which was older, the woman or the bicycle, but they were both pretty old. The woman had the yellowed skin of someone who has lived a long time in the tropics. Her white hair was cut carelessly short as though she couldn't be bothered to style it. She wore a faded denim jumper over a white tee shirt. Her arms and legs were wiry and thin, freckled with age spots. She came through the gate, pedaling as though all the furies in hell were on her tail.

"Oh my God," said Brenda. "What's she doing here?"

"Who?" Swot asked.

"I don't remember her name," said Brenda. "I can't believe she's still here."

The woman leaned her bicycle against the porch railing and then pulled a piece of paper out of her pocket.

"Take a look at this," she said,

"Margaret," said Brenda from behind Swot. "Her name is Margaret."

Margaret handed the piece of paper to Rory, and then turned to look at Father Amos.

"He hid the Miracle Child," she said, "so now what do we do? They'll keep killing until they find her."

CHAPTER FIVE

They sat on rocking chairs on Rory's front porch, but no one was rocking. They were all leaning forward to hear what Margaret had to say. Swot noticed that it was just the white people on the porch, although she couldn't count herself as a white person but she didn't think that anyone thought of her as an African either. Father Amos and Sister Angela had barely greeted the newcomer before they left in a hurry, presumably to warn whoever they could that Matapa was in their district; Mugabe and the driver still waited impassively next to Swot's grandfather's car.

Matthew had climbed the steps to the porch, but then he stopped and sat down on the top step, he could see and hear everything but he obviously didn't want to sit on one of Rory's sacrosanct rocking chairs; in fact Rory didn't seem to be any too pleased to have anyone on his porch at all.

"Wait just a minute," he had said to Margaret and then he disappeared into the house. Swot soon heard him moving about in the room directly behind where she was sitting. The window closed with a slam, and he pulled the curtain across.

Brenda leaned across to Swot. "He has something in there," she said. "It's something he doesn't want us to see."

"Like what?" Swot asked.

"I don't know, but Rory is not what he seems to be. Did you see the satellite dish?"

"It could be for his T.V.," Swot said. "I mean, he probably wants to know what's going on in the world."

"I don't understand why he came back," said Brenda.

"I thought you said he never left," said Swot.

She shook her head. "No," she said, "he must have left and come back. I heard he was drafted."

"Drafted?"

"Vietnam," she said. "That was the end of our fun."

"I thought my mother was the end of your fun," Swot said.

"Yeah, well, that too," Brenda admitted.

Rory came back onto the porch and sat down in a rocking chair. Now they all leaned forward and stared at Margaret.

"What's this about a miracle child?" Rory asked.

"It's all because of that damned nosey preacher from Ireland," Margaret said. This was the first full sentence Swot had heard from her, and it was obvious that she was one of those upper-class British people who sound like Queen Elizabeth, spitting out all her t's and d's and speaking slowly and clearly so that the poor benighted colonials could understand her.

"The guy who came through last year?" Rory queried, sounding even more heavily Virginian in the face of Margaret's determined Britishness.

"Yes, that man," she said, "Brother Frank."

"He seemed harmless," Rory said.

"Well, he was not harmless," said Margaret."

"He was an evangelist," Rory said. "We get them here all the time; it drives the local pastors crazy but we can't do anything about it. Some guy gets the idea that God's called him to preach, so he rents a sound system and starts going around the country, just collecting crowds and preaching to them. There's no law against it but it sure does make trouble."

"Unlicensed and uneducated," Margaret declared, "and they just come right into the school and demand to talk to the children, and I'm supposed to take time out of class. These children have better things to do than listen to every jumped up self-proclaimed evangelist who comes through here. We have our own clergy."

"You're still teaching?" Brenda asked.

Margaret glared at her. "So it is you," she said, "I thought I was mistaken, but it is you. You used to call yourself Songbird."

"That's right," said Brenda.

Margaret looked at Swot. "So is this...?"

"Yes," said Brenda. "This is my granddaughter Sarah, the result of my marriage."

"Some marriage," said Margaret.

" I assume you never married," said Brenda.

Rory interrupted the flow of nastiness between the two elderly white ladies. Swot was seething with curiosity about what could possibly have happened fifty years earlier that had kept them so angry at each other for such a long time.

"Brother Frank came through here about a year ago" he said.

"Yes," said Margaret. "To quote the Bible, "he came baptizing in the wilderness for the remission of sins," except that we already have people to do that; they're called priests. So this Irish bag of wind started proclaiming that his baptism was better than any other baptism because he baptized with water from the Jordan.   He wanted to preach in the market here, but no one came to listen to him Budeka is much more sophisticated these days; people have radios, some of them have televisions, they have dvd players, they're not like they used to be. If they want to be baptized they go to church; they don't need the services of some ignorant Irishman. He's still here somwehere, spouting his Irish blarney."

Margaret's sallow face turned red with anger as she spoke but Swot couldn't be sure if she was more annoyed with Brother Frank for his intrusive evangelism or for the fact that he was an Irishman.

"He baptized a baby;" Margaret continued, "they don't usually do that. Most of the evangelists that come through here don't believe in infant baptism so they leave the children alone, but not Brother Frank. He picked this baby out of the crowd and declared he was going to baptize her with his magic water from the Jordan; and that's what he did."

"That sounds harmless enough," Rory said, "It was just showmanship."

"Oh he's a showman," said Margaret, "but if you really want to see a showman you should see the witchdoctor at Kajunga."

"You really do have witchdoctors?" Swot asked, and then she remembered what Matthew had told her about his stepmother wanting to give him a charm from the witchdoctor.

"Oh yeah," said Rory, "plenty of witchdoctors."

"The witchdoctor was quite threatened by Brother Frank," said Margaret, "but he was no fool. He decided that he was going to finish what Brother Frank had started. So when Brother Frank moved on to go and annoy people in some other village, the Kajunga witchdoctor decided to bestow even more power on this poor innocent little baby girl. He declared that the child was special; she was already baptized in holy water from the Jordan, and now he added one of his own incantations over her, and declared that she was a miracle child, and that she could cure

AIDS."

"What?" said Rory.

"Cure AIDS," said Margaret, her face set and angry. "He declared that having sex with that child would cure AIDS."

"Sex?" Swot burst out. "I thought you said she was a baby."

"She's two," said Margaret.

"Two?" Swot repeated disbelievingly. "Who has sex with a two year old child?"

"You'd be surprised," Rory said softly.

"But what happened to her?" Swot asked. "Where is she now? What about her parents?"

"Her parents were terrified," said Margaret. "They knew the witchdoctor was going to sell her to the highest bidder."

"This is unbelievable," Swot said.

"No, it's not," said Rory. "This sort of thing happens."

"But a baby...."

"Yes, it happens to babies," said Rory.

"Witchdoctors make medicine with child sacrifice," said Matthew from his seat on the top step.

Swot stared at him and then looked at Brenda. Her face mirrored Swot's shock, but Rory and Margaret showed no sign of shock, they merely looked sad, and weary, and Swot realized that this was something they knew and lived with day after day.

"How can you live here?" Swot asked. No one answered her.

"So where is the baby now?"

"If I knew, I would not say," said Margaret, "but unfortunately I don't know. She was hidden by the white boy; the one who was killed.

"Is that why they killed him?" Swot asked. "Did the witchdoctor kill him? Killing him wouldn't help them find the baby. I mean, did they torture him and then kill him when he wouldn't talk? Does anyone else know where the baby is? How am I supposed to even_____"

Rory interrupted Swot's babbling. Swot welcomed the interruption because she knew that she needed help to stop the words and questions spewing from her mouth while thoughts ran around her head like squirrels in a cage.

"You said you have a note," Rory said.

"Yes. It seems to have come from General Matapa;" Margaret replied "it was left on my doorstep."

"General Matapa? So he's promoted himself," said Rory.

"Apparently."

Margaret pulled a sheet of paper from her pocket, and passed it across to Rory. It looked to Swot like a page that had been torn from a school notebook; rough textured paper with green lines and a ragged edge where it had been wrenched out. The writing was round and loopy, like a kid who had just learned to write, but there was nothing childlike about the message. Rory read the message aloud.

"General Matapa requires the Miracle Child. Give him the child and he will leave the region. "

"Perhaps he's bluffing," said Margaret. "I don't think Matapa is here."

"He's here," Swot said. "We saw some of his men."

"God help us," said Margaret.

"Do you have any idea where the child is?" Rory asked again.

"No," said Margaret pursing her lips and spitting out her words. "That obnoxious boy took her and hid her somewhere and he wouldn't even tell me what he'd done with her. I'm the one who has lived here all these years; I'm the one that people trust, but he just did it, without so much as a by your leave. God only knows what he did with her. He had no right; I'm the one who knows the family. I'm the one they trust. Coming here, trying to tell them how to run their lives....."

Her voice faded away into a series of mumbled complaints.

"So she's not with her parents?" Swot asked, interrupting the flow of vitriol Margaret was directing towards the deceased boy.

"Obviously not," Margaret replied condescendingly. "If she was with her parents, I would know where she is. Zach didn't trust them to keep her safe, and he didn't think I had any idea what to do."

She revved up her complaint engine again and glared at Swot when she interrupted her.

"Well, he had a point," Swot said. "Obviously everyone knows where her parents come from, so if they wanted the poor kid they would just go and get her. It makes perfect sense for Zach to take her somewhere. The only thing I don't understand is what anyone hoped to gain by killing Zach. He can't tell anybody anything now, can he?"

Matthew was scribbling away in his notebook. "May I speak?" he said at last.

"Speak away, kid," Swot said. "At this point your guess is as good as anyone else's."

Margaret looked at Matthew suspiciously.

"That's my Uncle Matthew," Swot said.

"One of my husband's children," Brenda said."

"Your husband!" Margaret sniffed.

"Well, at least I have one," said Brenda.

"I don't think they meant to kill him," said Matthew. "Sometimes people become angry and do things they don't mean to do. There was a fight and he was killed, and now they have to find a new plan."

"They?" Swot said. "Who are they? When did this Matapa person get involved? According to Margaret here the only people involved were the evangelist and the witchdoctor, so when did this war lord get in on the act?"

They all sat silently and considered the question.

"He's an evil son of a bitch," Rory said for the second time.

"So you think he killed Zach?" Swot asked.

Rory shook his head. "No, he wouldn't do that. If he actually killed an American, then the US would have to get involved and there would be hell to pay on all sides; no one wants to ruin the tourist trade. Matapa knows what side his bread is buttered; he won't step over the line."

"Where did Zach live?" Swot asked. "Was he in town here?"

Rory shook his head. "He was only about a quarter of a mile down the road from your grandfather's place. I suppose you'd call it a village, but in Virginia it would just be a wide place in the road."

"So what was he doing here?" Swot asked. "Did he come to town on his own, or did someone bring him?"

"He had a bicycle." Said Matthew.

"And where is the bicycle now?"

"Well, it's not here," said Rory.

"We should try to find it," said Matthew, scribbling in his notebook.

"And we should look through the rest of his stuff," Swot said. "Do you suppose it's still there where he left it?"

"Probably stolen by now," said Rory.

"Let's go and see," Swot said. She stood up out of the rocking chair and saw something move out of the corner of her eye. It was Mugabe, opening the vehicle doors. So, he was watching her every move; she felt very comforted by that fact, and just a little fluttery which was, of course, quite ridiculous because she was never, never, ever going to repeat the mistake her grandmother had made. She was going to be on the next plane out of Uganda just as soon as the road was fixed.

Matthew

Matthew scurried out of the way as the white people came down from the porch. The rainclouds had dissipated; the sun was shining and the mud puddles in Mr. Rory's compound were steaming in the heat. The white people looked hot and uncomfortable; he expected that they would soon start to complain. What did they want, he wondered; they complained when it rained, and they complained when the sun came out, and yet he had heard that in their own country they also complained of the cold. Perhaps they just liked to complain.

He had positioned himself so that he could hear their conversation, and that too had seemed to be full of complaints; apparently they did not approve of the way Ugandans lived their lives. He wondered why they cared; why they didn't just go home; why they thought that everyone should live as they lived.

He looked at Mugabe, his father's right hand man, who had stationed himself at the rear door of the SUV. Surely they could not fail to be impressed by Mugabe who radiated confidence and controlled strength. He watched as Swot climbed into the rear seat and he saw the way that she looked at Mugabe and he saw color creep across her pale cheeks. Well, apparently she was impressed with Mugabe.

He climbed into the vehicle and sat beside Swot and her grandmother while Mugabe took up his position in the front seat. The driver turned some dials on the dashboard and a wave of cold air streamed into the back seat. Swot's grandmother sighed happily and sank back against her seat. "Thank God for air conditioning," she said. Matthew shivered and tried to keep himself away from the stream of freezing air.

They bumped out of Mr. Rory's yard and onto the road. From the rear view window Matthew could see Miss Margaret standing in the driveway talking animatedly to Mr. Rory. He wondered if they were friends; they had both been in Budeka for a long time, and he thought that there may have been times when they were the only white people in the whole district. Perhaps they had once been more than friends; they must have been young once and Mr. Rory was a man, and once upon a time even Miss Margaret must have been a young woman.

They left the town far behind them, driving in the center of the road while lesser vehicles steered clear of them. Matthew knew that his father was a big man; and it seemed that even his vehicle earned respect. Soon they were back among the dense vegetation in the remnant of the rain forest. The driver pointed casually up into the trees and said something to Mugabe. Mugabe turned around and smiled.

"Monkeys," he said.

Matthew followed his pointing finger and saw black and white shapes leaping around in the tree tops.

Oh," said Swot, I'm really here. I'm in Africa, and there are monkeys. Monkeys; real monkeys," she repeated. She smiled at Matthew her face alight with wonder.

"Monkeys," she said again.

Matthew was surprised that the sight of a few Colobus monkeys could bring such joy, but he liked the effect. When Swot smiled her face was transformed.

"Stop," said Brenda's grandmother

"It's okay," Swot said. "I can see them from here."

"Oh not the monkeys," said the old lady, "I need to make a bush visit."

"A what?" said Swot

"I need to pee," her grandmother said. "I have no idea why Rory wouldn't let me into his house; I could have taken care of it in comfort. Anyway, I still need to take care of it."

Swot looked horrified although Matthew could not imagine why; bush stops were a part of everyday life.

Swot's grandmother tapped the driver on the shoulder. "Over there," she said, "there's a gap in the bushes."

"This is not safe," said Mugabe.

"Safe or not, I have to go," she insisted.

"I think you should listen to what he says," said Swot, and Matthew thought that she looked at Mugabe with something approaching awe. His opinion of Swot was immediately improved; at least she was one person who didn't think all Ugandans were incompetent.

"I'll only be a minute," said Swot's grandmother. She tapped the driver on the shoulder again. "Stop," she insisted.

The driver brought the SUV to a halt and the old lady climbed out and disappeared into the bushes beside the road. Mugabe also climbed out of the vehicle and stood, weapon in hand, staring at the place where the white lady had disappeared. He looked at Swot questioningly. Swot shook her head vigorously as if to indicate that she had absolutely no intention of going into the bush under any circumstances.

Matthew hesitated for a moment. He didn't want Swot to be angry with him, and he certainly didn't want to annoy Mugabe, but now that he thought about it, he really did need to make his own bush call. He was sure that he could go in among the trees and take care of his business before the old lady came back. He opened the passenger door and took hold of his crutch.

"Oh not you too," said Swot.

"Sorry," said Matthew.

The driver turned around and looked at him. "Hurry up," he said.

"I'm hurrying," Matthew responded tucking his crutch under his arm.

He scuttled across the road, taking the opposite side from the white lady; he certainly didn't want to come across her in the bushes. He took just a few steps off the road and into the elephant grass. Looking back he could see that Swot was fully engaged looking at the tree tops where the monkeys leaped and chattered. It occurred to him that he had never heard monkeys make so much noise and in fact their chattering had turned to hoops of alarm. He wondered what the white lady had done to upset them.

He concealed himself behind a clump of elephant grass and took care of his business, keeping an eye on the road to make sure that they would not drive away without him.

He saw the white women emerge from the bushes and then he heard a shrill alarm cry as the monkeys fled to the tree tops above him.

He saw Mugabe turn in his direction instantly alert as the three men they had seen earlier broke from the cover of the trees. They were on the opposite of the road from the white lady, the same side as Matthew, but they weren't looking at Matthew, they were looking across the road to the place where the white woman was walking out of the bush, straightening her skirt as she came.

Mugabe moved instantly, grabbing the woman's arm and dragging her towards the car. The three men backed away into the bushes just a few yards from where Matthew was standing.

Mugabe bundled Swot's grandmother into the car, and turned to face the three men. He raised his weapon. Matthew knew he had to move fast; faster than he had moved since the day he fell from the jackfruit tree. He started towards the road, his haste making him clumsy. His crutch tangled in the long grass and he fell forward. He scrambled to his feet casting around for the crutch. Before he could find it he was seized by rough hands and dragged into the road where he found himself staring back at Mugabe whose weapon was aimed directly at him. Whoever was holding him was using him as a human shield.

He stared at Mugabe, willing him to do something; shoot around him, shoot someone else. The rough hands dragged him backwards again; back into the long grass. He caught one last glimpse of Mugabe, still standing in the road, with his weapon still raised, and then he was thrown to the ground, then he heard the squealing of tires and the loud roar of the engine as his father's vehicle fled away.

CHAPTER SIX

Swot had been leading an uncensored life ever since she was eight years old and allowed free run of the family library. She had watched anything and everything on television; she had seen plenty of R rated movies, and she went to college when she was fourteen years old. She knew know a lot of bad words and she used them all on Mugabe; every single one of them, although she was pretty sure he had no idea what some of them meant. Nothing in her vocabulary was able to convince him to turn around and go and look for Matthew.

The driver roared down the road with Swot screaming invective at the back of Mugabe's head. When Brenda tried to get her quieted down Swot turned on her as well.

"You just had to do it, didn't you?" she said. "You had to make him stop."

"I'm sorry, Swot," Brenda said, "but I just had to go. How was I to know that Matthew would get out of the car? "

"You could have waited," Swot insisted.

"So could he," Brenda said.

They were all silent for a few moments and then Brenda said softly, "It's nothing like it used to be."

"What isn't?"

"This country; it was so friendly. We'd come up all the way from Cape Town and wherever we went the Africans were afraid of us. Oh we felt safe enough, but it was like we were in a bubble, some special privileged class and no one dared to touch us; and then we came here, and, well, it was just one big party. They had their independence and they were loving it, and we were Americans and they loved us; they loved Kennedy. We had a ball."

"So now what do you think?" Swot snapped. "Are you still having a ball?"

"No," said Brenda.

"And what the hell do you think they're going to do with Matthew?" Swot asked. "You heard what the driver said; they kill cripples."

"Perhaps they weren't Matapa's men," said Brenda.

"They were," said Mugabe, speaking for the first time.

"What will they do to him?" Swot asked.

Mugabe shrugged his broad shoulders, and they continued the journey in silence until they arrived at Grandfather Herbert's compound.

Swot went to her room. She had no wish to be any part of the moment when someone had to tell Jubilee that her son was missing. She imagined that the fat woman senior wife would probably want to tell her herself; she would probably enjoy telling her.

The rain had stopped, the sky was bright blue, and the heat in Swot's room was incredible. The fan was still motionless. No power. She slammed the door and hurled herself onto the bed. She wanted to cry, but no tears came, just a horrible sense of frustration and anger; and no place to focus that anger.

The door banged open and her grandfather strode into the room. He sat down on the single chair, a very frail looking item that would surely not hold his weight for very long.

"They did the right thing," he said. "Their duty was to protect you and your grandmother. Matthew was not their responsibility."

"He's your son," Swot said. "Don't you even care?"

She struggled to read the expression on his face.

"I care," he said eventually. "I have many sons, and I care for all of them."

"No you don't," Swot insisted. "You don't care about him at all. He's just a throwaway, isn't he? He's broken and you don't want him."

Grandfather Herbert rose to his feet. "Your guards did their duty," he said, "but they made a mistake in listening to your grandmother. They should never have stopped the vehicle. If you want to be angry, be angry with her."

He went out of the room, leaving the door wide open, and a few moments later Swot heard a loud wailing from outside. She knew what it was; Jubilee mourning for her son.

She looked out of the doorway. Jubilee was down on her knees in the dirt being comforted by some of the other women. The fat wife stood a short distance away taking in the scene but saying nothing. Grandfather Herbert went over to Jubilee and reached down to pull her to her feet. He spoke softly and she finally stopped her actual wailing, although she was still sobbing.

They made a strange pair, the grandfather immaculately dressed, stern and patriarchal and little Jubilee in her bare feet and dusty clothes. If this had been a father and daughter the scene would have made some sense to Swot's American mind, but Jubilee wasn't his daughter, she was his wife, and Matthew was his son. Swot slammed the door. "A plague on all your houses," she shouted to the empty room and then she climbed into bed and pulled the covers over her head.

Sleeping had always been her refuge and avoidance. She had spent hours, and days sleeping away disasters in her life, and found it quite easy once she got the hang of it. No date for the Prom – sleep it off. Best friend turning on you and calling you a know all – go to bed for a couple of days. Feeling lost and alone in a college dorm – don't get out of bed. A trip to Africa – sleep it off. Being responsible for some poor crippled kid being kidnapped by sadistic bastards who will probably kill him – well, that would make it hard to sleep but Swot could do it.

She did manage to sleep until well after dark and when she finally dragged herself awake she found that someone had been into the room and taken care of arranging the mosquito netting. She had to fight her way out of the net's clinging embrace before she could get across to the window and see what was going on. The compound was silent and dark with no lights showing in any of the windows, which meant that it was well after midnight. She opened the door and looked out. The sky was clear with a half moon and thousands of stars. As she watched, two figures flitted across the compound and over to the gatehouse. The gate itself was a huge metal construction topped with razor wire and admitting a car into the compound usually involved at least two men and a good deal of clanking and creaking. The only other way in was through a small man door, locked from the inside. The men came back out of the gatehouse, each wheeling a bicycle.

They passed through a patch of moonlight and Swot recognized that one of them was Mugabe. She had only been in Africa a short time but she was already over the idea that all Africans looked alike, and she had spent some time studying Mugabe. She hurried across the compound, heedless of the fact that she had nothing on her feet and reached the gate just as Mugabe was opening the man door. She thought she had been totally silent but apparently that wasn't the case and Mugabe was ready for her.

"Go back to bed," he said softly.

"Where are you going?"

"Go back to bed."

"No way."

While Mugabe and Swot continued their non-productive conversation, the other man was stealthily opening the man door.

"You either tell me, or I start shouting," Swot said. "What are you doing; stealing bicycles?"

"No," said Mugabe, "we are not stealing bicycles."

"Tell her to lock the gate when we leave," said the other man, now halfway through the gate and carrying the bicycle over the threshold.

"Lock the gate behind us," said Mugabe.

"Oh no," Swot said, and she stepped through the gate herself. For the first time since her arrival she stood outside the compound in the dark. The moonlight shone down on the rutted dirt road, and all around where she knew there should be little houses she could see only dark shapes; no lighted windows anywhere. In the distance a dog barked and something rustled in the bushes across the road.

Mugabe followed her through the gate, wheeling his bicycle. They stood together in the middle of the road. Although the lighting was not exactly bright Swot could see enough of Mugabe's face to tell that he was thoroughly pissed with her, although pissed was probably not the expression he would have used. She could also see that the other man was the man who had been driving her earlier in the day, or maybe by now it was yesterday.

"Go inside and lock the gate," said Mugabe. "We will find our own way back in."

"Not till you tell me where you're going."

"We're going to look for Matthew," said Mugabe.

"Really? " Swot said. "Why the big secret? Why are you creeping out like this?"

Mugabe sighed. "For a number of reasons," he said, "but mainly because your grandfather has not authorized us to go."

"What?" Her voice was growing louder and Mugabe shushed her. "He is not aware," Mugabe said. "Habati and I have made our own decision." He indicated the other man, the driver. So now she knew his name; he was Habati, but she knew nothing else about him; she knew nothing about either of them; just their names and the fact that they may possibly have been in the army.

"We did what we were told," said Mugabe, "and we protected you and your grandmother because that was required of us. We could not permit anything to happen to you."

"But Matthew___" Swot said.

"Matthew is one of our own. Matthew is our responsibility. Habati and I are ashamed that we allowed him to be taken."

"But you said___"

"I said that we did the right thing," Mugabe agreed. "We did our duty as employees of your grandfather, and now we will do our duty as members of Matthew's clan. We will go and look for the boy."

"Do you know where to look?"

Mugabe shook his head. "No, not really, but we will ask questions, and we will see what we can discover. We will go every night until he is found or...."

"No," Swot said, "don't even think like that."

"We have to hurry," Habati said. "We have far to go."

She looked at them standing in the moonlight. They were dressed in dark clothing but the light reflected from their faces.

"They'll see you," she said.

"We are prepared," said Habati, and he patted his side pocket. Swot assumed that he had a weapon; not the big weapon they'd carried earlier, which she thought was an AK47, although she didn't know much about that sort of thing. She guessed they had hand guns or something. Standing there in the road they both looked muscular and dangerous and ready to cope with anything.

"Are you secretly in the army?" she asked.

Mugabe shook his head. "Not now," he said, "but once. We know what to do."

He swung his leg over the back of the bicycle. "Lock the gate," he said.

Swot watched them until they were swallowed up by the darkness. A few moments later she heard the dog bark again, and then the silence returned.

She went back through the gate and closed the bolts. There was no way that she was going to sleep. She crawled back under the mosquito net and lay there looking up at the apex of the net, studying the way it fell in folds around the bed. There was comfort in that net and the way it shut out the shadowy shapes in the rest of the room. Under the net she was protected; inside the compound she was protected; everywhere she had been so far she had been protected. What about Matthew, she wondered. How was he sleeping; where was he sleeping; had he been able to keep his crutch? She thought of him trying to walk on his twisted leg and that was when she began to cry.

Swot didn't cry very often. She was not the crying type; she was more into temper tantrums, and fits of sarcasm. She was surprised how much she cried, how little she could do to end the process, and how exhausting it was to feel so much strong emotion. When she finally did stop crying, she wondered if perhaps she should pray. This was for her a totally new idea. Praying was not something she had ever thought of before but she was pretty certain that if she had gone missing Matthew would have been storming the gates of heaven on her behalf and doing it with complete faith that God would put things right.

She stared up at the white mosquito netting. Was God up there somewhere above the net, above the compound, and far beyond the African sky?   She didn't know if she was really praying, or just going over things in her own mind, but she addressed what she could of herself to what little she knew of belief in God and tried to cover all the bases. Keep Matthew safe, help Mugabe to find him; and strike Matapa dead. She felt that was pretty much everything that was needed.

She turned her pillow over to the dry side that had not been soaked by her tears, and somehow she slept.

CHAPTER SEVEN
Cecelia Byaruhanga; The Ursuline Boarding Academy, Budeka, Uganda

Cecelia lay awake in the darkness listening to the night sounds of seventeen other girls, all of whom seemed to be asleep. Theresa, in the bunk above was snoring softly. Cecelia was relieved that she had now gained enough seniority that she was not forced to take the top bunk. The bunks were stacked three to a tier and the girl in the top bunk could not even sit up in her bed; in fact her nose was only inches from the ceiling. Cecelia would have preferred the bottom bunk, but Mary was a prefect, so Mary had taken the bottom bunk.

The claustrophobic room contained six sets of bunks accommodating eighteen girls; too many for comfort or safety. The nuns knew there were too many girls in the room; the parents knew; the Board of Governors knew that the all of the dormitories were a health hazard, and a fire trap; but the Ursuline Academy was a good school and parents now wanted their girls to have a good education.

"Cecelia," a voice whispered from the bottom bunk, "are you awake?

"Mary," Cecelia said, "what's the matter?"

They spoke in English, because English was the language required by the nuns. Strict disciplinary action was taken against any girl who chose to speak in her own vernacular. The students at the Academy came from all over Uganda; if they were each allowed to use their own tribal language, the campus would be in chaos, and Cecelia was well aware that the Ursuline nuns did not approve of chaos.

"I heard something at the Prefect's meeting," Mary said.

Cecelia didn't need to be reminded that Mary was a prefect and that she was not a prefect. Well, maybe next year she would become one of the privileged, but for the time being Mary was the one who brought nuggets of news which she shared sparingly with the girls in the dormitory, offering them as special favors.

Cecelia kept quiet. She had no intention of begging for favors.

"Cecelia," said Mary again.

"Yes?" said Cecelia.

"They said the cell tower is down," said Mary.

"It doesn't matter," said Cecelia, "we're not allowed to use our phones."

"And the bridge across the swamp has washed out."

"What bridge?"

"The one across the river;" said Mary, "the one that connects us to Kampala."

"Oh that one," said Cecelia. She was dimly aware that the road from Kampala to Budeka crossed a swamp and a small, shallow river although she could not have named the river. Her father thought she should pay more attention to the geography of her tribal region, but she was really only interested in the geography of Kampala, and the world beyond.

"We're cut off," said Mary.

"Well, we're not going anywhere until the end of term," said Cecelia, "and they'll have it fixed by then."

"And..." said Mary, portentously, obviously dissatisfied with Cecelia's reactions so far.

"What?"

"Matapa has been seen here," said Mary.

Cecelia took a quick breath. Matapa, really?

"Are you sure?" she asked.

"Sister Josephine said that she'd heard rumors," Mary said.

"It's just rumors," said Cecelia.

"There's no smoke without fire," said Mary.

Cecelia heard Mary turn in her bunk, and felt the whole structure shake as the prefect prepared herself for sleep, leaving Cecelia to stare into the darkness.

She tried to dismiss Matapa from her mind. Rumors, nothing but rumors; the whole school was always full of rumors of one kind or another. Cecelia was now wide awake, and regretting the tea that she had drunk before she went to bed; the tea that was now sloshing around inside her and making her uncomfortable. She sighed; this was not going to wait for morning. Well, unpleasant as it was, a journey to the latrine would have to be made.

Cecelia slipped out of bed and lowered herself to the floor. Without the benefit of any kind of light she could still find her shoes on the floor by the bed, and her school cardigan hanging on a nail. Cecelia was fifteen years old, and she had been boarding at the academy for three years; she knew the routine; she knew how necessary it was to hang up her clothes, and keep her few possessions safely stowed in her locker. At home, during the long vacations, she could be a teenaged girl with a cell phone and a cd player and a closet full of clothes; but here at the Academy she was just another disciplined student, required to shave her head before the term started, to wear only her school uniform, and study, study, study to gain a place at University.

The girls in Cecelia's dorm could be considered fortunate, because their room was closest to the latrines; but they could also be considered unfortunate because, despite strict rules of hygiene imposed by the nuns, the latrine building was dark, damp and malodorous.

Cecelia eased the door open; a voice whispered to her from the darkness; Mary was still awake.

"Where are you going?"

"Latrine," said Cecelia.

"Watch out for snakes."

She stepped out onto the verandah that ran the length of the building. The tumultuous rains had finally ended but the night was damp, and she knew that the latrines would be wet and unpleasant. She gave in to a rebellious thought; the night was dark, no one was about; the nuns were asleep in the Mother House, the students were asleep; no one would see her. She sidled around the corner of the building, where the night was even darker.

No one will know, she thought, as she squatted by the wall, just a little more damp to add to the already muddy ground. Of course, if everyone did that every night the grounds would be disgusting; but just this once, what could it hurt?

Having taken care of her problem she headed back to the dormitory and then stopped abruptly as she heard a sound; voices whispering. Was it the nuns? Had they seen her? Oh heaven help her, there would be punishment for this.

A light flared in the darkness and shapes moved; someone was coming over the wall. Awareness came to her in a flash; Matapa; abduction; the fear that filled every schoolgirl and every teacher; men with guns coming over the wall. Over by the Mother House the dogs began to bark and the intruders no longer whispered; now they shouted and shone bright flashlights around the compound. Cecelia shrank back against the wall.

The raiders crashed open the doors one after another and the night was filled with the terrified cries of girls dragged from their beds. Cecelia knew what they wanted; they wanted the oldest girls; girls who could sustain a pregnancy, girls who could be sex slaves; they had no use for the littlest girls, and no interest in the nuns but they would kill anyone who stood in their way; or perhaps they would not kill them, perhaps they would just attack them with machetes, hacking off legs, and arms, lips, breasts. Cecelia knew what to expect; everyone who could read a newspaper, or listen to a radio knew what to expect; the terror that comes in the night; Matapa. She stayed in the concealing shadows as the intruders broke down the door of her dormitory. The dogs were loose now and the nuns came running from the Mother House. Gunfire rattled through the night, a dog yelped, the nuns fell to their knees, and she heard the voices of her dorm mates, pleading for time; time to get dressed, and then they were brought out of the dormitory, some in nightgowns, some in uniforms.

The nuns rose to their feet; they would do something, surely they would do something. Gunfire rattled again, another dog yelped. The youngest girls, seven or eight years old, were herded towards the nuns. Cecelia could see what was being offered; give us the oldest girls and we'll leave the little ones alone.

She held her breath. With a mixture of relief and guilt she realized that she was going to be safe; they were leaving without her.

Suddenly a beam of light shot through the darkness pinning her against the wall. Blinded by the light her captor was invisible to her, but she felt his hands on her and his arm around her waist, and she realized the futility of screaming; there would be no rescue.

Swot Jensen

Swot woke at dawn when all the roosters were fulfilling their duty as alarm clocks, and the women of the house were already chattering loudly in the compound.

She heard the main gate clang open and sprang out of bed to look through the window.

Mugabe and Habati came strolling in through the gate. They were dressed in their usual crisp white shirts, dark pants and sunglasses. There was nothing about their appearance to indicate that they had been in the bush all night.

She saw Jubilee dart across the compound. They saw her coming. Habati placed a hand on her shoulder. Mugabe shook his head. She turned away and went back into the shadows.

A few minutes later Brenda came into Swot's room carrying a mug of tea and a plate with two hardboiled eggs and a slice of bread. She sat down on the end of the bed.

"Will it do any good if I say I'm sorry?" she asked.

"No," Swot said, but she took the tea. Crying had dehydrated her. She started to pick the shells off the eggs. "I hate this place," she said.

"I know," said Brenda. "I'm starting to hate it myself."

"How can they do that?" Swot asked.

"Do what?"

"Think that they can cure AIDs by raping a little baby girl."

"I don't know," Brenda said. "The people I met here 50 years ago would never have done anything like that."

"So what changed?"

"I don't know if anything changed," said Brenda. "Perhaps it was always like that but I never noticed. I was pretty clueless."

"I'm sure you were," Swot said.

"But you have to realize," said Brenda, "that AIDS is something new. For you it's always been a fact of life but there was a time, not very long ago, when AIDS didn't exist. "

She stared up at the ceiling for a moment. Swot took a bite of the hardboiled egg and waited.

"If AIDS had existed in the sixties I'd probably be dead now," Brenda said, "and so would all the people I traveled with. Believe me, we were not careful and we didn't take precautions like people take today."

"If this is going to be a lecture on safe sex," Swot said, "I don't need it. I'm not having sex."

"And I'm not talking about sex," said Brenda. "I'm just saying that these people are terrified of AIDS and they have every reason to be terrified. All you've seen of this country so far is the city, and the road up to here."

"And a few monkeys," Swot added.

"I said I'm sorry," said Brenda.

"No," said Swot, "technically you haven't said you're sorry."

"Well, I'm saying it now," Brenda said. "What I'm really telling you is that there's a whole lot more of this country that you haven't seen; really remote villages, mountains, lakes, no electricity, no running water, no transport, certainly no computers, or tvs or anything like that. Where are those people supposed to get their information? How are they supposed to learn about AIDS and learn to be careful? Don't you think it's easier if they just believe that if they have this disease which they don't really understand, they can go to their witchdoctor and he'll give them a magical cure?"

Swot looked at her suspiciously. "You don't believe that, do you?" she asked. "You can't possibly think that there is any excuse; any excuse at all."

"I talked to your grandfather last night," Brenda said. "Oh, I really gave him a piece of my mind about everything that has happened since we arrived."

"And what did he do?" Swot asked.

"He talked to me," Brenda replied, "and he told me I had no right to judge."

"So he thinks it's okay? He thinks it's okay that someone wants to rape a two year old child? He thinks it's alright to kidnap Matthew and kill the Peace Corps worker?"

"No," Brenda said, "of course he doesn't. He's not a monster, Swot. However____"

"However what?"

"He is proceeding carefully. You have to realize that we're cut off until the bridge is fixed. The situation is highly volatile. These people have been through an awful lot since the last time I was here. Idi Amin____"

"Yeah, I read the history book,." said Swot.

"They didn't read it, they lived it," said Brenda. "They know what can happen when things get out of hand. Matapa is here somewhere and people are very nervous. What Herbert doesn't want is a riot because he doesn't have the people to control it."

"There are five soldiers in Budeka," said Swot.

"And what do you think five soldiers are going to do against a mob?" Brenda asked. "Have you ever seen a riot, Swot? Have you ever seen a violent mob?"

"No, of course I haven't, have you?."

"Don't you watch television?" Brenda said, "Iran, Iraq, Egypt."

"But that's not here," said Swot.

"It could be," said Brenda. "People are people, until they're a mob."

"Did you ever____" Swot asked, but before she could complete her question or hear Brenda's answer, they heard the clang of the outer gates being opened. Swot sprung to her feet and rushed to the door in time to see her grandfather climbing into the back of the SUV. Habati was at the wheel and Mugabe was riding shotgun, a pickup truck loaded with armed men waited on the road beyond the gate.

"Where's he going?" Swot asked.

"I don't know," said Brenda. "With no phones and no communications, I imagine he's going to Budeka to see what's going on."

"But what about Matthew?"

"I don't know," said Brenda.

"No you don't," Swot said angrily. She was tempted to tell her that Mugabe and Habati were at least trying to do something but she held her tongue. She was pretty sure that Mugabe wouldn't want her to tell anyone what she'd seen.

Swot picked up her breakfast plate and empty tea cup. "I'm going to take this to the kitchen," she said, "and I'm going to try to talk to Matthew's mother. She doesn't speak English, does she?"

"I don't know," said Brenda. "She might just be really shy and afraid to talk to you. Let me come with you."

Brenda's voice held a pleading tone. Swot knew that her grandmother was really sorry; of course she was sorry; Brenda didn't have a vicious bone in her body. She was really just a rapidly ageing sixties love child who had never wanted to grow up, but perhaps she knew something. Hard as it was for Swot to admit it, perhaps her grandmother did have something useful to offer; she had tried to live among these people in her youth, perhaps her experience would prove valuable.

The fat wife was coming towards them with a very determined expression on her face. Swot and Brenda stayed on the verandah and the fat wife stood one step below them.

"I want to talk to you," she said.

"So talk," Swot said.

The woman looked around. "Not out here," she said. "I come in."

"I don't think so," said Swot.

"Oh let her in," said Brenda. "Maybe she knows something."

"Yes," said the fat woman, "I know something."

Brenda and Swot went back into the bedroom and the wife followed behind and closed the door.

The fat woman looked at Swot. "Good morning," she said, "we have not been introduced, my name is Janet."

"Yeah, well, I'm Sarah," said Swot.

"I know," said Janet, "your grandfather has spoken of you."

The fat woman turned to Brenda, "Good morning Brenda," she said, "how was your night?".

"Horrible," said Brenda, "and how about you, Janet? How was your night?"

"My night was not good," said Janet. "We are very worried for the boy."

"Oh yeah," Swot said, "I bet you are."

"He is the son of our family," Janet said, "We are all worried for him."

She sat down on the chair, the one that Swot's grandfather had tested the night before. Brenda and Swot sat on the bed. They waited.

"He can be returned," said Janet eventually.

They waited again. Janet was perspiring quite heavily. She pulled a handkerchief out from the bosom of her dress and wiped her face. Again they waited. At last Janet came to the point.

"I have spoken to the witchdoctor," she said.

"Good for you," said Swot.

Brenda shushed her.

"What does the witchdoctor say?" Brenda asked.

"He says that he has spoken to the General."

"General Matapa?" Swot asked.

"Yes," she said.

"Where is he?"

"He will never reveal himself," Janet said, "but he will leave the region if we give him the baby."

"We've already been through that," Swot said. "He sent the same message to Margaret in Budeka. She doesn't know where the baby is, and anyway why would you even think of giving the baby to him?"

"Because if you give him the baby, he will release Matthew," Janet said.

She wiped her face again. Swot felt momentarily sorry for her. She knew what a terrible message she was delivering; Matthew or the baby?

"The lady or the tiger?" said Brenda under her breath.

"What?"

"You know the story," said Brenda.

Swot shook her head.

"We do not have tigers here," said Janet.

"There's always a tiger," Brenda replied. "Alright, you've delivered your message, such as it is, you can go now."

"The witchdoctor told Matapa that your granddaughter is clever; so clever that she'll be able to find the baby," Janet said. She looked at Swot. "Can you find her?"

Swot had no idea what to say.

"The General will not wait long," said Janet.

The wheels in Swot's brain started to turn. "He'll wait," she said. "Obviously he can't find the baby himself or he would have found her by now, so Matthew is the only card in his hand. He'll wait."

Janet heaved herself out of the chair.

"Don't let the door hit you in the ass on the way out," said Swot.

Janet gave her a puzzled look before she lumbered out of the room and closed the door behind her.

Swot had been holding her plate and cup the whole time that Janet had been delivering her message. She looked down at the plate and the eggshells; she found that she didn't seem to know what to do with them. Brenda took the plate from her hand, and pried the cup handle from her fingers.

"Once upon a time," she said. Swot looked at her in amazement. "What?"

"Once upon a time a low born courtier had an affair with the daughter of the king and when the affair was discovered he was forced to face a trial."

"Why are you telling me this?" Swot asked.

"To take your mind off other things," said Brenda. "Now, sit down and listen. The low born man had to face a trial. The trial was that he had to choose between two doors. Behind one of the doors was a hungry tiger, guaranteed to kill him; behind the other door is a beautiful woman who is hated by the princess, but if the young man chooses that door he will have to marry the princess's rival on the spot. Now, the young man thinks that the king's daughter will be able to find out what is behind each door and she will signal him what to do."

"I don't get it," Swot interrupted.

"You will," said Brenda. "Of course, the question is, will the king's daughter give up her lover by indicating the door with the other woman behind it, or will she be so jealous that she will signal him to open the door with the tiger? So the princess gives him a signal. He knows she's jealous, and he knows the tiger is real. So what should he do?"

"I don't know," Swot said. "What's the answer?"

"There isn't one," said Brenda. "It's the lady or the tiger. Choose."

"Oh I see," Swot said, "That's it isn't it; the lady or the tiger? There's no right answer."

"Not yet," said Brenda, "but if anyone can find an answer, you will." Swot stood up and went to the door. What had she been planning to do before the fat woman came to see her? Oh, yes, she was going to talk to Jubilee. Was she still going to talk to Jubilee? She actually had no idea. She opened the door and looked out. Janet was making her way out through the little man door in the main gate.

"Where's she going?" said Brenda from behind Swot.

"I don't know."

"We should find out," Brenda said.

Swot went out of the door and down the little step to the courtyard, and saw Jubilee coming towards her, eyes downcast. Her face was still gray with fear and she still wore the same dusty clothes she had worn the day before.

"Do you speak English?" Swot asked her.

She nodded her head.

"Do you know where Janet has gone?"

Jubilee shook her head.

"Well, let's find out," Swot said. She took Jubilee's arm and guided her into the little gatehouse where the boy who opened the gate would normally sit. They looked out the window to the street. Janet was standing in the road talking to a man on a motorcycle. Jubilee shrank back from the window.

"What?" Swot asked.

"Witchdoctor," she said.

"Really? That's the witchdoctor?"

"Yes."

Brenda had crowded into the little room with them.

"You're going to talk to him, aren't you?" Brenda said.

Swot nodded her head.

"Are you coming?" she asked Jubilee. Jubilee stared at her wide-eyed. Swot took that for a "no".

"I'll come with you," said Brenda.

So Brenda and Swot went out through the little gate and confronted Janet and the man on the motorcycle. He was, Swot thought, a very ordinary looking man, middle aged, skinny, wearing a striped shirt and sitting astride a dusty motorcycle of some ancient vintage. He looked at Swot as she approached. He glanced at Brenda for only a brief moment and then returned his gaze to Swot. As she drew closer to him she could see that the whites of his eyes were more yellow than white, and his face was marked by a pattern of scars; not accidental, more likely some kind of tribal markings.

Janet scuttled out of the way.

"You sent me a message," Swot said.

He nodded. "I hope you can do something," he said, and his voice sounded a little nervous. Swot had expected some kind of booming demon like voice, but this was the average voice of an average man. He lowered his head and scuffed his feet in the dust. "I did not mean to bring harm to the boy," he said. "You must tell the *effendi*, that I did not mean to bring trouble to his house."

"Oh," Swot said, "you're talking about my grandfather. So you're scared of him are you?"

Behind her Janet hissed some kind of warning sound.

"I am not afraid," said the witchdoctor, "but I wish the *effendi* to know that I did not encourage Matapa to take the boy. It is nothing to do with me."

"But you know where Matapa is?" Swot asked.

He shook his head. "Matapa found me," he said, "I did not find him. He wants the child; you give him the child and he will return the boy. You'll see, everything will be fine."

"Not for the child," Swot said.

He shrugged his shoulders. "The child is not your concern; just find her."

"And what will happen to her?" Swot asked.

Again he shrugged.

"If you find her Matapa will leave," said Janet.

Swot turned on her. "Do you really think it's that simple? " she said. "Even if I found her, which I don't think I can do, and even if I turn her over to your nasty friend here, which I will never do, what makes you think that Matapa will give Matthew back? Suppose he asks for something else?"

"He will leave," said Janet.

Swot looked at the witchdoctor. He seemed to be so very ordinary. She had expected him to have a bone through his nose, and feathers in his hair, and maybe a rattlesnake around his neck, but he was just a man on a motorcycle.

"How could you do that to the child?" Swot asked.

"I did nothing," he said.

"You're probably right," Swot said. "You probably did nothing, but you told people you'd done something. You told them that the girl could cure AIDS."

"She can," he said. "I have made my magic, and she can." Now he looked Swot straight in the eye, and she saw something lurking behind the yellowed sclera of his eyes; something powerful and evil. "Do you doubt my magic?" he asked.

"Yes, I doubt it," Swot said.

Behind her Janet hissed again.

The witchdoctor continued to stare at Swot.

"I think you are not protected," he said.

"I'm very well protected," Swot replied. "You'll never get inside these gates."

"I don't need to," he said. "I can curse you from outside."

"Oh come on," Swot said, "you might be able to get people in the village to believe in your curses, but you don't expect me to believe you do you?"

"Be careful," said Brenda softly. "Don't challenge him."

"But it's all nonsense," Swot said.

The witchdoctor leaned down from his motorcycle and picked up a handful of dust. He threw it in the air and watched it dissipate in the gentle wind.

"What was that," Swot asked, "was that your curse?"

He cocked his head sideways looking at her intently. "This is Africa," he said, "and you have African blood. I have sometimes succeeded in cursing white people but it is not easily done; our African spirits are not interested in white people and they require a great sacrifice. But you are not a white person and I see that you have no other protection; you are not a believer."

"I'm not a believer in you," Swot said.

The witchdoctor shook his head. "You do not have your own God;" he said "not like some people. You are not a Christian; you are not a believer. I can curse you; it will require very little magic. Find me the child and I will withhold my curse."

Before Swot could say another word he kick started his motorcycle and revved the engine until it screamed; then he took off down the road in a cloud of dust.

When the dust settled Swot saw that Janet was staring at her.

"What?" she asked.

"You were not afraid of him?" Janet asked.

"No, of course not," Swot said. "He's just a man."

Janet shook her head. "He's a very powerful witchdoctor," she said.

"Well," Swot replied, "I know you believe that, but I don't. You believe that his little magic pouch was going to cure Matthew's leg."

"It will," Janet said, "but Matthew will not allow it. I paid a lot of money for his leg to be cured."

"You would have been better off paying a doctor," Swot replied.

"We have no doctor," said Janet. "This is the way we do things. The boy was not grateful."

She turned and stomped off through the gate passing Jubilee who was creeping out to meet them. Jubilee came to stand beside Brenda and Swot in the road looking fearfully in the direction that the witchdoctor had taken.

"It's okay," Swot said. "He's gone; but I'm afraid I wasn't much help. I still don't know how to get your son back."

Jubilee stared at her in silence.

"Come on," Swot said as encouragingly as she could. "I know you understand me. Talk to me, please."

Jubilee's voice was very soft and made even softer by the habit she had of covering her mouth with her hand as though she was ashamed of her own words.

"He cursed you," she said.

"No, he didn't," Swot said, "he just threw a handful of dust around; that's not a curse."

Jubilee nodded her head. "He cursed you," she repeated.

"Oh well," said Swot, "then I guess I'm cursed. Let's not worry about that now. "

"You are not worried?" Jubilee asked.

"No, "Swot said. "I am not worried. I don't believe in any of it; not in God, not in evil spirits, not in curses; none of it."

Brenda put her arm around Swot's shoulder. "You'll be alright, Swot," she said.

"Of course I will," Swot replied.

"So what do we do now?" Brenda asked.

Swot looked at her grandmother. "We?" she said.

"I'm in this with you," said Brenda.

Swot would much rather have had Mugabe and Habati beside her with their muscles and their weapons and their mysterious military experience; but they were gone, and Brenda was all that was left.

"The lady or the tiger," said Brenda, "time to choose."

CHAPTER EIGHT

Brenda Songbird Carter

Brenda Carter's trip to Africa was not going exactly as she had planned, but that was no surprise to her because her plan had been a last minute thing based on nothing but a hunch. The idea of taking Swot to Africa had come as a sudden impulse and not out of any intense desire to be re-acquainted with the man she had impulsively married some fifty years before.

The thought had come to her when the whole family was seated around the birthday table, their faces illuminated by the guttering flames of Swot's 18 birthday candles.

"Blow out your candles, honey," said Swot's mother, Brenda's daughter, Monica.

Swot obediently puffed at the candles and a couple of them flickered and died.

"You can do better than that," Monica said.

"I don't see the point," Swot protested.

"The point is to look happy, make a wish, and be grateful for all your blessings" Swot's father said impatiently. "I have no idea what's the matter with you young lady, but you'd better snap out of it."

Swot puffed out a few more candles. She looked as though she was fighting back tears.

What?" said Swot's father. "Whatever it is just spit it out. I'm tired of seeing you moping around.

"I hate myself," Swot said.

"Honey, you can't hate yourself," Monica insisted. "You've done so well and we're so proud of you."

Tears trickled down Swot's face. "Okay, so I'm smart," she said, "but I'm so ugly."

Everyone at the table chorused their disagreement. Brenda joined in although she fully understood where Swot was coming from and recognized that her granddaughter was not completely mistaken. Swot wasn't really ugly, but certainly the mixed race heritage that had produced her beautiful mother and her handsome brothers hadn't worked quite so well on her.

Brenda's brain gave a little lurch and brought forth an unwelcome thought; this was her fault. She was the one who'd taken an African as her husband without any thought of the consequences on future generations, and without any thought of teaching her child what it meant to be African.

While everyone else was comforting Swot, Brenda set her mind on a different path. Comforting Swot and telling her that of course she was beautiful wasn't going to make it. What Swot needed was to know that she was the granddaughter of a man of some importance. The kid was feeling totally out of place amongst her American family but maybe she could find a more meaningful place in her grandfather's world. Brenda impulsively decided to give it a try.

"Come with me to Africa," she said.

Brenda wouldn't say that Swot jumped for joy but she did push her hair back and look Brenda in the eye and something connected. Brenda saw some small ray of excitement.

The plan was not working out the way Brenda had expected. First had come the rain turning the pleasant land of Brenda's memory into a quagmire of red mud and dangerous roads; then the murder of the Peace Corps worker, then the kidnapping of one of Herbert's children. If Brenda had expected Swot to have a similar experience to her own experience of fifty years earlier, then she was sadly disappointed. However, Brenda liked to look on the bright side, and she had found a bright side to even this miserable experience; Swot was connecting, she was getting involved, and she was thinking of someone other than herself and that was something.

They walked together from Herbert's house to the little cluster of homes where Zach had lived. The round huts and mud houses were very much as Brenda remembered; like an illustration from National Geographic complete with round eyed semi-naked children standing in doorways and peeking in wonder at the visitors. Brenda knew that her own mass of light hair and her pale skin made her especially interesting, just as it had so many years before.

Jubilee, who had reluctantly agreed to accompany them, shooed the children away as they approached the house.

"Oh, let them come in," Swot said.

"They will steal," said Jubilee.

Swot looked at Zach's little mud house pointing out the glass in the windows and the freshly painted door. "I guess this is the height of luxury judging by all the other houses," she said.

"I think the State Department sets minimum standards," said Brenda, "but that tin roof is gonna turn it into an oven."

A village woman hurried up to them with a key and unlocked the door. Jubilee shooed the children away again, and they retreated a few steps.

They stepped inside and Brenda looked up at the roof. "No holes," she said. The floor was cement and the windows were screened. The house had three small rooms; one appeared to be a living room furnished with a spindly looking sofa and a couple of chairs, one was a bedroom with a narrow bed and a closet, and the third was some kind of store room. Looking out of the back door she could see a latrine and a cooking area. Someone had installed a solar panel on the roof and a single bulb in each of the rooms; luxury by local standards.

"She assures me that the people here have taken nothing," Jubilee said. She was still speaking softly and keeping her hand over her mouth, but she was at least volunteering information.

Swot looked around at Zach's meager possessions. "No bicycle," she said. "We have to find the bicycle."

The bicycle was nowhere in the house, but Zach's laptop was on the bed. Brenda seized it with delight. "Look at this," she said to Swot. "I know what you kids are like, I'll bet this has everything on it, you know, e-mails, letters home, photos, everything."

Swot looked at the computer, obviously not as delighted as Brenda. "You're probably right," she said, "but there's no charge in the battery. She looked around the room. "I don't even see how he was charging it unless he was using the solar power, but I don't see an outlet or anything; and anyway we haven't seen much of the sun lately."

"We could take it up to the house," Brenda said, "and I could get Herbert to turn on the generator."

Jubilee tugged on Swot's sleeve. "Will this computer help us find Matthew?" she asked.

"I don't know," Swot said. "I'm trying to do one thing at a time to avoid falling completely apart." She looked at Brenda. "She doesn't understand," she said.

"I know," said Brenda. "She thinks we're wasting our time."

"Let me try to explain it again," Swot said to Jubilee. "The witchdoctor says that if we give him the baby, General Matapa will return your son."

"Yes," said Jubilee.

"So," Swot continued, "I am going to try to find the baby, but I won't give her to the witchdoctor."

"Then he will not return my son," Jubilee said.

"I'm not sure about that," Swot said. "If I can find the baby, then I think Matapa will have to come out of hiding to try to make a bargain with us."

Jubilee looked at her dubiously.

"I know," Swot said, "it's not much of a plan, but it's all I have. We have to start somewhere. I don't know how to find your son, but perhaps we can find out where Zach hid the baby."

"Assuming he's the one who hid the baby," Brenda added.

Swot turned on her "Don't complicate things," she said. "There are enough unknowns here; I can't handle any more. I'm going on the assumption that Zach is the one who hid the baby and that's how he got himself killed."

Brenda realized that her granddaughter was on the edge of panic; the responsibility was too much, the expectations too high. She needed to be encouraged not doubted.

"So let's take this place apart," she said, "and see if we can find a clue."

She opened the bedroom closet. Zach's clothes were arranged neatly inside; shirts and pants on hangers, and folded tee shirts and underwear on a shelf. The floor of the closet was taken up by a serious looking backpack and a pair of very new looking hiking boots. Poor kid, Brenda thought, he'd been planning on a hiking trip, maybe a safari. She dragged the backpack over to the bed and began to rummage through it.

"Bible," she said, "looks like he actually used it."

The Bible looked like it was intended for serious study, with a handsome but worn leather binding and his name stamped in gold on the cover. Zachary Ephron.

"Jewish?" Swot asked.

"No," said Brenda. "Old Testament and New Testament, so I don't think he was Jewish. Let's see what else is in here."

She removed some more items announcing each one as she placed them on the bed.

"Passport." She flipped the pages. "He was twenty two. Journal, there might be something in there, he seems to have done a lot of writing; postcards, nothing written on them; money, not very much; and an envelope." She lifted the flap of the small brown envelope and a black and white photograph fell out. "Now that's interesting," she said.

The photo was a black and white print of two men in uniform sitting side by side; a black man and a white man. The picture was old, curling at the edges, and the men were very young. The white man was small and slim with dark wavy hair and a prominent nose, the black man was much larger with broad shoulders. They both wore medal ribbons around their necks. She turned the picture over and looked at the writing on the back. The inscription had been written by someone using real ink and presumably a real fountain pen and the color had faded over the years. Someone else had written a modern transcription with a blue ball point pen. *Great Grandad with Sergeant Okolo, Kings African Rifles, Rangoon, Burma 1944.*

"I don't get it," said Swot looking over Brenda's shoulder. "Why was this kid carrying a picture of his great grandfather sitting with an African soldier? It had to mean something."

"Maybe he was just sentimental about his great grandfather;" Brenda replied, "some people are."

Jubilee took the picture from Brenda's hand. "I have seen this picture," she said.

"Really?" Swot asked. "Who showed it to you?"

"The boy, Zach, he showed the picture to everyone. He was looking for that man, that African."

"Why?".

"I don't know," Jubilee said, in a voice that implied how unacceptable it was that she didn't know, and how sorry she was to disappoint them.

"Do you think anyone knows?" Brenda asked.

"We can ask," she said.

"Well you'll have to do the asking," Swot told her "because I don't think anyone here speaks English."

Jubilee nodded her head. "They will not speak English to you," she said. "They are afraid."

"Of us?" said Swot.

"I think so," said Brenda. "Everyone here seems to be afraid of something. It's not like it used to be."

"So you keep saying," Swot snapped impatiently. "I don't know what you expected; it was all a long time ago."

"Yes, it was," Brenda agreed sadly, "a very long time ago."

Jubilee had no trouble assembling a group of women to look at the photograph; in fact the most difficult thing was to get them to move back far enough so that Swot and Brenda could get out of the door of Zach's little house.

Obviously the women had all abandoned whatever domestic tasks they were performing and come to see what the strangers were doing. Some of the women had babies on their backs, some had toddlers clinging to their skirts, and some were pregnant. Some women were pregnant, *and* had a baby on their back *and* also had a toddler clinging to their skirts. Brenda was struck by the idea that these women were living the life that she had abandoned. Looking around for women who might be her own age she saw several gray haired ladies standing in the crowd, their faces a mass of wrinkles, smiling toothless smiles. Yes, she could have been one of them; and Jubilee, passing the photo around and displaying a natural dignity, could have been her rival for Herbert's affections. She allowed herself a moment of sympathy for Janet who had no choice but to live with her husband's multiple wives, and the task of asserting control over his many children.

The women eventually chattered themselves into silence and Jubilee separated one of the gray haired ladies from the flock and brought her to Swot.

"She knows the man," Jubilee said.

"Really? She actually knows this old man?" said Swot.

"Yes," said Jubilee. "The old people know him. He is famous because he was a soldier for King George and he was given a medal."

Swot looked at Brenda. "King George?"

Brenda was secretly pleased to know something that Swot didn't know. "Before your time," she said. "He was the King of England in World War II. The back of the photo said the soldier was in the King's African Rifles, so I'm assuming that he was a Ugandan soldier who went to fight for the Empire; willingly or unwillingly."

"Is he still alive?" Swot asked Jubilee.

She nodded her head. "He is a very old man, but he is still living."

The older woman started talking to Jubilee. Jubilee was nodding and agreeing and occasionally making a little grunting sound of approval.

"Well?" Swot asked.

"Zach showed her the photograph and she told him where the old man lives. It is far, but she knows that Zach went to see him. He told her that the *mzee*, the old man, was a friend of his great grandfather; they were together in the War. When Zach came back from seeing the man he told her he had a very good visit. He said he would go again and take gifts because the old man and his wife lived in a very poor place with no food to eat."

"So where is this place?" Swot asked.

Jubilee asked some more questions.

"It is far," she said eventually.

"How far?"

"She cannot say. She has never been there. She says that the people at Kajunga Trading Center will know the path. If you show them the picture, they will know the man."

"Okay," Swot said. "So that's what we do."
Brenda had wanted Swot to be involved and to come out of her
shell of indifference, but this was moving too fast, and making very
little sense. "Wait a minute;" she said, "before you go hareing off
let's give this a moment's thought. What makes you think that
finding this old man has anything to do with finding the baby, or
finding Zach's killer, or getting Matthew back? You can't just go
charging off in all directions."
Swot looked at her. "You're telling *me* not to be impulsive?" she
said.
Jubilee tapped Brenda on the shoulder. "The old woman wants to
know if you wish to see the boy," she said.
See the boy! Did she want to see Zachary Ephron, dead for two
days, and lying in an unrefrigerated building in heat and humidity.
No, she didn't want to see the boy.
The old woman fixed her with a solemn gaze, and then said
something else to Jubilee, and pointed up the hill to a small cement
building set behind a wire mesh fence.
"She wants to know if their treatment of the body was
appropriate," Jubilee translated. "They don't know what you do in
America."
In America, Brenda thought, we don't do anything ourselves, we
leave it to the funeral director.
"I'm sure it's fine," she said.
"But perhaps if you look, you might find clues," said Jubilee.
"We should look," said Swot.
Brenda looked at her granddaughter; the girl was already on the
edge of emotional overload, she did not need to see whatever was
in that little building under the hot tin roof.
"I'll go," said Brenda, "you stay here and see if you can come up
with some logical reason to justify looking for the old soldier."
"But I should see him," Swot insisted.
"No," said Brenda, "you should not; there are some experiences
that you don't have to have; or at least not yet. I've seen plenty of
dead people, I can handle this."
She took the arm of her guide. "Lead on," she said.

Swot Jensen

Swot watched her grandmother walking away arm in arm with a dignified gray haired lady, and followed by a crowd of women and children. Although she would not have admitted it, she was relieved that Brenda had insisted on going alone. It was enough to have Zach Ephron's computer and his journal, she didn't want to face the reality of his dead body; not yet; not until she had answers. Jubilee gathered up her long skirt and dropped gracefully into a sitting position on the ground, her legs straight out in front of her. She looked at Swot expectantly. So, Swot thought, am I supposed to sit in the dirt? Is that what Ugandan women were expected to do; to sit in the dirt? She shook her head. No way was she going to be squatting in the dirt. She hadn't seen any men squatting in the dirt. She tried to imagine Mugabe squatting like that in the dust. No, he wouldn't do it.

She remained standing and started to flip through the pages of Zach's journal. The boy was talented. Each page was crammed with tiny writing and along the margins he had made little pencil sketches of the village and the people. On one page Swot saw a figure with a crutch. Matthew. On another page she saw the face of an incredibly aged man; a mass of wrinkles, a wispy beard and a thin fuzz of hair. There was no doubting the resemblance although more than seventy years had passed, this was the man who had gone off to fight for King George, and apparently he was still alive. Swot had no idea why she was fixated on this old man; but perhaps Brenda was right and it was just better than thinking about Zach, or Matthew, or the poor little baby girl.

She began to read Zach's account of his visit to Sergeant Okolo of the Kings African Rifles but she had only managed to decipher a couple of lines of Zach's cramped writing before she was rudely interrupted by the arrival of her grandfather's black SUV in a cloud of dust. Jubilee sprang to her feet and scuttled out of the way. Habati brought the vehicle to a halt and her grandfather descended, immaculate as ever in a dark suit and a red tie.

"I thought you went to Budeka," Swot said.

"Why are you here?" he asked.

"I'm investigating," said Swot. "Brenda is in the clinic looking at the ...body, and I'm looking at his journal."

"Ah," said her grandfather. "Why do you call your grandmother by her name?"

"I've always called her by her name," Swot replied. "That's what she wants."

"Do you intend to call me Herbert?" he asked.

"No, I mean, I'll call you whatever you want me to call you."

"You will call me Babu," he said. "It is a Swahili word."

"Yes, well, alright then...Babu."

"You must come back to the house," he said. "Fetch your grandmother and come immediately."

He climbed back into the car and closed the door. The vehicle edged forward and then stopped again as Jubilee approached. Grandfather Herbert, Babu as he wanted her to call him, wound down the window and spoke to Jubilee for a few seconds, and then the car went on its way in a cloud of dust. Swot saw Brenda coming out of the clinic followed by the crowd of women.

"He wants us to go back to the house," she shouted. "Are you finished?"

"Oh yes," Brenda said, looking pale, but determined, "I'm finished. There's nothing more to see there. They should bury the poor boy; they've done their best, but this is just not nice."

"So, any clues?"

"He was in one hell of a fight," she said, "and that's about all I could tell. Why does Herbert want us back at the house?"

"I don't know," Swot said "I thought he was going to Budeka but he couldn't possibly have gone there and back in this short time. Either he doesn't approve of us being out here, or something has happened."

She picked up Zach's backpack and his laptop and they trudged back to the house. Janet came storming out to meet them at the gate, and started berating Jubilee in whatever language it was that they all spoke. Swot had done absolutely no research before she left the States. She knew nothing of Uganda's geography, or climate, or local languages, or anything else. Her whole purpose in life up until then was to distance herself from her unwelcome African roots and to become as Scandinavian as her father's Swedish parents who had always seemed infinitely more stable than Brenda.

Janet scowled at Swot. 'He will see you in the dining room," she said. "He will see both of you."

Brenda and Swot went into the dining room. The room was dominated by a large table surrounded by mismatched chairs, including a couple of plastic chairs that Swot thought would have seemed more at home on a porch in New Jersey rather than a dining room in Uganda. The only significant piece of furniture was a large throne-like chair at the head of the table and this is where Swot's grandfather was sitting. She was struggling with the idea of calling him *Babu* because she was pretty sure that Babu was a character from a Walt Disney movie, or maybe that was Baloo. Whichever it was, it didn't seem a very dignified name for the stern figure seated at the head of the table.

Brenda and Swot sat down and Swot set the laptop on the table. "If you could turn on the generator," she said, "I could____"

Babu interrupted her. "I hear that you have been cursed."

Swot snorted dismissively. "He threw some dust around and told me that African spirits were going to get me because I have African blood."

"He was correct," said Babu.

"Oh don't be ridiculous," she said. "It'll take more than a handful of dust to curse me."

"You're wrong," her grandfather said. "I don't know if he actually cursed you or if he just threw dust in the air as a warning, but he could curse you, Sarah. It's quite possible for him to bring down evil on your head."

"Don't tell me you believe in that stuff," Swot said.

"It doesn't matter what I believe; " he replied, "it is what other people believe that matters. If people believe that you are cursed they will not come near you. I understand that you don't have your own faith?"

"I'm a realist," Swot said, "and I don't believe in God."
He gave her a very shocked look. Swot thought about her
conversation the night before with whatever cosmic being lived in
the heights beyond the African night sky. The conversation, or
prayer, or whatever it was had been strangely comforting.
"She doesn't mean it," Brenda said. "She's just finding herself."
Babu leaned forward in his chair. "Sarah," he said, "you are a bright
girl with a lot of courage but you will never survive here without
faith in something greater than your own brains; and you will never
understand my people, who are also your people, unless you
understand their spiritual beliefs."
"He didn't curse me," she said defiantly.
"You're probably right," he said, "but that is not why I want to talk
to you; both of you. I am going to send you to Budeka to stay. You
are not safe here, and we are not safe when you are here."
"Why?" Brenda asked. "What's happened?"
Babu sat back in his chair. "When I left here this morning," he said,
"I was going to Budeka to try to communicate with Kampala. I have
reason to believe that Rory Marsden has a means of
communication."
"The satellite dish," Swot said, "and the two radio antennas."
"Yes," he said.
"I thought there was something," Brenda said.
"I never reached Budeka," said Babu, "because we were stopped on
the road by some local people who were coming here to
communicate with me. Matapa raided a school last night."
"What do you mean by raided?" Swot asked.
"He took girls from the Ursuline Boarding School."
"Took them?" Swot couldn't fathom his meaning.
"He broke into the girls dormitory and took away ten of the oldest
girls."
"Why?"
Brenda touched Swot's arm. "That's what he does," she said.
"That's how he keeps the people in terror. That's why everyone has
been so frightened."
"He has taken the girls as sex slaves," said Babu, "and tonight he

will surely raid another school and take boys as soldiers. He will keep doing that until we give him what he wants, or until the army comes to chase him away."

"What about the soldiers we saw in Budeka?" Swot asked.

"We will talk to them when we return," said Babu. "It is possible they will take orders from me; but even so, they are only five men, and no ammunition."

"No ammunition?"

"They were traveling on public transport," Babu said. "They are not allowed to carry ammunition on public transport."

"I don't get it," Swot said. "They can make a rule like that and stick to it, but they can't catch someone who steals children?"

He shook his head "Chasing Matapa is like chasing the wind." He rose to his feet. "Go and pack your bags. I am taking you to Budeka where you will be safe."

"Aren't we safe here?" Brenda asked.

"No, you are not safe, and you are a danger to all the people in the house. We don't know who killed the boy from the Peace Corps, but it is possible that it was Matapa and that he has moved on to harming white people. You have to go into town where you can be protected. We have to make it quite clear that you are not here in this house."

Brenda rose from the table. "Everything's changed," she said.

"Yes it has," said Babu. "We have been through a lot since independence. We're not the people we used to be."

"Perhaps you shouldn't have pushed for independence," Brenda said.

Babu gave Brenda a look that would have blistered paint and she hurried out of the room. Swot rose to follow her. Babu stopped her.

"What have you found?"

"Not much," Swot said. "I have Zach's journal; there might be something in there, and if I could get his laptop charged I could see if he has anything that might help us. "

She sat down again and looked him in the eye. "What do you want me to do?" she asked. "If I find the baby, then maybe you'll get your son back, but what will happen to the baby? This requires the wisdom of Solomon."

"Ah," he said, "you can quote the Bible, but you can't believe it."

"It's just an expression," she replied.

"Do you think you can find the baby?" he asked.

"Well, I 'm assuming that Zach took the baby to someplace where he thought she'd be safe. If Margaret really doesn't know where she is, and if Sister Angela and Father Amos also don't know where she is, then Zach must have had some other friend or friends that we don't know anything about. That's what I'm hoping to find out from his laptop or from his journal. Maybe he has friends in Kampala, or some other part of the country. "

"And if you do find the baby....."

"I'm not handing her over," Swot said.

"No, of course not." Her grandfather allowed his head to droop for a moment; the first chink she had seen in his armor.

"This is too big for me," Swot said. "I'm just a kid. I don't know anything about sex slaves and child soldiers, and curses and witchdoctors and all these other things. I know you want your son back, but I don't know how to do it."

He gave her a sad little smile. "I do care for that boy," he said. "The problem with his leg was a big mistake; I should have done more for him. "

"Yes, you should," she said, although she didn't feel good about kicking a man who was already down, but she had to take her opportunity when she could. "And you should stop that awful senior wife of yours from beating up on Jubilee."

"That's enough," Babu said, but without much anger. "You don't understand our ways. Go and pack your bag, Sarah. "

Swot packed and took all of her possessions with her. Brenda said that she should leave some behind because they were going to come back, but Swot told her that she had no intention of coming back to her grandfather's unhappy house ever again.

They departed in two cars; Swot's grandfather riding alone in the Mercedes with Habati at the wheel and another of his anonymous sun-glass wearing henchmen riding shotgun. Brenda and Swot rode behind him in a double cab pick-up truck driven by Mugabe who had his AK47 on the seat beside him. The open bed of the truck was once again filled with guards. Swot felt extremely safe and extremely privileged as they roared down the road but she couldn't help thinking of all the other people who didn't feel safe at all. What would it be like when darkness descended on the little huts and houses tucked away in the tall elephant grass? Would the people lie awake listening for every rustle of the bush or crack of a twig, wondering if it was Matapa coming to kill them, or kidnap their children? What had happened at the school? Had anyone tried to save the girls? Where were they now? Swot's mind raced around in circles.

CHAPTER NINE

The little vehicle belonging to Father Amos was parked in the middle of the road. Swot supposed it was a sign of the general agitation that no one made any attempt to move it when Babu's little convoy came barreling down the road with Mugabe in the lead. They screeched to a halt. Mugabe rested his hand on the weapon next to him and the men in the back of the truck scrambled out, and stood like cartoon secret service men around the Mercedes while Swot's grandfather descended to bestow wisdom, or calm, or whatever else he could.

They were at the gates of the Ursuline Boarding School; the school where Matapa had kidnapped ten girls the night before. A noisy crowd waited outside the locked gates. It took a few minutes to realize what was happening. The throng was made up of parents who had come to retrieve their daughters; and the nuns were bringing the girls out one at a time and allowing them to squeeze through the gates to be reunited with their parents. A small group of adults stood off to one side. Swot did not think of herself as well attuned to the psychic energy of the Universe, or the spiritual temperature, or whatever else someone might want to call it but even she could feel the anger, fear, and sorrow that emanated from the group; the parents of the girls who had been taken.

Brenda and Swot climbed out of the pickup and stood to one side watching as Grandfather Herbert talked earnestly to the parents. A very British voice spoke softly in Swot's ear. "Things are going to become very ugly in a minute. You need to get back in your vehicle."

She turned to see Margaret, her white hair as disheveled as ever and wearing the same washed out denim jumper she had worn at Rory's house.

"It's not our fault," Brenda said.

"It won't matter," Margaret said. "They're looking for someone to blame. They're angry and they don't know what to do with their anger. In a place like this it only takes a spark."

"What about you?" Brenda asked. "What are you doing here?"

"They know me," she said with a toss of her head. "No one will hurt me. I am known and loved."

A movement passed through the crowd; a sudden change in energy. Swot saw her grandfather backing away, making a dignified retreat to the Mercedes. Mugabe leaned out of the window of the cab.

"Get back inside," he said.

"We're okay," Brenda said. "It's nothing to do with us."

Babu was inside the Mercedes now and the driver was rolling forward through the crowd. Someone started to beat on the roof of the car. Habati picked up speed. The gunmen leaped nimbly into the back of the pickup and Brenda and Swot scrambled back into the cab. At the last moment Margaret hurled herself in beside Swot.

"Hey," Swot shouted for the benefit of anyone who would listen. "It's not our fault. We didn't do anything."

The crowd had turned away from the dust of the Mercedes and the people were heading towards Swot's vehicle. The school gates opened and another little girl squeezed her way out. The mob, for by now it was more of a mob than a crowd, turned to see who she was. One of her grandfather's gunmen fired a shot; Swot assumed, or at least hoped, that he had fired into the air. The crowd hesitated for a moment and Mugabe gunned the engine, roaring down the road following the dust of the Mercedes.

"What was that?" Swot asked.

"Angry people with no way to vent their anger," Margaret said.

"But why us?" said Swot.

"They blame your grandfather for the fact that the bridge hasn't been mended and that the army hasn't arrived to protect them from Matapa."

"That's hardly fair," Swot said, "and why are you hiding in here; I thought you said that they knew you?"

"Discretion is the better part of valor," Margaret said primly.

"How will they get their children back?" Swot asked.

"They won't," said Margaret.

"But the army____"

"Will never come," she said. "They never do." Her face was alive with anger and bitterness. "The girls will be taken into the bush and given to the soldiers as wives. Some will die tonight trying to escape; some will die later in childbirth. They'll drag around with Matapa's army until they've forgotten where they even came from. They'll see and do things that we can't even imagine. They won't be rescued. They're as good as dead already."

"Not if he doesn't leave the district," Swot said. "If we can't leave the district, then he can't either."

"He can leave to the north," Mugabe said. "We are cut off from Kampala but Matapa can walk through the bush and leave. He can be in Sudan or Central African Republic if he just keeps walking."

"He says he's not leaving without the baby," Swot said.

"Ah," said Margaret, "the baby. Have you had any luck?"

"I don't know that anything could be called luck," Swot said. "If I find the baby and give it to him, then he'll give back Matthew but____"

"What?"

Swot looked at Margaret. Of course, she didn't know. The phones weren't working and no one had told her that Matthew had been taken. She wondered if the mob that attacked them knew about Matthew; if they knew they were attacking a family who had also lost a child. Would it even matter? Their anger had come to focus on the man they held responsible for their security; riding around in a big shiny car with a cadre of gunmen to protect him from kidnappers while some of their children had already been snatched in the night and more would be taken in the days to come unless Matapa got what he wanted.

They rolled into Budeka past the locked gates of Rory's house and up to the front of the little fake gothic cathedral and they parked next to the statue of the Virgin Mary. Swot's grandfather was greeted by the parish priest in a faded cassock and someone else who Swot guessed was the bishop, wearing a large gold cross and a much less faded cassock. When the formalities were completed they proceeded around to the back of the cathedral to a large low building protected by a high fence and metal gates.

"Oh," said Margaret, "they're putting you in the Speke Guest House."

"I don't remember this," said Brenda.

"It used to be the home of the district Governor, and I don't suppose he ever invited you in did he?" said Margaret. "Anyway you'll like it; they serve alcohol."

"What's that supposed to mean?" Brenda snapped.

Margaret shrugged her skinny shoulders. "Oh nothing," she said airily, "I just remember that you liked to drink."

"Yes," said Brenda, "I like to drink. In fact as soon as I get out of this wretched truck I'm going to have a drink; I might even have two. I might even buy a drink for Swot; in this country it's not illegal." Swot's ears pricked up. A drink? For her? That would be a first. There had been drinking on the college campus, but not for the likes of Swot. A girl could miss out on a lot of the fun if she went to college when she was only fourteen.

The entrance to the guest house was through a beer garden with round tables and umbrellas. The five stranded soldiers were lounging around one of the tables drinking beer straight out of the bottles. While Brenda and Swot went up to the reception desk where they were obviously expected, Mugabe went over to talk to the soldiers. Brenda was concentrating on completing the register and making inquiries about the bathroom facilities but Swot was totally distracted by the interaction between Mugabe and the soldiers. Hah, she thought, so much for not being in the army. The five soldiers had risen to their feet and they didn't sit down again until Mugabe waved them back into their seats and even then they gave the impression that they were kind of sitting at attention. No one saluted but they certainly did look respectful.

By the time Swot had returned her attention to Brenda and the whole question of whether the water was hot, and whether the toilet flushed, Babu was climbing into the pickup truck.

"Where's he going?" Swot asked.

"To the bridge," said Brenda, "to see if they've made any progress with the repairs. He's left us the Mercedes, and instructions that we're not to go anywhere."

"Oh," Swot said, "so where are we not going?"

"Well, I'm going to see Rory;" said Brenda, "apparently there's a gate from here directly into his yard.

"What if it's locked?"

"Then I'll stand and yell until someone comes," she replied. "Rory knows more than he's telling."

"Well good luck," Swot said distractedly. Her mind was on the fact that she could finally talk to Mugabe and find out what had happened the night before. She had been dying to ask him but a secret is a secret and he'd sworn her to secrecy.

"They're going to turn the generator on," said Brenda, "so you can get the laptop charged."

Swot rearranged her priorities. Get Zach's computer to charge, and then talk to Mugabe.

Margaret scuttled up to the reception desk. "I'm going to stay here," she said. "I'm sure no one would harm me, but ____"

"But you can't count on it," Swot said.

She lowered her gaze. "Discretion is the better part of valor," she mumbled. Swot guessed that was the mantra that had kept her safe for so many years.

"Are there any other white people in town?" Swot asked.

"Couple of missionaries," she said. "I hope they have the sense to come here."

"But if we're all in one place____"

"Oh I know;" said Margaret, "Cawnpore all over again."

"What?"

"The Indian Mutiny;" said Margaret, "all the white people hiding in one building; terrible business. "

She gave Swot one of her pinched little smiles. "Don't look so worried. I lived here through the very worst of Idi Amin and I haven't lost faith in the essential goodness of the people."

"Kidnapping girls____"

"No," she interrupted, "that's Matapa, and that's something quite different. No one here is going to hurt us if we keep ourselves to ourselves for a day or two."

"It didn't look that way outside the school."

"Grief does terrible things," Margaret said. "All we need to do is stay here and stay quiet and this will blow over. Matapa will move on. He always does."

Somewhere behind the building an engine started up with a loud clatter. The few people sitting around the tables lifted their heads and immediately rose to their feet. They came crowding onto the verandah pulling their cell phones out of their pockets.

"That's the generator," Margaret said. "Better enjoy it while you can. There won't be a cell signal, but at least their phones will be charged. "She looked at Swot gloomily. "If the cell tower is actually down it will take months to get it up again; and most of us have come to rely on our phones.

Swot lugged Zach's backpack into the bedroom and pulled out his laptop. She located the one live outlet in the room and plugged in the charger and then sat on the bed for a few minutes just to make sure the laptop didn't explode or catch fire. She had no idea what kind of voltage was coming through the outlet and how that would relate to Zach's American equipment. While she waited and watched the flashing green light on the charger she paged through his journal again. There was the picture of Matthew, and there was the picture of the old soldier, and there was....she looked carefully at the pencil sketch; a very old woman with a child in her lap. The child looked to be about two years old, and the woman looked about a hundred. She knew it was a stretch of the imagination but she couldn't help wondering; was this woman the wife of the old soldier, and was this the child? Something stirred in the back of her brain, or the pit of her stomach, or maybe in her soul. She felt a stab of comfort, as if someone or something had just told her that she was on the right track; not exactly a divine revelation but something. As she was a total stranger to the idea of divine revelations she set the idea aside as something to be considered later; perhaps in another night time chat with the cosmos.

She left the laptop to its fate and picked up the photograph of Sergeant Okolo. She wasn't going to admit to any more than a hunch but it was the only lead she had. She went in search of Mugabe and found him sitting alone at a table in the beer garden. The soldiers were nowhere in sight.

"About last night?" she asked.

He nodded his head gravely.

"Did you find out anything?"

"No, not so far. We will try again tonight. We will find him."

In the distance, above the clatter of the generator she could hear Brenda shouting for Rory. Apparently no one had come to open the gate for her.

"Do you know anything about Rory Marsden?" Swot asked.

"I have not asked?" he said. It wasn't really an answer to her question; Mugabe had a way of answering without actually answering. Rightly or wrongly Swot was more than ever convinced that he knew more than he was telling about many things; maybe even about the miracle baby.

"I want to go with you tonight," she said.

He shook his head and rolled his eyes.

"I have a clue."

"Really?"

"Well, not a clue, but a lead," she said. "It might mean nothing but I have a feeling."

"Do you know where Matthew is?" he asked.

She shook her head. "No, it's about the baby."

"We're not looking for the baby," Mugabe said.

"Well you should be, "she snapped. "You should be looking for both of them."

He dropped his head and refused to meet her eyes.

"This business of AIDS," he said, "has given Matapa power. The way his soldiers live; the way they take women and even go to prostitutes, they are sure to be infected. He doesn't offer them medicine, he offers them magic. If they believe he has brought them a cure for their disease they will follow him. That's all he wants."

"They'll kill her," Swot said.

"Yes," he said. "What they will do to her is unspeakable. I am ashamed for my people."

"Well, so am I," said Swot, "I mean, I'm ashamed for my people, the white people, and whoever the white idiot was who decided to pick that baby out of the crowd and make her into something special. "

She paused and Mugabe lifted his head again.

"We should not make this about black and white," he said.

"Are you kidding?" she spat back at him. "Everything here is about black and white whether you admit it or not."

"No," he said, "even without you mazungu we would still have a problem with tribe and clan. We don't need white people to make us fight; we can do that on our own. The problem with the baby is not about the mazungu evangelist; it is about the witchdoctor who profits from people's ignorance."

Do you believe he put a spell on her?" Swot asked.

"Of course not," he said.

"Do you think she deserves what's going to happen to her?".

"She's a baby," he replied. He shrugged his shoulders. "I have a daughter her age," he said.

Swot's heart almost stopped beating. In the midst of all the horror; the murder, the kidnapping, and being cursed by the witchdoctor, she knew that she had been keeping alive some sort of stupid fantasy about Mugabe. Well, that was the end of that fantasy. He had a daughter, so presumably he had a wife; a beautiful woman with shiny black skin and big brown eyes and a soft subservient smile; Jubilee on steroids. She decided not to think about her at that moment; she would think about her later, and anyway perhaps she was dead; women died in childbirth all the time. Perhaps he had never actually married her; that was also a possibility. She would have to think about all of that at a later time. She was not yet willing to let her fantasy die completely.

She sat down at the table, and showed Mugabe the photograph. He looked at it solemnly for a moment and then turned it over. He fumbled in his shirt pocket and produced a pair of reading glasses and Swot thought they made him look super intelligent. He read what was written on the back and handed back the photograph.

"I do not know him," he said, taking off the glasses and putting them back in his pocket.

"Apparently the people at Kajunga Trading Center know him," Swot said, "and apparently Zach visited him."

He raised his eyebrows inquiringly.

"I think that he took the baby there," she said. "We know he took her somewhere where no one else would look. As far as I can tell this old man is the only other connection he had and....

"Yes?"

"There's a sketch in his notebook, of an old woman holding a little child."

Mugabe made a noise that might have been a "tell me more" noise, or might have been a "you're full of it" noise.

"I thought that you could get someone to go to Kajunga and find out where the old man lives. Obviously I can't go because that would arouse suspicion, but after you find out where he lives we could go there tonight and see for ourselves."

"This will not help us to find Matthew," he said.

"It will give us something to bargain with," Swot replied.

"You would bargain with the life of a child?"

"No," Swot said, coming back to the essential weakness in her plan. If she had the child, what would she do because she would sure as hell not give her to Matapa or the witchdoctor?

"It would draw Matapa out," Mugabe said.

"It would," Swot agreed.

"I will send someone," he said.

"Do you need the photograph?"

He shook his head. "They will ask for the old King's soldier; that will be enough."

A shadow fell across the table and Swot looked up to see Brenda preparing to sit down beside her, and behind her was a waiter. "I'm having a beer," she announced. She looked at Swot. "Do you want one Swot?"

"Yes," Swot said, "I do."

Mugabe rose to his feet, inclined his head respectfully towards Brenda and departed.

"Nice man," Brenda said.

Swot nodded her agreement.

"Rory's home," said Brenda, "but he won't come to the gate. I'd love to know what's going on with him."

The waiter arrived with two bottles of beer, and a bottle opener. He snapped the lids and set the beer down on the table. The bottles were frosted; they had been in a refrigerator. At that moment Swot didn't care that she was about to have the first beer of her life; she was more thrilled by the fact that she was going to have the first really cold drink since she'd arrived in Uganda.

"Bottoms up," said Brenda lifting the bottle to her lips and taking a long pull.

Swot practically poured the beer down her throat. She wasn't really impressed with the taste, but the coldness was just wonderful. She sat back to savor the moment but there was no opportunity for real savoring because Margaret came running down the steps and across to the table.

"The children," she said, and then she stopped. "You're letting her drink beer?"

"Yes, I am," said Brenda. "What about the children?"

"Come and see."

They set the beer back on the table and followed Margaret through the reception area and out to the front of the building where they had a clear view of the main street into Budeka. Hundreds of children were making their way silently into town. They passed in a solemn procession, little barefoot children carrying blankets, and hardly speaking at all. Swot saw that Rory had opened the gates of his compound and was standing by the road watching them as they passed by.

"Where are they going?" Swot asked.

Margaret was close to tears. "I never thought I'd see this again," she said.

"What? What's happening?"

"Their parents have sent them into town to sleep."

"Sleep where?" Swot asked.

"Anywhere they can," Margaret said. "It's what they used to do in the Amin days, and later when Kony was here."

"Where are the parents?" Brenda asked. "Why aren't they with them? Those children are so little. If this was the US they wouldn't even be allowed to cross the street on their own."

"I know," said Margaret, "but this isn't the US and this is the best that anyone can do for them at the moment. The parents are at home protecting their property and they've sent the children here so that Matapa won't take them in the night. In the morning they'll walk home again. They'll keep this up until Matapa leaves. "

"Where have they all come from?" Swot asked.

Margaret snorted. "This isn't all of them," she said, "these are just the first ones to arrive. They'll be coming in all day from miles and miles away. Some of them won't even get here before dark, heaven help them."

She looked at Swot, and then at Brenda. "Well," she said, "you go and finish your beer; I have things to do."

"Can we help you?" Brenda asked.

She shook her untidy gray head. "You wouldn't know what to do," she replied. "You'd just be a distraction. "

She hurried away and Swot watched her as she was swept along by the tide of children. She picked up one of the smaller kids and hoisted him onto her hip. Still holding the child she stopped to speak to Rory and they surveyed the crowd together and then Margaret put the child down and went in through the gates to Rory's compound.

"Watch out for that one," Brenda said.

"Margaret?"

"It's her eyes."

"What's the matter with her eyes?" Swot asked.

"Wild. There's a wildness that wasn't there before, like she's just holding on by a thread," said Brenda.

"She's upset," said Swot, "and she's probably scared to death although she won't admit it. "

"Oh she's scared," Brenda agreed, "in fact they are all a lot more scared than they're willing to admit. The situation here could go out of control at any minute, and there's no one here to take control; all it takes is for one person to set the match."

"We're safe enough here," said Swot, but Margaret's words came back to haunt her. Cawnpore all over again, all the white people in one place.

"It's her eyes," Brenda said again. "Look at her eyes."

Margaret Veitch Budeka 1963

"They're still out there," Margaret said to Mrs. Fowler as they sat at breakfast.

"Disgraceful," said Mrs. Fowler. Her husband looked up from his morning Bible reading. "Can't you do something?" she asked.

He shook his Brylcreemed head. "I no longer have any authority," he said. "It's up to the locals to get rid of them."

"But they're on church property," said Mrs. Fowler; "that awful yellow van is still on top of the grave."

"It really is too much," said Margaret.

Mr. Fowler closed his Bible. "I'll have a word with the Bishop," he said, "perhaps he can say something to them."

"We don't even know who they are," said Mrs. Fowler. "What are they doing here? Where are they going?"

"From what I hear," said Mr. Fowler, "they are trying to drive that Volkswagen from Cape Town to Cairo; the three boys are Americans and so is one of the girls."

"The blonde one," said Margaret, "she's the American; the other two girls are from somewhere else. They're beatniks."

"Maybe you could talk to them," said Mr. Fowler to Margaret, "you're probably about their age."

"Oh I couldn't do that," said Margaret. "Really, I couldn't."

"I don't know what's the matter with their parents," said Mrs. Fowler, "letting them run around like that."

"More money than sense," said Mr. Fowler.

Margaret stood up from the table and brushed toast crumbs from her floral shirtwaist dress. "I'm off to work," she said.

"How are you getting along with the children?" Mrs. Fowler asked.

"We're getting used to each other," Margaret said evasively.

She went outside to the verandah and released the padlock on her bicycle and was soon cycling past the graveyard where the mini-bus sat with its yellow paint catching the bright rays of the morning sun. Drawing closer she saw that the bus was now missing its wheels. What did that mean? Did that mean they were never going to move on; never going to leave her in peace?

The tallest of the boys leaned over the broken railings and called out to her as she went by.

"Hi there," he said.

She brought the bicycle to a halt.

"Off to work?" the boy asked.

"Yes." She could think of nothing else to say. The Americans were a threat to the morals of the boys and girls in her classroom; they were the antithesis of everything that she had been brought up to believe but this boy...well, this boy was a different kind of temptation altogether.

"We haven't been introduced," the boy said. Margaret was very uncomfortable with the way she responded to the boy's accent; his slow drawl reminding her of the hero of every American movie she had ever seen. "I'm Rory," the boy said.

"Margaret," she replied.

"So what are you doing here?"

"I'm a teacher," she replied.

"From England?"

"Yes."

"Well," said Rory, "have you found any night life around here?"

She shook her head violently. "I didn't come for the night life."

The boy made no response and the silence dragged on. Margaret knew she should pedal away from temptation; away from this attractive American boy; this was not the reason that she had come to Uganda. If she had wanted to meet boys she could have stayed in England although to be honest she hadn't done very well at meeting boys in England; her desire to be a missionary had always put a damper on her social life. The boy was looking at her and grinning his easy grin, almost as though he knew what she was thinking.

"What happened to your wheels?" she asked; anything to break the silence.

"We're getting them fixed," he said "at least that's what they say."

"And then you'll be leaving?"

"We're in no hurry," he said, and he grinned again.

"Oh." She should say something else; but what? Could this be called flirting? Was this boy flirting with her?"

"Hey, Rory." A blonde girl emerged from the bus, tossing her long ringlets out of her eyes. She was wearing something skimpy and revealing. Baby doll pajamas, Margaret thought. What on earth kind of girl would walk around in broad daylight in nothing but a flimsy transparent smock and tiny bloomer panties?

"This is Songbird," said Rory.

"Really?" Margaret could not avoid the note of skepticism, and she knew she had arched her eyebrows; but it was so ridiculous, Songbird, indeed!

"No, not really," said Rory, "but____"

"Songbird is my traveling name," said the blonde girl. "Brenda is so confining, don't you think?"

Margaret had never given a thought as to whether or not a name could be confining; a name was a name.

"So you're a teacher," said Songbird with a wide, welcoming smile. "That's cool."

"I'm a missionary teacher," Margaret said, "from the Society for the Propagation of the Gospel."

"Whoohoo," said Songbird.

"Shush," said Rory.

"Stop by any time and propagate the Gospel," said Songbird.

Margaret realized that the American girl was not entirely sober and *it was only 8:00 a.m.*

Two more skimpily clad girls now stumbled from the Volkswagen. How many were sleeping in there, Margaret wondered and who was sleeping with whom?

"That's Annie," said Rory, waving a nonchalant hand at a small dark haired girl in a short white shift, "we picked her up in Cape Town, and that's Diana, she's from Bulawayo."

Diana was a brown haired girl whose hour glass figure was accentuated by brief shorts and a tight tee shirt. Dianna and Annie waved cheerfully and disappeared into the bush alongside the graveyard.

"I'm sure they could use the bathroom at the Fowler's house," Margaret said disapprovingly.

"Didn't want to trouble anyone so early in the morning," said Rory.

"It's not early," Margaret said, "most of us have been up for hours. Most of us have work to do."

"Ah," said Songbird, "but we are not like most people."

No, Margaret thought, you are certainly not, and thank goodness most people are not like you.

Songbird's glance slipped past Margaret and she broke into a broad smile.

"Oh look," she said to Rory, "there's that student we met last night. Isn't he gorgeous?"

Margaret turned around and saw a young African man in a dazzling white shirt.

"Hi Herbert," said Songbird, "why don't you come and have breakfast with us."

CHAPTER TEN

All through the long afternoon Swot watched the silent procession of children making their way into town. As the day wore on the children who arrived looked more and more weary, especially the girls who carried their younger brothers and sisters tied on their backs. Those who came later in the day looked even poorer than the ones who had come earlier. Although all of them were barefoot and dusty, the later ones didn't even carry blankets as they dragged wearily along the dusty road in the short twilight that would precede the darkness; a darkness where only the generator at the Guest House was providing any light at all.

Looking down the road into the town she could see candles and kerosene lamps flaring in some of the shop windows. As the short twilight came to an abrupt end, the Catholic priest came to the door of the cathedral with a flashlight and started to shepherd in the last of the children. Swot assumed that he was saving the cathedral as a place of last resort; a final refuge for the little ones who were still on the road in the dark.

Swot didn't like children; she never had, and she thought the reason was that she had never really been a child herself. Her confirmed status as a genius had made her aloof to the activities of children her own age. She had never seen the attraction of hitting a ball with a stick, or playing games of pretend, *"you be the Mummy and I'll be the Daddy."* No thank you. Liking or not liking children now had nothing to do with how she felt about the pathetic little shreds of humanity struggling into Budeka. God knows how far they had walked, she thought, and for once she meant it; only God could know how far they had come and only God, if he did exist, could keep them safe. It was not that she felt spiritual, nothing of the sort; she felt outraged. Who was this man, this self-appointed General Matapa, who could so terrorize a community that they would sooner send their children out onto the road in the dark, than run the risk that they would be taken by Matapa's soldiers? What had he done to inspire such fear, and why hadn't he been stopped?

Brenda and Swot ate by candlelight in the restaurant. It wasn't much of a meal; some kind of stewed meat that could have been beef, or goat, or really any kind of animal, and some boiled potatoes. Swot drank another bottle of cold beer. Apparently the management of the Speke Guest House set more store by keeping the refrigerator running and keeping the beer cold than lighting the restaurant; Swot could barely make out the faces of the other diners in the shadowy candlelight. She was drawn to the cold frosty beer like a bee to honey. She supposed she would have derived equal enjoyment from a cold soda, but with the beer there was an element of the forbidden and she was beginning to be attracted by forbidden things such as her plan to escape into the bush with Mugabe which was something that was certain to be forbidden if Brenda should get wind of it.

They were just finishing dessert, a slice of pineapple and a stale cookie, when Mugabe came into the restaurant. Swot saw him walk up to the buffet counter and start to fill a plate so she abandoned her dessert and walked over to join him. They moved along the table together with Mugabe taking a huge helping of food and Swot selecting a small potato as her excuse for being there.

"Well?" she asked.

"He is known," Mugabe said. "I will find him."

"I'm coming with you," she hissed.

To her surprise he nodded his head in agreement. "He was a soldier for the white men; he will think you are white. Yes, you should come. He doesn't know me."

"So you didn't grow up around here?" Swot asked.

He shook his head. "You ask too many questions," he said. "Go and eat your Irish."

"My what?"

"Your potato."

"So when__?"

"When all is asleep. I will knock."

Swot sat down at the table and sprinkled salt on her solitary potato.

"What on earth?" Brenda asked.

She was saved the trouble of making up a reason for taking the potato by the arrival of Margaret. As usual she was positively twittering with news and indignation as she made her hurried, bird-like approach to the table.

"He's here, "Margaret hissed.

"Who?"

"The Irishman," she replied. Margaret was apparently so angry with the Irishman that she was forgetting to be angry with Swot and Brenda as she pulled up a chair and leaned forward to impart her important news.

"He came in from Kajunga," she said. "Could you believe that he actually went there again, after what he did last time? I'm surprised they didn't throw him out on his ear."

"Maybe they just let the witchdoctor curse him," Swot said.

Margaret nodded enthusiastically. "I certainly hope so," she said. "If I knew how to cook up a curse, I'd curse him myself."

"So where is he now?" Brenda asked.

Margaret leaned even further forward so that her chin was practically resting on the table. "He's just coming in. Look."

Swot looked and saw a broad shouldered and somewhat sunburned white man making his way into the restaurant.

"The cheek of the man," Margaret hissed. "After all he's done."

"Does he actually know what he's done?" Brenda asked.

Margaret sat upright. "What on earth do you mean?"

"Well," said Brenda, "presumably he thought he was doing a good thing in baptizing the little girl..."

"No he was not," Margaret said.

Brenda continued as though she had not been interrupted. "He had no idea that the witchdoctor would do what he did, and he certainly had no idea that General Matapa would turn up here. Maybe, Margaret, it's not all his fault."

"Oh really," said Margaret. She sprang to her feet. "I am not going to sit in the same room as that man."

"Suit yourself," said Brenda.

Margaret made a hasty departure and Brenda smiled at Swot. "So, no dinner for Margaret," she said. "I'm going over to talk to him."

"Don't you dare," Swot said.

Brenda looked thoughtfully at her granddaughter. "For such a smart person you really do have a closed mind," she said. "I think we should hear his side of the story before we rush to judgment."

"I'm not interested in his side of the story," Swot said. "None of this would have happened if he had just minded his own business and stayed in Ireland."

"And you wouldn't exist," Brenda said, "if I'd minded my own business and stayed in Cleveland."

She picked up her beer bottle and strolled over to sit beside the

Irishman. If he was surprised to be accosted by an elderly white hippie lady he didn't let his surprise show. In a few minutes they were talking like old friends and Brenda was drinking another beer. Swot looked at her watch and wondered what on earth time all of these people would go to bed. Mugabe had said he would come when all were asleep. No one in her line of sight looked sleepy. The five soldiers were back at their table in the beer garden, Brenda was chatting away as though she had all night, and the staff was still banging around in the kitchen.

Swot went back to her room and checked on the state of Zach's computer which turned out to be a major disappointment. The computer would not boot up; apparently some internal part of the computer had been fried; she hoped that she wasn't the one who had fried it. Well, whoever was responsible the effect was the same; the computer was not going to give up any of its information any time in the near future. She unplugged the charger and plugged in the little bedside lamp and sat on the bed to read Zach's journal.

The first few pages of the journal introduced her to a man; a boy really; full of excitement about the time he was going to spend in Africa. He'd completed his Peace Corps training, packed his bags according to their directions, learned the basics of cultural immersion, updated his vaccinations and he was on his way. He sketched the airport in Washington DC while he waited for his flight; he sketched the Arrivals Hall at Entebbe while he waited for his luggage. He sketched the shoreline of Lake Victoria and the Peace Corps representative who came to meet him. His journal notes were naive and innocent; full of good intentions and his desire to help his fellow man. Swot thought that she would have liked Zach if she had ever had the chance to meet him, but she was equally sure he wouldn't have liked her. She would not have been Zach's type of girl.

She was just starting to read about his interaction with his hosts in Nawalyo and his reaction to Swot's grandfather's heavily protected compound when the lights went out and she was suddenly sitting in the pitch dark. An oppressive silence told her that the generator which had become part of the background noise had stopped running. A few moments later she heard the stumbling footsteps of annoyed guests leaving the bar in pitch darkness. She heard Brenda talking loudly about how a warning would have been a good idea before turning off the generator, and she heard the Irishman reply that most probably the generator had simply run out of fuel and no one was authorized to refill it.

Brenda shouted a goodnight and the Irishman replied with a God bless. Doors banged, footsteps ceased, and in an amazingly short time the guests fell totally silent. Swot groped her way to the window and pulled back the drapes and saw the empty beer garden dimly lit by a faint amount of moonlight. She stumbled back into the room and felt her way through her suitcase until she found a flashlight. She closed the drapes again, propped the flashlight up on the head of the bed and used its faint light to get dressed; dark jeans, a black tee shirt and a thick layer of insect repellant; then she turned off the flashlight to conserve the battery and lay down on the bed to wait.

A tapping at the window woke her. She had no idea how long she had been asleep but there was a quality to the dark silence that told her that everyone had been asleep for some time; everyone except the person knocking on her window. She cracked the door open and saw Mugabe's faint silhouette against the starlit sky. He took hold of her hand and her heart skipped a beat although it was soon obvious that his sole intention was to make sure that she didn't trip, fall, or slam into anything as they made their way to the gate. As they approached, a light flared in the gatehouse and Swot saw an old man sitting on a rickety chair and holding a bow and arrow.

"That's the guard?" she whispered.

"Poisoned arrows," Mugabe whispered back. "Be quiet."

The old man looked at them, nodded his head and turned away.

Mugabe slid back the bolts on the man door and they slipped outside into the starry darkness, with Mugabe still holding Swot's hand.

"Over here," he said and he shone a tiny flashlight into the bushes at the side of the road where it picked up the dull shine of the handlebars of a small motorcycle. Swot looked back along the road towards the town. Flickering light escaped from a few windows, oil lamps or candles, and further down the road a brighter white light; someone who owned a generator. She wondered about the children who had disappeared into the darkness. Were they all sleeping; all of them? Silence enveloped the cathedral where the latecomers had been taken in. Were they really sleeping or were they lying awake staring wide-eyed into the darkness too terrified to even move for fear of Matapa?

Mugabe kicked the motorcycle into life and Swot climbed on behind him. The headlight picked out a path along the patched and potholed road through town and then they left what little pavement there was behind and Mugabe picked up speed on the dirt road. Swot flung her arms around Mugabe and hung on for dear life. Whatever excitement she might have felt in holding onto her hero was completely dispelled by the sheer terror of roaring through the night with branches slapping against her arms and legs and night insects beating themselves to death against her face.

They finally arrived at Kajunga Trading Center which seemed to lie in even deeper darkness. Were all the people really asleep or were they too terrified to look and see who was roaring into town in the dead of night? Mugabe slowed down to a crawl and Swot could tell he was looking for something. Finally he found what he wanted and they turned off the supposedly main road onto a goat track where elephant grass crowded in on either side of them. She hid her face behind Mugabe's broad back, closed her eyes and endured the thick sharp grass hacking at her bare arms and wished she had worn long sleeves.

Mugabe stopped the motorcycle abruptly, turned off the headlight and silenced the engine. The night was no longer quiet and dark. A short way ahead of them the sky was lit by orange flames and people were screaming. Mugabe pushed the motorcycle in among the tall grass and motioned to her. "Stay here," he said.

"What is it?"

"Matapa," he said. "Don't move. Don't make a sound."

Matthew, The Crippled Kid

Matthew closed his eyes and tried to picture Jesus. His mother's most prized possession was an illustrated Bible given to her in her childhood. Whenever they had the chance to be alone and out of reach of the demanding senior wife, Jubilee would show Matthew the illustrations and tell him how Jesus was going to look after him; Jesus had a plan for his life.

The Jesus in the Bible had a white face, but Jubilee said that didn't mean that Jesus was a white man's god; Jesus was for everyone. The Jesus in the Bible had a white face because the Bible had originally been printed for white people. She showed him the address of the printer, written in small type in the front of the Bible; the printer was in London; far away, and the Bible had once belonged to someone named Peter Venables who had received it as a prize for attending Sunday School. Jubilee was very proud of that Bible, and the great distance it had traveled in order to find her so that she could sit by the fire and show the pictures to her son and promise him that his life would one day have a meaning.

Matthew's favorite picture in the New Testament was of Jesus, with his long brown hair, and compassionate light eyes, healing the crippled man. He wondered how the crippled man had felt when Jesus told him to get up and walk; how would he, Matthew, feel if a miracle worker came to his village and told him he could get up and walk? Zach had been like a miracle worker so far as Matthew was concerned. Zach had promised he would take him to a doctor, but now Zach was dead; taking with him the hope of a miracle.

The pick-up truck jolted down a steep embankment, hurling Matthew against the sharp edge of the wheel well and causing him to open his eyes and lose the image of Jesus he had spent so long creating. Reality, in the form of a scar-faced boy, poked his ribs with the butt of a rifle. The boy taunted Matthew in some language of his own. Matthew remained silent. He understood a word here and there of the boy's language, and he understood that the boy wanted to kill him. He also understood that the boy was forbidden to kill him, although Matthew had no idea why.

He had already spent a night and a day as the prisoner of Matapa. He had seen what happened to the girls from the Convent, and he had seen the casual cruelty with which the child solders treated each other, and yet he had not been harmed. He was bruised from riding in the back of the pick-up truck; he was humiliated by the fact that he had been tethered to a tree and given no chance to even urinate in private; the scar faced boy had watched the whole time and mocked the size of his penis; but he was still alive.

So far he had not seen the terrible General Matapa; in fact he had seen very few adult men; mostly he had seen boy soldiers revealing by their babble of languages and their tribal scarring that they were all far from their own homes.

He had expected to remain tied to the tree, chained up like a dog, but as night fell he was thrown into the back of this pick-up truck with his hands tied behind his back. The other boys, armed with guns and pangas crowded in beside him; two of the adult men climbed into the driver's cab, and they set off into the bush.

The boy with the tribal scars, the one who had poked him in the ribs, stared him in the face. "We burn," he said in English.

Matthew said nothing. The boy fumbled in his pocket and produced a lighter. He held it within inches of Matthew's face and flicked it with his thumb. The flame was a fierce orange flare and the boy brought it closer to Matthew's face; he felt the heat on his nose and lips. He summoned up another illustration from his mother's Bible; three men in a fiery furnace; he concentrated on remembering their names. Abednego, Shadrac, and who was the third?

"We burn," the boy said again. Obviously dissatisfied with Matthew's response, he closed the lighter and returned it to his pocket. "We burn village" he said. "You, you burn village."

Matthew shook his head.

The truck rounded a corner and the headlights picked up the outlines of a village; an impoverished place of thatched huts and mud houses. Dogs began to bark. The truck came to a halt and the boys scrambled from the back. "We burn village," the boy said, taking the lighter from his pocket again. He grabbed the rope that tied Matthew's hands together and tried to drag him from the truck. A shadowy figure loomed up behind him, one of the adults who had been in the cab. The adult man slapped the boy's head driving him backwards away from Matthew. A second blow sent him sprawling on the ground.

"Thank you," said Matthew. "I don't want to burn the village. Why are you burning the village?"

The man's face was in shadow, his expression unreadable. He dragged Matthew back into the bed of the pickup until he was backed up against the rear window of the cab. He took the loose ends of the rope and tied Matthew's hands to an eyebolt. "You are our hostage," he said. "You will stay here."

He walked away and left Matthew alone. Hostage; he was a hostage. He would be held until a ransom was paid. Matthew was filled with despair. Who would pay a ransom for him? He closed his eyes and again tried to comfort himself with the image of Jesus. He thought of the picture of Jesus surrounded by little children, well-dressed, light skinned little children; not crippled boys with torn clothes soaked in the urine of fear; and not ugly, scarred brutes with guns and lighters.

When the screaming started he kept his eyes closed

Swot Jensen

Mugabe stopped the motorcycle abruptly, turned off the headlight and silenced the engine. The night was no longer quiet and dark. A short way ahead of them the sky was lit by orange flames and people were screaming. Mugabe pushed the motorcycle in among the tall grass and motioned to her. "Stay here," he said.

"What is it?"

"Matapa," he said. "Don't move. Don't make a sound."

"But____"

He was gone; slipping away to disappear into the vegetation. Swot squatted down beside the motorcycle her heart pounding as she listened to the screams from the burning village. The flames flared higher into the sky and cast a dull red reflection on the metal parts of the motorcycle. She sank down closer to the ground. She might have stayed there, and what happened next might never have happened if something had not moved beneath her hand. She sprang to her feet. She was not alone. Snake; rat; lizard; lion? She had no idea what it was that moved but her imagination was running on overdrive and she knew she wasn't going to stay there to find out. Without really thinking about it she sprinted out of the bushes and onto the goat track, heading towards the only source of light; the burning village. Was this logical she asked herself? No, of course not, but logic abandoned her as soon as she put her hand on whatever it was that squirmed in the darkness and for once in her life she was just being a girly girl running away from whatever the danger was and seeking the strongest male around; Mugabe.

She stopped dead when she saw that two boys, their faces

illuminated by the flames, were heading in her direction. Her first assumption was that they were children running away from the village but then she saw that they were carrying weapons, and they had spotted her already. One of them pointed a gun at her; a large gun. Swot thought of every large lethal looking gun as being an AK47 and had no doubt that this was, therefore, an AK47. The boy looked way too young to be toting it around, but he seemed to know what he was doing when he aimed in Swot's direction and shouted something that she didn't understand, but she took to mean that she should stand still. She stood still and slowly raised her hands. The boys approached her. They were just boys; one of them looked to be about nine years old and the other was bigger, maybe ten or eleven; children who should, she thought, have been in school. They came closer and stared at her. They grinned and showed their white teeth in their dark faces. She grinned back. Children; just children.

The bigger boy continued to take aim at the general region of her stomach and Swot kept her hands in the air.

"Mazungu," he said.

"Yes, "she agreed, "mazungu." She took a step forward and the boy stepped back but he kept the gun trained on her. Now she could see his face clearly; the face of a child but the eyes of a killer; cold and dead. There was nothing friendly in his grin.

The smaller boy raised his weapon. They were jittery now, hopping from one foot to the other.

"You mazungu," said the big boy.

"Yes," Swot said, "you don't want to shoot me; big trouble for shooting a mazungu."

The little boy stepped forward and poked her hard in the stomach with the barrel of the gun.

"Hey," she shouted, doubling over.

"Hey," he replied and laughed. The other boy joined in. They giggled like school children.

"Mazungu," the little boy said again and he poked her again. "We kill you," he said.

"Stop that," said Swot. "Now you listen to me, I'm an American and if you shoot me you'll be in big trouble. Do you understand me? Big trouble."

"You big trouble," said the boy who had poked her.

Renewed screaming came from the village and both of the boys grinned proudly. The big boy gestured towards the sound.

"Matapa," he said. "You come."

"No way," she replied.

"You come," the big boy said. "We rape you, mazungu."

Swot stared at the boy. Rape her? He was a child. He grinned and it was not the grin of a child. "We rape you, we kill you," he said.

"Mazungu," the little one said, and this time he hit a hard blow behind her knees with the butt of his weapon. She fell heavily to the ground.

The older boy stood over her. "We rape you," he said and started to unbutton his ragged shorts while the little one, hopping from one foot to the other, nonetheless managed to keep his weapon aimed at her.

Swot found it almost beyond belief. Was this really going to happen? Was she going to be raped by an evil little ten year old kid? She was eighteen years old and so far she had managed to hang onto her virginity; waiting for the right moment and the right boy, and this was most definitely not what she'd had in mind. The older boy had put down his weapon so that he could go about his business with her. The little one was still taking aim at her, but he wasn't really concentrating. Maybe, Swot thought, he was getting excited at what he was about to see; maybe he was waiting his turn. She had no time to think about the consequences. She surged up from the ground and hurled herself at her potential rapist. With his trousers down around his knees he was already off balance and they went down to the ground together. He was strong but Swot was determined; this was just not going to happen to her. She kept a firm grip on her assailant as they rolled on the ground knowing that the kid with the gun wouldn't get a clear shot so long as she kept herself tangled around the other boy. For all she knew the little monster wouldn't think twice about shooting both of them, but it was a risk she was willing to take.

The big boy screamed at her in some language of his own, grunting, and kicking while she held onto his ragged shirt. She had no idea how long she could keep this up, and she had no plan beyond what she was currently doing. If she let up for even a moment the little kid would get a clear shot at her. All she could think of was that she would rather die than let this revolting boy do what he wanted; a fate worse than death? Yes. The logic center in her brain had ceased to function and she was acting out of impulse. This simply was not going to happen.

Suddenly the boy stopped struggling and his weight was lifted off her. She looked up and saw the outline of a man. Oh great, so it wouldn't be a ten year old; it would be a fully grown man. She staggered to her feet ready to put up whatever defense she could and saw that she wasn't about to be raped; she was about to be rescued.

The smaller boy was nowhere in sight but Mugabe had two guns tucked under one arm, and with the other arm he had a stranglehold around the neck of Swot's would be rapist.

"I told you to stay hidden," Mugabe said. He sounded angry and out of breath.

"Just kill the little bastard," Swot hissed, "or better still let me do it."

Mugabe shook his head.

"He was going to____" She ran out of words, and felt a sob rising in her throat.

"Yes," said Mugabe, "I know." He kicked the boy away from him "Go," he said.

"You're letting him get away with it?"

"We go," said Mugabe.

"But___"

"But what?" Mugabe said.

"He___"

"He is a child soldier," Mugabe said. "He has been stolen from his village and he has been brutalized and now all he knows is brutality. As soon as these boys are taken they are made to kill. Perhaps he was made to kill his parents, or his brothers, or his friends. It doesn't matter now. He has been made into a killer. He has eaten the hearts of his enemies."

"No."

"Yes," said Mugabe. "I think he has been many years with Matapa. Much killing."

"How do you know?"

"I heard him speak. He has been brought from Rwanda. Matapa was in Rwanda four years ago. That means he has been four years with Matapa. He has no other life."

Swot was still out of breath from the struggle.

"He was going to____"

"I know," said Mugabe, "but he failed. We must go."

"What about the village?"

Mugabe put his hands on her shoulders and gave her a none too gentle shake. "It is just one village," he said, "and the harm is already done. We have to remember why we are here, Sarah. The best thing we can do for the village is to make sure that Matapa leaves."

Somewhere ahead on the path a car horn sounded and an engine roared into life. Without being told Swot faded back into the long grass with Mugabe right behind her. A pick-up truck came at them out of the flaming village and then slowed to a halt just a few yards away. Fortunately the truck only had one working headlight which shone its beam onto the other side of the path. The driver sounded his horn again and Swot's two assailants appeared out of the bushes. The driver leaned out of the cab window and shouted angrily at the boys. They hung their heads; no longer soldiers, just two children who had lost their deadly toys. The driver berated them for some time and then Swot heard one of them say "mazungu". It was the only thing she understood of the conversation but it was all she needed to understand. They were telling the driver about the white woman they had found. The two boys climbed into the back of the truck and the driver pulled forward slowly, hanging his head out of the cab. He was looking for Swot.

As the pick-up edged past her hiding place Swot could see that the bed of the truck was jammed full of men and boys and bristling with weapons. Mugabe's arm was rock steady around her shoulders holding her in place. She did a good job of holding her breath until a little voice called out to her from somewhere in the bed of the pick-up.

"Sarah."

It was Matthew.

CHAPTER ELEVEN

Swot was really tired of having her face shoved into the mud. By the time Mugabe let go of her the pickup truck was nothing but a red rear light in the distance but her ears still rang with the sound of Matthew's frightened little voice calling her name.

"It was him," Swot said. "It was Matthew. We could have rescued him."

"No we couldn't," Mugabe said. "The truck is full of boys with guns; they'll shoot anything that moves. There was nothing we could do at this time."

"But he was calling me."

"Yes, I know."

"He needs help."

Mugabe pulled Swot to her feet. "He will not be harmed," he said.

"And how do you know that?" she demanded, swiping her hand across her face to get rid of the mud, and to deal with the tears that she was trying very hard not to shed.

"The boy is weak___"

"Yes, I know and that's why___"

Mugabe interrupted her impatiently. "They don't keep weak boys," he said. "You have seen them for yourself; do you think they would allow weakness?"

"They're evil little bastards," said Swot.

He nodded his head. "Exactly," he said. "A kind-hearted boy with a lame leg would not last five minutes with them, but they have allowed him to live. Why have they done that?"

"I don't know," Swot said angrily. "You tell me. You know everything."

"Because they need him," Mugabe said. "They need to keep him alive so that you will go and look for the baby. If they kill him they have nothing to bargain with. They won't kill him; not yet."

"But he called my name," she protested.

"I don't think that was what they planned," Mugabe said. "I think that Matthew heard what they were saying about finding a white girl and he guessed it was you."

"But he needed my help," Swot insisted, and this time she let the tears just run down her face, warm and salty.

"Yes," said Mugabe, "he needs help and we're going to give it to him. Remember, Sarah, he is of my clan and I have sworn to recover him. You are not alone."

"He was right there," Swot muttered.

"I know." He patted her on the back. "We have to go."

"But what about the village; aren't we going to help them?"

"There is no help we can give," Mugabe replied. "Other people will come; we have to go and find the old man. "

They retraced their footsteps and found the motorcycle where Mugabe had left it. He pulled it out of the weeds and climbed aboard. As soon as he had started the engine Swot climbed on behind him and they set off again, skirting the still smoldering village and heading deeper into the bush. Swot had no idea how Mugabe was navigating their path but he seemed to know what he was doing as he switched from one path to another following ever smaller tracks. Occasionally they would pass the huddled shapes of huts, a fenced borehole, or one time a cement building, white in the moonlight with a light in the window. At one point a creature scurried across the path in front of them; some kind of large cat, most certainly not anything domesticated.

Eventually they came to a halt under the spreading branches of a huge tree and Mugabe cut the engine.

"Is this is?" Swot asked.

"I believe it is," he said, looking up at the tree. "Yes," he said, "this is a weaver bird tree; we have arrived. I will go alone and wake the *mzee*. You will wait here. Do you understand me, Sarah? You will wait. Whatever happens, you will not move."

Swot nodded her head. She had no strength left to argue and no intention of moving. She had no idea how many more ten year old potential rapists might be hiding in the bushes but one per night was more than sufficient. She moved into the deep shadows beneath the tree and watched Mugabe as he approached a little cluster of buildings. A dog barked from somewhere close by and then a befuddled rooster crowed his morning alarm although morning was still hours away. The buildings remained in darkness. She strained her eyes to make out shapes, and saw that there was only one large round hut and the other shapes were chicken houses and goat pens.

Mugabe called softly in some local language; the only word Swot recognized was Okolo, the soldier's name. Mugabe edged closer to the door, still speaking softly and reassuringly. A voice answered him from within the hut. Mugabe turned on his flashlight and shone it on his own face, still standing a respectful distance from the door. At last the door opened and Swot saw the shadowy shape of someone dressed in white. Mugabe continued to shine the light on his own face while he conducted a short conversation. The shadowy shape retreated into the hut and a flickering light showed through the open doorway. Mugabe turned off the flashlight and came back to the tree to collect Swot.

"Haji Okolo will see us," he said. "He is a courageous old man. Most people would not open their door to a stranger in the night."

"So is that his name?" she asked. "Do I call him Haji, or Sergeant or what? I don't want to offend him."

"Haji is his honor," Mugabe said. "He has been to Mecca."

"Mecca? What does that have to do with anything?"

"When a Moslem has made the pilgrimage to Mecca he is then known as Haji. It is an honor."

Swot stopped dead in her tracks. "He's a Moslem?"

"Yes."

"But he fought in World War Two?"

"Many Moslems fought in that war."

"On our side?"

"Yes, they fought with the Americans. Do you have a problem with

Moslems, Sarah?"

"Well of course I do," she said.

"Not all Moslems are terrorists," Mugabe said. "In Uganda we live happily with many faiths. You will treat this man with respect, Sarah."

"Yes, I will but___"

"But nothing," he hissed. "He is a respected man and has done nothing to harm anyone and if you cannot put your ignorant American prejudice aside, I will not permit you to speak to him." Swot could tell that he was annoyed with her, really, really annoyed.

"Sorry," she said. "I wasn't thinking."

"No you were not," said Mugabe.

"So are you a Moslem?"

He didn't answer her. She followed him meekly into the lamp lit interior of the hut.

Swot couldn't say what she had expected to find inside the hut; she only knew that what she did see was a surprise. The interior was large and lit by a warm orange glow from a smoky hurricane lamp. The smoke curled up towards a high roof. The dirt floor was smooth and shiny with some kind of polish. The old man's bed was set off to one side, the covers thrown back where he had climbed out to open the door. The center of the hut was occupied by a grouping of low three legged stools. In the places where the lamplight lit the walls Swot could see a pattern of intricately woven rushes with items hanging on wooden pegs; items such as spears, arrows, a shield. She felt as though she was on a movie set and Tarzan would come swinging through the trees, or some Victorian explorer would pass by on his way to King Solomon's Mines. So this was Africa, she thought, the real Africa; the Africa that was rapidly disappearing from sight and memory.

Sergeant Okolo stood upright in the middle of the hut, leaning on a carved staff. He was tall and incredibly thin and his weather-beaten face was just as Zach had drawn it in his journal, down to the wispy white beard and the thin fuzz of white curls around the crown of his head.

"The Haji speaks English," Mugabe said.

The old man indicated that they should sit on the low stools. It took him a while to bend his shaky limbs and get into a comfortable position but eventually they were all seated and the conversation could begin. Swot didn't need Mugabe to tell her that she couldn't just dive into the subject of the child; everything about the traditional hut, the antique weapons, and the dignity of the old man told her that a certain amount of ceremony would be involved. She let Mugabe lead the way.

"Haji," he said, "we are sorry to disturb your night."

The old man shrugged his thin shoulders, "At my age," he said, "I need very little sleep."

His voice was a surprisingly deep bass; Swot had expected it to be thin and quavering but he spoke like a much younger man. "I sleep very lightly," he continued. "These days we are not safe in our beds."

Mugabe made a sound of sympathetic agreement, and then he paused. When it was obvious that the old man had no more to say on the subject of the dangers that surrounded him, Mugabe turned to indicate Swot.

"This American girl," he said, "is the granddaughter of the RDC."

"Eh," said the old man. He looked at Swot, and then he smiled showing a distinct lack of teeth. "I remember," he said. He took a moment in his own mind to remember. "She was the girl with the bright gold hair," he said.

"Brenda," Swot said.

He looked puzzled.

She corrected herself. "Songbird."

He smiled again. "Ah, yes, Songbird. So you are the child of Songbird?"

"I'm her granddaughter."

"Of course; I had forgotten how long ago it was. Americans in a yellow vehicle; like a little bus; I remember it well. Most people here had not seen Americans, but I had. I was with the Americans in Burma."

"Yes, I know," Swot said.

"The King gave me the Distinguished Conduct Medal," said Okolo. Swot looked at Mugabe. Could she start asking questions now? He shook his head and carefully and patiently led the old Sergeant into giving an account of his service in Burma seventy years earlier. Swot was well aware that they were in a hurry and that there was an important purpose to their visit but she soon became wrapped up in the old man's story and the long ago lost world that he described. The recruiting officer had come to his village to tell the young men that the faraway King needed them to protect the Empire. Swot tried to imagine how it was for those boys who had never before left their village. All they knew of the King and the Empire was what they had been taught in their little thatched school house. Most of them had never seen a white man, or a motor car, or an electric light bulb and certainly they had never seen a train or a ship but within days of signing up they were loaded on the train to Mombasa and then onto a ship and onward across the Indian Ocean and finally to the jungles of Burma.

Those four years of fighting for the King in the Kings African Rifles had changed Okolo's life. The boy who had never dreamed of moving beyond his own village came back as a man who had seen the world.

"And then they left us," he said at last.

"Who left?" Swot asked.

"The British."

"I thought you wanted them to leave."

"Yes," he said, "we wanted them to leave but they left too soon."

Mugabe made a derogatory noise that Swot took to mean that so far as he was concerned there was no such thing as "too soon."

Haji Okolo looked at Mugabe. "Do you really think we are better off?" he asked. "When the British were here we were safe in our houses; but now....."

"Now we are free," said Mugabe.

"And what have we done with our freedom?" the old man asked. "We have placed ourselves in the hands of dictators. We have killed our own people."

Mugabe shook his head and then looked at Swot. "This is the way the old people talk," he said, "but their world has gone."

"I served the King," said Okolo," and he gave me a medal."

"Yes, I know," she said.

The old man staggered to his feet. "I will show it to you," he said.

"That's really not necessary."

"Hmm," said Okolo, "I will show it to this man of yours."

"He's not exactly my man," Swot said hastily, "and that's not why we came."

She might as well have been talking to the wall. Okolo was down on his knees reaching under the bed. Swot looked at Mugabe and he gave her his usual eloquent shrug of his shoulders. "Be patient," he said softly.

Okolo emerged with a rusty old cookie tin. He reinstalled himself on the stool and then opened the tin and passed it to Swot. She looked inside and saw the treasures he had been keeping to remind himself of another day and another time. The medal was a silver disc with an engraving of a man wearing a crown. Okolo pointed a gnarled finger.

"That's the King," he said, "and on the back it has my name."

He took the tin back and ran his hands through his other treasures but without explaining what they were. Swot thought she saw a school report card, some old paper money, a sheet of yellowed paper with the word Citation written at the top, and then Okolo picked up a black and white photograph which he handed across to her. She saw Okolo as a young man in a dark suit standing proudly next to a young woman in a white dress; a wedding photo.

"You?" she asked.

"Yes," he said, "and my first wife."

"First?"

"The missionaries told us we were all to be Christians and to have only one wife." He grinned and Swot saw the young charmer hidden beneath the wrinkles of old age. "I married her so the missionaries would leave us alone."

"You didn't want to marry her?" Swot was now totally intrigued.

"Yes, I wanted to marry her; but I wanted to marry others. I have had four wives but she was the first."

"And now she's gone?"

"No," he said, "she is in Kampala."

"Ah," said Mugabe, who had been silent for some time, "when did she go to Kampala?"

A furtive expression stole across Okolo's face, and Swot could see him weighing up whether or not to trust them.

"Sergeant," Swot said, thinking that giving him his title would please him, "we know that an American boy called Zachary came to see you."

He nodded.

"And after his first visit he came back a second time and brought a child."

The old man said nothing.

"The child was in danger," she said, "and he asked you to protect her."

Still he said nothing. Swot swam forward into uncharted waters.

"Did your wife take the child to Kampala?"

He stared at her, his fingers moving automatically through his little pile of treasures.

"The American boy has been killed," Swot said.

His fingers stopped moving.

"Eh?" he said, and then "Who has killed him?"

"We don't know," said Mugabe "but we think we know why he was killed."

"Because of the child?" said Okolo.

"Yes," said Mugabe.

"He told me what the witchdoctor had done," Okolo said. "Such wickedness; to put such power on a child and in such a way."

"I don't think he actually did anything, "Swot said hastily. "Surely you don't believe that____"

Okolo pulled himself to his feet again. "The witchdoctor can do many things," he said, "but this thing he has done is evil. It is not our way. I told my wife to take her to Kampala where there is a powerful shaman who will remove the curse; then she can come home again."

Swot could feel herself falling further down the rabbit hole. "There isn't a curse, "she said. "It's all gobbledygook."

Mugabe raised his eyebrows. Swot assumed that gobbledygook was not a word in his vocabulary. She opened her mouth to speak again but Mugabe shook his head. He stood up, and Swot saw that although he was obviously taller than the old man, he took pains to keep his head lower as though he was some kind of mendicant.

"When did your wife leave for Kampala?" he asked.

"Yesterday," said Okolo. "She walked to the road with the child and then she took a taxi. She will be there already."

"No," said Mugabe, "she is not there. The bridge across the swamp is gone and there is no way to reach Kampala."

"Eh," said Okolo, "no one has told me this. I know the bridge; what has happened? "

"The rains have washed it away," said Mugabe.

"Such storms," said Okolo, "I cannot remember such storms before."

"We are alone here," said Mugabe, "and no help will come from Kampala." He lifted his head a little higher. "Matapa is here and he wants the child."

"Matapa," said Okolo. "Why is he here?"

"For the child," Mugabe repeated.

"Does he know you are here?" Okolo asked.

"No," said Mugabe, "that's why we came at night. We saw Matapa's soldiers back along the road, burning a village."

"The British would never have allowed such a man," Okolo said.

"Neither will we," Mugabe said. "What is the name of your wife?"

"She is called Florence," Okolo said.

Mugabe stepped back. "We'll send someone to the bridge to find your wife," he said, "and bring her back here."

Okolo shook his head. "No, not here; take her somewhere safe. If Matapa is here then none of us are safe. You take her to a safe place."

"We can take you," Swot offered, although she wasn't sure how they were going to get three people onto the motorcycle.

Okolo stood up straight. "I am the King's soldier," he said, "and I do not run from criminals. If he comes here I will kill him."

Swot's eyes strayed to the various weapons displayed on the wall. Okolo smiled. "I will use them," he said.

Mugabe jerked his head to indicate it was time for Swot to get up from the stool.

"Are you sure you don't want to come with us?" she asked.

"This is my home," Okolo said. "I will not leave my home." He gave her a strange sideways look.

"Have you been cursed?" he asked.

"No, "she said, "of course not. "

"Are you certain?"

"I saw the witchdoctor from Kajunga, "she admitted, "and he threw some dust around. It'll take more than a handful of dust to curse me."

The old man shook his head. "Be careful," he said, "that man from Kajunga is powerful and you have no protection; and I believe he has made a curse."

"Okay," she said, in order to keep the peace. "I'll be careful."

Somewhere close by a rooster crowed. Swot looked at Mugabe in alarm. Okolo extinguished the lamp and Mugabe moved to crack the door open. He nodded his head.

"It's almost morning," he said. "We have to go."

Swot and Mugabe went out into the pitch black. Maybe Mugabe knew with some inner sense that it was almost morning but to Swot it still looked like dark night. They found the motorcycle where they had left it under the weaver bird tree and Mugabe kicked it into life. They threaded their way back along the narrow track again avoiding the village that Matapa had destroyed. By the time they reached the Trading Center the sun was peeking over the horizon; when they reached Budeka it was full daylight and the gates of the Speke Guest House were wide open to welcome visitors; early-risers were assembled on the terrace for breakfast, and Swot's grandfather and grandmother were waiting for her with anxious, sour faces. They were not happy.

Babu said very little but Brenda made up for all the words he might have said, and then added some more of her own. Swot really couldn't blame her for being angry; after all she had been gone from her room all night without leaving so much as a note. She just found it ironic that when Brenda was Swot's age she had been running around Africa without any parental supervision, drunk, high, and ultimately pregnant, and yet she didn't trust Swot. She was well aware that Swot had never been drunk, that she didn't do drugs, and there was no way that she was pregnant so really Brenda could have cut her a little slack. On the other hand there was a warlord lurking in the bushes; someone had murdered the Peace Corps worker, and, although Brenda didn't know it, Swot had been very nearly raped by a ten year old punk. Swot decided to accept her tongue lashing and remain silent. She was, however, worried about what would happen to Mugabe because he was supposed to be the responsible adult.

Swot's grandfather's reaction to Mugabe was somewhat baffling. He uttered a few angry words but not very many, and Mugabe seemed to take them in his stride. They were speaking their own language so Swot had no idea what they were saying but she could tell that, far from being angry her grandfather was interested in what Mugabe had to say. As the two men faced each other Swot really couldn't say that Mugabe looked even remotely like an employee who was getting a reprimand. She remembered how he had lowered his head as a sign of respect for Haji Okolo but he didn't do this for her grandfather. Eventually they nodded at each other and Mugabe strolled off behind the building in the general direction of the gate into Rory Marsden's compound.

"I'm okay," Swot said to Brenda. "I just need some breakfast."

"Your grandmother was worried," said Babu.

"Yeah," Swot said, "well it's nice to have someone worry about me. How worried are you about your son?"

"Shut up, Swot," Brenda hissed. "Why do you have to make everything so unpleasant?"

"I saw him," Swot said, ignoring Brenda's interruption.

"Where?"

"We went past a burning village___"

"Yes," said Babu, "that's what Mugabe told me."

"And Matthew was in a pick-up truck with Matapa's men."

"They have not hurt him?"

"Not yet, "Swot said. "You should tell his mother."

"Yes," he said, "she will be informed."

"I'm going to get some breakfast," Swot said.

He laid a large hand on her shoulder. "Wait," he said.

"What?"

"You have courage but no caution," he said.

"Mugabe looked after me, "she said. "Did he tell you that we know where the baby is?"

"He told me," said Babu. "After breakfast you may come with me to the bridge and we will find the old woman."

"And then what?" Swot asked.

"The child's parents are here in town," he said.

"But you can't give her to them," she protested, "because then everyone will know where she is."

"I know," Babu replied, "but first let us find the child and then we will decide what to do next."

"You know," Brenda interrupted, "that none of this gets us any closer to knowing who killed the boy."

Swot found that her mouth was literally hanging open as she gasped. Brenda was absolutely correct; with Mugabe's help Swot had certainly managed to accomplish a lot in the last few hours, but she was no closer to answering the original question; who had killed Zachary Ephron?

"It doesn't seem so important anymore," she said. "I mean, he's dead, and nothing we can do will make him undead, but at least we can do something for the kid, and for Matthew".

"And I suppose we should just ignore the minor detail that there is a knife wielding homicidal maniac on the loose around here," Brenda said. She gave Swot a half-smile. "Oh take no notice of me; I know you're doing your best." She took her granddaughter's arm and led her up the steps to the terrace. "You can clean yourself up after breakfast," she said.

"Am I a mess?" Swot asked.

Brenda laughed. "Oh Swot, I'm so glad that you're not one of those image obsessed teenagers," she said. "Frankly my dear, you are a mess, but it doesn't matter; at least you're all in one piece. Now, I have to warn you that the Irish evangelist is still here and so is Margaret and there'll be more fireworks if they get near each other."

"That's their problem," Swot said. "I just want a cup of tea. I don't want to talk to anyone."

"And the witchdoctor was here," Brenda said."

"What?"

"That awful man from Kajunga; he was here earlier this morning and that Irishman gave him a hell of a telling off."

"Yeah, well, the Irishman started it."

"You should talk to him," Brenda said. "He's not what you would expect."

Swot sat herself down at a table and ordered tea and toast. Now that the action was over and the sun was rising steadily in the sky, she found it hard to believe all the things that had happened in the dark. The sky was blue and bright above them, flowers bloomed in pots on the terrace, smartly uniformed hotel staff went about their business, birds twittered in the trees. Swot could not connect the daylight world to the nighttime world of burning villages, and boy soldiers. If she had not seen it for herself; if she had remained safe in her bed at the guest house; she would never have known the kind of terror that stalked the lonely villages at night and caused old Sergeant Okolo to keep his weapons sharp and his door locked.

The Irish evangelist was eating alone at a table. He looked at Swot. She ignored him. Brenda hurried in and leaned confidentially across the table. "Rory's left his gate open," she whispered.

"So?"

"I'm going in."

"He doesn't want you there;" Swot said, "he made that perfectly clear yesterday when he refused to let you in."

"He can't refuse if I let myself in, "Brenda said.

"I don't know what you want with him, " said Swot. "You told me that whatever your relationship was, it was over before you even came here; and what about Herbert, your husband?"

"Hmm," Brenda sniffed, "some husband. Anyway that's not why I want to see him. He's up to something and I want to know what it is."

"Perhaps he genuinely wants us all to leave him alone," Swot said. "He's made a life for himself here and that's the way he likes it. It's been fifty years."

"A leopard doesn't change its spots," Brenda said, "and fifty years or not, he's up to something."

"Oh well, suit yourself," said Swot, pouring more tea into her cup.

"I certainly will," Brenda declared. She snatched up a sugar cube from the bowl on the table, popped it in her mouth and made her exit.

Swot looked with approval at Brenda's retreating back. She had two grandmothers; Christina, a sensible Swedish woman who was always stylishly dressed, took river boat cruises in Europe, and talked constantly about her book club; and Brenda. Swot could never find anything to say to Grandma Christina but she could always find something to say to Brenda. So far as she was concerned, Brenda had Christina beaten by a mile in the grandmother stakes; she was crazy, but it was a craziness Swot understood, and was learning to respect.

Swot was on her second cup of tea when the Irishman decided to get up from his seat and come across to her table. He was carrying a cup of tea and his hand was shaking so severely that he spilled most of the tea into the saucer as he set the cup down.

"Mind if I join you?"

Swot grunted. Yes, she minded but she wasn't sure what to do about it, and by the look of things he was far more scared of her than she was of him; so why did he want to talk to her?

"I've been praying for you," he said in his soft Irish voice.

"No need," Swot replied staring down into her tea cup.

"I hear the old man from Kajunga cursed you."

Swot looked up into his sunburned face. He was a handsome man with a round friendly face and blue eyes set amongst the beginning of wrinkles. His hair was dark and curly and edged with gray and he could have used a shave. She noted that his nose and the tops of his ears were peeling. She assumed that he must have been standing out in the sun the day before because that was the first day of sunshine since she had arrived. She guessed that he couldn't wait to get out into the marketplace and jam his religion down the throats of the ignorant hell-bound savages.

"I don't need your prayers," Swot said. "You've done enough damage already."

He hung his head. "I know."

"What on earth were you thinking?" she asked.

He sighed, and then took a long swallow of his tea.

"I take it you're not a Christian," he said.

"No, I don't think I am," Swot told him.

"If you don't think you are, then you're not," he said.

"Okay, then; I'm not."

"Do you believe in God at all?" he asked.

"I don't believe in discussing my religious views with complete strangers," Swot said haughtily.

"Do you believe in a power for good?" he persisted.

"Maybe," she replied.

"If you believe in a force for good, then you must believe in the equal and opposite force; the force of evil," he declared.

Swot thought about the experiences of the night before. "I believe in evil," she said.

"Then you are open to the witchdoctor's curse," he said.

She slammed her cup down on the table. "I wish everyone would stop saying that," she said. She started to stand up but he reached out a beefy hand and stopped her.

"Please," he said, "please listen to me for just a moment. I have to warn you. I've done everything wrong since I came here, please let me do something that is right."

Swot sat down again and glared at him. "Go ahead," she said.

"The little girl that I baptized____"

"Sentenced to death."

He took another deep breath. "You really are a troubled young woman," he said. "Where does all your anger come from?"

"We're not talking about me," she reminded him.

He nodded his head. "The parents brought that little girl to me because she was very sick," he said. "She had malaria and a high fever and they were frightened she would die. They didn't want her to die without being baptized; that's the only reason I did it."

"That's not what I heard," said Swot; "I heard you just wanted to make a display of your miracle water from the Jordan."

"And why would I do that?" he asked. "Water from the Jordan is no different than water from anywhere else? It's not the water that matters."

"So you didn't have water from the Jordan?"

"No, I didn't, but my interpreter thought it would be a good idea to say that I did. He wanted people to think I was something special. This is my first time here, you know, and I just picked up that interpreter in Kampala. I had no idea what he was saying most of the time. I had no idea that I was putting that little kiddie in danger."

"What are you even doing here?" Swot asked. "What gives you the right to run around Africa telling people that they're going to hell?"

"No," he said fiercely, "that's not what I'm telling them. I'm telling them how to get to heaven."

"Whatever," she said, shrugging her shoulders and reverting to the kind of careless teen speak she had abandoned years before.

"I'm serious," he said. "I'm all in favor of progress, and teaching people better ways of doing things, and sending foreign aid; doctors, nurses, engineers; I'm all in favor of that, but that's not what I'm called to do. The fact is that everyone here is going to die one day; you're going to die one day; and my duty is to tell people that they can go to heaven when they die. It doesn't matter how bad things are here; it can all be endured if we know that heaven is our home."

"That's a pretty miserable way of looking at things," said Swot. "Life sucks and then you die, but at least you'll go to heaven."

"It's better than the alternative," he said.

"How about life sucks and then you die, and that's it?" she said.

"Wow," he said, "you really are a miserable kid, aren't you?"

"I'm not a kid," she said. "I've finished college already."

"You're still a kid," he said. "Here's the thing; I don't want to be here; I would much prefer to be in Dublin with my family but God has called me to come here and spread the Gospel. So far I seem to have made a mess of things, but I believe that God will redeem my mess. I believe he has a purpose for my life, and for your life, and for the life of that little girl. I just want you to know that and to know that I'm praying for you. "

"I don't need prayers," said Swot, "I need to find that poor kid."

"Could we agree in prayer?" he asked. "Could we agree right now?" He reached across the table with both hands. Swot hastily shifted her chair backwards. She had no idea what he meant by agreeing in prayer, but she knew she didn't want to agree with him about anything. Okay, maybe he wasn't the monster she had first thought him to be; maybe he was just a gullible innocent who'd been led astray by an overzealous interpreter, but she still didn't want to sit at the table and hold hands with him and talk to a God whose only plan for Africa was to send white missionaries in to tell people that they shouldn't complain about this life because things would be better in the next one.

Swot's grandfather approached them. He nodded to the Irishman who immediately shoved his chair back and tried to rise to his feet, upsetting the tea cup in his haste.

"Sarah," her grandfather said, "we are leaving in five minutes; go and change your clothes."

"Where are you going?" the Irishman asked.

Grandfather looked at him as one might look at a small child. "We are going to the bridge," he replied.

"Not that it's any of your business," Swot added.

"Go and change," Babu repeated.

Five minutes later they left the compound. Babu and Swot were seated together in the back of the Mercedes with Habati driving and Mugabe once again riding shotgun, and Swot once again wearing Brenda's clothes. They were trailed as usual by the pick-up truck full of armed men. As they rolled past Rory's gates Swot saw Brenda emerge and wave frantically but Babu ignored her. Swot looked back through the rear window and saw Brenda standing in the road. Rory came striding through the gate and took Brenda by the shoulders; he seemed to be pleading with her, or maybe just trying to shake some sense into her. No surprise there, Swot thought, that was the effect that Brenda seemed to have on most people.

They continued their progress through the town leaving mud-spattered pedestrians in their wake. Swot turned her thoughts to her conversation with the Irishman who seemed to think she was going straight to hell. Of course she didn't believe him, or did she? She thought about the witchdoctor's curse and the three different people who'd told her that she had no protection. "If you believe in evil, then you must also believe in good". Really? She envied the Irishman. At least he believed in something.

CHAPTER TWELVE

They ran into signs of trouble just a few minutes after leaving Budeka although the first obstacle was nothing serious. A small truck which Babu referred to as a lorry was overturned at the side of the road. The road was jammed with people gathering up the charcoal that had spilled from the truck despite the protests of the truck's driver who ran from one person to another trying to recapture his trade goods. When the people failed to get out of the way Mugabe motioned for some of the men to come forward from the pick-up truck that was trailing them. Looking armed and dangerous they walked in front of the Mercedes for a few yards and parted the crowd so that Babu and Swot could continue their stately progress.

"Shouldn't they do something about the stealing?" Swot asked.

"What do you suggest?" said Babu.

"Tell the people to put the stuff back. It's not theirs."

Babu shook his head. "And then there would be a riot. Do you wish to die for the sake of a sack of charcoal?"

"It wouldn't come to that," she argued.

"It might," said Babu, "our people are now on a very short fuse. No supplies are coming in from Kampala and we are running short of necessities. People need charcoal for their cooking."

"So they should pay for it," she said.

"And who would they pay?"

"The driver."

"The charcoal is not his. The rightful owner is not here," Babu said. "If they give the driver the money he will take it and run away. Why should they do that?"

Swot really couldn't find a way to argue with that sort of logic so she just shrugged her shoulders; something that she had done frequently since she had arrived in the land of her ancestors. They drove on.

The road became increasingly congested. People were walking towards town, and about an equal number were walking away from town. Everyone seemed to be on the move, but no one seemed to have any destination in mind; they were just walking and dragging their children along with them. Swot saw more overturned vehicles with their loads spilled out across the road, and then she began to see vehicles that were still upright but just standing still in the middle of the road. Babu's armed henchmen climbed out of their truck again and walked in front of the vehicles shooing people out of their path. The road they were on had once been paved but now it was little more than a wide potholed track with deep ruts along each side. Their escorts were finding it harder and harder to shoulder their way through the crowd.

Mugabe leaned out of the window and called the pick-up truck forward to ride in front of them. They pushed on with the pick-up truck opening a path. Habati muttered something and pointed out of his window. Swot followed his pointing finger and saw the mangled remnants of a cell tower rising above the elephant grass in the field beside us.

"No signal," said Habati. They all laughed. Really there was nothing else to do.

They passed a bus. Some of the passengers were still inside, some stood outside; an enterprising vendor moved among them selling food. At first glance Swot might have thought that a carnival atmosphere prevailed but the further they went the more she saw resentment on people's faces as their escort strong armed their way through.

"We're getting close to the bridge now," Mugabe said, turning to speak to Swot over his shoulder. "These people have been waiting for days now. They don't know what to do."

"They should go home," said Babu. "Waiting here is not reasonable."

"Is there another way around?" Swot asked.

"Oh yes," said Mugabe, "but it is several hundred kilometers and a very bad road. They won't go that way."

"So they'll just wait?" she asked.

"They will try to find a way to cross," said Mugabe.

They were now almost at a standstill. She could see the tension in Habati's shoulders as he edged the big SUV forward. The vehicle tipped sideways as he set the passenger side wheels in the ditch and squeaked past a couple of stalled taxis. They stopped again. Now they were behind a large white SUV with a couple of huge radio aerials sprouting from its roof.

"UN," said Mugabe. "Even they can't get through."

"Go and help," said Babu.

Mugabe climbed out of the SUV and walked forward past their pick-up truck escort to talk to the driver of the UN vehicle. They moved forward a couple of feet. Mugabe came back. Swot's grandfather wound down his window to talk to him.

"We won't get much further," Mugabe said. "The vehicles at the river won't give way."

"So what will they do?" Swot asked.

"There is a rumor that the government is sending a ferry," Mugabe said but the look on his face told her that he doubted very much if a ferry would arrive any time soon. "There used to be a ferry further upstream. If they can get the motor started they will send it down to here."

"How many people are waiting?" Swot asked.

"Hundreds on this side," said Mugabe "but not so many on the other side. Mostly they have gone back to Kampala."

A woman pushed in behind Mugabe and spotted Swot's

grandfather through the open window. She started to shout. Babu wound up the window and Mugabe scrambled back into the passenger seat. The woman was still shouting and people were beginning to converge on the vehicle.

"What's going on?" Swot asked.

"They're angry," said Babu.

"With you?"

"With everyone," he said, "but I am here, so now they are angry with me. They want the bridge to be repaired."

"Is it a big bridge?"

He shook his head. "Not big, but important," he said, "with a cement causeway across the swamp. It was built by the British. It has not been maintained."

"But what do they expect you to do about it right now? "she asked.

"All I can do is talk to them," he said. "When I am here I represent the government. I can make promises."

"Will you be able to keep your promises?"

He shook his head wearily. "We are politicians," he said, "and that is what we do. We make promises we can't keep. I think the bridge was one of our election promises." He sighed. "I don't know why the people still believe us," he said. "They see nothing but broken promises. We promise them the moon and we give them nothing; we have nothing to give them."

The UN truck moved, the pick-up moved, and Habati edged their vehicle forward a few more feet. Swot wondered if moving forward was such a good idea. They were being jammed like a cork into a bottle; what would happen when they wanted to turn around and leave?

"Sarah," said Babu, "look at all those people. When the British left we were five million people, now we are thirty two million. Do you know how many of those people pay taxes?"

Swot looked out the window. Apart from the UN vehicle which looked very expensive she could see nothing but old battered vehicles that wouldn't have been allowed on the road in the US, and the people milling restlessly around looked uniformly poor.

"Taxes?" she asked.

"A government is run by taxing the people," Babu said, "that's basic economics, but these people have no money for taxes."

"No, I guess not," Swot answered thinking that this was not really a good time for a lesson in economics but her grandfather seemed determined to make her understand his position.

"We have no money of our own," he said, "and we rely on foreign donations. Look at these people, Sarah; don't you think they deserve something better than this?"

"They deserve to be able to sleep safely in their beds at night," she said, thinking of Matapa lurking somewhere in the bush.

"They deserve roads, hospitals, schools, and a better bridge," said Babu, "but I can't give them any of those things. It is quite possible that some foreign government has already given the money to repair the bridge, but the money has gone somewhere else; all I know is that it never came to me; it has stuck to someone's fingers, but not to mine. But these are my people and someone has to talk to them."

He tapped Mugabe on the shoulder. "We'll walk," he said.

"What about the baby?" Swot asked. "We came here for the baby."

"We will make inquiries," Mugabe said.

Swot started to open her door. She wanted to see the bridge. She wanted to see what was at the end of the long congested trail.

"Not you," said Babu. "You stay here. I will send back another man to be with you and Habati will turn the car around. After I have spoken to my people we will go back to Budeka."

"Don't forget the baby," Swot said.

He straightened his tie and brushed some imaginary dust from his lapels. Mugabe slipped out of his seat and came to open the door. Surrounded by his own henchmen Babu stepped forward into the crowd. An anonymous man with a weapon came to sit in the front seat. Habati wound down his window, surveyed the traffic situation and began the laborious maneuver of turning the Mercedes around. While he concentrated all his efforts on not running down any of the pedestrians Swot quietly opened the door and slipped from her seat. He never saw her leave.

Within about a minute she knew she had made a big mistake.

Sitting comfortably in the back of the SUV she had been safely above the crowd but now she was in the midst of it pressed in on all sides and carried wherever the mob wanted to carry her. When she tried to shove her way in one direction she found herself being shoved back. She didn't know if she had expected some sort of special treatment because she was to all intents and purposes a white girl, but the crowd wasn't cutting her any slack. People trod on her toes, elbowed her in ribs, and shoved her in the back. "Excuse me, excuse me," she shouted as she tried to move in the same direction as Mugabe and her grandfather. Of course it was ridiculous; nobody was going to excuse her and step aside. Although she couldn't imagine where anyone was going, nonetheless it seemed that everyone had a destination in mind. She tried to turn around and go back to the vehicle but she couldn't see where to go.

Quite suddenly a hand reached out of the mob and caught hers. She looked up and saw a large black man wearing a suit and tie and a wide smile. "You come with me," he said.

He dragged her towards him and shouted at the people who were in their way. She had no idea what he was saying but it seemed to have the right effect. Slowly but surely they started to move in the direction of the river. "You come, you come," the man kept saying encouragingly. At last they arrived at an open space where Swot could draw a breath and look at her rescuer. The suit and tie made a good first impression but his trousers were ragged. He wore black dress shoes but no socks, and he carried a battered brief case. They were standing in a small area of calm in the midst of the storm. A line of people snaked around them and ahead of them hundreds of people were being kept in place by a couple of uniformed guards. "This way, this way," said the man with the suit. "We go to the front."

"Front of what?"

"The queue," he said. "These people are queuing."

"Oh, you mean they're lining up for something," Swot said. "What are they waiting for?"

"For the ferry," he replied. "You come, we go to the front; you and me to the front."

She looked around. Now that he had explained the situation she could see it for herself. These people were waiting in a line; no pushing, no shoving, just standing and waiting; old and young, women with babies, children rolling around on the ground, men carrying suitcases. They were barely even talking; they were just standing and waiting; hundreds of people.

"You come," the man urged again.

"There's no ferry," Swot said. "Who told them that a ferry was coming?"

"It is coming," he insisted.

"Even if it comes, it can't carry all these people,"

"Yes," he agreed, "too many people. We go to front."

She hesitated.

"You mazungu," he said, "you go to front."

"Ah," she said, finally understanding. "You want to take me to the front so that you will be in the front."

"Yes," he said, "we go together."

"And you think they'll let me in just because I'm white."

"Yes," he said. "Tourists are all in the front."

She thought about it for a moment. The ferry didn't sound like a good proposition. Even if it arrived from wherever it was upstream, and even if they could keep the engine running, how many people could it carry and what would they do with the cars? She looked at the line of people waiting in the hot sun. What would happen if the ferry failed to arrive? What would happen if they couldn't get on board? Would they just stand there all night? And was it really true that all the white people were already at the front of the line, grabbing first place just because they were white.

"Come, come." The man pulled her forward. She made a snap decision to go with him; not that she had any intention of crossing the river, but he'd been smart enough to come and find her in the crowd and use her as his ticket to get him to the front of the line so that's what she would do. Without his help she would probably have been trampled to death by the crowd. She owed him a favor. They walked together towards the front of the line and no one protested when the guards waved them forward. Now Swot could see the river and the broken bridge. It was not what she had expected. She had no idea of the name of the river but she had expected that it would be wide and fast flowing and that the bridge would be a massive structure because her grandfather had said it was a good bridge built by the British.

What she saw was a narrow stream with marshes on either side, and the remnants of a causeway that had been built across the marsh leading up to a cement bridge. Obviously the rain swollen river had flooded the causeway and washed away part of the bridge. Now the waters were receding and the line of people and vehicles stretched out onto the narrow causeway and all the way to the broken railings of the bridge.

"They can't get a ferry up there," Swot said.

"It will come," her companion assured her. "It will come. We go to the front."

Before they reached the causeway they were stopped by a harassed looking official with a clipboard.

"You need to wait over there," he said.

"We go to front," Swot's companion insisted.

"Over there," said the official. Swot followed the direction of his pointing finger and saw a group of colorfully painted safari vehicles, another white UN vehicle and an ambulance waiting at the edge of the marsh. Someone, probably the safari guides, had erected shade canopies and set out chairs and a group of casually dressed tourists were sitting back watching the chaos all around them.

"We're not with them," Swot said.

"First we take the ambulance," said the official, "and then we take the *mazungus*. The ferry will arrive here; not at the bridge. You wait with them."

She looked at all the people waiting on the causeway. What on earth was going to happen if and when the ferry should actually arrive and they found that they were not first in line; that it was going to stop and pick up the white people first? What would happen if all the people on the causeway tried to turn around and get back onto dry land? The whole thing was a disaster waiting to happen; and the only people who were going to be spared were the tourists.

"We wait with them," her companion agreed. "Come."

A ripple of activity ran through the line of people. Swot turned to look behind her and was relieved to see her grandfather with his phalanx of guards glad-handing his way along the edge of the crowd. She doubted if he'd be pleased to see her, but she knew that she would have to throw herself on his mercy if she wanted to get back to the vehicle in one piece.

"We go," said her rescuer.

She remembered that she owed him a favor. It would only take a couple of minutes to walk over to the tourists and drop him off with them; then if the ferry ever turned up he would have to fend for himself.

"I'm going to say that you are my interpreter," she said.

"Yes, please."

They walked boldly into the enclave of white privilege. Swot pasted on her best and most confident smile and shook hands all around, bewailed the current conditions, complained about the heat and general discomfort and said that she would be back in a few minutes; would they mind if her interpreter waited for her? Her new friend said he would wait with the safari guides and drivers and very soon he was standing in a patch of shade chatting away to a group of dusty, competent looking men in khaki uniforms.

Swot walked back past the official with the clipboard who only had time to give her a puzzled look before he turned his attention to a heavily armed band of ragged men and boys who had come silently out of the bush behind him. A hissing, whispering sound spread through the crowd. "Matapa." She heard the word the same time as she recognized two of the boys; her would be rapist and his younger companion.

Swot saw her grandfather's guards react immediately, pushing her grandfather behind them and turning to face Matapa's raiding party. She was caught out in the open, a white girl in a flimsy skirt standing like something out of a Victorian melodrama between two opposing forces and then one of Babu's men opened fire.

She had never heard gunfire; not real gunfire. It was loud but not as loud as the resulting outburst of screams from the hundreds of people waiting so patiently in line. The screams soon formed themselves from meaningless shrieking into one word "Matapa" and then people began to flee the scene pushing and shoving just to get as far away as they could as fast as they could. Not everyone ran; some of them flung themselves flat on the ground. Swot hesitated for about half a second. She didn't have the instinctive reactions of the people around her; she had never been in a civil war but they had. Something whizzed by her head sounding like an angry supersonic bumble bee. She assumed it was a bullet but she had no idea where it came from but when another one buzzed by her left ear she knew that she was caught up in the middle of an African style gunfight at the Okay Corral and the only option available to her was to fling herself down on the ground and cover her head with her hands. Before she could take action, she felt herself grabbed roughly from behind and dragged forcefully backwards. She had no idea who had grabbed her but at that moment it didn't matter; if someone was giving her a way out of the mess, then she was all for it even if it meant being dragged backwards with her heels scraping along the ground. From then on things moved really fast.

When she thought about it later, she tried to put herself outside of the scene, and recall what she had seen for herself and what she knew must have happened. The scene played in her head in slow motion, like a fight scene from a Kung Fu movie or an old Western. Someone shouts "Matapa"; the crowd erupts in panic, mouths open, screams, people pushing backwards. Close up shot of Matapa's ragged band of children and youths firing randomly into the crowd. Babu and his men fling themselves down on the ground and return gunfire. A white girl stands in the middle of the crossfire with her mouth open, a scream struggling to rise in her paralyzed throat. As panic grips the people on the causeway they look for a way to hide. Men, women, and children jump or are pushed into the swampy water and the rapid flowing current carries them away. One of Matapa's men grabs the white girl and drags her backwards and out of the line of fire. The tourists spring out of their comfortable chairs and flee along the river bank. Matapa's men retreat into the bushes, still firing into the crowd and dragging the girl with them. The girl locks eyes with one of Babu's men; it is Mugabe. The girl finally manages to scream but it makes no difference because now she has been pulled away into the thick vegetation. What does Mugabe do? The girl doesn't know because he was lost from her sight.

The old pick-up truck that she had seen the night before waited for them amongst the elephant grass. Her captor hurled her into the bed of the truck and the rest of Matapa's little thugs climbed in behind her. They continued to fire as the driver revved the engine and plunged forward through the dense vegetation. Having at last found her voice, Swot screamed non-stop. She was still screaming when the shooting stopped and she didn't stop screaming until someone clapped a large, dirty hand over her mouth.

Congo Rain Forest 1968

The boy was far from his birthplace. The old man had led him deep into the endless forest walking for weeks, months, years, through the cool green shadows beneath the dense canopy of age old trees. They existed on roots and berries, and the flesh of monkeys the old man brought down with well-aimed stones. The stunned monkey would fall from the tree, and the boy would complete the killing. He would watch as the light left the eyes of his prey and remember how he had killed the boy at the convent; how the light had left the boy's eyes at the end of their dreadful battle; how the room had been soaked in blood; how his heart had turned to stone.

One night as they sat beside their fire the boy said. "I would like a new name."

The old man continued to chew on his mouthful of monkey flesh. "What did your mother name you?" he asked.

The boy shrugged his shoulders. "It doesn't matter," he said, "I don't want that name; I want a new name."

"What name will you have?"

"I will be called Mwene Matapa," the boy said.

"Eh," the man said, "where did you hear such a name?"

"I heard it from a storyteller," the boy said. "He came to our village when I was a child, while I was still with my mother; and he told stories of great Africans.. He told of the one they called Mwene Matapa, a great war lord of the Shona, long before the white men came."

"Yes," said the witchdoctor, "this story has been told for many years. All storytellers tell the same stories; I heard it when I was a child."

"Is it true?" the boy asked.

""It has some truth," said the man. "Mwene Matapa was indeed a great war lord from a land far to the South long, long ago. The white men have taken his land now; they call it Rhodesia; the Shona are defeated."

" I like the name," the boy said.

"But do you know the meaning?" the man asked.

The boy shook his head. "The story teller did not say."

The man allowed himself one of his rare smiles. "I think he was not a good story teller," he said. "The name has a meaning, it means Great Plunderer."

"A good name," said the boy.

"A true name;" said the old man, "the man who carried it showed no mercy; he had no weakness."

"I have no weakness; I have no mercy," said the boy. "I killed that boy with my own hands."

The old man nodded his head. "It was well done," he said, "but one boy is not enough."

"I will kill others."

The old man nodded again, and ripped off another piece of monkey flesh. "The name is already used by another," he said.

"Who has taken my name?" the boy asked.

"It is not your name;" the man said, "not yet. It is being used by a man of the Shona; it is said that he has fled from the white man's rule and has possessed the spirit of his ancestors. He has become a legend; the storytellers are beginning to tell of him. He has killed for the maumau in Kenya, he has killed here in Congo, and he will kill for others. The name is his, you cannot have it."

"I will take it from him," the boy boasted, "and the storytellers will then talk of me."

The old man looked at him in the flickering fire light. "It is possible," he said, "but you will need to be strong and powerful. You will need big magic."

"Can you make big magic?" the boy asked.

"Do you truly wish to find him and take his name?" the old man asked. "Do you have no other desires?"

The boy hesitated only very briefly. "I have no other desires," he said.

"To make such magic we will require a sacrifice," said the witchdoctor."

"Tell me what we need."

"An innocent," said the old man.

"What is innocent?" the boy asked.

"A baby."

"A human baby?"

"Yes."

"Where will I find such a baby?"

The old man picked at his teeth with a sliver of monkey bone, and then gestured with his hand. "There is a village," he said, "you will find it. Follow the smell of their fires. Bring me a baby, and we will make magic."

"And I will be called Mwene Matapa?"

No," said the old man, "I will not call you by that name; I will call you "boy"; but one day you will find this terrible man, this Mwene Matapa, and you will take his name from him. That is the magic I can do for you."

The boy rose to his feet. "I will return," he said, "and I will bring you the sacrifice."

The old man gazed deep into the fire. The boy turned and walked away into the darkness of the forest. He walked until the sun rose above the leafy canopy and the scent of the morning cooking fires drifted through the trees. He walked until he heard the sounds of a *village; dogs barked, women called, babies cried.*

CHAPTER THIRTEEN
Brenda Songbird Carter

Brenda waited anxiously on the verandah of the Speke Guest House
hoping that someone would come and tell her what had happened
to Swot, because quite definitely something had happened. The
whole town was buzzing with the rumor that something terrible
had happened at the bridge. Frank, the Irishman, had been up and
down the main street trying to get more information but so far all
he knew was that Matapa had carried out some kind of raid at the
bridge and that shots had been fired.

They had no more details until Margaret arrived at the Guest House
accompanied by the Bishop, and with Frank trailing along behind
them looking dazed.

"Well?" Brenda asked.

Margaret looked at the Bishop.

"What?" Brenda said. "Tell me, just tell me. What's happened?"

"We don't have the whole story," Margaret said, "but the Bishop
has been at the hospital. They've been treating people with gunshot
wounds."

"What about Swot? "Brenda asked.

The Bishop shook his head. "Nothing," he said. "The people I've
spoken to say that your... husband... is still there helping the
injured. I expect she's with him."

"Expect!" she shouted. "You expect? Can't you find out?"

"Hundreds of people are injured," Margaret snapped at her. "No
one has time to look for one girl even if she is your granddaughter."

"Did you even ask anyone?" Brenda said.

"The hospital is overwhelmed," Margaret replied. "They don't have
time to ask about just one person."

The Bishop smiled placatingly. "If your granddaughter is injured I
am sure they would take her to our private clinic," he said. "No one
would take her to the hospital; it's not a good place. But you
shouldn't worry, I'm sure she is with her grandfather and they will

come back when they can."

"And what am I supposed to do in the meantime?" Brenda asked.

"We could pray," Frank said. "Why don't you join me in praying for all the people in the hospital? I took a look in there and it's truly horrible; the people are just lying on the floor and there are only a couple of nurses to take care of them. I don't think there's even a doctor."

"The doctor is at the clinic," the Bishop said wearily.

"What's he doing there?" Frank asked.

"He's waiting for patients who can pay," Margaret sniffed. "That's what he does."

"The hospital is a hell hole," Frank said. "Can't you do anything?"

"He's not a government doctor," the Bishop said. "I can't make him do anything."

"Well I'm going down there to be with the people. They need prayers. Will any of you come with me?"

"I can't pray," said Margaret emphatically, her voice suddenly cold.

"Everyone can pray," Frank said.

Margaret shook her head. "God won't hear my prayers," she insisted.

The Bishop looked at her in surprise. "God hears all of our prayers," he said.

"Not mine," Margaret said firmly. "I'm beyond his reach."

Brenda momentarily forgot her fears for Swot and considered Margaret's strange declaration. Granted she hadn't seen her in the last fifty years but surely she hadn't changed that much. Fifty years ago she had been decidedly vocal on the subject of her prayers, especially her prayers for Songbird the sinner, and Songbird's relationship with Herbert who Margaret cast as an innocent caught in Brenda's evil trap. She had roundly condemned the fact that the marriage took place without the benefit of clergy, and she had been even more vocal about the amount of alcohol consumed during the celebrations and the suggestive nature of the dancing.

"God's forgiveness is always available to those who repent?" said the Bishop.

Margaret's face flushed. "I didn't say anything about forgiveness," she snapped. "Did I ask for forgiveness? Did I ask any of you to interfere in my business? "She looked at Brenda. "You come here after all these years and think you can just pick up where you left off___"

"Hey," Brenda interrupted, "calm down. I'm not your enemy."

"Oh that's right," Margaret said spitefully, "love and peace. You were all looking for love and peace."

"Margaret___"

"And then you just went swanning off and left me," Margaret said.

"No one left you" said Brenda, "if I remember rightly I offered you my place in the VW."

"Well it doesn't matter anyway," Margaret retorted, "because he came back. In the end he came back."

"I have no idea what you're talking about," said Brenda.

"Of course you don't," Margaret said, and then she clamped her mouth closed.

Brenda looked at the Bishop, he looked at Frank, and all three of them looked at Margaret. The flush slowly faded from her cheeks and she stared down at the ground refusing to meet their eyes. Brenda glanced anxiously at the sky. Very soon it was going to be dark and still no sign of Swot.

"Perhaps they're still looking for the woman with the baby," Brenda said, "that's why Swot went with them."

Frank's face lit up with delight. "You mean they know where she is?" he asked.

"Not exactly," Brenda said, "but they know that there was an old woman who was trying to take her to Kampala. Swot thought that she might be out by the bridge waiting with all the other people."

"Oh praise the Lord," Frank declared.

"Of course that doesn't bring young Matthew back," Brenda reminded him.

"No, no, of course not," said Frank, "but it's a start."

"Don't think you're going to get your hands on that baby," said Margaret, "she's mine."

"I don't think so;" Brenda said, "she belongs with her parents."

"Too dangerous," Margaret declared. "That's the first place the witchdoctor will look."

"She's right," said the Bishop. "We have to find a safe place to keep her; somewhere far away from here."

"No," said Brenda, "we need her so we can get Matthew back."

"Oh God, you're not thinking of giving her up?" said Frank, "You must believe me, I didn't mean any harm. I thought I was helping."

"That's what they all say," said Margaret. "You all come in here thinking you know what's best for us, and you don't know anything. When I think of that boy Zach___"

The Bishop interrupted her somewhat timidly. Brenda had the impression that he was just a little afraid of Margaret, especially as the wild gleam was returning to her eyes and her color was rising again. "Sister Margaret," the Bishop said, "we should not speak ill of that poor boy."

"He took her," Margaret said. "No one said he could take her. Who does he think he is?" She turned on Frank again. "You don't belong here; none of you belong here."

"You may be correct," said Frank, "but I'm here now and I want to be useful. I've had some first aid training so I'm going down to the hospital to see what I can do to help."

"That's right," said Margaret, "you go on down there and make trouble."

Frank looked at Brenda. "Will you come with me?" he asked.

Go with him to the hospital? No, she didn't think she could do that, but she was surprised that Margaret was so unwilling. The Margaret she had known half a century ago would have been down there like a shot, dispensing medicine and prayers.

"Oh God," said Frank suddenly. "Here they come."

"Who? What? "Brenda asked.

"The night commuters," said the Bishop; "children coming here to sleep. I'll have to go and unlock the cathedral. We'll take as many as we can tonight; things happened last night."

"Things?" Brenda asked. "What kind of things."

"Disgusting things," said Margaret; "filthy things; things that shouldn't be even talked about. They come here to be safe but they're not."

"Do you mean what I think you mean?" Frank asked.

"Yes, I do," said Margaret. "There's always someone ready to take advantage of a girl who can't fight back."

Brenda looked at the Bishop. He nodded his head. "Rape and defilement," he said. "It happens when the children have no one to protect them. It won't happen tonight; we'll take them into the cathedral. If only Matapa would leave and they could go home..."

"He needs to do more than leave," said Frank. "The bastard deserves to be shot. He's been doing this for years; why hasn't anyone caught him?"

"Because the Americans don't want him caught," said Margaret stabbing Brenda with an angry glare.

"Hey, don't bring America into this," Brenda said. "We're not involved in any of this."

"And don't you find that a little strange," said Margaret, "seeing that you Americans have appointed yourselves as the world's policeman?"

Brenda was not a political animal. Granted she had once carried banners proclaiming "make love not war" but that was many years ago and now she had no real political opinions at all. However, she was an American abroad and she wasn't going to let someone from another country, and most especially Margaret, get away with saying that Matapa and his band of thugs were a problem for the Americans to solve while everyone else sat on their hands and let their children be kidnapped, raped, defiled, and mutilated.

She was getting ready to give Margaret a brief rundown of all the good things that America had done in the world in the past fifty years when she was interrupted by the Bishop tapping her on the shoulder and pointing down the road. "Is it Swot?" she asked.

"No," said the Bishop, "it's Haji Okolo."

"Who?"

"The man that Swot went to visit," he said, "the King's soldier."

Brenda was stunned. "That was a secret," she complained. "Swot didn't tell anyone, not even me. I didn't know about it until this morning. Who told you?"

"There are very few secrets here," Margaret said.

Brenda stared at the approaching figures. The old soldier was striding out with the help of a long staff; his wife, who looked unbelievably ancient, tottered along beside him and between them came a tiny little girl in a pink dress. They stopped at the locked gates of Rory's compound and the old man pounded on the metal mandoor with his stick.

"It's her," Margaret shouted. "They've found her."

"Praise God," said Frank. Brenda considered it a trite expression but she had no doubt that Frank meant what he said and quite literally at that moment he was indeed praising his God.

Margaret gathered up the skirts of her shabby blue denim jumper and started to run. To Brenda's surprise the Bishop ran after her holding up the skirts of his cassock.

"Sister Margaret," he shouted, "be careful."

Margaret tried to ignore him but the Bishop was younger and swifter than she was and he managed to grab hold of her long before she reached the old man and the child. Margaret was furious, writhing and sobbing as the Bishop held her.

"Alice, Alice, "she screamed again and again.

Brenda would have been the first to admit that some of her memories of Budeka were half a century old and made dim the passage of time, but the Margaret who was now writhing and sobbing, and occasionally cursing, in the firm grip of the Bishop, was not the Margaret that Brenda remembered. In those long ago days Brenda had seen most things through a fog of alcohol and weed, but she had a very clear memory of Margaret, mousy and virginal with prim and proper blouses and skirts, sensible sandals and a hair do that she had to put up in curling rags every night. Brenda had no idea what had happened to Margaret in her long years of exile in Budeka or how she had survived two civil wars and the dark days of Idi Amin; but she had certainly changed. Young Margaret would never have attacked an African bishop, but old Margaret was now doing the best she could to wrestle him to the ground.

"Do you think we should do something?" Frank asked.

Brenda didn't have to answer that question because Rory chose that moment to open the man-door in his gates and step outside.

Presumably he heard the old man knocking with the head of his cane. He looked at the old man for a moment and then he looked at the Bishop struggling with Margaret. He walked past the old man and came striding across to rescue the Bishop from Margaret's clutches.

"It's Alice," Margaret screamed. "She's come back."

"Be quiet," Rory said.

"But it's Alice," Margaret screamed again. "I have to go to her."

"Shut up," said Rory, pulling her away from the Bishop. "Shut up and think."

"It's Alice," she said, yet again.

"Do you want everyone to know?" Rory asked.

Margaret stopped struggling and seemed to regain control of herself.

"If you keep screaming out like that, people will hear you and people will come to look," Rory said with the kind of patient tone that would be used on a five year old. "And if they come and look..." Rory said.

"Yes, yes, of course," said Margaret. "They'll recognize her."

"That's right," said Rory. "In a couple of hours this town will be absolutely full of children coming in for the night, and she'll be just another child. No one will recognize her."

Margaret was calm now and the Bishop released his grasp on her.

"It is her," Margaret insisted. "It's Alice."

"That's very strange," said Frank who was standing beside Brenda watching the whole incredible scene. "That's the child I baptized."

"That's what I assumed," Brenda said.

"But her name isn't Alice," said Frank. "I remember distinctly that they called her Speranza. I'd never heard the name before so I made a point of getting it right. There was nothing about her being called Alice."

The Bishop was smoothing his cassock and generally repairing the dignity he had lost in his struggle with Margaret. "That's the child," he said to Frank in an irritated voice, "I know the family. I have to say that I was very disturbed when I heard you had taken it upon yourself to baptize her. We had been preparing her parents for the baptism here at the cathedral."

"I didn't know that," said Frank.

"There are many things you didn't know," the Bishop replied. "We have our own way of doing things here and we don't need people like you to come in with your own brand of Christianity."

"I know," said Frank. "I'm afraid that I've been like a bull in a china shop."

The Bishop raised an enquiring eyebrow but Brenda decided not to interrupt with a translation.

Rory was coming towards them now with the little girl clasping his hand and the old man and woman walking beside him. Margaret was hanging back and looking over her shoulder to see who might be watching.

"Alice is an unusual name for people here," said the Bishop, "Mr. and Mrs. Fowler named their baby Alice."

"Did you know the Fowlers?" Brenda asked.

"Oh yes. Of course I was very young, but I remember them. I remember people complaining because Mrs. Fowler went all the way to Nairobi to deliver her baby; apparently Mr. Fowler didn't trust any of the doctors here."

"Where are they now?" Brenda asked.

"Oh good heavens," said the Bishop, "that was years and years ago. They left at the beginning of the Amin years. I think they went back to England."

"This is Haji Okolo," Rory said, indicating the old man, "and this is his wife, Florence. She's been looking after this child."

"Yes, I know," said Brenda. "Swot, Sarah, told me all about it. She was very impressed with your bravery."

"I was a soldier for the King," the old man said.

"Yes, Sarah told me."

"My wife wishes to say something," the old man said. "I will translate."

The old woman was struggling to get down on her knees and Brenda put out a hand to try to stop her.

"Let her do it," the Bishop said softly in Brenda's ear. "It is our form of politeness."

"No, really, she doesn't have to curtsey for me, "Brenda said.

"She's doing it for me," the Bishop replied.

Now Brenda was confused. The old man was a Moslem, and his wife had her hair wrapped in a scarf so maybe she was also a Moslem, but she was falling on her knees in front of a Catholic bishop. Brenda felt a stab of pity for Frank and his stumbling attempts to bring his western Christianity into Uganda's melting pot of religions, customs, and witchdoctors. The British were long gone and the Africans had reclaimed their own culture and presumably it all made sense to them.

The old woman began to mumble in her own language, and her husband leaned forward to hear what she was saying. Brenda studied her face, a mass of lines and wrinkles but with bright, enthusiastic eyes. She was incredibly thin, just dark skin draped over bones. As she knelt there on the ground it was as though she was a figure made up of the red African dust, and the dust was waiting to reclaim her. Brenda felt that the old woman might dissolve at any minute and just blow away and become one with the landscape.

"My wife says that she is sorry that she could not take the child to Kampala," said the old man. "She wanted to cross the river, but no one would help her."

"She doesn't have to apologize to me," Brenda said.

"She wishes you to understand," said her husband. "You are Americans; you are like the boy who came to see us."

"Well, yes, we are but___"

The old woman mumbled again and her husband translated. "He was a good boy; she is sorry for your loss and she wishes you to tell his parents that he was a good boy." He looked away from his wife and gave Brenda a half smile. "She has not traveled as I have," he said, "She doesn't know that the US is a very big country. She thinks you and Zach are from the same village. It is all she knows. She will be happy if you say yes."

Brenda thought about what this old woman had been through; somehow or another she had managed to carry that little girl all the way to the river. She imagined her struggling to find someone who would help them cross, and, when she couldn't get across, she had walked all the way back to her village. Plenty of people would have said that she'd done enough but she had been determined to do what Zach had asked her to do, so now she had walked all the way from her village and into town; all for the sake of one little girl; a little girl who wasn't even related to her; who wasn't even of the same religion. Brenda wanted the old woman to know how much her efforts were appreciated, and she could think of only one way to communicate with her. She was not as young as she used to be and her knees didn't bend the way they used to, but if the old lady could get down on the ground, then so could Brenda. So, with a certain amount of huffing and puffing, Brenda got herself down into a kneeling position. She looked up at the husband; he was smiling. "Will you translate?" Brenda said.

He nodded his head.

She took hold of the old woman's hand, dry and withered. "Thank you for trying," she said. "I will find the boy's parents and I will give them your message, and we will find a way to keep the little girl safe."

The old woman nodded contentedly.

Brenda looked up and found that Rory was holding his hand out to her. "You'll never make it on your own," he said, as he pulled her to her feet.

"I'll find them," Brenda said.

"That's not what I meant," Rory said.

"I know," Brenda agreed, "I could have been stuck down there for a long time."

The old woman managed to get to her feet without any assistance. She grasped Brenda's arm and looked her in the face and spoke again. Brenda noticed that she had no teeth.

"What did she say?" Brenda asked.

The old man said something to his wife in a stern voice. She shook her head and repeated whatever she had said the first time.

The old man shook his head. Brenda looked at the Bishop. "What is she saying?"

The Bishop frowned. "She is saying something, but I don't think it is true. I don't know where she would have heard such a thing."

"What?"

The old woman looked up at the Bishop, and spoke quite emphatically. Brenda looked at the Bishop and then at Rory. Rory looked alarmed, and so did Margaret. For the first time Brenda realized that Rory and Margaret could speak the local language although she didn't know why she had not realized it before; they had both been there for years.

"Well," Brenda said, "who's going to tell me?"

The Bishop put his hand on her shoulder. "She is saying that she is sorry about your granddaughter."

"What about my granddaughter?" Brenda asked. "Has something happened to her?"

"She's been taken by Matapa," said Margaret.

CHAPTER FOURTEEN

Taken by Matapa? Taken by Matapa! No, not Swot! Brenda had seen her leave in Herbert's showy black SUV, followed by a pick-up truck full of men. She should have been safe. Should have been...she should have been...

"It's just a rumor," said Rory. "This place is always full of rumors. I'm sure she's fine."

"Well," said Margaret, "you have to remember that the witchdoctor cursed her."

"Oh don't be ridiculous," said Brenda irritation taking the place of sheer panic, "you can't possibly believe in curses."

"When you've been here as long as I have___" Margaret said.

"She's fine," Rory said again. "You know how it is when a story gets started and it gets blown up out of proportion."

"But___" said Margaret.

"No," said Rory. "Leave it alone Maggie."

Maggie? That was new. Brenda had never heard anyone call her Maggie. She just didn't seem like a Maggie.

"I think we should pray," said Frank.

"Sure, you go and pray," Brenda said, "but I'm going to find out what's happened."

"I think the answer to your prayer is already here," said Rory.
Brenda looked up and saw Herbert's black SUV making its way
slowly, reluctantly, towards them. The driver pulled up next to
them and the back door opened. Herbert stepped out and Brenda
knew from the expression on his face that the rumor was true. She
wanted to collapse onto the ground; she wanted to scream; she
wanted to strike out at Herbert. She staggered towards him not
knowing what she was going to do but before she could reach him
the old lady appeared from nowhere and took hold of her arm in a
surprisingly firm grasp. Then she wrapped her arms around her and
held her tightly, speaking softly into her ear. Brenda had no idea
what the old woman was saying but it didn't matter; her thin,
cracked voice reached Brenda on some deep level and let her know
that she was not alone and her fear was not unique in this land
where children could be taken from their beds in the dead of night
and never seen again. Brenda couldn't ask how many children
Okolo's wife mourned, or how many trials she had endured, but she
knew that the old woman understood and somehow she also knew
that she was expected to be strong, and not give in to despair.

By the time the old lady released her, Brenda had her breathing
under control and was able to look Herbert in the eyes.

"Tell me," Brenda said.

Herbert told her everything he knew.

Mugabe climbed out of the vehicle and came to stand next to
Herbert nodding his head in agreement when Herbert explained
that he had told Swot to stay in the car. Neither of them had any
idea how she came to be where she was in the middle of a gunfight.
Mugabe seemed to be extremely distressed that he had failed to
protect her.

"It's not your fault," Brenda said. "I should have been with her. I
could have stopped her."

Even as she said the words she knew they weren't true. Swot was
Brenda all over again and when she made up her mind nothing
would stop her.

"So where has she gone? "Brenda asked. "Why aren't you still looking."

"They drove into the bush," Herbert said. "We couldn't follow. The people were too many."

"Too many?" Brenda said, "How could the people be too many?"

"We are always too many," said Herbert. "We are a small country with many people; and there were crocodiles."

The Bishop drew in a sharp breath. "Crocodiles," he said.

"What do we do now?" Brenda asked. No one answered her.

"We have to do something," she insisted.

"We wait for him to send a demand," said Herbert.

"He's already done that," Brenda reminded him. "He wants the baby."

"No," said Margaret leaping forward and scooping the little girl into her arms.

Brenda had forgotten that the child was even there; she had been remarkably quiet for such a tiny child.

"Put her down," said Rory.

"You can't have her," Margaret said.

"Put her down," Rory said again. "You're drawing attention to her."

Brenda looked around and understood immediately what he was saying. She had been so wrapped up in her own personal tragedy that she had been completely unaware of what was happening around her, but they were no longer alone. In addition to a group of eavesdropping adults who kept themselves at a respectful distance, they were also surrounded by children; the returning night commuters.

"I'm not giving her up," said Margaret.

Brenda looked at the little girl. She was a tiny scrap of humanity with skinny arms and legs, and sparse hair tinged with red tell-tale signs of malnutrition. She was just one child clinging to a tiny, insecure flicker of life. Brenda was horrified to realize that she was actually weighing the child's life against the life of her own granddaughter; the child's life in return for Swot and Matthew; two lives for the price of one. She shoved the thought into the back of her mind; she didn't know how it had even managed to surface. Surely she was better than that.

The Bishop stepped forward and pulled the little girl free of Margaret's embrace. "Let me take her," he said. "She can be with the other children. No one will know."

"You'd better change her clothes," Rory said. "Someone might recognize the pink dress. Bring her into the house, Margaret; I think I have something that will fit her."

"Oh," said Margaret, "do you still have____?"

"Yes," he said.

Margaret smiled and retrieved the little girl from the Bishop's arms. The poor little thing was being passed around like a football but she made no complaint. Did she even have a voice, Brenda wondered; the child had not made a sound. She reined in her thoughts; she knew what she was doing; she was trying to devalue the child's little life set against the genius of Swot.

"Come along Alice," said Margaret.

"I'm sure her name is Speranza," Frank muttered.

"You're wrong," said Margaret. She balanced the child against her bony hip and went on through the gate of Rory's compound, with Rory close behind her.

"What do we do now?" Brenda asked. "We can't just do nothing."

"We go to the Guest House and drink tea," said Herbert.

"Oh no, "Brenda protested. "We're not going to sit around drinking tea and waiting; what are we even waiting for?"

"For assistance," said Herbert.

"Oh, and who is going to assist us?" she asked.

"Word will reach Kampala," Herbert said. "The people on the other side of the river saw what happened. Assistance will come." He turned away from her, said something to Mugabe and then reached into his pocket and gave Mugabe a handful of money. Mugabe went over and talked to Haji Okolo and his wife and then he ushered them into the back of the SUV.

"Mugabe will take them to a Moslem Guest House," Herbert said. "They can't be allowed to walk back to their home tonight; and we will go and have tea, please."

Brenda really didn't know what else to do, and he did say please, so they walked together back to the Speke Guest House where

Herbert sat down heavily in a wicker porch chair, and gave a great sigh of relief. She took a good look at him and she didn't like what she saw. He was sweating profusely and the color of his face was tinged with gray. He pulled a snowy white handkerchief from his pocket and mopped at his face.

"Are you alright?" she asked.

"It has been a difficult day," he said, "and I am no longer young."

"Neither am I," Brenda said.

"I have a problem with my heart," he said.

"I didn't know. What kind of problem?"

"We are not sure how to proceed," he said. "I have been to Kampala, to Mulago Hospital, to see a specialist. He says that I should have surgery. I have a blocked artery."

Brenda dismissed his problems with a wave of her hand. "It's no big deal," she said. "It's a very common procedure; they'll put in a stent and you'll be perfectly fine. "

"The machines at Mulago are broken," Herbert said.

"What machines?"

"I don't know the names, but they are used by the heart surgeons. We have an excellent building, but the machines are broken. I have been waiting for six months."

"I hate your country," Brenda said. It wasn't quite what she meant to say; she had meant to use more tact but somehow the words slipped out of her mouth.

"There is much to hate," Herbert agreed, "but it is my country and I would like to make things better before I die."

"Oh you're not going to die," said Brenda.

"I think I will," he said. He heaved another great sigh and then leaned across the table to look her in the eye. "Songbird," he said, "can we talk as we used to talk? Can we talk without fighting? Can we be as we once were?"

"What about the children?" Brenda asked. "Do you want to take a trip down memory lane instead of worrying about what's happened to your son and your granddaughter."

"Worrying will not bring them back," he said. "We will make a plan in a minute but now I am very tired and I want to sit here for a few minutes and just talk about the past; very soon there will be no one who remembers how it was. Rory is growing old, Sister Margaret is not quite right in the head___"

"Oh, you noticed," said Brenda.

"We have all noticed," he replied, "but we are grateful for her long years of service to us. You never did like her, did you?"

"Oh Herbert," she said, "I didn't care about her one way or another. She was so busy with her good works, and trailing along behind us telling us that we were a bad influence on the natives."

Herbert laughed. "You were," he said. "You were a very bad influence."

"You loved it," she said.

He was beginning to look better, the color was returning to his face; the memories were doing him good.

"White girls had been forbidden," he said, "I had never talked to a white girl, and then you came; you and the other two girls_____"

"Annie and Diana, "Brenda said.

"What happened to them?"

"I don't know. When I got back to the States my parents practically locked me up."

"Were they very angry?" he asked.

"Oh yes."

"Because you had married a black man?"

"Married? "she said. "They didn't regard what we did as a marriage."

"Oh." He suddenly looked incredibly sad and very vulnerable. "I did everything according to custom," he said. "It took everything I had to pay the bride price."

The bride price? Fifty years later Brenda still felt ashamed about the bride price. None of them had bothered to find out anything about local culture and they were highly amused when Herbert had asked the boys in the group how much they wanted as a bride price. She didn't even know who came up with the idea of asking for three cows, but they had thought the whole thing quite hilarious and not to be taken seriously. They were all taken aback when a herdsman actually delivered three cows to the campsite, but it never occurred to them to refuse the offer, or to consider what it might have cost Herbert's family to give up three cows.

"Why did you leave?" Herbert asked.

"My parents made me," she said.

He shook his head. "No," he said, "you made a choice."

"I was afraid," she said.

"Of me?"

"Oh no, never. I was afraid for the baby, I was afraid for myself. I could never be a good African wife."

Herbert smiled. "It was a foolish thing," he said. "We were from different worlds."

"If you wanted a white wife you should have chosen Margaret," Brenda said, "she would have found a way to make it work."

"I didn't want Margaret," he said, "I wanted Songbird."

"We made a beautiful baby," she said.

"Really? I wasn't too sure. I'm afraid that Sarah is not___"

"No," Brenda agreed, "Sarah is not pretty, but I think that one day she will be beautiful; she just has to grow up a little."

She stopped abruptly; the moment had slipped away and they were back to facing reality; Sarah was gone and so was Matthew, and for all of Brenda's family wealth, and for all of Herbert's political clout, they had no idea how to get them back.

The waiter brought the tea and then murmured something to Herbert. Murmuring, Brenda thought, seemed to be a special Ugandan skill. She didn't know if the skill was in the speaking or in the hearing but she was getting very tired of being excluded from conversations.

"What?" she demanded. "What is he saying?" She knew that she sounded like a cross old lady and she faced the fact that she was no longer Songbird the freewheeling hippie who had tried for years to hang onto her youth; she was Brenda; she was a crabby old grandmother who had failed to protect her most precious possession. The thought of Swot somewhere in the bush with Matapa's thugs drove every other thought from her mind.

"There's someone to see me," Herbert said.

"Who? Is it anyone who can do anything?"

"It's the witchdoctor from Kajunga," said Herbert. He turned to the waiter. "Tell him that he may come," he said.

"You're going to talk to him?" Brenda said. "You're actually going to talk to him?"

"He is a powerful man," said Herbert. "It would not do to offend him."

"Are you afraid he might put a curse on you?" she asked.

"No," he said, "I am a Christian; he cannot curse me, but he can curse you."

"I'd like to see him try," she said.

Herbert scowled at her; the harmony of happy memories had vanished; they were once again two people, worried to death, and unable to even agree with each other.

The waiter murmured again; Brenda was pretty sure that he was protesting the idea of bringing the witchdoctor onto the premises.

"Let him come," Herbert said.

"Couldn't you just go outside and talk to him?" Brenda asked.

"Not at this moment," said Herbert and he pulled out his handkerchief and mopped his face again. Brenda finally realized then that he was too weak to go outside, and he really did need to sit and rest. She wondered what was wrong with the machines at Mulago Hospital and how long it would take for them to be fixed. Would they be fixed before Herbert died of a heart attack?

The waiter, eyes downcast, ushered the witchdoctor onto the verandah. Brenda heard a sort of hissing sound; and assumed it was the rest of the staff expressing their disapproval.

The witchdoctor was dressed much as she had seen him the day before in a dress shirt and pants smattered with dust from the road. This time she noticed that he had a little cloth bag hanging from a leather tie around his neck. Bones? Magic powders? She was not equipped to know.

He brought his hands together and gave Herbert a small bow and then broke into a torrent of words, accompanied by additional bowing. Herbert lifted his hand wearily. "Speak in English," he said. "My wife is interested in what you have to say."

'Oh no I'm not," Brenda said, but even as she was protesting she felt a slight flush of warmth. Herbert had actually referred to her as his wife; maybe it was just for the benefit of the witchdoctor, but it was an acknowledgement of what had happened all those years ago. Despite everything that her parents had done to deny the event, the wedding had taken place, she had been Herbert's bride; she had not just been some silly girl passing through on her way to somewhere else; she had been Herbert's wife; she still was Herbert's wife.

"Ah yes, Madame," said the witchdoctor, "I wished to apologize for what has happened to your granddaughter. It was not of my doing."

"You started the whole thing," Brenda said.

He shook his head. "It was started by that man," he said, pointing a grubby finger in direction of Frank the Evangelist who was making his way onto the terrace.

Brenda had noticed that Frank was in the habit of wearing a large wooden cross on a leather strap around his neck; now he lifted the cross and held it out in front of him in a way that might be more appropriate for an approach to Count Dracula; the effect might have been amusing if it were not for the way that the staff hissed and murmured among themselves, and for the chill that crept down Brenda's spine. Frank stalked towards the table holding the cross out in front of him while the witchdoctor grasped the little cloth bag that hung outside his shirt and muttered words that had no meaning for her. Brenda was gripped by sudden cold terror. She turned to Herbert for support but he had his eyes closed and his face betrayed nothing but utter exhaustion.

Brenda staggered to her feet. She was not sure what she intended to do, or what words she intended to speak, or whether she was going to just turn and run, and she had no chance to find out because the moment was suddenly interrupted by the sound of Margaret's plummy English voice.

"She looks so adorable," Margaret said. "The clothes fit her perfectly. Fancy Rory keeping them so long_____"

Margaret stopped speaking, Brenda's words whatever they might have been stuck in her throat, and Herbert opened his eyes.

Margaret had come up from Rory's compound and was approaching the terrace by way of the back stairs, holding the hand of the little girl. The child was dressed in a white dress patterned with yellow flowers and her sparse hair was decorated with a yellow ribbon. The witchdoctor tore his gaze away from the cross and looked at Margaret. Frank let the cross fall back against his chest. Margaret stared at the witchdoctor for just a brief moment and then she turned and fled down the steps dragging the little girl with her. The witchdoctor took a couple of steps forward but Herbert stopped him with a word in his own language.

Brenda, realizing the stupidity of Margaret's action tried to create a distraction. Perhaps the witchdoctor had not recognized the girl; perhaps. She started mindlessly rearranging the teacups and then grabbed hold of Frank's arm. "Will you have some tea?" she asked. Frank looked at her as though she had lost her mind but she continued to set out cups and saucers, determined that they should all act as though nothing had happened. Margaret, was looking after a little girl; so what? She was just one of the hundreds of little girls who had come into town for shelter; nothing special about that little girl; nothing special at all; just a kid from one of the villages.

"Sit down, "Brenda said, and Frank sat down beside her.

"Tea?" she asked the witchdoctor, although the words almost choked her.

The witchdoctor shook his head.

"No, thank you," he said. 'I will leave you now." He repeated his little bowing gesture and then departed the same way that he had arrived.

"Did he recognize her?" Brenda asked as soon as he was out of earshot.

Herbert still looked unutterably weary. "Of course he did," he said, "We shall have to do something. Where is Mugabe?"

"I don't know," Brenda said.

Herbert dug his cell phone out of his pocket, looked at it ruefully and replaced it. "We are back to the old days," he said. He lifted a hand and summoned a waiter. He murmured, the waiter murmured a reply. Once again Brenda failed to understand a single word. If she had stayed married to Herbert, she wondered, and stayed living in Uganda, would she now be a woman who knew how to murmur words that no one else could hear?

She lifted her teacup; her hands were shaking. "Frank," she said, "what just happened?"

"There's something wrong with that woman," Frank said.

"I'm not talking about Margaret," said Brenda. "I'm talking about you and that business with the cross. Something was happening?"

"Did you feel it?" Frank asked.

"I was terrified," she admitted.

"So was I," said Frank.

"Christianity is very new to us" Herbert said, "and the old gods are still here. " He looked at Frank. "It is best if you let us deal with things our own way; your coming here has created many problems."

"You can't blame him for everything," Brenda said. "General Matapa is home grown, isn't he?"

Herbert shook his head. "I have been told that he is from Congo," he said, "but the name Matapa, that's a Shona word, so maybe he's from Zimbabwe. It's hard to say. No one knows."

"No one knows?" Brenda said, and her voice grew louder. "No one knows! Why doesn't someone know? He's terrorizing your people and you don't even know who he is and where he comes from."

"His life is nothing but rumor and legend," Herbert said. "We know nothing for certain. Some say that he fought in Angola, for the Americans,"

"We never had a war in Angola," Brenda said.

"Secret wars," said Herbert. "The west has its hand in every war that is fought here. Men like Matapa were created by your wars."

"Oh come on, "said Brenda, "you can't blame us for everything. What he's doing is hurting you; it's up to you to do something about him. I don't understand why you can't make an all-out effort and find him."

"How long did it take the US with all its money and men to find Bin Laden?" Herbert asked.

Brenda didn't answer him. What answer could she give him? He had a point.

"But you must know something about him," Frank said, "something beyond the fact that maybe he comes from Congo. Whatever he did in the past doesn't matter anymore. What does he want now? Why is he attacking your people?"

"Our country was born in violence," Herbert said. "Under Idi Amin we lived with violence every day."

"Oh you're back in the past again," Brenda protested.

"Our current government is made up of people who fought to free us from Amin," Herbert said, "but not everyone who fought found a place in the government; some were left without the power they were promised."

"Okay," Brenda said, "so you're saying that possibly he was a mercenary who didn't get what he expected. What did he expect? Did he expect to get a comfortable position like you have?"

Herbert glared at her and Brenda wished that she could take back her tactless words. She hadn't really meant to suggest that Herbert held his position as some kind of payback for past favors; but now she thought about it, maybe it was the truth.

Frank interrupted the uncomfortable silence.

"I may be new to this country," he said, and he sounded angry, "but in Ireland we know all about being oppressed by the British, and I know how people try to justify hurting their own people for a political cause, but there is no excuse. What are his politics? What does he hope to accomplish? Have you even tried talking to him?"

"He has no reason," said Herbert, "and he has no politics. He is being used by other people for their own purposes."

"What other people?" Frank asked. "What other purposes?"

"We've set up peace talks," Herbert said, ignoring Frank's question; "but always he finds a reason not to come."

"What other people?" Frank persisted. "Who is using him?"

"Herbert," Brenda said, "he's taken your son; he's taken my granddaughter, *our* granddaughter, what is it that you're not telling us?"

Herbert mopped at his face with a handkerchief, and looked down at the table; he would not, or could not meet Brenda's eyes. "A lot has happened since we first met," he said.

"I know."

"We have fought a long bush war and we have removed a vicious dictator from power."

"I know."

"It's a good thing you were not here," Herbert said. "I was gone for many years; an exile in Tanzania waiting for our chance to fight our way back into power. You would not have been safe here."

"Herbert," Brenda said firmly, "that was then; this is now. What is it that you're not telling me?"

"I have never taken a bribe," Herbert said. "I am an honest man."

"I'm sure you are," she said.

He mopped his face again.

"We have a stable government now," Herbert said. "We have been in power since 1986. We have brought stability to this whole region."

Brenda shrugged her shoulders. "If you say so," she said.

"I do say so," he declared. "Where would you Americans be without us? Congo is in flames, Kenyans are rioting, Rwanda has had a genocide, Tanzania becomes more Moslem every day, but we remain stable and we continue to make you welcome."

Herbert stuffed his handkerchief back into his pocket and took a sip of tea. His hands were still trembling. "You would not like it if we had a change of government," he said.

Brenda looked at him impatiently. "You're not telling me anything," she said. "I'm asking a direct question and you are just rambling on about how long you and your friends have been in power. I know all of that, what is it I don't know? "

"I know what he's trying to tell you," Frank said. "I understand it completely."

"What?" Brenda asked.

"They were at war for years, one dictator after another, and all the people want now is peace. They want to know that they're safe in their beds at night."

"But they're not," she said; "not with Matapa around."

"Matapa does just enough to keep them feeling insecure," Frank said; "just enough to remind them why they need a strong army and a strong leader. Fear of Matapa is enough to keep them quiet and loyal and stop them from rocking the boat with demands for democracy and free elections. Your husband's government doesn't want to stop Matapa; they want to appear to be trying to stop him; but they don't really want him gone. Too much peace, and too much security gives the people time to think, and when people start to think and ask questions, governments fall."

Herbert took another sip of tea.

"If the government falls," he said, "what will take its place?"

"I don't know Brenda said. "Does it matter?"

""It matters very much," Herbert said. "It matters to Europe and it matters to America. If you want to know why Matapa has not been caught, ask your own government. Ask the nearest American you can find."

"Rory?" said Brenda. "You want me to ask Rory?"

She had no need to wait for the answer because a stray memory abruptly clicked into place and something she had heard half a century before suddenly made sense.

CHAPTER FIFTEEN
October 1963:

The VW bus had taken the journey from Cape Town in its stride; crossing the Karoo Desert, climbing the Drakensburg Mountains, and up onto the High Veldt; eight hundred miles at a leisurely pace and then Johannesburg had come into view, its skyscrapers piercing the horizon with the promise of comfortable beds, running water, and an opportunity to buy new clothes.

Songbird and Annie went shopping in the department stores on Eloff Street with Tommy trailing along behind to carry their packages.

"We could get a boy to do that," Annie had said. Annie was a South African who had joined them in Cape Town; when Annie said a boy could help them she meant that they could easily get an African to do their heavy labor; not a boy, but a man of any age, so long as he was not white.

"You don't need a boy;" said Tommy, "I'll come with you and keep you safe."

"I think I'm safe in my own country," said Annie, "it's you Americans who have to keep your eyes open."

"Make sure they don't buy too much stuff," Rory said, "we don't have room for any more stuff. Stick to the essentials and keep out of trouble."

Songbird strolled along beside Annie taking in the sights of Johannesburg's shopping district; the clean sidewalks, the tall buildings, the stunning window displays in the department stores. She was pretty sure that the only trouble she could get into in Johannesburg would be if she ran out of travelers checks because that would mean making a phone call home to her father; not a pleasant prospect.

As they came out of the final department store, loaded down with shopping bags, they found that a noisy crowd had gathered, blocking the sidewalks, and spilling out onto the street. Traffic was at a standstill and hundreds of young people, black and white, with the unmistakable look of university students, were chanting and waving banners.

"A demonstration;" Annie shouted, "and about time too." She grabbed Songbird's hand and dragged her forward into the mob. Above the sound of the chanting, the singing, and the shouts of protests, Songbird heard the shrieking of police sirens.

"Let go of me," she shouted to Annie, but Annie continued to drag her forward, For a few moments the three of them were caught up in the movement of the mob, and then she saw the crowd begin to thin as large, red-faced men in khaki uniforms surged towards them, beating the crowd indiscriminately with truncheons and receiving kicks and punches in return.

An officer grabbed Songbird around the waist, another held onto Annie.

"Rights for all students," Annie yelled.

"Shut up," said Songbird.

"We have a right to protest," said Annie as they were dragged to the back of a police van.

Songbird saw Tommy, standing taller than most of the students, and *still free of the mob.*

"Go and tell Rory," she shouted, and she saw him edge his way back into the doorway of a department store.

Within moments Songbird was on her hands and knees in the back of a crowded police van. She was still clutching the only bag she had managed to hang onto; no one was going to separate her from her new shoes.

"What have you gotten us into?" she shouted at Annie who had been flung in behind her.

"It's a student protest," said Annie, "the government wants to stop Africans from going to Wits."

"Speak English," Songbird said as she struggled to stop from pitching forward onto her face.

"Witwatersrand, my old university," said Annie. "They used to allow African students and now they don't; it's not right."

The rest of Annie's explanation was drowned out by the chanting of the student protesters who were jammed into the van alongside them.

"But we were just shopping," Songbird said. "We didn't do anything."

"But we look like students," Annie shouted. "Don't worry; we'll sort it out at the police station."

Sorting it out at the police station turned out to be a huge problem. Hundreds of protesting students had been swept up by the police and jammed into the Central Police Station. Songbird shrank back against a wall as the police forcibly separated the black students from the white students raining blows on everyone involved.

"What's going to happen?" Songbird asked.

"They'll book us," said Annie, "and then we'll go to court."

"You've done this before?" Songbird asked.

"Oh yeah," said Annie; "it's all part of being a student. Haven't you ever been to a protest?"

"No," said Songbird, "I haven't even been to college. My parents sent me to finishing school."

"No!" Annie sounded amazed.

"Yes," said Songbird.

"Well you wanted an adventure," Annie said, "and now you're getting one."

"Will we go to jail?" Songbird asked.

Annie shrugged her shoulders.

"I don't want to go to jail," Songbird muttered. Clutching her shopping bag to her chest she sank down to sit on the floor. "We're supposed to be watching elephants, and camping at waterholes," she said.

"Not too many elephants here," said Annie, dropping down to sit next to her.

The students had been in high spirits as they were herded into the holding pen but as time passed they grew quiet and Songbird could sense that high principles and student solidarity was giving way to personal fears as the police began to call them forward one by one.

"My parents are going to be so pissed," said Songbird.

"Maybe they won't have to know," said Annie. "Look."

Songbird looked and saw that Rory had entered the pen along with a red faced young police officer. She waved at him. He looked at her, scowled, and then jerked his head towards the door.

"He's getting us out of here," she said to Annie. "Come on."

Outside in the fresh air she tried to thank Rory, but he was not listening.

"You two cost me a fortune," he said, "now just get into the van and shut up. We're leaving."

"What?"

"We're leaving now," Rory said. "Everything's packed."

"But we haven't finished shopping," Songbird said, "and we wanted to go and see the Mine Dancers."

"Did you give them your name?" Rory asked.

"No."

"Did you give them my name?"

"No, of course not."

Songbird and Annie climbed into the van and Rory settled himself behind the wheel.

"We're about six hours from the border," Rory said, "and we're not stopping."

"What border?" Songbird asked.

"Rhodesia," said Rory.

Songbird crawled into the back seat and settled herself down next to Ben and Tommy.

"He's really mad," she said.

"I think he's just worried," said Tommy. "When I told him what happened he went white as a ghost."

"It wasn't that bad," said Songbird.

"I don't think he was worried about you," Tommy said. "He seemed to be more worried about his father. He went dashing off to make a phone call."

"Yeah," said Ben, "I think his father told him what to do. I don't know if you've noticed but he's always phoning his father."

"Really?" said Songbird who had not written so much as a postcard to her parents.

"His father is the one telling him what route to take; and he has this notebook where he writes down things and he takes it with him when he calls his Dad." Ben said.

"What sort of things?" asked Songbird.

"No idea," said Tommy, "but he never lets it out of his sight."

"We should try to sneak a look," Songbird said.

"No, "said Tommy, "I don't think you want to do that; you might be getting mixed up in something."

"It's Rory," said Songbird, "he's just out for a good time."

Tommy lowered his voice to a whisper. "Look," he said, "Rory's my fraternity brother so I can't say too much, but there was this rumor..."

"Yeah?" said Songbird.

"There was this rumor," Tommy repeated, "that his father was CIA."

"Really?"

"And we heard that Rory was being recruited right out of college."

"So what's he doing here?" Songbird asked.

"Exactly," said Tommy. "What indeed?"

Brenda was amazed that she was able to dredge up such a clear memory of that conversation. At the time she had dismissed Tommy's ideas as ridiculous. Rory drank, Rory smoked weed, and

Rory partied like a mad man; he was definitely not CIA material. She had no idea what had happened to Annie in the new integrated South African rainbow nation; she'd never heard from Tommy or Ben again, but she knew where Rory was. Oh yes; Rory was just a few yards away on the other side of a locked gate, refusing to let her inside his house.

Rory? Was it possible?

She looked at Herbert. He said nothing but his silence spoke volumes. She looked at Frank. "You're pretty smart," she said.

"You mean for an Irishman or for a Christian?" he asked.

She ignored the question. In the world where she had been born seventy years before, Irishmen were either policemen or steelworkers, and fundamentalist Christian evangelists belonged in a tent in the deep South.

"Is it Rory?" she asked.

"I think so," Herbert said. "Supposedly he has a few business interests that keep him here; some coffee farming, some import and export, but he has been here a long time, and he keeps himself separate from us. I don't think he likes it here, and he's angry all the time."

"Perhaps he's here because of Margaret," Brenda said.

Herbert snorted.

"Yes," Brenda agreed, "probably not Margaret."

"Probably not," said Herbert.

"And you don't know for sure about any of it?" she asked.

"He chooses not to know," said Frank.

"Well you'd better start to choose," said Brenda "and you can stop hiding behind your fake heart attack____"

"It's not fake___"

"I don't care," she said. "I don't care if you drop dead right here and right now; but you are going to tell me how to find Matapa. Now!"

"I don't know," said Herbert.

"Someone knows," she said. Everything that Frank had said was making sense. "Your government doesn't want Matapa found, so someone feeds them all the information they need to find him, so that they can look the other way; so they can look really hard in some other place. That's what they do, don't they? Who gives them the information? Is it Rory?"

"We're cut off," said Herbert, "no one has any information." He pulled his cell phone from his pocket. "No signal," he said.

"No signal," Brenda parroted back to him; "if you give me that again I'll shove that phone down your___"

"I believe him," Frank said before she could actually assign a final resting place for Herbert's cell phone. "They're not getting a signal; the tower is down. However, there are other ways to communicate."

"Radio," Brenda said, thinking of the aerials on Rory's roof.

"Satellite phones;" said Frank, "they don't need towers."

"I don't have a satellite phone," Herbert said in a weak voice.

"Maybe you don't" Brenda said, "but I'm betting that Rory does." She jumped to her feet, rattling the tea cups. "Come on," she said to Frank, "we're going to get to the bottom of this."

"But what about your...er...husband?" Frank asked.

Herbert was slumped in his chair, his face gray with fatigue.

"Leave him where he is," Brenda said.

She turned away and saw Mugabe hurrying across the verandah.

"Hey you," she said; "your boss needs you."

Mugabe looked at her and then at Herbert. "Please sit," he said.

"No," Brenda shouted, "I will not sit."

"Please," he repeated softly, "there is something I must tell you."

"Don't bother," she said, still shouting; "I already know all about it and Herbert's plan to stay in power. What's your story? Who are you working for? CIA? Al-Qaeda? Who pays your salary?"

"Please sit," said Mugabe again, pulling out a chair and patting the seat invitingly. Out of the corner of her eye Brenda saw the restaurant staff fleeing the scene, frightened away by the crazy old white lady who was apparently trying to give her husband a heart attack.

"The news is not good," Mugabe said, "and you must sit and be calm."

"I will not sit and be calm" Brenda said "I'm going to see Rory."

"It's about Madame Margaret," said Mugabe.

"Oh to hell with Madame Margaret," she shouted. Frank hissed his disapproval, but Brenda was beyond caring.

"Very well," said Mugabe, still speaking softly, "you come, and you will see for yourself."

He released his hold on the chair. "You come," he said. "Come." He turned and walked away towards the gate that separated the Guest House from Rory's compound. Well, that was where she wanted to go, Brenda thought, so she followed.

Frank started to follow and then he stopped and looked at Herbert. "You go ahead," he said. "I'll stay with him."

"Fine," said Brenda "you be a good Samaritan if you want to. He doesn't deserve any help, not after what he's done."

"We all do wrong," Frank said piously. Brenda ignored him.

As they approached Rory's compound she heard the sound of someone crying; no, not crying, someone sobbing; someone wailing as though their heart would break. The gate stood open. They stepped inside and as she rounded the corner to the front of the house she saw the source of the noise.

Margaret was on her hands and knees on the lawn, her forehead touching the stubbly grass, her entire body convulsing as she sobbed. Rory knelt beside her patting at her spiky gray hair.

"Rory," Brenda shouted, not at that moment caring about what it was that had upset Margaret. "Who are you working for?" she demanded. "Who's paying for you to be here? What gives you the right to___"

"Shut up," said Rory. "Just shut your mouth Brenda."

"I will not," said Brenda. "I want to know___"

"Just shut it you stupid, stupid woman," Rory said, "or you'll get us all killed."

For a moment she thought he might be talking to Margaret but he had actually stepped away from her, leaving her to roll on the ground in paroxysms of grief, and he was heading angrily in Brenda's direction.

"I've worked it out," Brenda said. "It's taken me fifty years but I've worked it out. You had to get us out of the police station didn't you; you had to get us over the border because no one was supposed to know that you were there. You were spying for your father, weren't you?"

"Shut up," said Rory, his mouth next to her ear. "I have no idea what it is you think you know, or what this has to do with my father but I need you to stop shouting."

"Because I'll give your big secret away?" she said.

"No," said Rory, "because we have a problem; a big one."

He looked down at Margaret. "She couldn't do it," he said, "she couldn't keep the poor kid hidden; she had to show her off."

"This is what I was trying to tell you," Mugabe said. "The man from Kajunga has taken the child."

"He pulled her from my arms," Margaret sobbed, sitting up and looking at them.

"He will give her to Matapa," Mugabe said.

"I'm sorry", Brenda said, "that's awful but___"

"It means we have nothing left to bargain with," said Mugabe. "When the child has been delivered to Matapa there will be no reason to keep the hostages alive. Matthew and Sarah will die."

Congo Rain Forest; 1970

The boy was now almost a man, tall and slim with fierce dark eyes. "Must I leave the forest before the power has come?" he said to the old man, as they sat by the fire. They were far to the west now in the never ending forest, and the boy's birthplace was nothing but a distant memory. "Try again," said the old man, and the boy who was becoming a man threw dust on the fire and called to the spirits of the forest. The fire sputtered and died.

"You will never have the power, but you may yet succeed," said the old man. "The name you seek cannot be found here, so you must leave; our time is finished."

"What must I do?" asked the boy.

"You must use the powers you have, and not wish for the powers that have not been given to you," said the old man.

"It is the blood of my white father," said the boy. "It is because of his blood that the forest spirits will not obey me."

"You cannot change your blood," said the old man. "You must

accept what you are."

"And what is that?"

"You are a killer; you are the destroyer, you will become Matapa.'

"Where is he?" asked the boy. "Can your magic find him?"

"To the west," said the old man, "he is fighting for the Americans."

"No," said the boy, "the Americans are not here."

"They are secret," said the old man. "Go to the west, you will find the fight, and you will find money from the Americans."

The boy hesitated. "Am I ready?" he asked.

"No," said the old man, "but I have done what I can to make you ready."

"Why?" asked the boy. "Why have you helped me?"

The old man grinned showing his teeth filed to sharp points.

"You are my revenge," he said.

"For what?"

"For many things," said the old man. "For the teachers who beat me, for the miners who kicked me, for the white women who scorned me, for the settlers who took my land, for the Belgians who took my country, and now I am sending you to them, blood of their blood. "

"How will you know that I have succeeded?" asked the boy.

"Because I will be with you," said the old man.

"No," said the boy, "I cannot take you."

"You are going to kill me," said the old man, "you know it, and I know it. Perhaps today, perhaps tomorrow; you are going to kill me."

The boy hung his head for a moment. "I am," he agreed.

"I know," said the old man, "and when it is done you will be strong."

"But I will not have your power?"

"No."

The next morning the boy left the forest, leaving behind the bones and the skin, but not the heart, of the man who been his guardian. He walked west to the place where Congo became Angola to find the man who called himself Matapa.

CHAPTER SIXTEEN
Cecelia Byaruhanga: Early morning, north of Budeka

The early morning light filtered down through the canopy of trees as the sun rose on Cecelia's second morning at Matapa's squalid camp. The first night had been the worst; the worst night of her life, the worst thing she could possibly imagine. The second night had been similar but she felt that God had allowed her mind to go to another place; to detach itself from her body and what was being done to her. On the first night she had been raped multiple times; there, she had said it, admitted it to herself and allowed the words to take up residence in her brain but not her soul; never her soul. Yes, she had been raped first by the men, and then by the boys but she was still Cecelia; she was still someone; still a daughter of the Ursuline Convent.

When the sun rose on the first morning the kidnapped girls had been unable to look at each other; each one carrying their own shame with downcast eyes. The men had left them alone all through the long day and they had nursed their cuts and bruises, and endured the terrible pain and shame that hid between their legs. The acts had been repeated the second night but not so violently; Cecelia had the impression that some kind of selection process was taking place; that they were each being chosen to be the possession of just one man; and there had been a distraction; the arrival of the mazungu girl.

The pick-up truck carrying the captured girl had roared into camp just before sunset, slithering down the muddy track to the bottom of the gorge where the ancient rain forest provided perfect cover for Matapa's squalid tent encampment. The white girl had spent the night sitting under a tall tree in the center of the clearing and none of the men had touched her. The crippled boy had spent the night beside her and had fallen asleep with his head on her shoulder. Now, as the camp stirred for the day, she could hear them talking.

The boy touched the mosquito bites that decorated the girl's arms "Malaria," he said. "That's malaria."

The girl smiled and hugged his skinny shoulders.

"Malaria is the least of our problems, "the girl said; she sounded like an American. It seemed to Cecelia that the girl and the boy knew each other although she could not imagine how this could be. The boy had been in the camp the night before, and he was obviously not one of Matapa's soldiers; he was too small, too weak, and not even able to walk properly. She had no idea why he was still alive.

Sometime during the night another girl had crept across the compound to sit beside the newcomers. Cecelia looked at the other girl with pity, mixed with dread. The girl was barely in her teens; a blood stained cloth was wrapped around her waist and she was clasping a new-born baby to her barely developed breasts. The baby was a tiny scrap of flesh wrapped in a ragged cloth; its hands groped feebly at its mother's inadequate breast, and its mouth searched blindly for the nipple that the mother was trying to force into its mouth. The baby didn't seem to have the strength to latch on, and the mother didn't seem to have any milk to offer. While Cecelia watched the child finally gave up its feeble efforts to feed and lay still in her mother's arms. The child mother hung her head, cradling the little creature against her bony chest.

"Oh God," Cecelia thought, "that could be me. I could be pregnant."

As if to reinforce Cecelia's fear another girl stepped out of one of the tents; this girl was closer to Cecelia's age, fourteen or fifteen years old, her hair grown into a wild halo of tight curls. She stopped in front of the white girl, arching her back wearily and revealing a well-advanced pregnancy. She looked down at the exhausted mother and the silent baby and shook her head.

"She will not live," she declared. "The mother is too young."

"Will the mother live?" the white girl asked.

The pregnant teen shrugged her shoulders. "Perhaps not," she said, and moved on, making her way towards Cecelia.

"You should get up and move around," she said. "You will feel better. Tell your friends to get up. You must show yourselves to be hard workers. If you work hard someone will choose you as a wife; it will be easier for you."

"How long...?" Cecelia asked, surprised to find that she still had a voice. She realized that she had not uttered a sound since her last high pitched scream as the soldiers took her from the convent grounds. She had been silent, all of the girls had been silent; there was nothing to say and they knew what would happen if they protested. If they wanted to live they must do nothing to anger Matapa's soldiers; this was common knowledge; the only advice that anyone had ever given. If you make the soldiers angry they will start to cut you; cut off your lips, cut off your breasts, cut off your hands; they are animals; do what they say and you might live.

"How long have you been here?" Cecelia asked.

"I think it is maybe two years," the girl said, speaking English. "They took me from Sudan."

"And the baby?"

"My second," said the girl. "The first one died; for this one at least I know who the father is. He is my husband."

"Husband?"

"Yes," said the girl. "It is the best you can hope for; that someone takes you as a wife. Tell that to your friends; it will be easier for them."

"Have you ever tried to run away?" Cecelia asked.

The girl shook her head. "I have seen what happens to those who try," she said.

"Someone will find us," said Cecelia.

The Sudanese girl flashed a quick, intelligent glance. "No one will look for you," she said, "but they might look for the white girl."

"Who is she?"

"I don't know," the girl replied, "but they have never taken a white girl before. Perhaps Matapa has gone too far this time; perhaps she is the one who is going to set us free."

Swot Jensen

The child mother suddenly slumped against Swot, leaning her head on Swot's shoulder. The baby was now very still. Swot turned her head away. For once in her life she had no idea what to do. Nothing she had ever experienced had prepared her for what she had seen the previous night, and what she was seeing by the light of the rising sun.

After Matapa's band of boy monsters had thrown her into the back of the pick-up truck she had lost track of time. The journey had seemed interminable as she was jostled around and bruised against the bare metal floor of the truck bed. Eventually they had arrived at the edge of a steep gorge. The truck lurched and swayed its way down a mud-slicked switchback of a road until they were deep into a heavily forested valley. Trees closed in around them and monkeys shrieked in the tree tops above.. The truck splashed across streams moving ever deeper into the rain forest until they finally came to a clearing and a haphazard camp site made up of incongruously brightly colored backpacker tents surrounding one much larger olive green army tent.

Swot had no idea how many people were in the camp, but it seemed there were not many. The boy soldiers roamed the perimeter cradling their guns, their eyes bright with the desire to shoot something; anything, but preferably a person. There were women and children in the camp; young women who kept their gaze focused on the ground and moved among the men as though they expected that at any moment any one of the men might strike out at them. The children were mostly naked toddlers, their limbs covered in scratches and bites, their hair sparse and faded, and their bellies swollen with worms.

They had arrived early in the evening and to Swot's relief she and Matthew were more or less left alone to hug each other and huddle on the ground. The sun set with Equatorial abruptness. Swot was grateful for the fact that the flickering firelight only afforded her occasional glimpses of what was happening to the girls from the convent. She could hear the brutal voices of the men, but the girls were silent, enduring their treatment without a sound, without a protest. It was not until morning that she heard them weeping quietly and then whispering softly to each other. The morning light also showed her the girl who had crept up beside her, the girl with her tiny bundle of sadness clasped to her chest.

As the sun rose higher in the sky, the convent girls began to stumble to their feet. As if by instinct they moved to pick up yellow jerry cans heaped at the edge of the clearing, Swot realized that they were following an age old rhythm that had existed for them from early childhood; the women and girls of Africa rising in the morning to collect water. They were apparently comforted by the familiarity of the task as they moved in a straggling line, followed by the boys with guns and returned a few minutes later walking upright, their hips swaying for balance, and carrying the jerry cans on their heads. One of the girls approached Swot and offered her a plastic cup filled with muddy water. Swot shook her head.

"You must drink," the girl said. "They will not make tea, you must drink this."

"Do you have any idea what's in that water?" Swot asked.

The girl glanced around and then squatted down in front of Swot "We have to stay alive," she said.

"That water will kill you," said Swot.

"I am aware of that," the girl said reprovingly, "but we must do what we can and we have to drink."

"Not yet," Swot replied..

"Why have they left you alone?" the girl asked. "Is it because you are a mazungu?"

"I'm a hostage," Swot said. "They won't hurt me." She felt bad saying it; she was a hostage; she was safe; she had not been raped by half a dozen men. How could she speak so smugly to the poor girl kneeling in front of her with two swollen eyes, and a trickle of blood seeping out from beneath her school uniform skirt?

"Will someone come for you?" the girl asked. "Will they come for all of us?"

"I hope so," Swot said.

"I am praying," said Matthew.

The schoolgirl looked at Matthew. "Why do they keep you?" she asked. "You are not a mazungu?"

"Jesus will save us," Matthew said.

"Last night I prayed to the Virgin," the girl confessed, "but she did not save me."

"You're still alive; and while there's life, there's hope," Swot said.

She sounded corny and stupid even to herself.

"I am Cecelia," the girl whispered.

"Sarah," Swot said; she had already abandoned the idea of being Swot. She felt as though Swot Jensen, genius, know-all, and child of privilege, had been left behind at the broken bridge. Now she was Sarah, an eighteen year old who knew nothing and who was terrified that someone was going to drag her into one of the multi-zippered, multi-colored stolen tents and steal the virginity that she had been treasuring; steal it, trample on it, abuse it in every way and leave her to give birth to a tiny, helpless and hopeless infant.

Cecelia inched forward and looked at the girl who had slumped against Swot's shoulder. "I don't know where she comes from," Cecelia said. "She gave birth last night, we heard her screaming. She is not from here; she has no English."

Poor kid, Swot thought, dragged from her home and giving birth among strangers who could not even speak her language. Cecelia moved a corner of the rag that wrapped the infant. "The child is dead," she said.

"What do we do?" Swot asked.

Cecelia slipped the baby from her mother's arms. The mother heaved a long sigh and sank lower to the ground, resting her head on Swot's lap. When, Swot asked herself, had she become Earth Mother to this girl?"

Cecelia pulled the rag up and over the baby's face and walked away with it clasped in her arms. She gave it to one of the men who stood outside the army tent. He took it and went inside, and Cecelia walked away out of sight.

Matthew was muttering under his breath. Swot thought that perhaps he was stringing together whatever swear words he knew, and she was willing to add some more of her own, but then she realized that the muttered sounds were in fact prayers.

"What are you praying for?" she asked. "What makes you think that God is going to get us out of this?"

"I prayed for the baby," Matthew said, "that her soul will go to heaven."

Suddenly Swot wanted to cry. A great sob tried to work its way up her throat. Any moment now the young girl who slept with her head in Swot's lap would wake up and find her baby gone. What could Swot say to her; they couldn't even speak the same language? She looked up at the canopy of trees above her, much as she had looked up at the top of the mosquito net in her room at her grandfather's house, and tried to imagine what kind of being, what kind of creator, could possibly allow the horror of Matapa's camp. Then she thought about the baby with its tiny grasping hands, and its blind groping for comfort; what comfort would it have found in this place?   Perhaps death was a mercy; perhaps for some of these people death would be the ultimate mercy and that was exactly what Frank had told her as they sat at the Guest House; first we take care of Heaven; then we take care of life.

Swot's musings on life and death were interrupted by a flurry of activity among the young men and boys who were supposedly standing guard over her, and she heard a vehicle roaring down the slippery track that led to the gloomy encampment at the bottom of the gorge. The girl whose head was in Swot's lap stirred slightly but her eyes remained closed. A beat up pickup truck emerged from the trees; not the pickup Swot had seen before; evidently Matapa's army had more than one vehicle.

The pickup came to a sliding halt at the edge of the clearing and a tall skinny man emerged. He was wearing army camouflage that looked as though it had just been washed and ironed, and he carried himself with an air of command. The boys guarding the captives suddenly gave the task their full attention, waving their guns menacingly in Swot's face. The tall man took a couple of steps towards Swot. He took off his sunglasses and looked her up and down disapprovingly and then turned away and headed for the largest of the tents; Matapa's headquarters, or so Swot assumed. The guards muttered among themselves and then one of them poked Matthew with the barrel of his weapon. Matthew scooted away and the guard poked him again.

"Hey, leave him alone," Swot said. "Pick on someone your own size."

The guard looked at her; of course it was the boy who had been so determined to rape her just two nights before. She found it difficult to distinguish between the skinny young thugs who tormented the prisoners, but this one she knew; he was a little heavier than the others, perhaps he was first at the feeding trough, and his face was somewhat broader, and two of his front teeth were missing. Yes, she knew this one and he knew her and they were not destined to be friends. He turned his attention away from the Matthew and kicked the girl who was sleeping in Swot's lap.

"Hey, stop it," Swot said.

He grinned his evil gap-toothed grin and kicked the girl again. The girl's eyes fluttered open, and she began to move her arms groping for the baby. Her eyes opened wider and her panicked gaze swept around the clearing. Finally she focused on Swot's face as she struggled to sit upright. She was asking Swot a question, and Swot had no need of an interpreter. Where was the baby? Where? Where? Swot had no idea what to say to her; all she could do was shake her head, and try to make sympathetic noises, but her sympathy was a troubled thing. Should she really sympathize with the fact that the poor kid would not have to try to feed her pathetic little infant? She had been raped and abused; how could she even love the child of her rapist; surely she was better off without a baby to care for?

Swot thought that perhaps it was a good thing that she couldn't speak the girl's language because she knew she would have said all the wrong things. What did Swot know about maternal love, the most love she had ever felt was a vague sense of duty towards her parents, and a passing responsibility for a guinea pig that Brenda had misguidedly given her one Christmas?

The young thug aimed another kick at the girl; presumably he wanted her to stand up. Swot flung her arms around the girl and the boy's boot landed squarely on Swot's elbow letting her know that the little monster was not playing around; it was a hefty kick intended to hurt and hurt it did.

Before the boy could renew his attack a woman came storming across the compound and jabbered at him in a scolding tone. She was a large woman, middle aged or even older and she was apparently very much in charge. When she had finished railing at the boy she dismissed him with a pointed finger and he skulked away to stand at a distance and glare at Swot.

The older woman squatted down beside Swot and examined her elbow. Swot pulled her arm away; she didn't need sympathy, certainly not from any member of Matapa's band. The other girls, the ones who had been taken from the convent, crowded around the older woman. The woman started to ask questions, and finally Cecelia, the girl who had introduced herself to Swot, whispered a response. The older woman nodded her head. She looked at Swot and then at the girl whose head rested on Swot's lap. The girl's eyes had closed again; she was very still. The older woman rolled her onto her side and Swot saw that the ground beneath her was soaked in blood. She heard the other girls murmur unhappily as they looked at the blood; obviously they had first-hand knowledge of birth and death, and maternal mortality, and they knew what they were seeing.

In college Swot had read some medical books so she had book knowledge of the process and patchy recall of a video of a birth that had been shown in High School. The videoed birth had taken place in a clean delivery room where, after a good deal of effort and encouragement from those around her, a healthy young woman had delivered a strapping baby boy who had been placed in his mother's arms. Smiles all around, grinning father, congratulatory nurses; some routine process by which the placenta was delivered and then off home to the wonderful world of American babyhood. The older woman passed her hand across the girl's forehead, perhaps checking for a fever. Finally she unwound one of the many layers of fabric that were wrapped around her waist and placed it under the girl's head. She looked around at the other girls taking in the state of their clothes and then she issued a command.

"Sarah." It was Cecelia, the girl who had asked Swot if she thought they might be rescued. "Sarah," she said again, "this woman is offering to give us clothing. She is responsible for us. She will look after us."

"Well, she's not doing very well so far," Swot said.

"I think she does what she can," Cecelia said. "Do you want new clothes?"

"No," said Swot. "I'm fine. My clothes haven't been..."

Her voice trailed away. What was she going to say? My clothes haven't been ripped off me? I haven't been raped and beaten? I'm a white girl; I'm special; they left me alone last night when they were doing God knows what to you?

"I'm fine," she repeated. "What about the...little mother?"

"There is nothing that anyone can do," Cecelia said. "She is bleeding too much. She was too young." She looked around at the other girls. "We are all too young," she said.

The older woman issued another command, and Cecelia turned to follow her, and then turned back again. "You should come," she said. "You should not be separate."

Separate; an interesting word; Swot wondered if there was any advantage in being separate, or would it be better to somehow bond with the other girls; not that bonding had ever been her strong point.

"You come," said the older woman in a voice that could not be denied.

Swot rose reluctantly to her feet and followed along behind the other girls, and the gun toting boys followed behind her until they were waved away by the older woman. Then she led the girls into a clearing in the trees where some bushes gave a small sense of privacy. She opened a battered old suitcase and brilliantly colored cloth spilled out. The girls seemed to momentarily forget their distress as they fell on the fabric and began to drape it around themselves.

The woman came to Swot, holding a length of dark green fabric; by far the most subdued of the fabrics Swot had seen. She stumbled through an introduction in English.

"I am Angelique," she said. "You will wear this."

"No, I won't," Swot said. "I don't need it, give it to someone who needs it."

"You must look *comme les autres*," Angelique said, breaking into French halfway through the sentence.

French was not a difficult language for Swot; it was one of several European languages that she had soaked up as a kid. She answered her in the same language.

"I'm alright," she said. ""I don't need new clothes."

"I know," said Angelique. Her accent was unfamiliar, but the French was easy to follow. "I needed you to come here so I could talk to you."

She took the length of ugly fabric and began to adjust it around Swot's waist, tucking and pleating and speaking softly under her breath.

"Some of these men and boys speak French," she said, "so we must speak softly. I do not very often meet a girl like you___"

"You mean a white girl," Swot said.

"I have never actually spoken to a white girl," Angelique said. She was behind Swot now, making adjustments to the cloth and taking her time about it. "What I mean is that I do not very often meet a girl who might have the courage to escape. Most girls are broken as soon as they arrive here."

"Broken?"

"Last night," she said, "what they did to those girls is to break their spirit and soon they will realize that they need to find a man to protect them from the other men; and when they belong to one of our men and they become pregnant; well they don't try to run."

"Do you belong to a man?" Swot asked.

"I belong to Matapa," she said quietly.

"Oh."

"He took me from my village when I was fourteen. It has been many years, maybe as much as twenty."

Swot looked down at the top of Angelique's head as she continued to make obviously unnecessary adjustments to the skirt that she was fashioning for her. Swot had taken her for an old woman but if what she said was true, then she was no more than thirty four.

"You are still close to home," Angelique said, "and if you run you will find a place to take you in. People are looking for you and for the other girls; this is the only chance you will have. Soon we will move on and you will be far from your family. They will forget you;

they will stop looking for you."

"No, never," Swot said.

"Perhaps it will be different for you, you are a white girl, but for the other girls, there will be no help when we move beyond this place."

"Did you ever try to escape?" Swot asked.

Angelique sat back on her heels and looked up at Swot. "Matapa took me when I was fourteen and he was still a handsome man; I was not afraid of him at first. Of course, at that time he was not the true Matapa."

Swot wondered what she meant by "not the true Matapa". Was Matapa more of a title than a name? Had there been some other Matapa?

"I bore him many children," Angelique said, "although none have survived."

"None?"

"This is a hard place to raise a child," Angelique said.

"But if you have no children here," Swot said, "why don't you leave? "

Angelique shrugged her shoulders. "I don't know where I am," she said, "and I don't know my way home. If I run from this place who will help me; I would just be an old woman on the road; robbers would kill me."

"Do you even know what country this is?" Swot asked.

"Yes," she said, "I am not ignorant; I know this is Uganda, but I have not seen a map or even a book since the day I was taken. We have traveled in the bush for so many years, but I have never been to a town; I have never spoken to another woman; only to the girls we capture."

"So where are you from?" Swot asked.

"Congo," she said.

"Can't you get back there, I don't think it's very far?"

"Congo is big," she said, "and I am from the west; it is far; it is very far. I don't know if my village still stands. I don't know if I have a family there. I don't know if anyone remembers me."

She stood up and stepped back to admire her handiwork. Swot thought that she had been crying quietly as she told how far she was from her home, but now she swiped her hand across her eyes and said "If you are going to run, you must do it tonight, and you must go alone."

"I have to take the boy, "Swot said.

"The cripple?" Angelique replied. "Him, they will kill."

"I know."

"But he cannot run. What is he to you, he is not your brother?"

"He's my responsibility," Swot said, "and I will not leave without him."

"Then you will not escape," said Angelique, "and I am wasting my time."

"No really___"

"I have given you this cloth because it is green and you will not be seen so well among the trees."

"Thank you."

"But if you take the boy," she continued, "you will not move fast enough."

"I will find a way," Swot assured her.

"Bon chance," said Angelique in a tone that implied that Swot would need more luck than she could possibly get.

Angelique led them back out of the clearing. The girls had somehow recaptured some of their lost dignity by the way they had tied and draped the bright fabric around themselves. Without their school uniforms they looked much more mature, not schoolgirls, but women. Swot dragged along behind in her drab green skirt glad of the fact that it did little to improve her appearance; the last thing in the world she wanted to do was attract the attention of any of Matapa's men.

She returned to her former place under the tree.

"I'm still praying," Matthew said encouragingly as he scooted back beside her.

" I wish I knew how," Swot said.

"It's just like talking to a friend," Matthew said.

"If only," Swot replied.

The man in the crisp camos appeared through the doorway of the old army tent, the headquarters, or so Swot assumed.

"You," he shouted. "You white girl; you come here."

"Don't go," Matthew said hanging onto the back of Swot's tee shirt.

"I don't think I have any choice," Swot said.

"Take me with you," Matthew pleaded. "Don't leave me alone with him." He directed a rapid glance at Swot's chief tormenter. She didn't want to imagine what would happen to Matthew if he was alone so she hauled him to his feet and wrapped one of his skinny arms around her shoulders.

"I'm coming, "she said. "We're both coming."

The tall man shrugged his shoulders. Matthew and Swot shuffled reluctantly across the clearing. So this was it; they were finally going to meet the great and dreadful Matapa. Swot had a suspicion that he was not going to turn out to be a timid imposter à la Wizard of Oz. The flaps were open on the old green tent but the interior was a dark mystery. What did he want with her? What would he do? He was an unknown; no one even knew what he looked like; this man, this warlord who had murdered and mutilated his way across a great swath of Central Africa. No one knew where he had come from, or even his nationality; perhaps he had been part of the army that had ousted Idi Amin thirty years before, or perhaps he was someone else. Perhaps the original Matapa was long since dead and buried and some other perverted thug had taken his place.

As they approached the tent, and the revelation awaiting them, a skinny boy emerged from the interior holding some kind of instrument in his hands. He looked up at the trees and then down at the lighted display of whatever he held in his hands. The newcomer, the tall man in camos, shouted at him impatiently and pointed up at a clear patch of sky above their heads.

"If you can't see the sky, the phone can't see the satellite," he said impatiently but in very clear English. The skinny boy stopped dead in his tracks, apparently overcome with terror. Swot tried to make sense of what she had just heard. A phone; they had a phone; they had a satellite phone! That was it; that was the secret of their communications ability; they didn't have to rely on cell towers; they had a satellite link.

The boy moved forward and stood in the spot where a tiny ray of sunlight beamed through a clearing in the trees. He nodded his head; obviously the phone was receiving a signal.

"What do I do now?" the boy asked.

"You dial the number," the man said.

"What number?" the boy asked, his voice shaking in terror.

The tall man grabbed hold of the instrument and slapped the boy on the side of his head. "Why are you playing with this thing?" he asked.

"I'm supposed to learn how to use it," the boy said. "I am the new communications officer."

"Who told you that?"

"The general said I was supposed to learn," the boy repeated, "because my English is good."

The tall man nodded his head. "Your English is good enough," he said, "but there are other boys with good English, so you'd better get this right."

"Yes Sir, Lieutenant, Sir," the boy said eagerly. "I will get it right.

The lieutenant turned and looked at Matthew. "That boy speaks English," he said, "and that girl, she speaks good English."

"He's a cripple," the boy said. He didn't bother to say why Swot's ability to speak English was unimportant; it was implied in everything that she had seen of Matapa's ragged band; girls had no value.

The lieutenant returned the phone to the boy's trembling hands. "Who are you phoning?" he asked.

The boy showed him a piece of paper. "I am to phone this number. It is a test."

The man nodded. "Let me see you do it," he said.

The boy carefully aligned the phone in the beam of sunlight and began to dial a number.

"No, no, no," the man said, grabbing the phone again and turning it over. "Don't you know anything?" he asked impatiently. "You need the code. Here, look on the back of the phone. You dial the code and then you dial the number. Now do it."

The boy squinted at the back of the phone, mouthing the numbers written on the label. Swot automatically analyzed his problem; he had to memorize the numbers before he could turn the phone over and actually dial them; not the most efficient system. She wanted to suggest that they should put the code numbers on the front of the phone; it would be more logical. She almost said something and then she stopped herself. What did she care where they put the numbers? Why would she help them to be logical? For a brief moment her interest in the existence of a satellite phone with an ability to call anywhere in the world, had made her forget her situation. She clamped her mouth closed, and watched the boy dial in the code, and then he consulted the slip of paper and dialed in his test number. They all waited. Swot could hear various clicks and beeps from the phone. She thought about what was actually happening; the phone had searched the small area of sky available to it, and had located a communications satellite; it was bouncing a signal from the satellite to another phone. A few more clicks and beeps and the connection was made. She heard a man's voice saying hello.

"This is a test," the boy said, full of self-importance and apparent relief that he had completed his task.

"Where are you?" said the man on the other end of the satellite beam. "What are you playing at? I never agreed to this____"

The lieutenant grabbed the phone from the boy, and the voice on the other end was abruptly cut off.

"Turn it off and keep it off," the man said. "Keep it off, do you understand me?"

The boy cowered from the blows that were being aimed at his head. He was a skinny little kid and Swot supposed that she should have felt sorry for him; he had only done what he was told, but she couldn't waste any of her energy and brain power on sympathy because she was too busy dealing with what had just happened. She had recognized the voice at the other end of the phone. The voice was pure Virginia; Rory Marsden.

Angola 1975

The boy from the Congo had proved himself to be a fierce fighter.. The Portuguese colonists had fled from their homes and estates in Angola, just as the Belgians had fled from Congo, and the fighting was fierce between the tribes; a perfect place for a young man who was willing to kill without asking questions.

It was in Angola that he found the man he had been seeking, the battle-scarred Shona mercenary who had taken the name of his mythic ancestor, Mwene Matapa, the Great Plunderer. When the boy attached himself to Matapa's band of mercenaries he found a connection to something new; something beyond his imagining; Americans! They were a great secret, these Americans, to be spoken of only in whispers. The Americans were there, but they were not there; they stood behind Matapa, they supplied weapons, information, and dollars, but they were not there; to the rest of the world they were invisible.

The boy from Congo learned to read and write the language of the Americans and made himself useful in every way possible. They seemed to like him; they recognized his white blood; they treated him like a long lost son and he hoped they might take him with them to America when the day came to abandon their allies in Angola. But then the day did come and suddenly they were gone; all of them; fleeing in transport planes, droning high overhead and leaving the Africans to fight their own war and leaving the boy to, once again, decide his own fate.

No one in Matapa's encampment could say whether the war had been won, or which side might eventually emerge as the victor, but the Americans were gone, and so was the money. The boy from Congo began to ask questions, knowing that Matapa had no answers. "Where do we go now? When the sun comes up tomorrow, where will you lead us?"

On the night when the last of the American planes departed, Matapa hid in his tent, tossing restlessly on his mattress pad, longing perhaps to return to his childhood home by the waters of the Zambezi. In the small hours of the morning, moonlight flooded the tent as the boy from Congo lifted the tent flap, and the shadow

from his tall figure fell across the old man in his bed.
Matapa fumbled for the knife he kept beneath his pillow, but it was
too late; the time had come for change; time for the boy from
Congo to claim the name he had so long coveted. The old Mwene
Matapa would never see the fertile lands of his childhood again; his
bones would lie where he fell on the blood stained soil of Angola.
In the morning the boy from Congo claimed his title, he was the new
Mwene Matapa, the new Great Plunderer; and he would lead his
band of killers to the north, where they could dip their knives into
the blood of Ugandans.

CHAPTER SEVENTEEN

Swot didn't dare lift her eyes from the ground or let anyone see the expression on her face. Someone shoved her in the back and she began to walk as slowly as she possibly could, dragging Matthew along with her. Her mind was racing. Rory Marsden had answered the phone; she knew it beyond any shadow of a doubt. Rory Marsden answered a phone call from Matapa's camp. Her mind was processing the implications of that simple fact. Rory had answered the phone, but the cell tower was down; she had seen it herself lying beside the road, a mass of twisted metal; no way had it been repaired or resurrected in the few hours she had been away. Rory answered the phone, ergo Rory had a working phone; a satellite phone. So if Rory had a satellite phone why had he made such a point of telling everyone that they were cut off; that he could not talk to the American Embassy; that he could do nothing to help the local population when Matapa's raiding party began their kidnapping spree? Bottom line; who was Rory Marsden and whose side was he on?

Matthew dug Swot in the ribs and she realized that they were now inside the gloomy interior of the green army tent. She dragged her mind away from Rory Marsden and looked around. A row of folding tables along one side of the tent held electronic equipment; cell phones, a laptop, and the base station for the satellite phone. The kid who had called himself the communications officer was carefully replacing the phone in its charger. Swot had no idea what they were using to charge the phone; she had seen no signs of a generator, but obviously they had some method because the charger showed a green light. Perhaps a solar panel, she thought. She reined in her wandering intellect. What did it matter how they charged the phone, the fact was they had a phone and it worked? On the other side of the tent two young girls sat on either side of an army cot. One girl held a water bottle, clean, commercially bottled water, along with a plate of chicken. She broke off a leg bone and handed it to the man in the bed. He sucked weakly on the meat and then allowed the bone to fall onto the ground beside the bed. Swot judged the length of his illness by the accumulation of uneaten chicken bones piled on the floor. Outside of the tent his followers were subsisting on filthy water and thin gruel; inside the tent their leader was spitting out meat and bones and leaving them to be foraged by a small party of ants. Another of the captured girls held a bowl of water on her lap and sponged his forehead. So this was it; General Matapa; not a powerful commanding figure but a painfully thin, pale faced man, his forehead shiny with perspiration. "Come here," he said in a weak voice, gesturing for the two girls to move aside.

Swot stepped forward with Matthew still clinging to her side. Even in the dim light of the tent Swot could see that Matapa was a sick man with sunken cheeks and a livid eruption of blisters on his colorless face.

Matthew hung back, clinging to Swot's arm.

"AIDS," he whispered.

"Yeah," she said, "I guessed as much."

She was not at all surprised to find that Matapa had AIDS although maybe she had not expected it to be so advanced. All kinds of information had been thrust upon her in high school including colored illustrations of the various lesions and tumors that accompanied the advanced state of the virus. She didn't need Matthew to tell her that she was looking at an extremely sick man with very little hope of recovery. So that was it, she thought, Matapa's interest in the miracle child was not just for the benefit of his boy soldiers; it was for his own benefit.

Matapa's illness came as no great surprise, but Matapa himself gave her quite a shock. Matthew put it into words.

"He's a mazungu," he whispered.

"Perhaps it's because he's sick," she whispered back.

"He's white like you," Matthew said.

"Come here," Matapa repeated.

They took another faltering step forward.

"Don't touch him," Swot said to Matthew; not bothering to whisper.

Matapa struggled to sit upright and one of the girls rushed forward to put a couple of pillows behind his back. The effort of sitting up caused a coughing fit. Swot sprang backwards, pulling Matthew with her; no way was she going to intercept any of this man's germs. The rational part of her brain remembered that no one should be afraid to be near an HIV positive person; that the virus was not airborne, that it was only contained in body fluids, but the irrational part of her brain, the one she was just beginning to discover, was horrified by the man's symptoms and was urging her to flee for her life.

"You can't hide from it, girlie," Matapa said in a hoarse whisper.

"It's avoidable," Swot said self-righteously. "You brought it on yourself."

"Oh yah," he said, "and what do you know about it, girlie?"

She tried to place his accent; not Ugandan, not British, something else, slightly German, a touch of French; the accent of a man who had learned his English from wanderers of all nations. However, he seemed to have learned it well; despite the outlandish accent, and his obviously weakened condition, the words came to him easily.

"So what do you think?" he asked. "Not what you expected, eh?"

His attempt at laughter ended in another coughing fit. One of the girls wiped his mouth with a bloodstained rag. Swot wanted to tell her not to touch him again; to stay away from his body fluids, to wear a surgical mask; to do something to save her own life, but what would be the use, surely she was already infected? Surely they were all infected. If he hadn't passed the AIDS virus on to them, he was most certainly passing on his current pneumonia.

The man in the bed took a sip of water before he managed to speak again. "So" he said, "we're not so different are we, you and I? Touch of the tar brush as they used to say when I was a kid. So your daddy was a black man."

"My grandfather," Swot said.

"Ah," he said, "not quite so close to home. Yah, I heard about you, visiting the big man, huh? So what do you think of us?"

She said nothing, but Matapa wasn't discouraged. Despite his coughing fit he seemed anxious to talk.

"You're wondering about me, aren't you?" he said. "Yah, where does that man come from? Well, girlie, I come from Congo; straight from the heart of hell."

"Heart of Darkness," Swot said.

"Oh, so you read it, did you?" he said.

"Yes, I read it," she said.

"So you know about Congo?"

"So what?" she replied, not intending to have a literary discussion. Yes, she had read Joseph Conrad, and she had read King Leopold's Ghost, and she had read all kinds of other horror stories about the Congo; she had read enough that just the word "Congo" sent a shiver down her spine.

"My daddy was a settler." Matapa said; "He ran out when the real killing started. Didn't like it when the blacks started killing the whites; wrong way round you see, girlie; not part of God's plan; whites kill blacks; that's what they thought. Kill them, starve them, beat them to death; and have your bit of fun with the women. Yah, nothing wrong with that, white man takes a fancy to a local girl, no one cares. So what, you say, well I tell you; so what. So what if there's a baby; nothing to do with him, not the great white settler; not when he has to leave in a hurry; not when the knives are coming out at night; so what happens to his son? What happens to the little half-caste that no one wants? He took off and my mother leaves me with the nuns. So what, girlie, if the nuns disappear in the night; so what if I'm left there all alone? I survived; I learned to kill."

He broke into another fit of coughing. Matthew's hand slipped into

Swot's and held on tight.

"Congo," Matthew said.

"Yeah," Swot whispered back. She looked at the man in the bed. "So you're not the real Matapa?" she said, and her conversation with Angelique made a little more sense; Angelique had said that the man she married had not been the real Matapa, not then, but later.

"I am the real Matapa now," he declared. "I killed the other one; I ate his heart. We are one."

Swot felt herself swaying and for a moment she feared that she would faint, and take Matthew down to the ground with her. To her surprise she found that Matthew was now the one exerting strength; holding her upright. Ate his heart! Did he really mean that? Had he eaten the other man's heart?

"The Americans liked me," said Matapa.

"I don't think so," said Swot.

"War makes for strange friendships," said Matapa.

"This isn't a war," Swot said, "and it's nothing to do with America."

"Isn't it?" said Matapa, and Swot remembered the voice on the phone; pure Virginia.

."No," she said, "don't make excuses, you're just a murderer, plain and simple."

"Yah," he agreed, "but it's a living, girlie. "

"You call this living?" Swot asked.

"I'm going to be cured," he said.

"With phony magic from a phony witchdoctor?" Swot said, "No one can cure what you have."

A light flared momentarily in Matapa's lackluster eyes. "When the nuns abandoned me," he said, "when they climbed into their little old bus and headed for the border they took their white man's god with them, and left me alone with the African gods. I've made my sacrifices to those gods, girlie; I've given them the blood of babies and virgins and they have promised me a cure."

"I don't believe in your gods," Swot said,

A laugh rattled up from his chest. "I heard about you and the witchdoctor," he said. "I heard he cursed you."

"No he didn't," Swot said. "I don't believe in his curses. It's all nonsense."

The rattling laugh welled up again. "So what do you call this, girlie? You're here in my camp; is this where you wanted to be, or you think maybe this is part of the curse?"

"I don't believe in curses," Swot repeated, "and you'll never find that baby, and even if you did, whatever obscene, revolting things you plan to do with her isn't going to cure you."

"Yah," said Matapa, "I hear that the witchdoctor is saying we can cure all the boys in the camp just by defiling this baby. Yah, I heard that, but I'm not going to do it."

"You're not?" said Swot.

"No girlie, I'm not. I'm a very sick man, I need big medicine, not sex with a little baby girl. This witchdoctor, the one who cursed you, doesn't know how to make big medicine. I will do it myself. I will sacrifice the child; I will make medicine for everyone."

"Sacrifice," said Swot, "what do you mean?"

"I will kill her," said Matapa, "and I will eat her heart."

No," said Swot,

"Yes, girlie," said Matapa, "and if that doesn't cure me, then perhaps I will kill you and eat your heart. I think there is medicine in you; white man medicine."

"You're disgusting," Swot said.

Matapa shifted his gaze and seemed to focus on something behind Swot. He raised his eyebrows questioningly.

"Yes," said a voice behind Swot's right shoulder. "He has her."

She turned to look at Matapa's lieutenant.

"Ah," said Matapa, smiling widely and showing a row of discolored teeth, "we found her, girlie. Your friend the witchdoctor has her."

CHAPTER EIGHTEEN
Matthew

They had found the baby! Matthew gasped, and Swot squeezed his hand really hard. He knew what she was telling him; don't draw attention to yourself. So far the man in the bed had not even looked at Matthew, but it would only be a matter of time. The man was evil; Matthew could feel the evil in the very air of the tent; ancient evil; the kind that had once dwelt in the never ending forest.

"Jesus, help me," he prayed silently, "please help me." He had confidence in the Jesus of his mother's bible, but even his confidence allowed room for a small amount of doubt; not really a question of *could* Jesus overcome Matapa, but more a question of *would* he?

"It doesn't matter whether you found the child or not," Swot said, "she can't cure you."

"I told you," Matapa replied; "I have sacrificed to the gods of the forest, they will not let me die."

That was it, Matthew thought; that was the evil in the room.

"Everyone dies," Swot said.

"No," said Matapa, "I have eaten the hearts of my enemies; I will not die." He sank back against the pillows and waved his hand in dismissal. "Bring her back later," he said.

"And the boy?" the lieutenant asked dragging Matthew forward. Matapa looked at him with little interest and then turned away. "Yah, bring him back as well," he said; "they can both watch."

The girls ministering to Matapa closed in around him, and recommenced wiping his face with the bloody rag. Swot slung Matthew's arm around her shoulders and helped him out of the tent; she seemed to be gasping for air, and Matthew realized that they had both been holding their breath, as if they could not bear to even breathe the same air as Matapa.

The lieutenant remained inside and closed the tent flaps. Swot led Matthew back to sit beneath the tree that had sheltered them in the night.

"You were very good," Matthew said softly. "No one else has ever found out so much about Matapa. No one knew who he was, but now you know. He told you everything."

"And why do you think that was?" Swot asked, sinking down onto the ground beneath the tree.

"He was frightened of you," Matthew said.

"I doubt it," she replied.

"Yes, he was," Matthew insisted. "He blames everything on his race, because his father was white, but he's not white, but then he sees you, and you don't blame anyone. He knows you're not afraid of him; not even afraid of the forest gods. You're not even afraid of the witchdoctor," he added in a sudden burst of confidence, "and that's why the curse didn't work."

"You don't think I'm cursed," said Swot, "really? So what do we call this, just bad luck?"

"Yes," said Matthew, "it is just bad luck."

"Well, I think our bad luck just got worse," said Swot.

"What do you mean?" said Matthew. He could not imagine how the situation could get any worse.

"Oh nothing," said Swot. "Don't worry about it, not yet." She was silent for a moment, staring down at the ground, her face grim.

"He still didn't tell you his name," Matthew said.

She looked up. "Who?"

"Matapa. He didn't tell you his real name, but he told you more than he's told anyone else. We could tell the army what we found out."

Swot stared at the ground again and then she took a deep breath and looked at him. "They're not going to let us go," she said.

"But they found the baby..."

"Men like Matapa don't keep their promises," she said.

"But he liked you," Matthew protested.

"He wanted to show off," Swot said. "He had to tell his story to someone. He wanted to impress me with how clever he is, and how evil he is."

"But..."

"We know too much now," Swot said. "The only reason he told me any of it, was because he knew I would never have the chance to tell anyone else. Matthew, unless we do something to help ourselves, we're not going to last the night."

Matthew stared at her; she was right, of course she was right; she was a genius and he was just a stupid kid who didn't have the sense to see the danger they were in.

"I will pray," he said resolutely.

"You do that," she said.

"And you will pray with me," he insisted.

She shook her head "I don't know how to do that," she said. "You pray for both of us."

"I need you to pray with me," he said. "Jesus said that when two or three are gathered together, then he will be there. We need him to be here."

Sarah shook her head. "I don't know how," she said.

Matthew heard a monkey screeching angrily in the forest canopy above him, and a shower of leaves fell around them as the trees began to shake.

"The forest gods are here," Matthew said, "Matapa has brought them with him. We must be together."

He took hold of Sarah's hands and closed his eyes. He couldn't tell if she was praying but she allowed her hands to remain where they were while he prayed. He imagined his silent words winging their way upwards to the heights of heaven, far, far above the reach of the forest gods; to a place of light where no other gods could exist.

Swot suddenly pulled her hands away. He opened his eyes.

"What is it?"

"Over there," she said.

He saw that the boys were making their way deeper into the forest; they carried shovels and behind them came one of the older men with a bundle thrown over his shoulder; a bundle wrapped in brightly colored cloth.

"Are you done praying," Swot asked, "because I have a couple of questions?" She sounded fiercely angry.

Matthew waited. In his experience the best way to deal with an angry person was to keep quiet and to avoid giving them any reason to become even angrier.

That's her," Swot said, "that's the girl with the baby; they're going to bury her.

Matthew nodded his head.

"Did you ask your Jesus why he didn't save that girl?"

Matthew shook his head. "I don't understand everything," he said, "but now she is at peace."

"Oh great," said Swot, "you sound like that idiot evangelist saying that all you can do for the poor is tell them that they'll go to heaven one day."

"Did you pray?" Matthew asked.

"None of your business," she replied.

Matthew kept quiet, his attention focused on the burial party making their way into the woods.

"Well," said Swot suddenly, "I don't plan to die here, and no one's going to bury me in the backwoods."

Matthew's heart leaped. "Do you have a plan?" he asked.

"Yes, I do," said Swot, "it just came to me. It's crazy but it's worth a try."

"What is it?"

"We have to get our hands on that satellite phone, "she said. "We can call for help, and then if we can manage to leave it turned on it will broadcast our position. Someone can get a satellite fix on us."

Matthew didn't understand much of what she had said about the phone broadcasting a position, and a satellite getting a fix on them, but he understood the main point of her plan; one way or another she was going to make a phone call.

"Who can we call?" he asked.

Swot hesitated. "I don't know. Give me a moment, let me think."

"My father?" Matthew suggested..

She shook her head. "There's no cell phone coverage. It's no good calling anyone around here; all the phones are dead. Do you know any other numbers; people who aren't from around here?"

"No," said Matthew. "I have never been allowed a phone; perhaps someone else has a satellite phone,"

"Rory Marsden," said Swot, "but I'm not calling him."

"Why not?"

"Because he was the one that answered the phone just now; that was his voice. How come Rory Marsden is on calling terms with Matapa?"

"I don't know," said Matthew.

"Exactly," said Swot, "and that's why we can't call him."

"Can we call Mugabe?" Matthew asked. "He's very strong."
"Yes, he is," said Swot, "and no we can't call him; we don't even know his number, and anyway his phone won't work."
"Unless he's gone to some other place," Matthew said, trying to be optimistic.
"He has not gone to some other place," Swot said angrily. "He would never just abandon us; he's been out looking for you. He says you are of his clan."
"Yes, I am," said Matthew, "but I am not important."
"Well, he thinks you are," said Swot.
"Do you know any phone numbers?" Matthew asked.
She shook her head. "No one in Uganda," she said.
"But it doesn't have to be in Uganda," Matthew said. "You can call anyone in the world, can't you?"
She grabbed his hands. "Matthew, you're brilliant," she said. "I can call anyone in the world."

Swot Jensen
Anyone in the world? Who? Who did she know who could do anything? Did she even know any phone numbers? At home, in Cleveland, she had a cell phone full of contacts but none of the numbers were in her memory. Wait; she did know a number; she'd known it since she was a little kid. She knew her home phone number. She could phone home. She could talk to....her dad! Dad would know what to do.
"Matthew," she said, "I know what___"
"Shh," said Matthew, stumbling to his feet. The girls from the convent were filtering in through the trees highly visible in the bright cloths that had supplanted their school uniform; a couple of the older girls came with them; the pregnant one following behind along with the Angelique.
"We are going to hold a service," Cecelia said to Swot.
"What?" Swot's mind was not in Uganda; her mind was in her father's study in Cleveland and she was trying to work out whether he would be at home, or would he still be in the office? What was the time difference? Suppose all she got was the answering

machine?

"They are burying our sister," Cecelia said.

"I know."

"We are going to pray," Cecelia said.

"We'll come," said Matthew, hopping to his feet.

"I don't see the point," Swot said, still wrestling with the question of time difference.

"I don't think I can get over there by myself," Matthew said softly. Oh great, she was his human crutch! "Can't you use a stick or something?" she asked.

"I will look for one," Matthew said, "if you will help me."

She hauled herself to her feet and draped his arm over her shoulders. Matthew gestured towards the forest. "Over there," he said.

"That's the funeral," Swot complained. "I don't want to go there."

"That's where they keep the firewood," Matthew said. "I'll see if there are any good sticks."

"Okay," Swot growled and they fell into line behind the mourners. They were burying the poor dead girl in a little clearing close behind the back of Matapa's tent. Swot reasoned that Matapa had no intention of making this gorge his permanent home or he would choose a different site for the graveyard; she was pretty sure that bodies accumulated at quite a rate around Matapa and his followers. Her sincere hope was that Matapa would soon be adding his body to the accumulation; not that it would make any difference; apparently the title of General Matapa could be passed from one evil jerk to another, ad infinitum.

The girls assembled around the gravediggers and Swot watched out of the corner of her eye as the older men lowered the girl's small body into the grave. Then Angelique stepped forward and handed over another small bundle, wrapped in rags; the baby. The convent girls started to sing, one took the lead and the others followed, their voices weaving intricate rhythms and harmonies. Much to Swot's surprise the boys put down their shovels and joined in, building another layer of harmony. Their song rose into the steaming equatorial air carrying with it all the richness of their culture, all the dreams and hopes that had once been part of this little girl, all the future that might have existed for her tiny baby. Swot imagined that the captured girls were offering their prayers to the mother they all trusted; the Virgin Mary of their Convent; but she had no idea what dark gods were being worshipped by the ragged, thuggish boys of Matapa's army; they sang with the voices of angels and lived the life of Satan's demons.

The girls continued to sing as the boys filled in the grave. Matthew hopped over to the wood pile and began sorting through the dead wood. Swot remembered the home made crutch he used in his father's compound; no doubt Matthew was an expert at finding just the right crutch to fit his growing body.

One of the older boys stopped his work on filling in the grave and shouted at Matthew. Cecelia stopped singing and shouted back to the boy. The gravediggers continued their labor and Cecelia came to speak to Swot.

"I told him the boy was looking for a crutch so he could walk alone," she said.

"You're right," said Swot. "He can't rely on me all the time."

"Take me with you," Cecelia said.

"What?"

"When you escape, take me with you."

"We're not going to escape," Swot said bitterly' "how do you expect me to escape?"

"You will think of something," said Cecelia. "You are a mazungu, you will not die here."

"That's what you think," said Swot. "Believe me, I don't have any special powers, I can die just like___"

Matthew interrupted her gloomy prognosis by hissing at her from his place in the wood pile.

"What?" she asked.

He hissed again, and then put his finger to his lips, and opened his eyes really wide, more or less beckoning her with his eyebrows.

"He wants to talk to you," Cecelia said.

"I can see that," she replied.

"Perhaps he has found something."

"In the woodpile?"

Cecelia shrugged her shoulders. The choir took up another song, even more heartbreaking than the last one, and the boys shoveled to the rhythm.

Swot sidled over towards the woodpile and Cecelia followed her. As they stepped into the undergrowth Matthew hobbled towards them with a newly discovered forked stick tucked in his armpit.

"Come this way," he said, "and do not scream."

"Why should I scream?"

"You will want to scream, but do not make a sound and do not run away."

"Okay," Swot said. She turned to Cecelia intending to send her away, but she was close behind, dogging Swot's footsteps so they moved forward together.

"Now stand still," said Matthew, "and look down."

Obediently Swot looked down and practically jumped out of her skin.

"Do not scream," Matthew whispered.

Swot swallowed the scream that was rising in her throat as she took in the fact that a huge snake was sliding through the undergrowth within inches of her feet. Its tail was hidden in the long grass on one side, and its head had already moved across the clearing and was lost from sight. The snake was an iridescent blue black moving like a ribbon of flowing water.

"Ah," said Cecelia, "I see."

"What?" Swot asked. "What's to see? It's a snake."

Matthew shook his head. "Not a snake," he said. "Safari ants."

"Ants?"

Swot bent over for a closer inspection.

"Do not move," Matthew said.

Swot stayed where she was and stared at the flowing stream in front of her, and now she could see that it was not a snake; it was a column of ants, millions, maybe billions of shiny black ants moving with a single purpose.

"If you disturb them they will bite," said Cecelia. "They are looking for food; they will eat anything they find."

Swot had been thinking about poking them with a stick; she rethought the idea.

"They can devour an elephant," Matthew said. "They can kill a sleeping man; they can kill a man who is in his bed."

"Well that's all very interesting," Swot said, "but I don't see....." But then she did see; she saw exactly what Matthew had seen; the column of ants was moving in a straight line, and if there was no change in their direction that line would lead them to the rear of the green tent; the tent where Matapa lay immobile in his bed.

"Will they go in there?" Swot asked.

"I think so," said Matthew. "When the colony is hungry they send out scouts to find food; if the scouts have found food in Matapa's tent, they will lead the colony to the tent."

"Chicken bones," Swot whispered. "He had chicken bones and there were ants on the bones."

"God is good," said Matthew.

"All the time," Cecelia said.

Matthew nodded; Swot shrugged her shoulders.

"It's not God, it's nature," she protested.

"All nature is in God's control," Matthew said. "I have prayed for a miracle."

"Eh," Cecelia said admiringly.

"Okay, okay," Swot said, "let's not argue. You can say it's a miracle if you like; the point is what are we going to do?"

They both looked at Swot. Her mind was racing. She had no idea how long it would take for the ants to reach the tent; if that was indeed where they were heading. Even in the short time she had been standing in the clearing, millions of ants had marched past her feet and the end of the column was nowhere in sight. She tried to gauge their speed; slow and steady, and the tent was not far away. If they were not already making their way under the tent flaps, they wouldn't be long; not long at all.

"If one of Matapa's people sees them, will they be able to stop them?" she asked.

Cecelia shook her head. "They will need poison," she said. "When they find food, nothing stops them, and if anyone is in their way....."

Swot looked at the ants; she really had to find out for herself. Everything logical in her cried out against the wisdom of making a plan based purely on the possibility that a miraculously summoned column of ants could eat an elephant, or a man in his bed. She extended her sneaker clad foot and touched the outer edge of the column. For a brief moment the column hesitated and then it flowed on while a couple of ants detached themselves from the column and crawled across her shoe, and then a couple more, and then a few more.

"Get back," Matthew hissed.

The ants moved from her sneaker to her socks and then started up her legs; and then the biting started, pinpricks of pain advancing up her legs. She sprang backwards, beating at her legs. Cecelia pulled her away.

Swot started to beat harder at her feet and legs.

"Don't," said Matthew, "someone will see you."

The bite of the safari ant was ferocious. "Are they poisonous?" Swot whispered. The column had moved on and she knew that she only had a few outriders chewing on feet and legs, but it was enough for her to believe that enough of them together would most definitely eat an elephant.

"No poison," Cecelia said. "Just pick them off."

Pick them off? Swot tried to hide herself behind a tree while she hitched up her skirt and pulled and squeezed at the vicious little creatures that had dug their jaws into her legs. Behind her the singing had stopped, and the burial party broke into a babble of sound. She had drawn attention to herself and the boys; the guards; were heading towards them.

"Just walk," Matthew hissed.

Yeah, sure, just walk, and pretend that no one and nothing was chewing her foot. Matthew hobbled along beside her.

Cecelia shouted something to the guards.

"What did you say? Swot asked.

"That you were, you know, in the bushes because...."

"Okay," Swot said. She tried to get her mind back around the situation. She fully accepted the fact that there was going to be an enormous disturbance in Matapa's tent the moment the ants appeared; the question was how to take advantage of it?

"We're going to grab the phone," she said to Matthew. "As soon as anything happens, I'm going to grab the phone."

He nodded his head.

"So we're going to make our way around to the front of the tent, so we're close as possible."

He nodded his head again.

"And we'll get the phone," Swot said.

"And then what will we do?" Matthew asked.

"Then we'll run like hell into the woods, and I'll phone my father," Swot said.

She looked at Matthew's crutch. "How fast can you run?" she asked.

"I can help him," Cecelia said.

"I didn't say...."

"I'm coming with you," Cecelia said.

"If they find us...." said Swot.

"I know," Cecelia replied, "but if we stay here we will die; I will not let them touch me again; never again."

Swot looked at her determined young face. For a few moments she had been so busy concentrating on her own problem that she had forgotten what the poor kid had been through the night before; a fate worse than death; yes, Swot understood what she meant.

"We have to find a clearing," Swot said. "The phone has to be able to see the satellite."

Matthew and Cecelia looked at her blankly. ""You don't have to understand," Swot snapped, "you just have to do it. We'll go through the trees, not up the road. Do you understand, we will not go up the road?"

"We are not stupid," Cecelia said quietly.

"I know," said Swot, "it's just that my mind works very fast."

"We are not slow," said Cecelia.

"No, of course not; I'm not suggesting that you are, but...." Swot interrupted her stumbling explanation with a sudden burst of reason. "Oh what the hell?" she snapped. "I don't have time to explain and I don't have time to take your feelings into account. Both of you just shut up and do what I tell you and we might get out of here, and I'll be politically correct later, when it's all over. Matthew, whether you like it or not, you can't run as fast as I can, and there's nothing I can do about that right now, so as soon as the trouble starts you head into the woods and stay just to the right of the ants; you know where they're coming from and no one else does, so just keep going until you find a clearing, and you go with him Cecelia."

"But___," the girl protested.

"Stay with him," Swot said, "and keep him moving."

Before she could say anything else the shouting started followed by an enormous eruption of activity from within the green tent. The flaps were flung open and the two girls emerged screaming, then the lieutenant hopping from one foot to another and barking orders. Behind him came the kid who had called himself the communications officer. They were all slapping at their clothing and hopping from one foot to another. For a moment Swot wondered if they were just going to run away and leave Matapa to his fate, but then she heard the boy soldiers pounding on the ground behind her and they charged past, heading towards the tent.

"This is it," she said. "Get going."

Matthew and Cecelia turned and scurried into the undergrowth. No one raised a finger to stop them; all attention was focused on the green tent. This was it. Whether by good luck, natural coincidence, or the force of Matthew's prayers; they had their opportunity. Swot was going in.

CHAPTER NINETEEN
Brenda Songbird Carter

Brenda stormed from room to room in Rory's house, flinging open doors and finding very little inside apart from shabby furniture and stores of food. Just one door remained, and that door was locked. She pounded on the door and then hurried back into the living room to face Rory. "Why is that door locked?" she shouted. "Give me the key, let me look inside. I know you have something in there. What is it? Is it a radio, a satellite phone? I want to open that door."

Rory ignored her. He had wrestled Margaret onto the sofa and was doing his very best to shove a couple of pills down her throat while she resisted him with all her might.

Mugabe raised his hand, palm upwards like a police officer stopping traffic. "Be patient, please," he said.

"Patient! Patient!" Brenda shouted adding her screams to Margaret's sobs. "They have Swot; how do you expect me to be patient? Now she's saying they have the kid___"

Margaret sobbed louder than ever and Rory somehow managed to pour some water down her throat. Her sobbing ended in a gurgling sound as she swallowed the water and the pills.

"They're sleeping pills," Rory said. "She'll be asleep in a couple of minutes; I gave her enough to knock out a horse. Please, Brenda, please be patient."

"I don't have time to be patient," Brenda said. "If that little slime from Kajunga has the baby, he'll be heading straight to Matapa and Swot won't stand a chance."

"No," said Mugabe, "he will wait."

"Why? Why the hell should he wait? Brenda's mind was racing. She was filled with fury and anxiety; her heart was practically pounding out of her chest and Margaret's alternating sobs and screams were driving all logical thought from her brain.

"Because the witchdoctor doesn't know where Matapa is," Rory shouted. "Now shut the hell up, and let me think."

"You know where he is," Brenda shouted back. "You know exactly where he is."

"No," said Rory, "not exactly."

"Bastard," said Brenda

"Please Madame," said Mugabe.

"Oh you be quiet," she said turning on him, "I don't even know whose side you're on." She turned back to Rory. "What's behind that door," she asked, "and why is it locked?"

"Because I keep my computer in there," Rory said, "and in this country people steal things."

"I think they steal in every country," Mugabe said.

"Yeah, yeah, you're probably right," Rory said. He leaned down and smoothed Margaret's hair. "She's calming down," he said.

He was right; Margaret was no longer actually screaming, and her sobs had become gulps.

"Why on earth did she do that?" Brenda asked. "You told her not to draw attention to herself."

Rory continued to smooth Margaret's hair.

"It's nothing," he said.

"Oh, it's something," Brenda assured him. "This whole place is full of secrets."

"Just leave it alone," said Rory."

"No," said Brenda. "Rory, they have my granddaughter, how can I possibly leave it alone?"

"I won't let them hurt her," Rory said.

She turned to Mugabe. "Did you hear that?" she asked. "He's admitting it; he's admitting he knows where they are."

"No, I don't, "said Rory, "but I think I can communicate with them. I'm sure I can persuade them to let your granddaughter go; they have nothing to gain by keeping her; not if they have the child."

Margaret was still sufficiently awake and attentive to emit a choked scream and stare at Rory with wide terrified eyes.

"No," Margaret muttered, "no, no, no." She attempted to sit up and Rory pushed her back down.

"Nothing will happen," he said.

"Liar," Brenda shouted. "Don't believe him, Margaret. He doesn't care what happens to that kid."

Margaret looked at her with unfocused eyes. "She's his child," she said, "he won't let them take her." Her eye lids drooped and she was obviously fighting to stay awake. "You didn't come in time," she said. She closed her eyes again, and this time they stayed closed.

"Your child?" Brenda asked, momentarily forgetting about Swot. "That little kid is your child?"

"No, of course not," said Rory.

"Then what is she talking about? Come on Rory, stop with all this mystery. Tell me the truth about something; anything. Give me a reason to trust you."

"There was a baby," Rory said. "A little girl; Margaret called her Alice."

"Yeah, I know, I heard her."

Rory shook his head, still looking down at Margaret, now sound asleep.

"It's been fifty years," he said.

"What?"

"After you married Herbert," Rory said, "Margaret and I..."

"And there was a baby?" Brenda asked.

He nodded his head. "There was a baby; I never saw her, I didn't know."

"Where were you?"

"I was with the others, doing what we had all planned to do; driving to Cairo. I didn't know about the baby." Rory shrugged his shoulders. "Maybe Margaret tried to write to me, but i didn't get the letters; we were on the move."

"You always got your letters," Brenda protested.

"Letters from home," he said, "not letters from Margaret. So after we reached Cairo___"

"So you made it," said Brenda stabbed by a sudden pang of envy; her friends had finished what they set out to do, but she had gone home in disgrace and somehow, fifty years later, that missed opportunity still mattered.

"Yes, we made it," said Rory, "and then we all went our separate ways and I went home, and then I went...well, never mind."

"Where;" Brenda demanded, "where did you go?"

"It's not important," he said. "The fact is, Margaret had a baby."

"So where is she now?"

Rory shrugged his shoulders. "I don't know."

"Does she know?" Brenda asked, looking at Margaret who had begun to snore in the way that heavily drugged people snore.

"No," he said. "The Fowlers took her."

"The missionary people?" Brenda said. " Are you saying they stole your child?"

"They didn't steal her from me," he said. "I guess they stole her from Margaret, although I don't think anyone thought of it as stealing at the time. Margaret couldn't tell anyone she was pregnant or she'd be sent home in disgrace, so they said that Mrs. Fowler was pregnant, and they all went to Nairobi, so when the baby was born, and it was a white baby, everyone believed it was Mrs. Fowler's baby; no one thought Margaret would have done anything like...that. When they went back to England they took Alice with them; there was nothing Margaret could do about it."

"So she's how old?" Brenda asked.

"She's a grown woman, the same as your daughter," Rory said, "She's middle aged, I guess, but Margaret doesn't think of her that way; she still thinks of her as a baby."

"She's not right in the head, is she?" Brenda said.

"No," said Rory, "she's been going downhill for a while. She had a bout of cerebral malaria, and she hasn't been the same."

"I never did like her," Brenda confessed, "and neither did you. So why...?"

"You married Herbert," Rory said.

They stood there in silence for a moment looking at each other and considering the choices they had made over the span of fifty years. Brenda gave a fleeting thought to what might have been and then returned to the present.

"Okay," she said, "now that's out of the way, how about you tell me the truth about everything else. You're CIA, aren't you? You were always going to be CIA."

"No, not always; I tried to get out of it."

"So what Frank says is true," Brenda said.

"I don't know what Frank said," Rory blustered.

"He says that you're here to make sure that Matapa stays around and destabilizes the country."

"No," said Rory.

"Yes," said Mugabe.

"And what are you?" Brenda asked, turning to Mugabe. "What branch of the government are you? Who are you working for?"

"Not for the CIA," said Mugabe.

"He's been watching me," said Rory.

"You've destroyed our democratic process," Mugabe said.

"No," said Rory, "I've been keeping you free of Al-Qaeda."

"We can do that without the help of the CIA," Mugabe said.

"So now what are you going to do, Rory? " Brenda asked. "Are you planning on letting those children die; after all what's a few more deaths; you have enough on your conscience already, a few more won't make any difference? How does it make you feel seeing all those little children coming into town? How do you feel about burning villages, and kidnapped schoolgirls? How do you feel about all of this, Rory Marsden? Are you proud to be an American?"

"Very proud," said Rory, "although I don't expect you to understand. Someone has to do the dirty work so that America can face the world with clean hands."

"We don't need your help," Mugabe said.

Rory turned to face him. "I'm not here to help you," he said, "I'm here to keep America safe; we don't need another failed African government.___"

"Our government has not failed," Mugabe protested.

"Because we won't let it," said Rory. "So long as there are people like Matapa around, your government has an excuse to keep control; terrified people don't want democracy, they want soldiers."

"We can take care of ourselves," Mugabe said.

Rory ignored him. He looked at Brenda. "My father was CIA," he said, "and I didn't understand what he did; he would never talk about it."

"Because he was ashamed," said Brenda.

"Because it was a secret," Rory replied. "I used to be like you, thinking everything was love and peace and democracy but I grew out of it. I went to Vietnam, I understood."

"Vietnam," said Brenda. "Who the hell could understand Vietnam?"

"I could," said Rory, "after I saw the big picture."

"You've been brainwashed," she said.

Rory shook his head. "I have two numbers for you," he said, "nine and eleven."

For a moment her mind went blank.

"The World Trade Center; the Twin Towers," Rory said.

"That," she said, "was no excuse for what you're doing now."

"It's every excuse," Rory said. "We're in a war, and in wartime people get hurt."

"We're not part of your war," Mugabe said.

"You're in the front lines," Rory said. "You're at the crossroads. "If we allowed a violent overthrow of your government then_____"

"Oh stop it," Brenda said, "I don't even care why you're doing this; all I want is to get Swot back."

"I know," said Rory. He put his hand into the pocket of his jeans and pulled out a bunch of keys. "I'm going to try," he said. He left Margaret's side and unlocked the door to his inner sanctum. Brenda followed him into the small, windowless room with Mugabe close behind her. Rory flicked a switch and the room lit up.

"Solar," he said, "and car batteries."

The room held a desk and a rough wooden table loaded with electronic equipment, screens glowed, lights blinked; unlike everyone else, Brenda thought, Rory was not out of power and not out of touch with the wider world. He picked up something that looked like a cell phone from the eighties. A wire trailed from the phone to a bank of car batteries beneath the table, and another wire snaked across the ceiling and disappeared through a hole in the wall.

"This is my only hope of finding Swot," he said, "and you have to be patient."

"What is it?" Brenda asked.

"It's a satellite phone," said Mugabe,

"It's the only link I have to Matapa," Rory said. "If and when he turns on his phone I can get a GPS reading of his position; I can't do anything until he contacts me."

"You could phone him," said Brenda.

"I've tried that already," said Rory. He ran his hand through his hair and she could see his frustration. "I've been trying to reach him for days. He was just supposed to show himself and then move on through; and no one was supposed to get hurt; we just wanted to remind people that he's still around.   We didn't plan any of this; you have to believe me."

"I don't know why I should," Brenda replied.

"Because___" He never finished his sentence. "Someone's at the door," he said.

With a surprising display of strength for a man of his age, he shoved Mugabe out of the room, and grabbed Brenda's arm pulling her along with him and closing the door firmly behind him. Margaret was where they had left her, snoring on the sofa, her mouth wide open. Someone was calling Brenda's name and banging on the front door.

"Brenda, are you in there? Brenda?"

"It's Frank," she said.

"The Irishman?" Rory asked.

"Yes," she said, "he's the one who helped me work out what you were doing and why."

"You can't tell him," Rory said.

"I can do what I like," Brenda replied, heading for the front door. Rory turned away from her and dashed back into his secret room. She heard the click as the door locked behind him.

"That's not going to help you," she shouted furiously.

Mugabe walked calmly past her and opened the front door revealing not only Frank, but also the Bishop.

"Something's happened," Frank said.

"Is it the children?"

"No, it's your husband."

For a moment Brenda forgot who her husband was; her mind was fully occupied with other things; plus for the past fifty years she had been without a husband. Frank mistook her incomprehension for distress.

"It's a stroke," he said, "that's what the doctor says. You should come; he's asking for you."

"Herbert?" she said, trying to drag her mind away from the problem of Rory and the locked door.

"You need to be with him," said the Bishop. "Come with us, we'll take you to him."

"I can't come with you," she said, looking back into the room.

"I'll stay here," said Mugabe. "You go with them; I can take care of this...problem."

Brenda looked at the set of Mugabe's shoulders, the way that he held his body, and sensed his controlled power. Yes, she thought, Mugabe will take care of this; for the moment.

CHAPTER TWENTY

A car and a driver awaited Brenda outside of Rory's gate, the engine idling and headlights illuminating the potholed dirt road. Brenda climbed in with the Bishop and Frank and the car bumped onto the main street and into the center of town. The buildings were mostly shrouded in darkness with the occasional flicker of light from an oil lamp, but in the darkness people were still moving up and down, still talking, and still going about their business. They stopped in front of the one building that was blazing with electric light.

"Private clinic," said the Bishop. "We thought it best."

"So what happened?" Brenda asked.

"He fell to the floor," Frank said, "just after you left. He was very distressed, you know, when you left him."

It sounded like an accusation and Brenda responded accordingly. "I had things to take care of," she said.

"And...?" Frank asked.

"I'll tell you later," she said, "but the long and the short of it is, you were right; he is what we thought."

"Ah," said Frank.

"Come," said the Bishop.

They climbed out of the car and went in through the front doors of the clinic. The room inside was brightly lit, clean, modern; on a par with a modest doctor's office in the U.S.

"This is the best clinic we have," the Bishop said.

"If this is where the doctor waits for his private patients," Frank said, bitterness creeping into his tone, "then it's nothing like the hospital."

"We could not send a man of your husband's stature to the government hospital," the Bishop said. "In the hospital they would let him die."

"Yes," Brenda replied, "I gather he's not popular with the people."

"It is not easy for our people to trust those in authority," the Bishop said cautiously.

"Perhaps there will be a rebellion," Frank said, and then he smiled apologetically. "Sorry," he said, "What can I say? I'm Irish, we're all for rebellion."

An inner door opened and a smiling African man appeared in a crisp white coat, a stethoscope slung around his neck.

"You are the wife?" he asked sounding surprised. Brenda assumed that no one had told him that the RDC's wife was a wild haired old white woman.

"Yes," she said, "I'm his wife. What's happened to him?"

"A small stroke," said the doctor. "We are going to treat him. " He thrust a piece of paper at her. "This is what we will need. You can obtain it from my pharmacy next door."

"What?"

"We understand his arteries are blocked; this is what they told him at Mulago. We will give him blood thinners; you can obtain them from my pharmacy."

"What are you talking about?" Brenda asked. "Why haven't you treated him already?"

"We are waiting for you to buy the drugs," the doctor said.

"Me?"

"Yes, he says you will pay. I think he will also need water, and some other things; pajamas, a little food, some clean sheets___"

"You haven't treated him?" Brenda repeated. "Don't you know anything? If it's a stroke, he needs blood thinners now; I don't know much but I know that much. Why are you waiting?"

He smiled apologetically. "We are waiting for you to buy them, Madame."

"And meantime you're doing nothing?"

"He is in bed. He is comfortable."

Brenda shoved her way past the doctor and through into the examination room. Herbert, still fully dressed, was flat on his back on an old iron hospital bed. He looked at her with wide, frightened eyes.

"Can you speak?" she asked.

He mumbled something. She came closer.

"Need the drugs," he said, struggling to produce the words.

"I know," Brenda said, "and this little shit is going to give them to you."

He shook his head.

"What?" she asked.

He shook his head again.

"Can you move your arms and legs?" Brenda asked. Many, many years ago, when she had just returned from Africa Brenda's father had a stroke. He remained paralyzed down his left side for the rest of his life, although he did regain his ability to speak and tell her what he thought of her marriage to Herbert. From the day that she had seen her father reduced from a powerful authority figure to a weakened shell of a man, Brenda had lived in fear of the very idea of a stroke. She made it her business to know about strokes and the importance of the first three hours; she knew that Herbert should already be receiving treatment, not lying around waiting for her to go the pharmacy on his behalf.

Herbert made flopping movements with both of his legs and his right arm; his left arm remained limp and unmoving; he looked at it in fear.

"It'll be okay," Brenda said, "they can do wonderful things these days," She looked around the room, clean, neat and almost devoid of equipment, "although I doubt they can do very much here."

She turned to the doctor. "What the hell are you waiting for?" she asked.

"I'm sorry," said the Bishop, "but this is our way. Someone must pay for the drugs before they are given to the patient. The supply is very small and most people cannot pay. There are so many people."

"Yes, Brenda said, "but____"

Frank pulled a wad of paper money from his pocket. "How much do you need?" he asked.

"Don't____"

"This isn't the time to stand on principles," Frank said. He handed his roll of money to the doctor. "Go and get what he needs and bring me the change," he said.

"You can't trust____"

"Yes, I can," said Frank.

The doctor left the room clasping the roll of money. Frank leaned over the bed and took hold of Herbert's limp hand.

"I will pray for you, brother," he said. "I'm believing for a complete healing."

Herbert managed to smile with half of his face, while the other half remained slack and unmoving.

"He will need you to stay with him," the Bishop said to Brenda, "and bring him whatever he needs. That is our way."

"That's what nurses are for," Brenda argued.

"No," said the Bishop. "Patients are cared for by their families. It is our way."

"Well that's ridiculous," she said. "I don't have time to care for him."

"He's your husband," the Bishop said, sounding both shocked and disappointed.

Brenda looked down at the man in the bed; the man she had shut out of her life for the past fifty years. What had she been thinking? What on earth had made her think that she could bring Swot to this alien place and demand that she call it home? Why had she been lording it over Herbert's other wives; the ones who knew how to kill a goat, and cook over a charcoal fire, and give birth to baby after baby, and live within the harsh hierarchy of a polygamous household? She didn't belong here. She didn't belong with this man. They were strangers to each other with nothing to unite them except a long ago passion that had produced a child whom Herbert had never even seen.

"He's not my husband," Brenda said, "and I'm not his wife."

Herbert made a grunting sound. She went to him and took hold of his other hand, the one that could still clasp her hand.

"It's over," she said. "I'm not going to torment you any longer. You have your wives, and I can't be one of them."

He gave her his lopsided smile.

She leaned close to him and whispered in his ear. "I loved you," she said softly, "and you were the sexiest thing I had ever seen."

He made another grunting sound; she thought it was laughter.

"I'm going to send someone to get Janet," she said, "she's the one who should take care of you."

She looked up at the Bishop. "Could someone go and get his wife," she asked. "I'll give you money. I'll pay for everything but I don't belong here."

The Bishop nodded his head, kind but somehow smug; surely he'd known all along that she didn't belong with Herbert; surely everyone had known since the day that she had returned that she didn't belong with Herbert; she didn't even belong in Herbert's country. She wondered briefly what they thought of Swot because, although she, Brenda, might have no claim on Herbert or on Uganda, Swot was a very different case.

The thought of Swot brought a stab of remembrance and a return of the panic that she had pushed into the background while she had meditated on her relationship with Herbert.

Selfish bitch she said to herself, and about herself; doubly selfish because she had only been concerned about Swot while Herbert had a double loss; his granddaughter and Matthew, his son.

"You go," said the Bishop. "One of the nuns will come while we wait for the other wife."

Well, at least he didn't say the "real" wife. She planted a quick kiss on Herbert's forehead while he was in no position to forbid it and they went out to the waiting room.

The doctor hurried in through the outer door clasping a brown paper bag. "You are leaving?" he asked.

"Everything is under control," said the Bishop.

"Ah," said the doctor and he headed for the inner room.

"Wait a minute," Brenda said.

The doctor hesitated.

"Do you have the change?" she asked.

"Change?"

"From my friend's money."

"Ah, yes," the doctor felt in his pocket and handed a wad of money to Frank.

"And the receipt," Brenda said.

"Ah."

"Forget it," said Frank. "Just let it go."

"No," said Brenda, "we need the receipt."

"This doctor is an honest man," said the Bishop.

"Oh yeah," said Brenda. "If he's so honest how come he's not down at the hospital treating all the other people; people with no money."

Frank took hold of Brenda's arm. "There are some things you can't fix," he said. "Is this really the hill you want to die on? Is this the place where you want to make your stand?"

Brenda took a deep breath. "No," she said, "you're right, this isn't my fight and I'm not going to make it my fight; Rory Marsden is my fight."

"Okay then," said Frank, "then let's go and fight that fight and leave this doctor to get on with his work."

"I just want him to know that I'm onto his game," Brenda said.

"And now he knows," said Frank, "and it doesn't make a scrap of difference. Let's just thank God that this man is available to take care of your husband, and he seems to know what he's doing. Perhaps God is preserving your husband's life for some special reason. Perhaps he has a special task for him to do; perhaps he has something special for you to do."

"Must you bring God into everything?" Brenda asked.

The evangelist smiled. "He's already in everything," he said. "He doesn't need me to bring him in."

"So it's God's fault that Swot's been kidnapped?" Brenda said.

"I wouldn't put it like that," said Frank, "but ___"

"But nothing," said Brenda, "you talk to God if you want to; I'm going to talk to Rory Marsden."

Frank's driver returned Brenda and Frank to Rory's house and they went in through the unlocked front door. The flickering oil lamp revealed Margaret still snoring on the sofa but Mugabe was nowhere in sight. The door to Rory's inner sanctum was still firmly closed. Brenda brushed past Margaret and thumped on the door.

"Open it," she shouted. "Open this door you bastard."
She heard Frank's hiss of disapproval or maybe disappointment that half an hour in the presence of a near-death experience had not cooled her temper.
"Get out here," she shouted.
The door rattled; someone was pulling back a bolt. The door swung open but the figure that emerged was not Rory Marsden; it was Mugabe.
"What are you doing? Where is he? "Brenda asked as she shoved her way past Mugabe.
"He has gone," Mugabe said.
"But how...?"
Mugabe pointed up at the ceiling where a panel had been removed. "Across the rafters, into the bedroom and out the back door. I became suspicious but I was too late," he said. "I entered the room the same way he left," he added."
"How long has he been gone? "Brenda asked.
Mugabe shrugged his broad, eloquent shoulders. Brenda looked around the room; the equipment was dead; no red lights, green lights or flashing lights, no glowing screens, and most especially no satellite phone.
"He turned everything off," she said, somewhat redundantly.
"And he took the phone," said Frank who had crowded in behind her and who was, like Brenda, stating the obvious.
"Well," Frank patted Brenda's shoulder, "I think this is good news."
Brenda gave him the benefit of what Swot called her "stink eye".
"No, really," Frank protested, "he's gone to get them."
"No," said Mugabe, "he doesn't know where they are."
"But he could use the phone to find out," said Frank. "He could home in on its signal, couldn't he?"
"It's not that simple," said Mugabe.
"If he had a GPS___" said Frank.
Mugabe shook his head. "He would need a satellite signal locator; if he is truly CIA, then maybe he has one."
"You seem to know an awful lot," said Brenda. "How come you know so much?"

Mugabe ignored her question.

"If he really knew where Matapa has his camp, "he said, "I believe he would have gone to rescue your granddaughter. He is honorable in his own way."

"How can you say that after everything he's done?" Brenda asked.

"He has been serving his country," Mugabe said. "I cannot agree with what he has done, but I can understand it. He is correct when he says that Uganda stands at the cross roads, and the West is very worried about us and the possibility that we will become a Moslem nation. Many people here were swayed by money from Muammar Gaddafi; he helped us to build roads, and factories, and mosques, and he even paid people to convert to Islam, and for Moslems to take Christian wives. He was a friend to our President."

"Gaddafi's dead," said Frank.

"And other leaders of other countries are waiting to take his place," Mugabe replied, "and the US government is very worried about that. Is it surprising that a man like Rory Marsden would try to stop that?"

"Not with the lives of children," said Brenda.

Mugabe shook his head sadly. "African children," he said, "do not have the same value in the eyes of the world."

"Oh that's just horseshit," said Brenda.

"Not from what I've seen," said Frank.

"So are you going to just stand here and justify Rory's behavior," Brenda asked, "or are you going to do something?"

"I am going to talk to the King's soldier," Mugabe said shouldering his way past Brenda and into the living room. "Matapa has been operating close to the man's home and I believe that Haji Okolo may know more than he realizes. I will question him."

He looked down at Margaret who was now drooling in her sleep.

"Stay with her," he said, "until I return. Perhaps she knows something."

"Not on your life," said Brenda. "I'm coming with you."

"No," Mugabe said, "you are not. It is a Moslem Guest House, you will not be welcome."

"I am not asking for a welcome," Brenda said.

"We will learn nothing if you go there and make your mazungu demands," Mugabe said, and there was an edge to his voice. So far he had been polite but firm; Brenda had a feeling that he was reaching the end of his ability to be polite and his true feelings were leaking out around the edge of his stoicism.

"I just want to hear what he has to say," she protested.

"If you come with me," Mugabe said, "you will cover your head, you will walk one pace behind me, you will___ "

"I will do no such thing."

"Then you will not come," said Mugabe and he swept past her and out of the door without another word.

"Well, he told you, didn't he?" said Frank.

"Yes," said Brenda, "I guess you could say that. Things are not the way they used to be."

"I'm sorry," said Frank, "this must all be very hard for you."

"Incredibly hard," Brenda said, and was surprised to feel tears pricking at the back of her eyelids. She turned her back on the Irishman's sympathy. She didn't need sympathy, not now, she needed something to do. She distractedly examined the books on Rory's bookshelves; a collection of out of date paperbacks, with yellowed pages and dog eared covers, and then tucked into the farthest corner, she found a picture in a cheap frame, its color faded by the passage of years; six laughing white kids lined up in front of a battered Volkswagen mini-bus. She carried the picture to the light.

"That was us," she said to Frank.

They looked at the picture together.

"You haven't changed much," Frank said, "that's you, isn't it?" He stabbed his fingers at the tall blonde in the center of the frame. Oh yes, Brenda thought, that was her with her hair an unruly mass of yellow curls, her neck swathed in several layers of chunky beaded necklaces, and her legs hidden by a chiffon skirt. She remembered the skirt, it was the one that she had tie dyed herself by using stones from their campsite, and a package of red dye she had found on a dusty shelf in the back of a general store in Bulawayo. She knew that she had made quite a mess of the sink in the Ladies washroom and she had walked away from the mess without cleaning up; she had been walking away for her whole life; always leaving others to clean up her mess..

"No," she said to Frank, "I haven't changed much; I'm still hanging onto my youth; pathetic isn't it? When that picture was taken you weren't even born."

"I meant it as a compliment," Frank said.

"I know."

Frank pointed at a figure lurking in the background of the picture. "Who's that?" he asked.

Brenda squinted to get her eyes in focus; even if nothing else had changed her eyes had most certainly changed, and not for the better.

"That's Margaret," she said. She couldn't see the face clearly but she recognized the flower printed shirtwaist dress and the tightly controlled brown hair.

"She looks unhappy," Frank said.

"Your eyes must be better than mine," Brenda said, "but you're right, she didn't approve of us; we had come for a good time and she had come to minister to the heathen. She would have approved of you."

Brenda returned the picture to the bookshelf.

"There's nothing you can do here," Frank said.

"I'm well aware of that," Brenda said sharply, "everyone has made it very clear that they don't need my help."

"I thought that perhaps you should lie down for a few minutes and try to get some rest," Frank said.

"Oh that's right, let the old lady take a nap," said Brenda. "Perhaps there's a rocking chair."

"I didn't mean___"

"Oh yes you did, she said as she stalked out of the room. She knew where Rory's guest room was and suddenly she wanted to lie down. Frank was correct, there was nothing else for her to do, and she was tired. The golden girl in the tie dyed skirt would not have been tired, but Brenda wasn't the golden girl any longer; she was a woman of seventy who was facing up to the fact that she had never done anything really useful in her entire life.

She stumbled into the darkened room and flung herself down on the bed, squeezing her eyes closed. The picture of the six travelers laughing and Margaret scowling seemed to be projected on the inside of her eyelids. She focused in on Rory standing there smiling nonchalantly. Had the whole journey been a lie; a cover story so Rory could spy for his father? Had they all been tools of the CIA? Her exhausted brain tried to grapple with the thought that everything, even her marriage to Herbert, and the birth of her daughter; the very fact of Swot's existence, could be laid at the feet the CIA. She was too tired to be angry; too tired to feed any more fuel into the fires of her anger or to hold onto her straying thoughts. She slept.

When she awoke the sun was shining at full strength through the bedroom window and the sounds of an African morning filtered into the room. Women called, children laughed, a goat bleated loudly and then was silenced, rattletrap vehicles passed by on the road, but no roosters crowed, no birds sang. Brenda sat up, filled with panic. Had she slept through the dawn bird chorus and the morning alarms of the roosters? What on earth time was it?

She stumbled out into the living room where she found Frank coaxing Margaret to drink the cup of tea she was clutching in her skinny hands. Her eyes were rimmed in red but she was calmer than the night before and more connected to reality.

"Any word?" Brenda asked.

Frank shook his head.

"What time is it?"

"Past eleven."

"What?"

"You needed the sleep," Frank said.

Margaret stood up shakily and handed the tea cup back to Frank.

"I'm going home," she said.

"Are you sure it's safe?" Frank asked.

"They have what they want," Margaret said, "so they don't need me. They already have Brenda's granddaughter."

The look she gave Brenda contained some small shreds of

sympathy.

"Do you want my driver to take you?" Frank asked.

Margaret shook her head. "I have my bicycle," she said.

"No you don't," Brenda said, her mind clearing as she remembered that Margaret had come with them in Herbert's car. "You weren't riding your bicycle."

"It has been brought here," Margaret said, "and anyway I have another one." She stopped abruptly. "I have two bicycles?"

To Brenda the last remark sounded more like a question than a statement, as though Margaret could not understand why she had two bicycles.

"I need to go," Margaret said. She set the teacup down. "Thank you for your prayers," she said to Frank, and then she let herself out of the front door.

"So you've been praying," said Brenda, "wouldn't you have been better off looking for Mugabe, or Rory, or talking to the police?"

"I don't know how to do those things," Frank said, "but I know that God does."

"What did you pray for?" Brenda asked. "How could you even put it into words, there's so much?"

"There's never too much for God to handle," Frank said. He pulled a small battered Bible from his shirt pocket. "The Lord has given me a word," he said.

Brenda rolled her eyes. Possibly, just possibly, she was beginning to feel a need for this God who had sent Frank to the back country of Uganda, but she wasn't ready for phrases such as the one he had just used. The Lord has given me a word, indeed! How corny was that?

"Mugabe isn't coming back for us, is he?" she asked.

"Apparently not," Frank said, thumbing through his Bible.

"And we don't have any other plan?"

"No," said Frank.

"So we're screwed," Brenda said.

Frank leaned forward, his Bible open in front of him. "God gave me this from the Psalms," he said.

"What do you mean by gave you?"

"Sometimes God gives me a chapter and a verse from the Bible."
"I still don't understand," said Brenda, wishing that she could.
"He puts it into my head," Frank said. "Just listen; "Psalm 104: O Lord, how manifold are your works! In wisdom have you made them all; the earth is full of your creatures."
He closed his Bible.
"That's it?" Brenda said.
"That's it."
"What does it mean?"
"I have no idea."
"But you find that comforting?" Brenda asked.
"Yes," said Frank.

CHAPTER TWENTY ONE
Swot Jensen

Exactly as Swot had predicted, the invasion of safari ants created panic in Matapa's squalid encampment. The boy soldiers, forgetting their pretensions of maturity, ran wildly, firing their weapons at everything and nothing; the already frightened girls just ran in circles and screamed. Swot joined in the running and the screaming and tried to stay away from the random gunshots. Unlike everyone else her running was not without purpose because, although she was waving her arms and yelling like everyone else, she was running towards Matapa's tent and not away from it. Out of the corner of her eye she saw Matthew and Cecelia slip away into the thick underbrush.

When she sensed that the screaming was coalescing into coherent words and that someone would soon realize the cause of the panic, she prolonged the confusion by shouting as loudly as she could in French and German, and a little Chinese she had picked up along the way. She was actually in the doorway of the green tent before the majority of the little thugs charged with guarding her realized that they were not under attack by men with guns, just ants with sharp teeth.

She was on her way into the tent to grab the phone and make her getaway when her way was blocked by Matapa's lieutenant. She was behind him and he didn't see her because he was concentrating on the man in the bed, but, nonetheless, he was blocking the doorway. The ants had swarmed across the discarded chicken bones of Matapa's meals in a great black tide and were following the scent of meat up the legs of the cot and across the blanket; millions of them heading towards Matapa who was struggling to rise from his bed.

Although the ants were already biting at their ankles several of the boys had apparently been helping Matapa to get to his feet but now the lieutenant waved them away. Swot had no understanding of the actual words spoken by him and by the boys but she didn't need words in order to know what was happening; the lieutenant was showing his hand and making his grab for power. All he had to do was to make sure that the man in the bed was abandoned to the mercy of the ants, and within a few minutes he would be able to claim the throne and become the new Matapa. No one outside of that tent would ever know what had happened.

The boys hesitated looking from one man to the other while the ants chewed on their ankles and the tide rolled forward up the bed. The moment was frozen in time and there was no way Swot could move forward and grab the phone without being seen. She felt pinpricks of pain at her ankles; the ants were finding a new food source. Her feet moved of their own volition, stepping sideways and backwards in an agitated jig. Matapa's glance moved beyond his treacherous lieutenant and focused on her.

"Hello girlie," he said in English, "are you still here?"

When the lieutenant turned his head to look at Swot, Matapa pulled a pistol from beneath his pillow. His hand trembled so much that his target could have been the lieutenant's head, or it could have been somewhere around Swot's left shoulder. She froze, choosing to believe that she was not the one that Matapa was trying to hit. He fired and the sound cracked through the tent. She felt the wind from the bullet as it whipped past her shoulder. Before anyone had time to react Matapa fired again and the second bullet found its mark. The lieutenant crumpled to the ground with blood trickling out of his mouth and unidentifiable materials spewing from the back of his head.

Swot wanted to move, to run, to scream, but her brain, the brain of which she was so proud, switched itself into analytical mode calmly recognizing that the bullet had penetrated the sinus cavity and that accounted for the blood in his mouth, and the substance that was coming from the back of his head was brain tissue and... and what? She pulled her brain back under her own control and forced herself to absorb the fear and shock and move on, focusing on what was happening around her and not on the minutiae of the lieutenant's wound.

Matapa threw off the blankets, scattering the tidal wave of ants. Slowly but steadily he got himself onto his feet. The boy soldiers rushed to his aid, very certain now as to what side their bread was buttered. As if the millions of ants were connected by just one brain they changed direction and began to swarm across the floor towards the blood that was pooling around the lieutenant's head.

Swot screamed; in the circumstances it seemed to be what any normal girl would do, and she was desperate to appear normal and so she let all of her emotions rise to the surface in a series of blood curdling screams, and while she was screaming she stepped out of the way of Matapa and his attendants as they headed for the door. While she was screaming she was also slapping at the ants that were crawling around her feet, and some of her shrieks were quite genuine; being attacked by safari ants was like being attacked by malevolent demons armed with tiny sharp scissors, cutting and slicing away little pieces of flesh. Swot kept her eyes cast down at her feet in ostrich mode; if she could not see Matapa, then she had to believe that he could not see her. She knew the idea was ridiculous, but she could not bring herself to look up and so she saw only a parade of feet as the boys helped Matapa out of the tent. When the feet were no longer visible, she ran forward into the great sea of shining predators. Thousands of ants squelched beneath her feet as she lunged for the phone pulling it loose from the charging station and concealing it behind her back and then she made a dash for the open air.

She was only seconds behind Matapa as she slipped out of tent.

Somehow he was still on his feet, the pistol still in his hands and his soldiers gathering around. He saw her at once.

"Hey girlie," he shouted, "what are you doing in my tent?"

For a moment her heart stopped beating, and then it started to pound. What was she doing in his tent? Good question.

"I didn't know..."she said, and the tremble in her voice was very real. "I didn't know what was happening. I thought___"

"You thought maybe I'd died," Matapa said with a wheezing laugh. "Take more than a few ants to kill me, girlie."

"Oh," Swot said, "I didn't know. Ants? Were they just ants?"

"Just ants," Matapa said. "Yah, how do you like our African ants, girlie?"

Swot used her free hand to slap at the ants that were still chewing on her legs and making their way up her skirt. Matapa didn't seem to notice that she was only using one hand.

"So," he said, "you see how we take care of things around here?"

"Yes," said Swot, and again she didn't have to force the tremor in her voice.

"So don't be trying anything," Matapa said.

He turned and snapped a command and the pregnant girl Swot had met the night before came forward with a battered plastic garden chair. Matapa sat, still holding the pistol. Swot stood where she was, not daring to step away, but feeling her opportunity passing as the scattered members of Matapa's camp began to reassemble; any moment now someone would come up behind her and see what she held concealed behind her back. The phone was too big to push into her waistband or slide up under her tee shirt. How long would it be before someone realized that Matthew and Cecelia were missing? She tried to console herself with the thought that they might have had time to climb out of the gorge but she knew it was foolish to hope that Matthew had made enough progress. Perhaps Cecelia would abandon him. Would Cecelia do that she wondered, would she just leave Matthew to his fate?

Matapa issued another command and his two nursemaids approached him on their knees and began to pick away at the stray ants that still clung to his arms. Swot hated Matapa with every fiber of her being but she had to admire the stoicism with which he had ignored his own discomfort while he reasserted his authority. Matapa's acknowledgement of the biting ants seemed to free everyone else to do the same thing and the whole group gave themselves over to slapping and picking at their own and other people's arms and legs.

Angelique approached Swot.

"I'm okay," Swot said in French, "I've got it under control." She waved her free arm. "Look no ants.

Angelique came closer.

"No really," she said.

Angelique's face was set with grim determination.

"Please don't," Swot said, but Angelique ignored her protest and squatted at Swot's feet. She began to pick off the ants that clung to the hem of Swot's improvised skirt. She pushed at Swot's legs; she wanted her to turn around. Swot refused to budge. Angelique pushed again. Swot stood still. With a little snort of annoyance Angelique hitched her way around to Swot's back.

"Eh." It was a soft surprised little sound; Swot knew that Angelique had seen the phone in her hand.

"Please," Swot whispered.

"Where is the boy?"

"He's gone," she said.

"Eh;" another soft sound of surprise and approval.

Angelique came around to the front again, still on her knees.

"You go into the bushes and take off your skirt," she said loudly in heavily accented English. "You go. You be private."

Swot hesitated.

"You go," Angelique said loudly. "Go over there." She indicated a patch of bushes. "Go now," she whispered in French, "and then run."

"Thank you," Swot said.

"You run," Angelique repeated. "You say where we are. You tell people."

"I will," Swot said.

"I want to go home," said Angelique.

243

Swot stepped away into the bushes and headed uphill as fast as she could. Behind her, she could hear Angelique chattering away as though she was still talking to Swot. She was giving Swot as much time as she could. Swot climbed rapidly, moving beyond the sound of Angelique's individual voice until the sounds of the camp were just a jumbled babble of sound far below. So far the sound had not congealed into any organized cries of alarm; they didn't know yet that their prize mazungu was missing. She imagined that she was not at that moment a priority; priority must surely go to the fact that Matapa had just killed his lieutenant and now the lieutenant's body with its attendant blanket of carnivorous ants was stopping anyone from getting into the tent; stopping anyone from seeing that the satellite phone was no longer on its charger.

Swot moved as quietly she could through the undergrowth. She did not dare to follow the muddy path up the hill and she had told Matthew and Cecelia to keep to the right and head upward. She tried to do the same thing, hoping that she would soon come across them. She could see a patch of sunlight ahead; a clearing in the forest; her first chance to get a signal for the phone but she hesitated, wondering if she was still too close to the camp.

She passed through into the patch of light and called for Matthew. No answer. She called again; nothing; she must have bought them enough time to move even further up the hill.

She blundered back into the undergrowth and then realized that she was leaving a path of broken branches and beaten down bushes that could be tracked by anyone with any kind of tracking skills. She forced herself to slow down and step carefully. She could see two areas of sunlight ahead; two clearings in the forest. She looked down at the ground; no footprints; no broken twigs, no sign that Matthew and Cecelia had passed that way. She renewed her grip on the phone. Much as she hated to admit it, Matthew and Cecelia were not her priority; her priority was reaching beyond the gorge and letting someone know where she was, and, more importantly, where Matapa was.

She stepped carefully to the left heading for the closest patch of light and came out into a clearing where several huge old trees had fallen across a little stream. Something moved in the branches overhead and she heard a chorus of jabbering alarm calls. Black shapes careened through the branches around her setting the tree tops swaying. Not gorillas she told herself, there are no gorillas here; chimpanzees, just cute, friendly little chimpanzees although the sounds they were making were neither cute nor friendly. Swot knew that she couldn't stop until she was clear of their chimpanzees' territory because their territorial fussing would give away her position. She moved on, heading uphill towards the next patch of sunlight. The chimpanzees let her pass unhindered and peace was restored to the forest.

The next clearing was larger and, looking up, Swot could see a wide swathe of blue sky. She turned on the power button of the phone, pulled out the antenna and aimed it at the sky. A green light blinked and the screen glowed pale blue; she thought she had never seen such a beautiful sight. Her fingers trembled as she started to dial, She had only one phone number committed to memory; every other number was stored on her own cell phone at home. No one memorized phone numbers; no one except little kids, and when Swot was a little kid the only number she needed to memorize was her home phone. That was all she had now; genius or not, she only knew one phone number

She started to dial and then stopped, no, no; country code; what was the country code? Did she know what it was? Yes, of course, she had commented on it to her father before she left home. How come, she asked him, that the US has the number 1 as its country code; do we think we are so important? Her father had laughed and told her he didn't know the answer but he hoped that travel would broaden her mind and that she would be a good representative of her country and her family, and that she wouldn't be too much of a show off.

She redialed, and the phone gave her an error message. Error! What was the error? What was she doing wrong? At last she remembered and she was ready to kick herself for wasting precious time. How could she have forgotten something so important? How could she have forgotten how the now deceased lieutenant had raged about using the access code? She turned the phone over, studied the code on the reverse side and tried to push aside her panic and commit it to memory. She dialed as fast as she could before the number could slip away and entangle itself in the memory of the ants, and the lieutenant, and the bullet whizzing past her ear.

She completed the code, listened to a few more clicks and buzzes, assumed they were a good sign and punched in her home phone number. More clicks, more buzzes, and then a faraway sound, the sound of her home phone ringing in faraway Cleveland. "Don't go to voice mail," she prayed. She heard her father's voice. "Hello, you have reached Erik Jensen, I'm sorry we can't take your call....."

CHAPTER TWENTY TWO

Swot's mind was racing. How long could the message be? Thirty seconds? Maybe less than thirty seconds. She tried to assemble a couple of sentences that would convey the horror of their situation, the existence of Matapa, because most certainly her father had no idea he existed, and instructions to call the American Embassy, and then...and then what? Oh yes, home in on the satellite signal.

She was ready, the phone beeped just like every other voice mail: leave a message at the sound of the tone.

The words were on the tip of her tongue, but what came out was a hiccup of a sob and a plaintiff cry of "Dad, Daddy, pickup the phone."

Damn, she thought, she had wasted precious seconds; she would have to dial again. She was about to break the connection when she heard a sharp intake of breath and a voice on the line saying "Swot, is that you?"

"Dad?"

"No, it's Andrew."

Her brother, she didn't want to speak to her brother, she didn't even like her brother.

"What's up Swot?"

"Where's Dad? I need Dad."

"He's not here," said Andrew, "it's the middle of the day. What do you want? Have you run out of money already?"

"No, no." She drew in a deep breath. Okay, so this wasn't her father; it was Andrew. She had never been close to her older brothers; never been interested in their endless sporting activities; never respected their limited academic achievements; but time was running out. She would have to tell someone.

"You still in Uganda?" Andrew asked.

"Andrew, listen to me and don't ask questions."

"Hey," said Andrew, "chill out, Swot."

"No," Swot hissed into the phone, "you chill out. Andrew this is serious, dead serious."

"You been captured by cannibals?" Andrew asked.

"More or less," said Swot.

"What?"

"I'm serious," she said. "I'm really serious. We're all in trouble here. There's this guy, General Matapa..."

"General what?"

" Matapa, he's a sort of war lord," Swot said.

"Okay, so____"

"No, not okay. Don't talk any more, Andrew, just listen to me. I don't know how much time I have."

"Okay but___"

"Shut up," said Swot.

"Hey," said Andrew.

"This is what you have to do," Swot said. "You have to phone the American Embassy in Kampala."

"Why don't you phone them?"

"I don't have a phone."

"Yes, you do, you're talking on one."

She could hear the delight in his voice; she knew how much he resented her; how much both of her brothers resented her. So far as they were concerned she was an obnoxious know-all and Andrew was thrilled that just this once he had caught her saying something irrational. She would never live this down; if she lived at all.

"Stop it," Swot hissed. "Please Andrew, just listen; I am deadly serious." She had a sudden irrational need to cry, and she knew that another sob was starting in her throat.

"Swot," said Andrew, "are you okay?"

"No, I'm not, I'm really not."

"Okay, take a deep breath and tell me about it," Andrew said his voice suddenly serious.

Swot told him as much as she could in a shaky voice and short gasping sentences. The stolen child, the abducted girls, the death of the cell phones, Matapa, Matthew (she supposed that strictly speaking Matthew was also Andrew's uncle but that was not important; there was no time for explanations), and then Rory Marsden's betrayal, whatever that might mean.

"Call Dad," she implored, "get him to call the Embassy. He has to do it now. I can't stay hidden for long and he's going to kill the baby; he's going to eat her heart."

"Swot!" Andrew was teetering on the edge of disbelief.

"It's true," Swot said. "You have to believe me."

"Do you know where you are?" Andrew asked.

"No," she said, "but we're in a kind of gorge and I'm going to leave this satellite phone switched on; they should be able to get a GPS fix on it."

"I don't think that's how it works," said Andrew.

"They'll know what to do," Swot said desperately. "They'll have something."

"But Swot___" said Andrew.

She heard a commotion in the trees down below her. The chimpanzees were shrieking again, and shaking the tree tops; someone was climbing the hill and voices were calling; she could hear them above the shrill cries of the chimpanzees.

"I have to go," she said to Andrew.

"Swot," said Andrew.

"What?"

"Be careful."

"Yeah," she said, "I'll be careful but you'd better do what I told you."

"I will," he said, "don't worry. I'm going to take care of it."

The need to cry was returning. "Don't go," she whispered but he had already broken the connection and the phone was silent in her hands, the green light still glowing. All she could do now was hope that Andrew had been wrong about the Embassy having no way to track the signal; surely they had some kind of device; if not GPS, then something else; her plan was tenuous enough without Andrew throwing any more obstacles in her way.

Choosing stealth over speed she crept out of the clearing, easing her way into the undergrowth. She knew that she had been careless on her first mad dash from the camp, leaving a trail of broken twigs, and muddy footprints, but after that she had been careful. If the trackers were on her trail now it was because they had heard the disturbed chimpanzees; but that was it; when they reached the chimpanzee territory they would find no further clues; she was quite certain of that. She moved cautiously through the bushes; they would expect her to go uphill, making a dash for the road, so she angled herself slightly downhill. All she had to do was keep the phone safe, keep the signal on and keep away from Matapa's thugs and ....Matthew and Cecelia, how could she have forgotten about them? They were waiting for her somewhere, but where?

She worked her way sideways across the hillside moving towards the general direction that she had sent Matthew and Cecelia. She suspected that she had moved too far up the hill, and moved too fast; Matthew would not be moving so fast, hobbling on his improvised crutch.

She continued her furtive progress through the undergrowth swallowing her fear of whatever might be hidden in the damp soil beneath her feet, snakes, lizards, more ants; she couldn't afford to take them into consideration. For someone who had grown up in a wealthy Cleveland suburb of landscaped lawns, chlorinated swimming pools, and paved walking trails she thought she was doing pretty well. She didn't realize how tightly she was holding her feelings in check until something grabbed at her ankle. She jumped backwards, and allowed herself a small squeak of alarm before she remembered that she must be silent. She could hear her pursuers thrashing around in the bushes some distance away, but the chimpanzees had quieted down again; if she had screamed the way she wanted to scream, she would have been heard, no doubt about it.

The something, whatever it was, grabbed her ankle again. She looked down; a hand, a girl's hand; Cecelia. With a sigh of relief Swot sank down into a crouch and peered into the bushes.

"In here," said Cecelia.

Swot crawled into the small clearing behind the bushes and found Cecelia and Matthew waiting for her. "I talked to my brother," Swot whispered, "I think he understood. We have to keep the signal open, and I think we have to get clear of the trees."

"We should climb up to the top of the gorge," Cecelia said, "but I don't know about Matthew___"

"I can do it," Matthew said.

"I don't think you can," said Cecelia. She turned to Swot. "He is tired already," she said, "and he is slow."

"I'm not leaving him behind," said Swot.

"But___"

"No," said Swot. "Let's go; all of us; up the hill."

The uphill slope was slippery with mud and dead leaves and grew steeper as they climbed. The road that led down into the bottom of the gorge followed a series of switchbacks across the hillside, but if they were to stay clear of the road they had to go straight up the hill. Within a few minutes Swot knew that, despite his best efforts, Matthew was not going to make it. His crutch slipped in the mud for the last time and he lay face downward panting with exhaustion. He looked at Swot with defeat in his eyes.

"You have to leave me behind," he said.

"No."

"You must. I'll hide; I'm very good at hiding. If I stay still they won't find me, and then when help comes..."

If help comes, Swot thought to herself.

"You know he's right," said Cecelia.

Swot was surprised by her own indecision. She had always been logical, and logically the best thing to do was to leave Matthew behind so why was she having so much trouble making the only logical decision? Well, whatever the difficulty, the decision had to be made.

"Are you sure?" she asked.

"Yes," said Matthew. "Go."

Swot and Cecelia went, moving faster now, scrambling on their hands and knees up the hillside until they were above the tree canopy and the sky was a blue bowl above their heads. As they cleared the tree line the light on the phone began to blink, and the phone buzzed.

"Someone's calling," said Swot.

"Keep it quiet," said Cecelia.

"I'm trying." Swot stared in panic at the phone's number pad as it continued to buzz.

"Answer it," said Cecelia.

"No."

"Perhaps it's your brother," Cecelia said.

"And perhaps it isn't," said Swot, amazed at the fact that her brain seemed to be so full of concern for Matthew that she was unable to cope decisively with any new input.

The phone continued its urgent buzzing and Cecelia grabbed it from Swot's hand, pressing buttons indiscriminately until the buzzing stopped and was replaced by a voice.

"Hey," said the voice.

"Hello," said Cecelia.

"Who is this?" asked the voice.

Swot recognized the voice; Rory Marsden. At last her mind cleared and she was able to think again. She pulled the phone from Cecelia's hands and stabbed at the red button, severing the connection.

"You can't turn it off," Cecelia said. "How will they find us?"

"If we leave it on, he'll find us," Swot said.

"Who was it?" Cecelia asked.

"Someone I don't trust," said Swot.

"You have to turn it back on," Cecelia insisted.

Swot clasped the phone to her chest and forced herself to be still and to think. Brenda's words swum into her mind; the lady or the tiger; here it was again. Turn the phone off and avoid Rory

Marsden, turn the phone on and allow someone, anyone, to find Matapa's camp. She turned the problem over and over in her mind. What did she really know about Rory Marsden? Well, she knew that he had only pretended to be out of touch with the American Embassy and the world in general, because apparently he still had a working phone. She knew that Matapa had Marsden's phone number and she knew something else; yes, she knew that Rory was angry with Matapa. What was it he had said; he had said that he hadn't agreed. Hadn't agreed to what; to kidnapping Matthew; to kidnapping Swot?

"We have to turn it on again," Cecelia repeated.

Yes, Swot thought, the girl was right; they had to keep the phone on. Her whole plan relied on the tenuous thread of contact; her brother phoning the Embassy; the Embassy tracking the signal. She pressed the green button and the lights glowed again. The plan was rubbish, she thought, ridiculously optimistic rubbish, but it was all she had.

"Let's go," she said. They started to climb again. The rim of the gorge was not far above them now; hopefully they would come out onto the road and then they would...Swot had not thought that far. The light was brighter now, the trees were thinning; they were on the final slippery stretch of hillside crawling on their hands and knees and grabbing at roots and branches to haul themselves upwards.

Cecelia was ahead, her feet slipping and sliding and sending mud cascading down onto Swot's head. Blinded by the shower of dirt, Swot moved sideways, grasping at a clump of grass.

"I can see the road," Cecelia shouted. "We made it."

Swot saw the other girl pull herself over the lip of the gorge and disappear from sight. Desperate to follow Swot tightened her grasp on the tough grassy clump and pulled herself upwards. The grassy roots gave way and suddenly Swot was clasping at air. Her feet scrabbled for purchase among the leaves and stones and found none. She started to slide, her face buried in the mud. Her hands worked of their own accord, her right hand reaching groping for a hold, her left hand releasing the satellite phone. She had only a brief moment to register the fact that the phone was gone, falling into the leafy canopy below, before she too was falling and screaming, screaming, screaming.

Matapa struggled to breathe. Unless he could be rid of the curse he would die here in this patch of green forest that reminded him so much of the great forests of his childhood. He would not die; no, he had come too far to be destroyed by the petty evil spirits that had taken up residence in his chest, scarred his face, and brought unending weariness to his body. He would make magic, he himself, the great Matapa would bring about his own healing.

He set aside his memories of the old man who had journeyed with him as he grew to manhood; the old man who had told him that he had no talent for witchcraft. The years had passed, Matapa had grown strong, nothing was beyond his reach; all he needed was the sacrifice.

He had heard what the white men said of this curse; that it was not the work of an enemy but a natural thing, a random sickness transmitted by sexual acts. He heard other people, African men, saying that this strange thing, this illness was something manufactured by the white man in an attempt to destroy the virility of the African man; to make him fearful of going to women and to make sure that no babies could be born. Matapa dismissed both of these ideas with contempt. He knew the white men; he had fought alongside them and he had seen them go to prostitutes and village women; he had even seen some of them raping their captives; they would not do that if they themselves had poisoned the deep private places of the African women so that lying with them would bring about their own death. No, Matapa knew full well what this thing was; it was a curse, a new skill learned by the witchdoctors and used throughout Africa. Someone had used this curse on him, and was now using it on his followers for many of them had the same signs on their bodies, running sores, raging fevers, coughs, and night sweats. He would cure them all. It was in his power.

He shifted his weight on the spindly plastic chair. The camp was ruined; they would move on; he had given the order. As soon as the child was brought to him, as soon as he had made the magic, they would move out.

He thought about the American; the one who had told him to frighten, but not to kill. This, he knew, was impossible for how could the fear spread if he did not kill? Now the American was angry and no doubt he would soon withdraw his protection. Yes, it was time to move west, back to Congo where they had no need of American protection. The work in Uganda could be done by someone else; Matapa was ready to go back to the forests of his home.

A terrified boy came to speak to him, his voice so soft and so full of fear that Matapa was forced to lean forward in the chair to hear what the boy was telling him.

"The phone is not here."

Matapa looked at the wreckage of his tent, his personal possessions spread around the ground.

"You have not looked enough," he said.

"It's not here," the boy said. "I have looked. Someone has taken it."

"Who?" asked Matapa.

"Perhaps the mazungu girl; she saw me using it."

"Find her," said Matapa.

"We are all searching."

"What about the boy, the cripple?"

"He has gone with her."

"Then they will not go far," said Matapa. "Find them."

Matapa leaned back in his chair; the short conversation had made him breathless. He needed the magic; without it he would not have the strength for the journey out of the gorge, and he would not have the strength to fight off the next challenger for his title.

He closed his eyes and tried to recall the way in which his mentor had prepared the sacrifice; the knife, the fire; the drums. He no longer believed what the old man had said, telling him that he had no power for great magic. He was Matapa now and he had the power; he knew it. He had eaten the old man's heart; the old man lived in him.

The sound of a vehicle making its way down the switchback road into the gorge made him open his eyes. Yes, this was it; the truck he

had sent to Kajunga to collect the child.   The truck rolled into the
clearing. The driver opened the door of the cab and then turned and
reached back inside. When he turned back he had the child in his
arms, a little girl in a yellow dress. Matapa smiled. At last!
The men riding in the back threw something from the truck bed,
something that landed with a heavy thud on the muddy ground and
shouted a string of curse words such as Matapa had not heard since
he had been abandoned by the Americans in Angola; the girl; the
one who was almost white. He raised his voice in triumph.
"Hello girlie," he shouted, "you should have run faster. Now I will
have a powerful sacrifice."

CHAPTER TWENTY THREE
Cecelia

Cecelia Byaruhanga was a city girl, raised in a comfortable modern
home in Entebbe. Her father was employed at the Entebbe Airport,
and her mother ran a thriving import-export business. Every
Christmas Cecelia flew with her mother to Dubai for the latest in
fashion and electronics. Cecelia's life was marred by only one thing;
the fact that the ancestral home of her father was in Budeka. Family
tradition required that Cecelia should be exiled from the bright
lights of Entebbe, and the even brighter lights of Kampala, and be
sent to the shabby classrooms and overcrowded dormitories of the
Ursuline Academy in Budeka where she could maintain her mystic
connection to her clan, her tribe, and most of all, the family land.
Now she stood in a ditch at the edge of a goat path in a state of
disoriented panic. Nothing in her past experience had prepared her
for this moment. She had no idea where to turn for help or even
how to find the nearest village. What little she knew of rural life led
her to believe that the apparently uninhabited scrubland around
her was, in fact, quite densely populated with peasant families but
what she had learned of cautious city living also warned her that a
girl wandering alone in the bush was a prime target for robbers,
rapists, or any combination of the two.
She looked back into the gorge where the American girl had made

her sudden descent through the tree tops, her screams fading into silence as she tumbled through the branches. The falling mazungu girl had taken Cecelia's hope of rescue with her and now Cecelia had no idea whether or not the satellite phone was still sending out a signal.

She wondered if she should just set out along the barely discernible track; the direction really didn't matter; if she walked far enough she would surely encounter someone. On the other hand, perhaps she should go back into the gorge and try to find either the phone or the girl, Sarah. Of course Sarah might already be dead; a fall like that would surely inflict serious injuries; and there was the whole question of the boy; the one who was hiding somewhere down there clutching his improvised crutch and waiting to be rescued.

Cecelia heard the high pitched whine of an approaching motorcycle and instinctively shrank back into the bushes. She needed time to think, in fact she needed time to pray; she couldn't imagine what the nuns would say if they had been told that Cecelia Byaruhanga's first impulse had not been to ask the Virgin Mary for help and that she had chosen instead to fill her head with thoughts of rape and robbery. Well, she would let this motorcycle pass, and then she would pray, and trust that the next vehicle would be one sent by one of the saints in whom she placed her trust; maybe even St. Cecelia, her own personal saint.

The motorcycle was approaching cautiously, slowing down, and then finally coming to a complete standstill just a few yards from the place where Cecelia was hiding and peeking through a screen of elephant grass.

The man on the motorcycle removed his helmet and ran his hand through his hair; white man's hair. He set the helmet on the motorcycle's gas tank, and reached into the pocket of his padded jacket, producing a square black instrument of some kind; not a cell phone but something with a glowing screen. Then he reached into his other pocket and brought out a phone, the twin of the satellite phone that the white girl had stolen from Matapa. He punched some buttons, stared intensely at the phone, and then punched the buttons again.

Well, Cecelia thought, she may not be as sophisticated as the American girl, but she could put two and two together and she had a very good idea that what she was seeing was more than a coincidence. The man on the motorcycle had some kind of device that was homing in on the signal from the satellite phone exactly as Sarah had predicted. He had been following a signal but now it seemed that the signal had disappeared; he was obviously puzzled, looking at his phone, looking at the electronic device, but finding nothing. Well, that answered one question; the phone was no longer working; not surprising considering the height it had fallen. She imagined that its mangled remains were caught up in a tree somewhere far below.

Who was he, this white man on a motorcycle? She only knew of one such man in and around Budeka; Rory Marsden. She had never heard anything bad about him; in fact she had never heard anything specific at all, but he was an American; the girl, Sarah, was an American, this man had to be the answer to a prayer that she had not yet even prayed. Sending up a silent thank you to St. Cecelia, she stepped out of her hiding place and called out his name.

"Mr. Rory?"

He looked up.

"Where the hell did you come from?" he asked.

The American Embassy, Kampala, Uganda

Maurice VanBuren looked at the small group of men and women gathered in a secure, windowless room in the basement of the US Embassy. He was confident that nothing any of them said or did in this room would be heard or seen by anyone else, not even the Ambassador. He was uncomfortably aware of the fact that US Embassies all over the world functioned behind barricades and barbed wire intended to keep out all citizens of any nation other than the US. In fact the guards at the gate of this particular embassy barely acknowledged the right of US citizens to enter the stronghold of their own nation. As for those who applied for a visa to enter the US; they were directed to another building, another guarded office where they would most probably be informed that they were not welcome to visit the US for any reason whatsoever. A siege mentality had overtaken the entire building and nowhere was this more evident than in the crowded room where the official topic under discussion was the murder of Zachary Ephron.

Malia, VanBuren's assistant, a frighteningly efficient African American woman from Boston, had already delivered her opinion.

"It's an isolated incident," she said, "something local; no indication that it's connected to anything political."

"How do we know?" This from Davis, one of VanBuren's top agents, tipped back in his seat, his sweat stained safari shirt unbuttoned to reveal a lion's tooth strung on a leather cord around his neck. With his overlong hair and sun-browned face he looked exactly like the person he purported to be but was not; an itinerant safari guide, with a taste for hard liquor and well-heeled tourists.

"It's not going to be a problem," said Malia.

"How do we know that?" the agent asked again.

"Local intel," said Malia.

"Marsden," said Davis. "Do you trust that guy?"

"I trust him on this," said VanBuren. "The situation with the kid is not going to be a problem. The Ambassador called his parents."

"Not a call I would want to make," said Davis, and the other agents in the room murmured their agreement.

"Neither would I," said Van Buren, grateful as ever that he had never married, never fathered children, and never created a situation where someone would grieve over him. "The Ambassador has promised a speedy return of the body. His staff are sending in a helicopter; there's no other way in."

"Yeah, I heard about the ferry," said Davis. "That thing hasn't run since the British left; they're not gonna get it running now."

"The ferry's not our problem," said VanBuren. "Our problem is Matapa."

"Well," said Davis, "I already warned you about him."

"I'm aware of your warnings," said VanBuren, "and I'm not saying you're wrong, but Marsden's always been able to control him in the past."

"And now he's gone rogue," said Davis.

"That was always a possibility," said Malia. "We know Matapa's unstable, but we thought___"

"What we thought doesn't matter now," VanBuren interrupted. Malia shot him an annoyed glance. Hey, VanBuren thought to himself, if you want my job you can have it; you try keeping all these balls in the air.

"Here's what we all know," said VanBuren. "Matapa___"

"We don't even know the guy's name," Davis said.

"Shut it, Davis," said a voice from the back of the room. "Some of us want the facts."

Davis slid down in his seat, stretching his long legs out in front of him and fixing his gaze on his battered safari boots.

"Three nights ago," VanBuren said, "Matapa raided a boarding school and___"

"Marsden's lost control," Davis said.

VanBuren ignored the interruption. "He took prisoners, teen-aged girls, he also took the son of the local Commissioner, Herbert Barongo, God knows what he has in mind for that kid."

"We got all this at yesterday's briefing," Davis complained.

"Here's what you didn't get," said VanBuren, "because Marsden has apparently chosen not to tell us; Matapa also took the Commissioner's granddaughter, an American citizen by the name of Sarah Jensen. "

"Herbert Barongo was briefly married to an American woman in the sixties," said Malia by way of explanation, "and it seems that the granddaughter was visiting him."

"How old?" asked a voice from the back of the room.

"Eighteen," said Malia.

Davis continued to stare at his boots. "What does Marsden say?" he asked.

"Marsden's not saying anything," VanBuren said. "We didn't get this information from Marsden; we got it from the girl's father in Cleveland who made a call to the Ambassador."

He felt the sudden change in the atmosphere of the room. Davis drew in his long legs and sat up straight, chairs were shuffled, and he heard sudden intakes of breath.

"Newspapers?" asked a young woman from the back row.

"Not yet," said Malia.

"How?" asked another voice.

"Well," said VanBuren, "according to the father, the girl somehow got her hands on Matapa's phone and called her brother; asked him to track the signal and find her."

"Smart kid," said Davis.

"According to the Ambassador the girl has a genius IQ," said Malia.

"Why didn't Marsden tell us about this?" asked the female agent in the back row.

"The man's past it," said Davis, "and he's been here too long."

"We think he'll try to take care of it himself," said VanBuren.

"What?" said Davis. "The guy's seventy years old, and how long is it since he's been retrained? Has he ever been retrained?"

"He's a special case," VanBuren said, "a local asset. No one else could have done what he's done, not even you Davis. You've made it with your great white hunter act for the past ten years, try doing it for fifty years."

"If we don't produce results, the father will go public," said Malia, "and some idiot reporter is sure to connect it to the Peace Corps kid, and before we know where we are we'll be airlifting the Embassy staff out of here."

"It's not going to come to that," said VanBuren, thinking, not for the first time, that Malia was no longer happy in the role of assistant; she was ready for a transfer, even an upgrade; preferably to an Embassy on the other side of the world where she could take charge and give free rein to her desire to make doomsday predictions.

"So did we?" asked Davis.

"Did we what?" said Malia.

"Track the signal," said Davis.

"We had a brief contact," said VanBuren. "It might be enough."

He looked around the room, making an assessment of his agents and coming to the conclusion that it would have to be Davis.

"You own a suit?" he asked.

Davis flicked a lock of lank black hair out of his eyes.

"Me?"

"Yeah, we're the funeral party; you and me in the helicopter to pick up the boy. Can you think of a better way to go in?"

Davis shrugged his shoulders. "You're right," he said, "it's a good way in. Yeah, I own a suit."

"Go get dressed," said Van Buren. "Dark tie, white shirt, nothing fancy. We have to move on this. The chopper is waiting for us."

Davis rose to his feet. "And you're coming?" he asked.

"I am," said VanBuren.

"It's been a while."

"Yes, it has. Anything else you want to say?"

"Marsden?"

VanBuren shook his head. "I have no idea. He might be on top of this, he might be dead; we haven't heard. The place is cut off, no one's going in or out until the bridge is mended, or the ferry is working; so we take the chopper and we go see."

"Should we inform the Ugandan government that we won't be running Marsden and Matapa any longer?" Malia asked.

"Not yet," said VanBuren.

"Anything else I should know?" Davis asked.

"Yeah," said VanBuren, "Mugabe Is In Budeka."

" Mugabe," said Davis, "my God, whose side is he on?"

"Hard to tell," said VanBuren.

Brenda Songbird Carter, Budeka

Brenda paced around the beer garden like a caged lion. She seethed with impatience and frustration. Lunchtime had come and gone, the sun had passed directly overhead and was on its way to the western horizon and still there had been no word.

Frank nursed a beer and watched her making her way round and around the garden while the beer he had ordered for her remained on the table, sweating in the heat of the sun.

"Come and sit down," he said yet again.

"What's the point of sitting down?" Brenda asked. "Sitting down won't get us anywhere."

She stopped to look at the Irishman, recognizing the concern on his face. He's frightened I'm going to keel over, she thought. He thinks I'm too old for this. She sighed; maybe she was too old but what difference did that make; Swot was her granddaughter, and someone had to do something?

She lowered herself reluctantly into a chair and leaned forward, her elbows on the table, her face only inches away from the Irish evangelist.

"He's not coming back is he?" she said.

"Who?"

"You know who," she growled, "Mugabe. He's found out something from that old sergeant and he's not telling us what it is."

"Yes," said Frank, "I think that's probably what has happened. There's nothing you can do about it. He seems to be a very competent individual."

"Yes," said Brenda, "very competent. I wonder why he was pretending to be one of Herbert's guards."

"Pretending?"

"He's no run of the mill rent-a-thug," Brenda said.

She took a swallow of the beer; warm, bitter, pointless. The solution to the crisis did not lie in beer drinking. "How's the praying?" she asked.

Frank raised his eyebrows.

"I'm serious," she assured him. "I doubt if God would listen to my prayers, but maybe he'll listen to you; you being one of his own."

"He listens to all of us," Frank said.

"But has he told you anything else?" Brenda asked. "Last time I asked you told me something about nature or animals and ___"

"No," said Frank, "I don't know anything else, but I know that it was a true word; it meant something."

Brenda sprang to her feet again.

"We can't do this," she said, "we can't just sit here."

She looked around at the peaceful beer garden. A man in overalls was trimming the hedge; the waitresses were leaning on the bar their heads close together, whispering; smoke from the cooking fire rose from behind the kitchen.

"What's the matter with everyone?" Brenda asked. "Don't they care? This man's been terrorizing the country for years; he's stolen their children and burned their villages and they don't seem to care. Why aren't they rioting in the streets? Why do they put up with it?"

"Rioting is a dangerous thing," Frank said, "and people get hurt."

"Yeah, yeah," said Brenda, "I know you're Irish and you have all this experience at rebellion and oppression and all the rest of it, but doesn't this strike you as wrong? You would think that someone would do something?"

"I'm sure that someone is doing___"

"Well I don't see anyone doing anything," Brenda interrupted. She took another long swallow of the beer. Her heart was ready to pound out of her chest and her mind would not be stilled. "If no one else is going to do anything, then we'll have to do it," she said. She slammed the beer bottle down onto the table. "Do you still have your PA system?"

"Yes, but..."

"Will it work without electricity?"

""It runs off a car battery."

"Okay," said Brenda, "you go and set it up, and see if you can find your interpreter. We're going to talk to some of these people; correction, we're going to talk to all of these people."

"They already know everything," Frank said, "and apparently they've learned to live with it."

"No," said Brenda. "They don't know everything. They don't know that their own government is behind this."

"They might," said Frank; "they seemed pretty fed up with your husband."

"But they don't know about Rory, do they?" Brenda asked. "They don't know that the good old United States is protecting Matapa. What do you think they'll do when we tell them that Rory is a CIA agent?"

"You can't do that," Frank said.

"Why not?"

"He's an American, you're an American, blowing his cover would be, well,...treason."

"No, it wouldn't," Brenda said, "it would be freedom of speech."

"You must hate him very much," Frank said.

"Hate? No I don't hate him."

"But you want him dead," said Frank.

"Oh, it wouldn't come to that," Brenda said.

Frank looked around at the peaceful scene where Brenda seemed to be the only agitated person. "Northern Ireland," he said, "British troops on every corner. My parents took me across the border from Dublin to Belfast and young as I was I could feel it."

"Feel what?"

"The fear; it was on every face; the British Tommies, just boys really, patrolling in their armored vehicles, terrified of ambush; the women, all they wanted was for their kids to be safe; and the kids, full of hate. Everyone knew someone who had been killed and not just by the soldiers; the IRA killed its own traitors, blew up houses, and burned people in their cars." Frank paused and took a deep breath. "I found God, and I found my own peace," he said, "but I haven't forgotten what it feels like. It's here, it's like a sleeping tiger; this might look peaceful to you, but it's not; everyone here is terrified; they've been through enough, they don't want to wake the tiger."

"I have to get Swot back," said Brenda.

"And you're willing to kill Rory to get it done?" Frank asked, "And not just Rory; if you tell people what's really been happening here, they'll go after your husband, and the soldiers, and anyone else they think might be responsible. "

"I don't care about Rory," Brenda said.

"What did he do to you?" Frank asked.

"He lied," Brenda said, "we thought we were out on an adventure, having fun, seeing the world, but we were just his decoys. He didn't care about us; none of it was real."

"And all of it was fifty years ago," Frank said. "You need to grow up."

"I'm seventy years old," said Brenda, "I think I'm grown up."

"Then act like a grown-up," Frank said, "and think of some way out of this mess that doesn't involve getting Rory killed and inciting an international incident."

"It won't___" said Brenda.

"Oh yes it will," said Frank. "If you let these people know that Rory Marsden is a CIA agent and that he's working with their own government to keep Matapa safe, that'll probably bring down the government; and America will lose its foothold on this part of Africa; maybe all of Africa. And then___"

"And then what?" Brenda asked, as she tried to comprehend the reality of Frank's apocalyptic forecast.

"And then then the Islamists move in," said Frank "and that is what Rory's been trying to avoid for all these years. Uganda becomes a haven for terrorists, and your American War on Terror expands across Africa."

"No," said Brenda, "you can't hold me responsible for all of that."

"All it takes is one little spark," said Frank.

"No," said Brenda, "no, no, no." She buried her head in her hands, squeezing her eyes closed, trying to shut out the sight of Frank and his terrible accusations. Surely he was wrong; he was exaggerating, he was leaping to wild conclusions. All she wanted to do was to stir up the population of one small town; she could be their savior, their Joan of Arc, she could lead them out of their current apathy and into action. If they all stood together and resisted this terrible man, this Matapa; surely they could rescue the kidnapped children and drive Matapa out. Of course they would have to know where to look for Matapa but if they knew that...Mugabe knew but Mugabe had disappeared. What had Mugabe learned and who had he learned it from? The old soldier, Sergeant Okolo; he must have told Mugabe something.

Brenda rose to her feet.

"You can't do it," said Frank. "I'm not going to let you."

Brenda ignored his protests. "I need a scarf," she said.

Frank sat back in his chair. "What?"

"For the Moslem Guest House," said Brenda, "I need a scarf to cover my head. Are you coming with me?"

"No," said Frank, "I am not."

"Then I'll go on my own," said Brenda.

She hurried out of the beer garden ignoring Frank's continued protests. He was following her; she knew he would; and perhaps there was some sense in what he was saying, but Brenda was beyond sense, her mind fixed on just one objective. She hesitated at the edge of the road; which way? She had no idea how to find the Moslem Guest House; maybe there was more than one Moslem Guest House. Well, surely it would be in the town, not out in the bush. She turned towards the main street and hurried on. Her sandals kicked up spurts of red dust and the sun beat down relentlessly. She could hear Frank coming along behind her; not speaking now, just following; following the crazy old lady.

A motorcycle pulled up beside her and she stepped back in alarm. The driver's eyes were concealed behind dark glasses but he was grinning at her in a friendly way. She scrutinized his face; no, he was no one that she recognized.

"Boda, boda, lady," he said.

"What?"

"Boda, boda. You going into town?"

"Yes, yes I am. Are you offering to take me?" she asked.

"Yes, Madame," said the young man. "Five hundred shillings."

"Okay," said Brenda.

"You climb on," said the driver.

"You be careful," said Brenda and she started to straddle the back of the seat.

"No," said the driver, "you sit sideways." He pointed to another motorcycle that had passed them by. The passenger was a woman who perched sideways on the seat, a baby on her lap.

Brenda arranged herself carefully on the seat.

"Where do we go?" asked the driver.

"Do you know of a Moslem Guest House," Brenda asked.

The driver turned his head and looked at her.

"You are a Moslem?" he asked.

"No, I'm a ...Oh never mind, do you know where the Moslem Guest House is?"

The driver shrugged his shoulders. "They are many," he said.

Brenda thought for a moment. "Just take me to the clinic," she said.

"Which one?" said the driver.

Brenda was beginning to feel totally helpless. She could see Frank hovering at the side of the road, ready to step in and haul her off the motorcycle.

"Anywhere," said Brenda, "just take me into town. I'll take it from there. Go on, get going."

The boda-boda driver revved the engine into a high whine and the motorcycle lurched forward. Brenda grabbed the driver around the waist and they inserted themselves into the flow of traffic heading for the town center.

CHAPTER TWENTY FOUR
Sergeant Okolo

Erasto Okolo, formerly of the Kings African Rifles, was enjoying his ride in the big black Mercedes. He sat rigidly upright in the back seat and wondered how it would be to ride this way every day, like a minister, or a politician. As his thoughts turned to ministers and politicians he turned to the man seated beside him.

"How is your father?" he asked.

"He is well," said Mugabe.

"And when do you expect him to return?"

Mugabe stared straight ahead. "Perhaps what we do today will make a difference," he replied.

"Perhaps," said Okolo.

The two men were silent for a few moments.

"Where is he now?" Okolo asked.

"Belgium," replied Mugabe.

Belgium; Okolo thought about Belgium for a moment. His memory was still sharp, he still remembered the maps of his childhood; faded by exposure to the sun, spotted with rust marks from the leaks in the thatched schoolhouse roof. He remembered the teacher pointing with his cane; the one he also used for chastisement and correction, at the map of Europe; the tiny island that was Great Britain, and the multicolored mass that represented the other nations of Europe. Belgium was a nation to be mentioned with disdain because Belgium held sway over the vast central forest to the west of Uganda; the land they called Congo and they had turned it into a land of horrors where the native population was routinely abused, and murdered.

"Why did he choose Belgium?" Okolo asked.

"He was unable to obtain a visa for any other country," said Mugabe.

Yes, thought Okolo, that was not surprising. He knew Mugabe's father, or at least he knew of Mugabe's father, and his implacable opposition to the current government. To befriend Mugabe's father was to make an enemy of Uganda; and few countries would take the risk. Mugabe's father had run for President in the last election and had been arrested on a trumped up charge. The newspapers had been full of stories about the daring rescue of the presidential candidate, breaking him out of jail, escaping across the border into Rwanda. Some believed that the jail break was planned by one of the candidate's sons, perhaps the one who was rumored to have trained with the Israeli Special Forces. The stories had been disturbing to Okolo, reminding him of the Amin days when good men were forced to flee under cover of darkness while other good men had simply disappeared.

"I was surprised to find you here," Okolo said.

"I am my father's eyes," said Mugabe.

"And the man you are working for; the Commissioner, does he know who you are?"

"He does," said Mugabe.

Okolo slowly digested that piece of information and he chose not to comment. Mugabe was working for the Commissioner, the President's personal representative. The Commissioner was employing the son of a notable dissident. Okolo had grown old and wise by keeping his opinions to himself whenever possible especially when it came to politics.

He turned his attention back to the night that Mugabe had appeared at the door of his hut, asking for information about the American boy and the child who had been put under his protection. The safest course would have been to tell Mugabe that he knew nothing but once the young man had told him who he was and what they were seeking, and once Okolo had seen the almost white girl, with her strange intelligent face, he had forgotten about safety. Something in him had risen up in protest against the fact that the lives of his neighbors were again being disturbed by armed men who came in the night to burn and destroy. A lifetime ago; he had fought in the white man's war for the freedom of Europe, and the King had given him a medal as proof of his valor. But that night when the scent of burning villages was carried on the breeze he knew that his precious medal meant nothing at all if its owner had long since become a coward.

He was not surprised that Mugabe had come to him at the Guest House, leaving behind the Commissioner's angry white wife and removing his shoes respectfully as he crossed the threshold. Did he know anything? Did he have any idea where Matapa might be hiding?

Okolo had not been sure, not at first, but the more he thought about it the more he realized that it might be true.

"There is a gorge," Okolo said, "very deep. No one lives there."

"No one?" Mugabe sounded surprised. Uganda's population was growing by leaps and bounds, there were very few places where absolutely no one lived.

"The place is filled with evil spirits," said Okolo. He looked at the modern young man with his smart suit and colorful neck tie. Did such a city bred man believe in evil spirits?

Mugabe nodded his head. "I know of such places," he said.

"My wife tells me," said Okolo, "that other women have observed movement lately, deep in the gorge. I told her it was chimpanzees; we know that there are many in that place, but she told me that chimpanzees do not light fires."

"No, they don't" said Mugabe.

So that was how Okolo had come to be riding in the large black car that no doubt belonged to the Commissioner, with Habati, the Commissioner's driver, at the wheel,

The sun was now low on the western horizon; twilight would be short and darkness would be complete. The road was little more than a goat path wending its way across a grassy plateau. The car slowed, the driver peering forward through the front windshield, attempting to find the ever more elusive trail.

"I think we are near," said Okolo. "I have walked this path but I have never come here in a vehicle." He knew he was becoming confused; on foot he would be able to recognize the shape of a tree, the arrangement of a cluster of boulders, but the car cut him off from any contact with nature. They slipped past a tree that had been destroyed by weaver birds, their nests hanging in the dried-out branches, choking the life from the tree.

"It is here, I think," said Okolo. "Let me walk. I will find it." Habati brought the car to a halt. Okolo climbed from the car and reached back inside for his long walking pole. Mugabe climbed from the other side resting a deadly black assault rifle across his shoulder. Okolo found himself wishing for his spear and the other traditional weapons that he kept by him in his hut.

The two men walked forward together with the Mercedes purring along slowly behind them.

"Here," said Okolo, pointing to the place where the trail made a sharp turn to the left. "We are very near." They made the turn and left the vehicle behind them. The sun was now only inches above the horizon; its golden rays flashed on something bright in the bushes.

Mugabe signaled a halt and then he moved forward slowly to investigate. He pulled the bushes aside to reveal a girl cowering among the weeds. She rose slowly to her feet, hanging her head, refusing to meet their eyes.

"Who are you?" Mugabe asked.

"No one," she said.

Okolo's glance flickered to the gold chain around the girl's neck; he knew about such chains, and what they meant. He extended his arm and caught hold of the girl's shoulder.

"No," she said.

"I won't hurt you," he said, saddened by the thought that a girl like this should be so full of fear.

He dropped his hand to the neck of her shirt, and felt her tremble.

"What are you____?" Mugabe asked.

Okolo showed him the cross suspended on the chain. "This girl is from the Convent," he said. "We are in the right place."

"Why are you here?" Mugabe asked. "Where is the American girl?"

"She is down there, "said the girl, "we were together but she fell. The white man has gone down there."

"What white man?" Mugabe asked.

"I don't know." The girl sounded terrified. "The white man who lives in Budeka; he told me to wait here."

Okolo pushed his way through the weeds, and saw where the ground fell away at his feet. He was standing at the top of a steep trail that snaked down into the rain forest below. He had always known of this place; long ago this was the place where witchdoctors had hidden from the Christian missionaries. As he watched, a flame flared far below, casting shafts of light up through the tree canopy, and then the sound started; the drums he had not heard since his long ago childhood; the drums of sacrifice.

Swot Jensen

"Come and sit here girlie, "said Matapa, patting the battered plastic chair next to him.

Swot sat, not because she wanted to, but because she had no choice. Her chief tormenter; the ten year old with the AK47 was behind her making sure she didn't make another break for freedom. Swot doubted if she could make a break even if the chance arose. She ached from head to toe from her wild plunge through the trees. It was possible that she had escaped without actually breaking any bones, but she knew that her right ankle was at the very least sprained, and her left arm was just about useless with pain radiating from her shoulder at the slightest movement. Being dumped on the ground from the back of the pick-up truck had added a severe blow on the head. Perhaps she had suffered a concussion, really she had no idea, and what did it matter anyway; she was back in the camp; the fire was alight, and the witchdoctor from Kajunga was pounding on a drum.

She wondered how they would do it. Why the fire? What were they going to do to her; what were they going to do to the little girl? Swot looked at the child being held by Angelique. So that was the one; the miracle child; the little scrap of humanity whose existence had created the whole situation. She was a strangely silent little girl perched passively on Angelique's hip, wearing a starched and ironed yellow flowered dress, and gazing around with wide untroubled eyes; truly an innocent.

"Where is my phone?" asked Matapa.

"What you really want to know," said Swot, "is whether or not it's still transmitting."

"Is it?" he asked.

"Of course," said Swot, although she had no idea whether or not the phone was transmitting. She knew that it had transmitted for some period of time, but now she had no idea, although she suspected that it would have been broken into pieces as it fell through the trees.

Events were moving too fast; even if her brother had managed to get a message through to the Embassy in Kampala, there was very little hope of rescue before Matapa did whatever it was he planned to do with knives and drums and fire.

The pounding of the drum was making it hard for her to think of anything except the evil that seemed to blanket the valley floor, weighing down on her shoulders, crawling up her spine, and bringing with it the memory of the witchdoctor throwing his handful of dust and telling her that she had no defense.

She glanced sideways at Matapa realizing that she had not heard his terrible cough in some time. He seemed more alert, more energetic, and much more dangerous than the critically sick man he had been that morning.

For no apparent reason, except for the fact that there was nothing she could do about it, the boy poked her with the barrel of his weapon. She reached out and grabbed hold of it; she had nothing to lose, and perhaps it would be better just to be shot.

"Stop it, you little monster," she said. "Just stop it."

"He's just having his fun with you," said Matapa.

"Since when has this been anyone's idea of fun?" Swot asked.

"My mother was raped by a white man," Matapa said, "the boy just wants to return the favor."

"It's not going to happen," said Swot.

With some difficulty Matapa rose to his feet. He steadied himself on the arm of the chair for a moment, and then walked away towards the fire. He passed by Angelique holding the child in her arms and paused to pass his hand across the child's head. The child screamed; the first sound she had made. Matapa laughed and moved on to the place where the witchdoctor squatted with a drum between his knees.

The boy jerked the barrel of the weapon from Swot's hands and aimed it squarely at her chest.

"He wants me alive," Swot said.

The boy said nothing. The flickering firelight lit the sharp planes of his face, and the unwavering stare of his eyes. Swot wondered who he was, where he had come from and if he was really capable of killing her.

Angelique came towards her carrying the still screaming child. The boy swung around, aiming his weapon at Angelique who simply looked at him as a mother would look at a recalcitrant teenager. She lowered herself into the chair that Matapa had vacated and settled the child on her lap soothing her in soft phrases until the screaming ceased.

"I am sorry," said Angelique in French, "I had hoped you would be the one to escape."

"It's alright," Swot replied, also in French, "because they found me, they're not looking for the others."

"Ah," said Angelique, "where are they?"

"Yes," said the boy in heavily accented French, "where are they?"

"You didn't tell me he spoke French?" Swot said accusingly to Angelique.

Angelique looked at the boy.

"Where are you from?" she asked.

"Rwanda," the boy said, and there was sadness in his voice. "from Kingali."

"You are far from home," said Angelique. "We are all far from home."

Swot looked at the shadowy shapes of Matapa's supporters moving around in the firelight. The convent girls were still huddled together under the watchful eye of a boy with a rifle, but the other women of the camp moved freely with little children trailing behind them. The tents were already packed and loaded on the lorry along with bundles of clothing and bedding. She could see only a handful of adult men, leaning against the hood of the truck, cigarette ends glowing in the dark.

She looked at the boy from Rwanda; so far from home. He could speak French; she could communicate with him; they could move beyond his few phrases of English, all of which were threats to rape or kill; somewhere beneath the dull, beastly exterior was a boy who had once had a home.

"Why do you stay?" she asked.

The boy frowned as though he had never even considered the question.

"How long have you been here?"

He looked down at the ground.

"You can answer the questions," Angelique said.

The boy was silent.

"You have a gun," Swot said, "you could use it to escape; there's no one to stop you."

The boy continued to stare at the ground. The barrel of the weapon was no longer pointed at Swot's chest; he had allowed his attention to wander. Perhaps he was thinking of his home; maybe he was remembering his mother.

"Don't you want to see your parents?" Swot asked.

Angelique hissed and Swot realized that she had made a mistake. The boy looked up from the ground his face a mask of anger.

"I killed my parents," he said.

"You what?"

Angelique reached out and touched Swot's arm. "It is required," she said.

"They're required to kill their parents?" Swot asked.

"Yes."

"I shot them," the boy said, "and I went with Matapa."

"They have all killed their parents;" Angelique said, "it is the first thing that they must do; if they don't, then they themselves are killed. "

Swot stared at the boy trying to put herself into his shoes; he had killed his parents. She thought about her own parents, her laughing black haired mother, and her stoic blond father and herself at this boy's age, or even younger, being given a gun and told to shoot them. The thought made her stomach turn, but this had not happened in Cleveland with bright electric lights, security alarms on the windows, and the police just a 911 call away. No, this had happened somewhere in Rwanda in the rural darkness of a land that had already ripped itself apart in a bloodbath of genocide and this boy, this child, was an heir to all that fear, and all that guilt.

"It's not your fault," she heard herself say. "No one will blame you." The boy made a small non-committal sound, but at least he was listening.

"Wouldn't you like to go home?" Swot asked.

"We can't go home," the boy said. "Matapa would never let us."

"He can't stop you," Swot said. "You all have weapons, and there are only a few men."

"No," said the boy.

"Yes," said Swot, "you can do it. If you do it now, then you will be free; you'll be able to go home. People will understand; they know what Matapa does; they'll know it's not your fault."

The boy's gaze flickered from her to the shadowy shapes of the men leaning against the lorry.

"Matapa is sick," Swot said, "and one of those men will kill him eventually."

"He will grow strong with the sacrifice," the boy said.

"If he kills me," Swot said, sensing her opportunity, "the Americans will come after you, and then there'll be no going home for anyone."

"She speaks the truth," said Angelique.

"I've already told the Embassy where I am," Swot said.

"Eh," said the boy.

"Truly?" asked Angelique.

"Yes," said Swot. "They'll come for me, I know they will, but if they come too late, and they find that you've actually killed an American citizen, well..."

"We are not responsible," the boy said.

"They're not going to believe that," said Swot, "not when they see that you're armed to the teeth, and that there are only a couple of men with you, and then when they find out that you've already killed the Peace Corps worker___"

"No," said the boy, "we have not killed him. We have killed no one here."

"But you're going to," said Swot, pressing her advantage and setting aside the issue of who had killed Zach Ephron. "You can't let them kill me."

The boy looked at Angelique who was continuing to soothe the child on her lap.

"Tell him," said Swot.

Angelique lowered her head until her cheek was resting against the top of the child's head. "So many babies," she said, "we have lost so many babies."

"You don't have to lose this one," said Swot. "Please, Angelique, you know this is wrong; this magic is never going to work."

Angelique shook her head. "It will work," she said. "I have been with that man for many years, and I have seen much magic."

"Alright," said Swot, switching gears, "let's say the magic does work, then what? Matapa recovers; he gets his health back, he's ready to murder his way around Africa for another twenty years; is that what you want?"

Angelique looked up at her, tears running down her cheeks.

"I am afraid," she said.

"So am I," said Swot.

"How would we do it?" the boy asked.

'Talk to the other boys," said Swot.

"I cannot leave this place," the boy said. "I must guard you. If I leave, they will see."

Angelique rose to her feet. "I will go," she said.

"He will kill you," said the boy.

"If I die, I die," said Angelique. "I have allowed too much evil for too long." She tightened her hold on the little girl in her arms. "This child," she said, "has such innocence; perhaps she is magic."

"No," said Swot, "don't start thinking like that. She's just a baby."

"Yes," said Angelique, "perhaps it is just the innocence of all babies; perhaps I had forgotten."

She set the baby on Swot's lap and simply walked away. The child turned and slipped her frail arms around Swot's neck and rested her cheek against Swot's shoulder.

"It's alright," Swot said to the top of the child's head. "We're going to be alright; she'll do it."

She put her arms around the slight little body, surprised by the sudden wave of protectiveness that surged through her. For a moment there was nothing but the firelight, the drums, and the warmth of the small body on her lap, and then she heard the high pitched sound of a motorcycle coming at speed down the hillside. The men who had been lounging beside the parked vehicles sprang into action and the drumming ceased as the witchdoctor stirred up the fire sending flames shooting high into the air and illuminating the valley floor. Swot caught sight of Angelique talking to the boy who was guarding the convent girls. She glimpsed movement on the hillside above the camp; a boy escaping, or maybe Matthew returning. Please, not Matthew. Let him escape. Matapa turned from his place beside the witchdoctor and draw a pistol from his belt. The boy from Rwanda was suddenly attentive taking steady aim at her with his weapon, and the little girl tightened her grip around Swot's neck.

The motorcycle skidded into view and by the time it came to a halt the rider was surrounded by armed men. Even before the rider spoke Swot recognized the shock of white hair; Rory Marsden.

TWENTY FIVE
Brenda Songbird Carter

Brenda Carter was staring at a framed picture of her younger self; the same picture she had seen at Rory's house, but she wasn't at Rory's house and the picture was not hidden away on a bookshelf, it was set on a bedside table, and she was on the bed.

She sat up and tried to look around the room but the movement provoked waves of pain behind her eyes. She let her head drop back onto the pillow, and closed her eyes. After a few moments she tried again but this time she only lifted her head slightly and shifted her position on the pillow. Better, yes, much better. She was on a narrow bed in a small, sparsely furnished room; presumably a private room at the private clinic; no doubt Herbert was next door in a similar room.

It was all coming back to her now and she knew what had happened but along with the memory came the panic. She couldn't lie here comfortably in bed; she had things to do. Where was Frank with his PA system? What she needed to do was rouse the population and lead a march on wherever it was that Swot was being held. How long had she been lying here? She stared up at the light bulb that was illuminating the room. Had the power returned? No, she could hear the distant clanking of a generator. Nighttime; but how late? She raised her arm to look at her watch; just after seven o'clock. There was still time.

It was all the fault of the wretched man with the motorcycle and his stupid instruction that she should perch herself on the seat like some Victorian lady, and then Janet, stepping out into the street right in front of them, and Frank coming along behind on another motorcycle. The whole thing had been a complete disaster, and right outside the clinic. She had seen Janet coming across the street from the pharmacy, bringing medications for Herbert, she supposed, and she had immediately thought of going into the clinic and asking Herbert to tell her where she could find the old Sergeant. She wasn't sure that Herbert would approve of her plan to get the townspeople involved, and maybe he would even stand up for Rory Marsden, but it was too late to worry about subtleties ; it was time these people started to stand up for themselves.

All she'd done was slap at the driver's back to get him to stop and she hadn't expected him to swerve the way he did and she certainly hadn't expected Frank to be right behind her on another motorcycle. Of course Frank hadn't fallen off in the middle of the road because he had been securely seated but Brenda had fallen. She remembered the jolt of hitting the road, and a moment of looking around to see what had happened, and then nothing; and now they had her trussed up in bed in the clinic.

She tried sitting up again; much better this time. Once again her gaze fell on the framed picture. Why would it be here in the clinic? It made absolutely no sense and perhaps she was hallucinating after all. She looked around at the rest of the room and the truth slowly began to dawn on her. This was not a room in the clinic; this was a bedroom in someone's house; not Rory's house, she knew what his house looked like, someone else's house.

The single ceiling light left shadows in the corners of the room but now that she was more awake she could see the bulk of other pieces of furniture; a wardrobe, a mirror, a small dresser, and framed photographs on the dresser. She swung her legs over the side of the bed; her head swam a little but slowly the world returned to focus. Well, she had no idea where she was, or who had been kind enough to let her use their bedroom but she would have to thank them later, right now she had things to do.

Apparently someone had taken her shoes, or perhaps she had lost them in her fall from the motorcycle; oh well, no matter; she would go barefoot.

The door was locked; now who on earth would want to lock her into a room? Well, she'd just have to go out of the window. She opened the curtains revealing the inky darkness outside, apparently this person had the only generator in the neighborhood; or perhaps this was the only house in the neighborhood. The windows were barred; ornamental, wrought iron bars, but nonetheless they were bars, so, she wouldn't be going out of the window.

Perhaps her benefactor had locked the door for fear that Brenda would be hysterical or amnesic when she came around; she had to remember that most people saw her as an old lady, and not the way she saw herself. All she had to do was bang on the door and someone would come and release her. She realized that her thoughts were a little slow; she was disoriented; not surprising considering the last thing she remembered was falling from the motorcycle and landing at Janet's feet. Just take a few deep breaths she told herself, and then get on with it.

She pounded on the door; no one came. She pounded again, she shook the door handle, she shouted, but the house remained obstinately silent with nothing but the distant grinding of the generator. Was she a prisoner? Surely not, unless this was something that Frank was doing to keep her quiet.

She walked over to the dresser and picked up a couple of photographs, carrying them over to look at them in the light. Here was a black and white picture of a child; a little girl with blonde curls and a big ribbon in her hair, and here was the child again sitting on her mother's lap. Brenda looked closely at the mother; Mrs. Fowler. Oh yes, this was the missionary Mrs. Fowler, the bastion of British rectitude and correctness in the face of Brenda's loose morality and impulsive marriage. So, if this was Mrs. Fowler then the baby was...gears shifted in Brenda's brain. Mrs. Fowler wasn't the mother of this child; this was Alice, Margaret's daughter, the one that the Fowlers had stolen. If this was a picture of Margaret's daughter, then this was Margaret's house, but why had Margaret locked the door?

Brenda went back to the bed and took another look at the framed picture of her traveling companions, wondering why Margaret would keep it by her bedside.

"We've all changed, haven't we?" said a voice behind her.

Brenda swung around. Margaret was standing in the doorway.

"I thought you'd like to see it," she said.

"Why have you kept it?" Brenda asked.

"Because I'm in it," said Margaret. "You were all ignoring me, but I was in your picture."

Brenda set the picture back on the table. "Thank you for looking after me," she said, "but I have things to do."

"No, I don't think so," said Margaret.

Brenda pushed past her and Margaret made no objection.

"The front door's locked," she said quietly.

"Then unlock it," said Brenda.

Margaret set her lips in an obstinate line. "You're not going anywhere," she said.

Brenda took a deep breath and resisted the urge to put her hands around the other woman's skinny throat. "I have to help Swot," she said, "and the little girl."

"Alice," said Margaret.

"She's not Alice," Brenda said, "Your Alice is grown up. She went to England with Mrs. Fowler."

"Oh, you don't have to remind me," said Margaret. "If I ever set eyes on that woman, I will....."

"Why didn't you go and look for her?" Brenda asked

"Who?" said Margaret.

"Mrs. Fowler," said Brenda, "and Alice."

"Alice is here," said Margaret.

"But you just said...."

"Alice is here," Margaret said, "Rory has gone to get her."

"You're not making any sense," Brenda said impatiently, and then she remembered what the Bishop had said; cerebral malaria; Margaret had been infected with cerebral malaria; Margaret might never make sense ever again.

"I know Rory's gone to get her," Brenda said, "but don't you think we ought to help him?"

"Rory is very capable," said Margaret, "you should know that, he drove you all the way from Cape Town."

"We all helped," said Brenda.

"But Rory was in charge," Margaret insisted. "Really you were all Just passengers."

"Passengers," Brenda muttered, "stooges more like; CIA decoys."

"I beg your pardon," said Margaret.

"Oh nothing," Brenda said. "Really Margaret, I think we need to give Rory a hand. He can't do everything on his own. Why don't you just unlock the door and I'll go and see___"

"You don't even know where you are," Margaret said.

"No, I don't."

"We're not in town."

"But we could get into town," Brenda said. "You seem to be able to get into town."

"I ride my bicycle," said Margaret.

"Then perhaps I could ride your bicycle," said Brenda, feeling as though she was humoring a three year old one minute and petting a wild animal the next minute. From one moment to the next she was unsure which way Margaret's mood would swing but the swings seemed to be triggered by her memory of her stolen child.

"Can you even ride a bicycle?" Margaret asked. "Aren't you too old to ride a bicycle?"

"No older than you are," said Brenda.

Margaret seemed to arrive at a decision. "We'll go together," she said. "I have two bicycles."

"Where are they?" Brenda asked.

"In my store room," said Margaret, jangling her key ring. "I'll show you."

Brenda followed Margaret through the tiny kitchen and waited while she unlocked another door. She ducked inside the dark room and emerged with a battered old bicycle. "I've had this since I first arrived," she said, wheeling it out into the light.

"I remember," said Brenda.

"You can ride that one," Margaret said, "and I'll ride the other one." She ducked back into the room and emerged with a much newer bicycle, a man's bicycle.

Brenda looked at the bicycle, a red frame, sturdy handlebars and the saddle set up high. A suspicion was creeping into the back of her mind; if she could just bring it to light; it was there, but not quite there.

Margaret seemed to have forgotten her earlier anger and she was staring at the bicycle in puzzlement. "I don't know who set the saddle so high," she said. "How am I supposed to ride it like that?"

"It's really a man's bicycle," said Brenda.

Margaret was rummaging around in a kitchen drawer. "I have a spanner here somewhere," she said.

A man's bicycle, Brenda thought. That's what was worrying her. Margaret had a man's bicycle. The thought finally dropped into place.

"Margaret," she said, "does this bicycle belong to the Peace Corps worker?" she said.

"It used to," said Margaret, "but he's not using it any more, is he?" She turned from the kitchen drawer with a knife in her hand. "I'll have to use this," she said.

Swot Jensen

Rory Marsden strode forward and the light from the fire turned his hair from white to orange and revealed a face contorted with fury. Swot could see that she was about to lose her opportunity to persuade her guard to free her. The boy was no longer wavering; he kept his weapon trained on her, his face was grim and his focus was on the angry American.

"We can still do it," Swot said.

"Who is he?" the boy asked.

"No one," said Swot; "it makes no difference."

"Is he American?"

"Oh yes," said Swot bitterly, "he's American."

"Matapa will kill him," said the boy.

"No," said Swot, "I think they are friends."

"You bastard," Rory shouted. Swot made the mental switch from the French she had been speaking with her captor to Rory's Virginian English, although bastard sounded much the same in either language.

"I told you," Rory shouted, "no Americans, you don't touch the Americans."

Matapa stood alongside the witchdoctor on the opposite side of the fire from Rory. "Hurry," he said.

The witchdoctor emptied the contents of a small wooden bowl onto the fire and the flames turned from orange to blue. Swot saw astonishment and fear on the faces of Matapa's soldiers; the boy beside her gasped.

"Copper and salt," Swot said to her guard. He frowned; she searched her French vocabulary but the words would not come, and what would they mean to him even if she said them?

"It's not magic," she said, "it's just metal. He threw metal on the fire."

"Leave," Rory shouted, "just leave now; leave everyone behind. Take your men and go."

"No," said Matapa, "first I make the sacrifice."

The witchdoctor threw another handful of powder on the fire; this time the flames were green.

The little girl on Swot's lap, oblivious to the danger, gasped in amazement at the changing colors. Swot tightened her grasp on the frail body.

"It's not magic," she repeated. "It's all show."

Rory kept his gaze on Matapa as he moved closer to Swot.

"Hi kid," he said. "You alright?"

"What do you think?" said Swot.

"Where's Matthew?"

"I don't know," said Swot. "And if I did, I wouldn't tell you."

"This wasn't meant to happen," Rory said.

"Oh," said Swot, "and exactly what did you think would happen? "

Rory turned away. "Let them go," he said.

Matapa came towards them through the cloud of smoke that billowed around the fire. Behind him, in the ever changing colors of the flames, the witchdoctor began to chant.

"You can take the girlie," Matapa said, "but I keep the baby."

"I can't let you do that," said Rory. Swot saw his hand creeping to the back waistband of his pants. By the time she realized that he was trying to pull out a weapon Matapa already had a pistol in his hand. She had a vivid memory of the speed with which Matapa had dispatched his lieutenant just a few hours earlier; of the blood and the brain matter oozing from the man's shattered skull. She knew that Matapa wouldn't hesitate, not even for a moment but then he did hesitate; they all hesitated, because a terrible throbbing roar was coming from somewhere overhead, and a bright white light flooded the valley.

The sound of Matapa's shot was drowned by the throbbing but Swot saw Rory fall at the same moment she realized that the sound was the sound of a helicopter hovering above the tree tops. The light filled the valley drawing every eye and the downdraft of the rotor blades sent the tree tops shaking. Dad, Swot thought, it's my dad, he did it. She waited with baited breath for what might happen next; perhaps American Special Forces descending on rope drops from the helicopter, but her unfortunate gift of logic told her of the impossibility of her hope. The helicopter could hover and light up the scene, and terrify Matapa, but no one could descend through the tree canopy; and where would her father have found Special Forces at such short notice?

Rory was not dead; he rose to his knees, and crawled towards her. "Get away from here," he said. "Take the kid and go

"Who is it?" Swot asked looking upwards at the light; she didn't even think to ask him how badly he was hurt; she didn't care.

"No idea," said Rory, "but someone's locked onto the satellite phone signal. Now get out of here."

Swot looked at the boy with the gun. "Please," she said.

"No," said the boy. "Matapa will make the magic; he will cure us."

Rory Marsden groaned and collapsed forward onto the ground. The witchdoctor threw another powder onto the fire; red flames soared into the night sky, competing with the light from the helicopter.

Brenda Songbird Carter

The drone of the helicopter had broken Margaret's concentration and given Brenda a chance to put the Peace Corps worker's bicycle between herself and the knife in Margaret's hand. For a moment the thrumming of the rotors shook the little house, and then the helicopter headed away but the moment had been long enough for Margaret to forget whatever it was that she had been planning to do with the knife. As the sound died away Margaret looked down at the knife and then at the bicycle.

"I can't use this," she said. "I have a spanner somewhere."

"You'll need a wrench," said Brenda encouragingly.

"A spanner is a wrench," said Margaret, "we speak English here."

"Yes, yes, of course," said Brenda.

Margaret turned around and continued to rummage in the drawer while Brenda concentrated on the simple fact of the helicopter. For the past forty-eight hours it had seemed that the outside world had ceased to exist; as though some unknown apocalyptic event had destroyed all civilization except for the tiny pool of humanity remaining in this remote region of Uganda; but now the real world had returned in the form of a helicopter, flying low over Margaret's house. Outside powers were finally intruding on their isolation and she had to assume those outside powers knew about Matapa, and the kidnapped children; perhaps they even knew of Rory's connection to the CIA; perhaps they were here because of Rory. Brenda felt as though a huge burden had been lifted from her shoulders. Someone else knew what was going on, someone competent had acquired a helicopter and was flying in to rescue the children and she was no longer alone; no longer in charge. She had never liked to be in charge; she much preferred to drift through life as a passenger with no desire to be the driver.

"He took the baby," Margaret said, "and he wouldn't tell me where she was."

"You killed him," Brenda said. "You're the one who killed Zach. You murdered him."

"No," said Margaret, "not murder; an accident."

"Accident?" Brenda's voice was rising in indignation. "I saw the body Margaret, that was no accident; how many times did you stab him?"

"I don't know," said Margaret, "but I didn't mean to kill him. He wouldn't tell me."

"Of course he wouldn't tell you," said Brenda, "because you're crazy as a loon. "

"I'm not, I'm not crazy," Margaret said, "You just don't understand."

"Rory told me that you had cerebral malaria," Brenda said. "It's not your fault, but ____"

"Rory," said Margaret. "Why was he talking to you? What did he say about me?"

"Just that you'd been sick."

Margaret slammed the drawer shut.

"I don't remember much," she said, "I can remember what happened years ago, but I forget what I had for breakfast. " Her hands were shaking as she grasped the handlebars of the red bicycle. "What will they do to me?" she asked. "I can't go to prison;

the prisons here are terrible."

You should have thought of that, Brenda said to herself, before you murdered an American citizen. She stopped the words before they came out of her mouth. What was the point of trying to score points by stating the obvious?

"Perhaps Rory could help," she said. "Apparently he has some influence in the American Embassy."

"Sometimes it seems like yesterday," Margaret said. "You were all so...."

"So what?"

"So free," said Margaret. "Your hair, your clothes, just the way you moved your bodies. I was so envious. The Mission Society told me what to bring, how to dress, even how to do my hair, and I thought it was the right thing to do, and then you all came along and you seemed so happy. "

"We were happy," Brenda said, "We didn't have a care in the world. Of course we didn't know that we were all just cover for Rory's intelligence gathering."

"He was in love with you," said Margaret.

"No," said Brenda. "it wasn't serious, none of it was serious."

"He only came to me because he couldn't have you," Margaret said. "Just one night, and then he was gone. When I found out I was pregnant I didn't know what to do; I didn't even know how to reach him. When I told Mr. Fowler he said such horrible things to me; they were going to send me back to England, and then Mrs. Fowler said she would take the baby so long as it was a white baby. They didn't believe me; they didn't believe it was just the once, and that it was Rory; they thought I'd been with the local boys; they thought I was like you."

Brenda bit her tongue and let the remark go unchallenged. It came as no surprise that the Fowlers had a low opinion of Brenda Songbird Carter.

"They stole my baby," Margaret said. "They told me they would always be here and I could see her at any time, and then they left; they just ran away. Everyone ran away and I was here on my own."

Brenda reached out and covered Margaret's gnarled and work worn hands as they gripped the handlebars of the bicycle. "Look at us," she said, "two old women still fighting about something that happened fifty years ago. We can't change the past but we can do something about the future."

Margaret shook her head. "I killed that boy," she said.

"You weren't yourself," said Brenda. "I don't think it's just the malaria; I think maybe it's Alzheimers."

Margaret looked at her blankly. "Never heard of it," she said, "is it some new American disease? We don't keep up with that kind of thing here. We just go from day to day with malaria, and dysentery."

Perhaps it's better that way, Brenda thought. Why bother Margaret with a description of a disease that had no cure? Let her think it was malaria; let her think she might even recover. She tried to imagine what it would be like for Margaret to go on trial; for the details of Margaret's past to come to light; the baby, the Fowlers, Rory and, inevitably, Rory's connections to the CIA.

"This is a very good bicycle," said Brenda.

Margaret gave her a quizzical look, white eyebrows arched above faded blue eyes.

"I guess it would be stolen pretty quickly if it was, say, left unlocked outside your house."

"Oh yes," said Margaret. "You can't leave anything unlocked around here. Everyone has needs, and stealing isn't looked on the same way here. You'd have to live here to understand."

"Yes, of course," said Brenda. "Why don't you unlock the door, Margaret, and I'll take this nice bicycle outside?"

Suddenly the pale eyes were in sharp focus and Margaret's face was no longer blank and distant. So, Brenda thought, she hasn't lost all her marbles.

"Not outside my house," Margaret said. "Further down the road. People from other towns use this road, the bicycle could end up anywhere, it might even leave the country."

"Yes," said Brenda, "it would be good if it left the country."

"I'll take it," said Brenda. "You don't know your way around."

"But I think I should come with you," Margaret said.

They left together, with Margaret wheeling the bicycle and Brenda walking behind, just in case.

Matthew

Matthew slid downwards through the bushes; down was easier than up. He had spent too much time trying to crawl up to the rim of the gorge thinking that he could catch up with Swot and Cecelia somewhere on the road above. His efforts had proved exhausting and pointless. His twisted leg was nothing but a useless reminder of the day he had fallen from the jackfruit tree and all the misfortune that had come to him because of the fall. He had used precious moments of energy visualizing his distraught mother, and wondering if his father would even care what had happened to him, or whether he would just be glad to be rid of the need to feed and clothe his crippled offspring.

He had still been trying to climb when he heard Swot fall; he heard her scream; and he heard the crashing of branches as she fell down through the tree canopy. He even tracked the path of the satellite phone as it bounced through the treetops and he saw it come to rest high up in a tree, beyond the reach of any creature except for the chimpanzees.

He was still undecided about whether he should go up or down, and still lying exhausted in the bushes when the pickup truck roared down into the valley and came to a halt just below his hiding place. He heard the men talking, and he then heard Swot. She was alive, and she was angry, and from what he could hear, they were putting her into the back of the pickup.

That was when he decided to go down and not up. If Swot was down there somewhere, then he was going to be with her. He slid down through the trees, so much easier than climbing upwards. At last he reached the flat land around what had been the campsite, although the tents were already down.

He pulled himself upright and leaned against a tree where he had a good view of what was happening. He saw the witchdoctor from Kajunga climb out of the pickup and hand a small child to the woman from Congo. So that was her, the miracle child.

The witchdoctor went immediately to the circle of stones that had marked the campfire; he stirred the still smoldering ashes and fed small sticks until the fire was fully alight.

Matthew had seen Swot talking to the boy who was guarding her; for a moment he thought that she had persuaded the boy to let her go, but then the witchdoctor began to throw his magic powders onto the fire, and Matthew had felt the stirring of evil spirits. Would Swot feel them he wondered; she had no belief in spirits, perhaps they would not make themselves known to her. As for him, he knew that the air around the valley seethed with evil.

He needed a crutch; there was nothing he could do without a crutch. He would have to go back to the woodpile. He crawled through the bushes, confident that he would not be heard; every eye was fixed on the witchdoctor, every ear was listening to the beating of the drum.

He was within a few feet of the woodpile when someone kicked him, and then landed on top of him. He rolled over, determined to protect himself from the blows of his attacker, but no blows came his way. Whoever had landed on him was as afraid as he was, breathing ragged, sobbing breaths. The light from the fire flared green and showed him a boy struggling to his feet. It was the boy who had been selected to make phone calls; the one he had seen learning to use the satellite phone. The boy stared down at him.

"Don't say anything," said the boy in a pleading tone. "Don't tell anyone I'm here."

Matthew shook his head.

"I lost the phone," said the boy. "He'll kill me, I know he will."

"Where are you going? "Matthew asked.

"I don't know," said the boy, "but I'm not going to stay here."

He stared at Matthew, finally realizing who he was.

"Why are you here? I thought you had escaped."

"I can't leave her behind," Matthew said, indicating Swot and her guard.

"Why," asked the boy; "she is a mazungu; what is she to you?"

"She's of my clan," Matthew said, and saying it made him feel manly; not a crippled boy, but a man of his clan, doing the work of the clan, protecting its members.

The other boy grunted an agreement; he understood the responsibilities of the clan.

"Good luck," he said.

"Wait," said Matthew. "Do you have a weapon?"

The boy pulled a handgun from the pocket of his ragged shorts.

"Can I have it?" Matthew asked.

The boy hesitated.

"You should not be found with a weapon," Matthew said. "If you have a weapon they will think you are a soldier of Matapa, but if you have no weapon, they will know you are innocent."

"How can I go without a gun?" the boy asked.

"Wait at the top of the cliff," said Matthew. "There is a girl there, you can go together. She will show you."

He held out his hand, and the boy handed him the gun. "Do you know how to use it?" he asked.

"I think so," said Matthew. He tucked the weapon into the waistband of his shorts, hoping that he was not about to shoot himself.

The boy turned away and disappeared into the bushes, and Matthew resumed his painful crawling towards the woodpile to search for a crutch that would allow him to stand upright and somehow protect Swot. He could still feel the evil spirits in the air, but he ignored them; they had no power over him.

The King's Soldier

Sergeant Okolo attempted to maintain his dignity in the face of the impetuous driving by the RDC's driver. He was not accustomed to such speed but he understood the need; in fact it was possible that he understood more than young Mugabe and his companion. The helicopter that had appeared out of the night sky and now hovered above the tree tops shining a searchlight into the gorge was not so much a help as a hindrance, and presented a real danger for the impulsive young man, although Mugabe seemed to be ignoring the danger.

The helicopter meant one of two things, Ugandan Army, or

Americans, and whichever was the case it would not be a good idea for Mugabe to be involved. Okolo knew enough about politics to know that Mugabe's father was a real threat to the government in power, and as for the Americans; well who could say what would happen if they felt threatened or embarrassed and had to save face?

The driver flung the vehicle into the final hairpin bend and then screeched to a halt to avoid a boy with a crutch who was unaccountably standing in the middle of the trail. The boy never even turned his head, his entire attention on the scene before him as he tried to keep his balance while he took wavering aim at a boy soldier who was guarding the mazungu girl.

Okolo was still trying to take in the situation when Mugabe sprang from the passenger seat and grabbed the boy by the waist. The boy turned, startled, and dropped the crutch as Mugabe bundled him into the back seat next to Okolo.

"I'm going to shoot him," the boy said, making a grab for the door handle.

Okolo pulled him away from the door, and held onto him.

"I'm going to shoot all of them," the boy declared.

"I understand," said Okolo, although in fact he didn't understand at all. "but we should leave it to the experts. You have done your best."

"They shot Mr. Rory," said the boy.

Okolo drew in a sharp breath. He knew who Mr. Rory was; Mr. Rory was an American, but who had shot him? Mugabe slammed the rear door and reached into the front of the vehicle for his weapon. "Stay there," he said to the boy.

The driver left the engine running, the headlights blazing and followed Mugabe into the clearing where they were greeted by a hail of bullets. Okolo grabbed his protesting companion and pulled him down so that they crouched behind the front seats.

He knew that he should remain hidden and out of harm's way; old men did not belong in modern warfare, but he was desperate to see what was happening. He had a strong suspicion that if anything happened to young Mugabe the repercussions would be felt nationwide. He peered cautiously through the gap between the seats and recognized that he was seeing the results of intense and expert training in the way that Mugabe and Habati rolled into the shadows away from the hail of bullets. He half-expected to see gunfire from the helicopter but no help came from that source. Whoever was in the helicopter was observing but not participating. Cowards, Okolo, thought. Whatever side they were on, how could they watch the scene below them and do nothing? How could he himself watch and do nothing; he who had been given a medal by the king? "Stay there," he said to the boy beside him.

"I'm coming with you," the boy said.

"No," said Okolo. "Someone has to remain alive to tell what has happened. You stay, and you watch, and you will tell the story."

"I have a gun," said the boy.

"Use it if you have to," said Okolo.

"I will," said the boy.

With extreme caution, Okolo opened the door of the vehicle and edged his way around until he had a clear view of what was happening. The hail of bullets was coming from a group of men who had gathered beside an open lorry. They were firing into the bushes where Mugabe and Habati had taken shelter.

He looked up at the helicopter whose bright lights were revealing too much. What was really needed was a distraction. Perhaps he was not just a useless old man resting on the citation he had received 70 years before; perhaps he still had something to offer. He felt around on the ground and gathered a handful of small rocks, and then he moved away from the shelter of the vehicle; no point in putting the kid in danger. He approached the lorry. He had no need of stealth, the helicopter was making enough noise to drown out any sound he might make, and the witchdoctor had added his own sounds to the chaos, pounding on the drum and chanting.

He saw the Commissioner's granddaughter clasping the small child and limping hurriedly away from her guard; a boy too young to be holding the massive weapon that he appeared hesitant to use. The white girl's mouth was moving, she was arguing with the boy.

He turned his attention from the girl and back to the men who were

firing into the bushes; he had only the faintest hope that Mugabe
and his companion could have survived the onslaught of the rapid
fire but he wasn't ready to give up on them. His arm was not as
strong as it once was, but it was strong enough. He began to throw
the rocks, one after another. The first three missed their targets
and then he found the range and his aim was as accurate as it had
been in his youth guarding his father's cattle and able to bring down
a hyena with a well-placed stone. He threw, one rock after another,
striking the men hard, concentrating on their heads and shoulders.
It was as he had hoped; they turned towards him. He had given
Mugabe the chance he needed and he saw the men fall as Mugabe
and Habati burst from the shadows. Without even checking on the
fallen men, Mugabe headed towards the place where the
witchdoctor's fire was still sending blue and green flames into the
night sky to mingle with the bright white light from the helicopter.
Mugabe fired as he ran and the witchdoctor's chant changed
abruptly to a gurgling scream and then silence.
The white girl, still holding the baby and still limping, ran towards
Mugabe. The boy soldier who had been guarding her raised his
weapon and Okolo let loose another stone. The boy turned in
Okolo's direction, eyes wide with panic; Okolo saw his own death in
the boy's face as the boy took aim at him. He thought of the
promises of the Koran, he was Haji, he had a place in Paradise, and
then a gunshot exploded beside him and the boy guard fell,
clutching his arm. Okolo turned around in time to see the boy with
the crutch, the one who had been told to stay in the vehicle,
toppling backwards from the recoil but still clutching the handgun.
"You were supposed to stay in the car," he said, as he pulled the
boy to his feet.
Together they watched the white girl hurling herself at Mugabe,
throwing her arms around him. Okolo had no idea what she said, or
whether or not Mugabe returned her fierce embrace because at
that moment the light from the helicopter was extinguished and
the clearing was lit only by the firelight and the headlights of the
Mercedes.
Okolo saw, or thought he saw a tall figure slipping away into the

shadows; someone fleeing the clearing and disappearing into the shadows of the forest. He felt the weight of the last stone in his hand but knew the distance was too great; the quarry had escaped.

CHAPTER TWENTY SIX
Swot Jensen

The evangelist seemed not to be surprised by the news but Swot's grandmother was filled with amazement.

"Ants," she repeated. "The answer was ants?"

"Yes," said Swot. "Without the ants we wouldn't have had a chance."

"I told you it meant something," said Frank. "God always means what he says."

"They were a miracle," Matthew said.

Brenda appeared to be awestruck.

"Swot," she said, "that man gets messages from God."

Swot pushed the thought aside; she didn't know what to do about it; not yet. Brenda seemed to have made up her mind; Frank had given Brenda a Bible and Brenda was reading it. Swot wasn't sure how she felt; grateful, yes definitely grateful. Was she ready to believe that some force existed in the universe, a force that controlled all of nature, and yet cared about her personally? That was what Frank would have her believe but that kind of belief would require more exploration; but not now, not when her whole world was changing around her; and Mugabe had disappeared again. No, she couldn't think about Mugabe; she would have to think about something else; change the subject.

"Do you think we'll ever know who killed him?" Swot asked.

"We don't even know if he's dead," Brenda replied. "They haven't found a body."

"I don't mean Matapa," said Swot, "I meant the Peace Corps worker; Zach. We still don't know who killed the poor kid."

"No we don't," said Brenda, "but we can't know everything, can we?"

"Don't you think we should___"

"No, I don't," said Brenda firmly. "I think we should leave that subject alone; leave it to the Embassy and the police."

"Really?"

"Yes," said Brenda.

"But we could help them," said Swot.

"They don't need our help," said Brenda. "Please, Swot, don't ask any more questions."

"I don't understand," said Swot.

"I'm asking you to leave it alone," said Brenda. "Just trust me on this one."

"But___"

"I think that man over there is trying to get your attention," Matthew said.

Swot looked across the crowded beer garden. The man from the Embassy, the good looking one with black hair and a lion's tooth on a cord around his neck, winked at her and jerked his head to one side. She gave him her most discouraging glare and turned back to talk to Brenda.

The party at the Speke Guest House was in full swing; and like most farewell parties it had devolved into beer drinking and expressions of undying friendship. Even Janet, the senior wife, had taken time off from nursing her husband and was sitting at a table talking to Jubilee and Matthew.

Swot knew that tomorrow it would all be over, and this group of people would probably never meet again. Early in the morning the helicopter would carry VanBuren back to Kampala along with Rory, Margaret and Brenda. They would be the first to leave because they had a plane to catch; the Embassy wanted Rory out of Uganda as soon as possible. He had already said goodbye to his comfortable little home and returned to the Guest House with just one suitcase; not a lot to show for his years of clandestine activities. And Margaret; Margaret was going home for the first time in fifty years, with Rory and Brenda beside her and all of Brenda's financial resources at her disposal to help her find her daughter. What a surprise that had been; Margaret had a daughter and Rory was the father, and Brenda had transferred her energies from fixing Swot to fixing Margaret.

The helicopter would be making a second flight later in the day to pick up Swot and Matthew, and a very nervous Jubilee who was delighted that her son would finally have his operation, and terrified of the idea of flying.

The man from the Embassy winked at Swot again and this time he jerked his thumb in the direction of the shadows along the back wall of the beer garden. Swot scowled at him and he broke into a wide grin and rose to his feet. He had abandoned his suit and tie and was clad in a sweat-stained safari shirt and khaki pants decorated with innumerable pockets. He elbowed his way through the crowd which included the Bishop, and Sister Angela and a good many people unknown to Swot, until he stood close beside her, too close.

"What does a guy have to do to get you on your own?" he asked.

"Just go away," said Swot.

She should have been happy, and perhaps she should even have been flattered that this obviously sophisticated and worldly man wanted to be alone with her, but she couldn't summon any interest in him or in the party. She was pleased that everything had worked out; that the convent girls had been reunited with their parents, that the boy soldiers were going to be rehabilitated, that Angelique was going to finally find her way back home, but her happiness was pierced through with doubts. So Matapa had eluded them; it didn't matter; he was alone and sick; his time was over. No, Matapa was not the source of her doubts; every thought she had twisted itself around to Mugabe and the moment that she had flung herself into his arms and he had done...what? What had he done? Had he returned her embrace? Had he held onto her as tightly as she held onto him? She had no idea and in the chaos that had ensued there had been no chance to find out and now two days had passed and she had seen no sign of him. Habati continued to drive the Mercedes around the town, his eyes unreadable behind their dark glasses and if he knew anything, or had any opinion, he was not sharing it with Swot.

"Someone wants to see you," said the Embassy man.

"Me?"

"Yes, you. He's waiting outside the back gate."

"Who is it?" Swot asked.

The Embassy man grinned again, his teeth white in the gathering gloom. "Who do you think it is?" he asked. "I'll give you as much time as I can, but you won't have long; I have to get him out of town tonight."

"You?"

"Yeah, we're driving west; two safari guides, Simba Davis, that's me, and my African partner, scouting out the land for our clients."

"Why" Swot asked.

"Because he can't stay here," said Davis. "They won't let him stay, not now."

"They?"

"Don't ask questions," said Davis, "just seize the moment."

"Just go," said Brenda who had apparently overheard every whispered word.

Swot did as she was told, threading her way unnoticed through the crowd and sliding into the shadows along the wall. She heard the metallic rattle of a gate being unlocked and saw a change in the density of the shadows as a door was opened in the wall. She stepped through without fear; she knew who was on the other side. He stood beside a dark green Land Cruiser, bundles of supplies strapped to its roof. He was dressed as a safari guide, khaki pants, safari shirt, a vest adorned with multiple pockets.

"You're leaving," she said. She had meant it to sound accusatory, but it came out as simply sad.

"I have to," Mugabe replied. "I don't have time to explain but I think you will read it in the newspapers. I will join my father in Belgium."

"Belgium?" She couldn't imagine him in Belgium. What did she even know of Belgium; cathedrals, medieval houses, chocolate? He didn't belong in Belgium; he belonged here in the land of red earth, and singing insects.

"Where will you go?" he asked.

She had not thought beyond Kampala and Matthew's surgery; her father arriving on the night flight to be with her, Brenda gone to

England,
"I suppose I'll go home," she said.
"Yes, of course."
The silence was heavy between them. She should never have hugged him, never have thrown her arm around his neck, holding him so close that the child she was still carrying had burst into tears. She had to ask. "Will you take your wife with you?"
"I have no wife," he said.
Her heart skipped a beat.
"But you have a child," she said.
"It is possible to have a child with a woman who is not your wife," said Mugabe. "I made a mistake; one that I will not repeat."
He shuffled his feet in the dust.
"I wanted to apologize," he said.
"No," said Swot, "you don't have to apologize for anything. You saved my life. You saved everyone."
"But when I found you; when I greeted you, I...."
He seemed to run out of words.
"Oh, you mean that," she said, feeling for the first time in her life the power of being a woman; not a girl, a woman. "I think that was mutual."
"Really?" He was smiling now. "How old are you, Sarah?"
"Eighteen," she said, "I'm legal."
"But still very young," he said.
She heard the clang of the gate being opened. Mugabe looked down at her. "Come to Belgium," he said,
Belgium! She could only imagine what her father would say about Belgium; but surely there were universities in Belgium; post-graduate courses totally suited for an American student.
Simba Davis appeared out of the gloom and opened the door of the Land Cruiser.
"Time to go," he said.
This time there was no crying child between them as Mugabe gathered her into his arms, and held her for a long moment.
"I'll come," she said.
"I know," he replied. He dropped into the driver's seat and started

the engine.

Swot stood by the side of the road until the Land Cruiser was lost from sight, driving west into the heart of the continent. She let herself back in through the gate. Her father would never understand, but Brenda; yes, Brenda would understand that Sarah Jensen had found what she was looking for and this time there would be no running away.

EPILOGUE

Matapa moved slowly. Three days had passed since the night of the helicopter; three days in which the strength had drained from his body and the fever had returned. He was nearing the end of the gorge, the tree canopy thinning above his head, the light losing its friendly green glow. Soon the little stream he was following would pour itself into the larger river and spread across the grassy plains. The chimpanzees were far behind him, chattering in the tree tops, and ahead would be the world of the predators and prey, lions, and cheetahs, antelope and zebra; a world that was not in his blood as the forest had always been.

He was being followed; he had known it for several hours. The follower was skilled and stealthy but Matapa still sensed his presence; not an animal, a man. His life was behind him now, his time as the legendary Mwene Matapa was over, beaten by the white man's cursed disease. If he had only been able to make the sacrifice, then perhaps he could have survived; even allowed another man to take on the title, and he himself could have returned to his home.

The light ahead was now very bright, a world of sunlight on dry yellow grass; a world he could not enter. He would wait here in the green shadows; wait for the man who was following him. He doubted that it was the American; the elderly white man possessed no tracking skills. No, his pursuer was an African; skilled in the ways of the forest; as skilled as Matapa had been in his boyhood when he was the witchdoctor's apprentice.

There was a time when he would have been able to conceal himself among the dark green undergrowth and wait in silence for the follower to come into range, but silence was impossible now when the coughing fits came upon him.

Clasping his chest he held the cough at bay long enough that he could take measure of the surrounding sounds, bird calls, the rustle of small animals, the wind in the branches, the snapping of a twig. He turned his head towards the sound and the man was there in front of him; an old man, tall, and thin, clad in a bark skin loin cloth and carrying a long spear.

Matapa reached for the pistol he had tucked into his belt but the cough would no longer be held at bay and his hand moved of its own accord and clutched his chest to ward off the tearing pain. Thus it was that the spear pierced his hand before it pierced his chest. If his hand had not slowed it, the spear would have pierced his heart and he would have died immediately, but as it was he had time to search the face of the man who had hunted him down and to hear the words spoken over him.

The old man leaned in close, speaking in slow, careful English. "I am Erasto Okolo," he said, "and you have disgraced our people."

The old man leaned even closer, his eyes widening in surprise. "You are not of our people," he said. "Where have you come from, why have you done what you have done?"

Matapa looked up at the sunlight filtering through the trees, remembering another forest, and the light of his mother's village. "Why?" The question echoed through his mind. "Why?"

He remembered the way his mother had pried open his clutching fingers; the nun who had spoken to him with no kindness in her voice; and the old man who had led him back into the forest and shown him its darkest secrets. He closed his eyes, shutting out the last of the green light.

The boy from Congo was beyond thought and beyond feeling when Sergeant Okolo pulled the spear from his chest and began the long journey back to his home village.

About the Author: Eileen Enwright Hodgetts was born in England. She emigrated to South Africa at the age of twenty one; returned briefly to the UK and then emigrated to the United States. She lives in Pittsburgh, Pennsylvania, with her husband Graham. They have two children and four grandchildren.

From 1999 to 2010 Eileen was the director of Encounter Uganda, a multifaceted, faith-based mission to Uganda. Encounter Uganda concentrated its efforts on bringing practical as well as spiritual encouragement and relief to one small area of Uganda. The mission resulted in the creation of a hospital, a coffee farm, a well-drilling initiative, and numerous personal involvements by the two hundred and fifty people from four nations who made up the mission teams.

Eileen Enwright Hodgetts is the author of two additional novels both available from Amazon.com
Whirlpool, a novel of Niagara Falls
Dragons Green, a modern European adventure.

See also: More than One Wife, Polygamy and Grace
an exploration of African polygamy; co-authored by Archbishop Stanley Ntgali, Primate of the Church of Uganda and Eileen Enwright Hodgetts

For more information visit www. *eileenenwrighthodgetts.com*

Made in the USA
Charleston, SC
21 May 2013